"It's not often you find a book that so perfectly captures the messy complexities of modern mid-life marriages and manages to also be a riveting page turner, yet with *Reservations for Six*, Palmer somehow pulls it off. I inhaled this book in two days, but these six characters so fully came alive for me that I'll be thinking about them for much, much longer. Absolutely brilliant." — **Colleen Oakley**, *USA Today* bestselling author of *The Invisible Husband of Frick Island*

"*Reservations for Six* is a wonderfully wise, acutely observed story of love, lust, relationships and marriage. Palmer's insight into the variegated wants and whims of the human heart is revelatory. This is a fun, fast, and insightful read." — **Jessica Anya Blau**, author of *Mary Jane*

"Six birthday-goers make reservations while having reservations in this falling dominos tale about the ins and outs of love. Thought-provoking and full of heart, a portrait of friendship, three marriages, and the importance of discovering one's true path through the myriad complexities of life. Not to miss!" — **Julie Valerie**, author of *Holly Banks Full of Angst*

"It's often said that it's impossible to know what's really going on in someone else's marriage, but you can get deliciously close in *Reservations for Six*, Lindsey Palmer's smart, compelling, and completely believable novel about three couples negotiating infertility, infidelity, and incompatibility between the sheets as they approach forty. With great wisdom and empathy—and well-placed shots of anger and humor—Palmer portrays the particularly tricky years of marriage that are the middle for some, but spell the end for others. I thoroughly enjoyed spending time with this ensemble of intelligent, well-meaning, and often confused friends as they struggled to know when to compromise and when to dare change." — **Karen Dukess**, author of *The Last Book Party*

"A realistic portrayal of couples facing emotional crises." — *Kirkus Reviews*

"Pull up a chair and watch the drama unfold as these six friends manage the roller coaster of midlife." — *Library Journal*

"[*Reservations for Six*] reveals the challenges of marriage as well as the rewards... Palmer has a sure hand with her characters. Overall, this offers a shrewd but affectionate portrayal of marriage in middle age." — *Publishers Weekly*

Reservations for Six

Reservations for Six

— a novel —

Lindsey J. Palmer

Wyatt-MacKenzie Publishing
DEADWOOD, OREGON

Reservations for Six
Lindsey J. Palmer

ISBN: 978-1-954332-32-4
Library of Congress Control Number: 2022930689

Cover illustration by Cienpies Design | Alamy Stock Photo

The characters and events in this book are fictitious. Any similarity to real persons,
living or dead, is coincidental and not intended by the author.

Wyatt-MacKenzie Publishing
DEADWOOD, OREGON

www.WyattMacKenzie.com

Dedication

To my family

CHAPTER 1

Nathan's Birthday

The whole thing was perfectly choreographed, with the finesse and ease of a Broadway production still going strong ten years into its run. Mickey arrived at Giorgio's a minute before their eight p.m. reservation, headed to the table in the back, and set the show in motion: ordering the first two bottles of red, the bruschetta and olives and burrata, then setting out place cards that had grown frayed after a decade of use. Mickey would be at one end, with her husband Matco to her left, beside Louisa, and Nathan would sit at the other end—the birthday crown was placed ceremoniously at his setting—with Abe and Amy on the opposite side. Everything in place, Mickey assumed her spot, touched up her lipstick, and waited for her husband and her four best friends to arrive.

Spotting Nathan's boyish frame, Mickey shouted out, "Birthday boy coming through!" knowing it would cause him to bloom with embarrassment. Nathan was followed by his wife, Louisa, just two inches shy of his six feet, though she seemed to have grown even taller since having the twins a couple years ago. Her curly hair had a personality of its own, and she'd always been broad-shouldered, but motherhood had enhanced her curves, making Mickey's best friend even more beautiful in Mickey's eyes. Louisa heaved a cake box onto the table and shed her giant parka.

"Man, it's cold out there. I'll never ever get used to January in Massachusetts."

Mickey cupped her palms into makeshift earmuffs to warm Louisa's ears. "New England winters will put hair on your chest!"

"Exactly what I need."

"Here, drink up, warm up." Mickey distributed generous pours of wine.

Nathan took a gulp. "Thanks. It's been a day."

"A *birthday!*" Abe appeared, clapping him on the back. "Our resident elder, how does it feel on the front lines, forging forth into a new decade?"

Nathan groaned. "It feels like creaking knees, a receding hairline, and—"

Mickey cut him off: "Such bleak talk! I think you meant to say, it feels wonderful to be surrounded by the love of my nearest and dearest."

"Sure, that." Nathan finished his wine and reached for the bottle in one swoop.

Abe extended a folder to Louisa, stamped in all caps: "MS. BAUER." "This was in your mailbox." The two were colleagues at the local high school, River Mill, where Abe taught history and Louisa had climbed her way up from English teacher to vice principal. They'd both started on the same day nearly a dozen years ago, and been pals ever since.

Mickey intercepted the folder. "Come on, no one's getting sucked into work tonight."

She directed everyone to their seats, as if they didn't know them by heart, and Abe plunked the birthday crown onto Nathan's head. "You really are balding, aren't you?" Nathan shoved him away with affection.

"How long until our other halves show up?" Mickey said to Abe. She was marooned at one end of the table, flanked by empty seats on either side.

"Any minute now," said Abe, always the optimist.

"Well, I predict they don't make it in time for apps," Mickey replied.

She was right. The tablecloth was already a wreck of bread crumbs and olive oil, and their spouses were on the verge of ordering for them when Amy and Mateo swooped in one after the other, all apologies. A bug in Amy's code, a crisis on Mateo's team, blah blah blah—they'd all heard it before. The only people who believed Amy and Mateo would ever leave their offices before eight o'clock were Amy and Mateo themselves.

Mateo made the rounds kissing cheeks, before landing at Mickey and massaging his wife's shoulders. "That hits the spot," she sighed. "Today was all upper body." Mickey, a gym owner and triathlete, was perpetually in need of stretching and loosening.

"This is why you married me, right?"

"That and you knocking me up." It still amused Mickey all these years later: how she'd had to let out her wedding gown to accommodate her burgeoning belly. It had long ago returned to six-pack taut, and the baby bump had grown into a full-fledged teenager: Melody, age seventeen, was as feisty as her mother, as natural of a leader as her father, and the treasure of her parents' lives.

Amy nodded hello to her friends, then took her place next to Abe, nuzzling his nose.

"You two are still such lovebirds," Mickey said, "and after how long?"

Everyone picked up on the cue, bellowing in unison, "Ten years!" The first of these birthday dinners had been exactly a decade ago, on Nathan's thirtieth birthday. Louisa and Mateo had invited along Abe and Amy, their respective coworkers—it was a set-up, and an instant match. The six of them had been gathering at Giorgio's for all six of their birthdays every year since. It was a tradition, a good-luck charm, and a celebration all rolled into one.

They ordered their usuals: lasagna, chicken parmigiana, cacio e pepe, spaghetti carbonara, chicken marsala, mushroom risotto, Caprese salad. Most of them had been on various diets over the years, flirted with paleo or Whole 30, eliminated sugar or gluten, abstained from drinking on weekdays or altogether. But when it came to each other's birthdays, they were all in. Even Mickey, who otherwise stuck to a clean, vegetarian regimen that, along with her rigorous workouts, occasionally fooled people into thinking that she and her teenage daughter were sisters.

Louisa watched her friend dig in to her mountain of pasta. Mickey did everything with gusto, always had. It was one of the first things that had drawn Louisa to her. Mickey had been Louisa's R.A. her freshman year of college, the older girl's room a revolving door of fun. Despite her busy social calendar, the senior had made space for Louisa, drawing her out of her shyness and into her inner circle. Louisa had soon realized that as popular as Mickey was, her friends were party friends—mostly up for big nights out, and dancing around to blasting music while pre-gaming for big nights out. Whereas Louisa was someone Mickey could truly confide in. The two of them often lounged around in their PJs and stayed up half the night talking. They swapped stories of lonely childhoods: Mickey being a late-in-life accident of parents who were over it after having raised three sons and Louisa being the only child of two workaholics who had little time or patience for parenting. They talked about their classes and crushes, their fears and fantasies of the future, and by the end of the semester, they were inseparable. They'd only grown closer in the nearly two decades since.

Mickey looked even better now than she had back then, while Louisa was still hanging onto a handful of the fifty pounds she'd gained while carrying her twins. It was impossible for her to fathom fitting exercise into her day or abstaining from the stress chocolate stashed in her desk. Watching her friend eat so heartily, Louisa consciously pushed aside her envy; she preferred to feel in awe, thinking of Mickey like a muse who existed on a higher plane.

Mickey noticed Louisa observing her. "Open wide, Lou." She

3

delivered an expertly coiled forkful of spaghetti into her mouth. "So good, right?"

Louisa nodded, mouth full. Mickey didn't think any less of her because of her love handles. Plus, the food was heavenly—Louisa couldn't believe that this and the Kraft Mac & Cheese she served her kids could both be called pasta.

The group ate family style, everyone reaching over everyone else for bites and bottles and little plates piled with forkfuls of this and that. The waiters knew them—the birthday crew—and flitted about the table, refilling glasses and bread baskets, uncorking bottles of wine and bringing out more sauces without being asked. An observer might be excused for thinking the friends didn't have much to say to each other, since few words were exchanged during this phase of the evening. In truth, no one felt the need to drum up conversation for conversation's sake. They were comfortable, at home in their little sextet, bellies growing fuller and heads fuzzier with good wine.

Louisa took a break from her plate to sit back and marvel at her life. Sure, she was so sleep-deprived she could've used an entire year to catch up. And most days felt like a breakneck sprint, her to-do list stalking her like a sleazy creditor. But that was expected, given her demanding, thankless job at the school, and her demanding, generally thankless toddlers. It also meant that she and Nathan sometimes went days without exchanging more than cursory greetings and kid logistics—long gone were their days of romantic gestures and spontaneous dates. But despite all that, how lucky that Louisa had populated her life with such wonderful people, and that they'd built this chosen family still going strong through everyone's early middle age.

Louisa settled her focus on her husband, perched over a napkin scribbling notes. It had once made her swoon to watch his big hand wrapped around a golf pencil, his mind brimming with ideas that he simply had to get down right away. She patted his leg fondly. He flinched—she must've startled him.

"I love you guys," she said to the table, and was met with nods and *mm-hms*. Everyone was flush with food and drink and feeling sentimental.

Amy snuggled up to Abe, laughing at his impression of a student's presentation about North Korea's imports and exports. Amy was content to sit in front of a monitor all day writing code, but she was grateful for her husband's ease in the world, and how he pushed her to be more outgoing. The booze was making her flirtatious: she delivered a butterfly kiss to her husband's cheek. Mateo caught her eye and winked, and she darted away from his gaze, embarrassed to have her intimacies noticed.

Abe slipped his arm around Amy's waist. He loved their friends, and their birthday tradition, which was inextricably tied to his relationship with his wife, since the very first Giorgio's dinner had also been their first date. Though if it were up to him, they'd cut it off early tonight so he and Amy could get home and down to business. It was her last day ovulating, according to his Mini-Maker app. When they'd started this venture nearly two years ago, Abe had offered to track Amy's cycle. She'd agreed only reluctantly, but quickly got used to it, seeming relieved to be spared the burden of doing it herself. Abe knew that for many couples, baby-making sapped the excitement from sex—he'd heard all about it at his infertility support group—but he felt the opposite. To Abe, combining pleasure with such a sacred mission elevated the experience to previously unimaginable heights. And though they'd yet to get pregnant, making love during that time of month hadn't lost its thrill for him.

Mateo scanned the table, observing the women: Amy, his clever friend and former colleague, brilliant and chic, always holding her cards close to the chest. Louisa, who'd turned confident and steady with motherhood, like she'd finally grown fully into herself. And of course, Mickey, who was now delivering instructions about the cake presentation to Kimmy, that waitress who clearly wanted to get in his wife's pants. Mickey was an indiscriminate charmer—of men and women of every physical type and personality. She still wore the bright red lipstick she'd worn when Mateo first met her, at that party Nathan had brought him to in grad school. He'd barged through a door to what he thought was the bathroom, but instead found two women kissing on a bed. The strawberry-blonde one caught Mateo's eye, and gestured for him to come join. Mateo demurred, too shocked and shy, but he'd been determined to find her later. He still couldn't believe he'd convinced her to come home with him that night—and to stick around ever since.

No one at the table noticed when Nathan disappeared. His palms were sweaty and the room had started spinning. He knew he'd gone too far in trying to take the edge off, and found his way to the restroom mostly by instinct—the restaurant's layout was as familiar as his own home. He pissed for what felt like an eternity, then splashed cold water on his cheeks and forced himself to face the mirror. Vision a little swimmy, he struggled to bring his reflection into focus. All this love and friendship and celebration—it had become cloying, like a strong perfume in a small space. It seemed to Nathan like half the reason the group kept up these birthday dinners was so they could congratulate themselves on being such dear, devoted friends.

When the ritual began, Nathan was turning thirty—an age that had seemed so grown-up at the time, with everyone else still coasting out the end of their twenties, ribbing him about his old age. Nathan *had* felt old, but in a mature, wise way. He'd felt optimistic, too, looking ahead to years upon years of adventures, so much life ahead.

But then it was like he'd blinked and was forty. *Forty.* Half his life might've been behind him. Hell, his own dad had only made it to sixty. Nathan saw his future laid out before him: as a husband and father and worker bee, still scraping by on his salary of a non-tenure-track lecturer, always being reminded by Louisa of his inferiority at parenthood, worn thin on time and energy, and meeting up a few times a year with these same friends to sit around this same table at Giorgio's, another decade gone by. It honestly felt like no future at all.

Nathan felt sweaty, then chilled, then sweaty again. The whirring exhaust fan pulsed in his ears; the walls closed in. He reached into his pocket for a tissue, but found only the crumpled paper where earlier at the table he'd jotted down a list of video games to try. He lurched through the door to the restaurant, pausing to steady himself against the wall.

Then he spotted it: the behemoth of a cake, held by that waifish waitress, Kimmy, and lit up with—*groan*—forty candles. A math professor, Nathan was normally all for precision, but in this case, no. Birthday candles to match one's age was for children, not a middle-aged man whose life was so monotonous that the appearance of a cake was meant to count as grand excitement. Nathan wished the waitress would trip and send the cake flying; he yearned for escape. But all his friends were waiting for him; his *wife* was waiting for him. The thought made him cringe, but in the end, inertia won out. Nathan knew what was expected of him. He ducked in front of Kimmy's path and returned to the head of the table just in time.

"Happy birthday to you, happy birthday to you..." His loved ones sang with the same enthusiasm as he and Louisa had last fall when Phoebe and Finn turned two. How come people didn't age into a different birthday song, something less jolly and humiliating? Nathan grinned and bore it, right through the final line when the cake and its army of candles was plopped down before him, now his burden to bear.

"Make a wish!" Abe called out. Louisa took Nathan's hand—hers was clammy and hot. "Shout it out!"

This was tradition, Mickey's idea originally. Her theory was that a wish kept secret got buried, like it had never been wished for in the first place. Whereas sharing the wish aloud with your friends was like notarizing it, welcoming it to the world, so it could be nurtured and nourished. So many of their achievements had started as shouted-out wishes at this very table: Mickey's gym, Mateo's businesses, Abe and Amy's house, Louisa's promotion, Louisa and Nathan's twins (not that they'd wished for a pair).

Nathan sucked in all the air he could manage, then blew with all his might, obliterating every last flame mocking his age. It was invigorating. For the first time that evening, he felt powerful and in control. He hadn't planned to say a thing—not here, not now—but he was caught up in the moment, so he drew in another breath, turned to his wife, and blurted it out: "Louisa, I want a divorce."

CHAPTER 2
Louisa

Louisa tried to concentrate on the road. She'd been blindsided—by the news, not to mention the delivery of it in public, in her favorite place, in front of her closest friends. All she wanted was to be home, buried under her comforter, drifting into a deep, dreamless slumber. But you can't always get what you want—this, Louisa realized, was emerging as a theme of the night.

After Nathan's big announcement, she now had to contend with traffic. Why there was traffic at ten o'clock on a Tuesday night was anyone's guess. The world seemed to be conspiring against her. She was driving, of course—Nathan was in no state. Moments after he'd made his declaration, Mickey, god bless her, had the cake whisked away, and she must've handled the check, too. Amy and Mateo retrieved everyone's coats, then Abe ferried Louisa and Nathan out to their car, assuring Louisa he'd cover for her in the morning if she wasn't up for work. Now Louisa was stuck inching along the highway, accompanied by her snoring, booze-reeking, hankering-for-a-divorce husband slumped over in the passenger seat. When they finally got home, she'd have to make sunny small talk with their babysitter, shelling out the contents of her wallet and acting like all was well as the girl wished Nathan a very happy birthday.

A very happy birthday, indeed. Even if Nathan had wanted to explain to her the bombshell he'd dropped at Giorgio's, Louisa knew that talking to her husband after so many drinks was an exercise in futility.

But this was new. Never before had they discussed divorce. The word was barely a part of Louisa's vocabulary. Her own parents were still married, still happy enough in their way, neither one having let up on the seventy-hour workweeks they'd maintained throughout Louisa's childhood. Nathan's parents had been a cheerless pair, but a pair they'd remained until both had died within six months of each other a few years ago. As Louisa helped Nathan to bed, she considered him: this man she'd been loving for nearly half her life, who now wanted to leave her. She felt slightly ridiculous climbing into bed beside him, but also a bit worked up and self-righteous, since surely *she* was not the partner meant to decamp to the couch. She guessed she was supposed to be bawling from misery and heartbreak—and maybe she was in shock, because her main feeling was confusion. Lying awake late into the night, Louisa tried to piece together the puzzle of Nathan's wish.

Was their relationship perfect? Hardly. Most of what they talked about was Phoebe and Finn and the household and their schedules. And Louisa knew she'd grown more irritable with Nathan since they'd become parents—but he was constantly buying the wrong size diaper or forgetting the kids' lunches at home. And when they did manage to get time together to relax, they tended to collapse on opposite ends of the couch and tap mindlessly at their respective phones. And okay, it was hard to remember when they'd last had sex—had it been three Saturdays ago, or had a whole month passed them by? But lately, Nathan seemed to want it as little as Louisa did. Plus, they fought about money. A criminal portion of their income went to daycare and student loans, and they did a monthly dance to figure out which bills they could put off versus which ones they couldn't. The rent on the house had risen steadily over the years, but they'd never worked up the energy and coordination to move somewhere more affordable, never mind to buy their own home.

So, yeah, if they were filling out a form about the health of their marriage, they'd check a lot of the boxes that you weren't supposed to check. However, to Louisa, all this stuff seemed par for the course—and temporary. She understood marriage to be a commitment, and believed that problems were meant to be solved, not abandoned. She and Nathan both had demanding careers, and twin two-year-olds, for god's sake. While they'd once spent entire weekends lazing around in bed, indulging in movie marathons, and excitedly swapping ideas about the world, their lives had changed. They'd clean up their act when Phoebe and Finn were a little older and they had some breathing room. Anyway, whoever went into marriage expecting it to be all sunshine and ice cream was a fool. Was Louisa's husband a fool?

Whatever was troubling Nathan, they'd work it out. They'd find ways to reconnect—prioritize date nights, read self-help books, whatever it was that couples did in these situations. Maybe this was a good thing, Nathan raising an alarm that they'd slid into some kind of marital danger zone and needed to make changes. Yes, it was definitely a good thing. Convinced of these points, Louisa pulled the comforter tightly around her and drifted to sleep.

Louisa carried Phoebe and Finn down to the oval rug, indulging in their sweet morning squirms. She relished her daughter's soft cheek against her own, her giggly insistence on singing "Old Mac-Donald" and shouting out a succession of animals increasingly unlikely to reside on a farm: a fish, a moose, an elephant, a unicorn. Louisa's favorite time of day was when her kids started up their harmony of mewls from their cribs, anticipating their morning snuggles. She herself woke at five, the alarm zapping away the thin gauze of sleep; then a cold shower, an outfit, and her war paint, all while racing against the clock until the twins woke up.

Both sets of little arms had reached out to her when she entered the nursery, the sweetest sight. Sometimes Louisa carried them into her bedroom, one kid per hip, and they'd all pile into bed together, where Nathan would just be coming to. They'd sing songs and make funny faces, a happy little foursome for a few precious moments before everyone disbursed to their days.

But not today. Nathan remained deeply asleep, and honestly, Louisa was relieved. Seeing as how the morning rush was no time to discuss the desire for divorce, her preference was to not interact with him at all.

Louisa heard the toilet flush, followed a few seconds later by Finn's shout of "Oh no, Mama!"

In the bathroom, she found her son wide-eyed, holding a handful of Legos, and pointing at the toilet, which was overflowing. Half an inch of water had already collected on the tile floor.

"I'm wet!" Finn declared superfluously, before dumping the rest of the Legos into the toilet bowl. Louisa stood there wondering if this was Finn's rebellion against the fact that his sister had mastered potty-training months ago, whereas he liked to pretend he was too good for the mini-toilet that he didn't yet have the self-control to visit reliably.

"Mama, I'm wet!" *Shit*—water continued to pool all around them, and Louisa was just standing there. You'd think such cries would rouse Nathan, but no, he was dead to the world.

"Okay, out, out." Finally, she mobilized, drying her son's feet and her own, then changing their socks. Nathan appeared in the doorway, eyes bloodshot and skin sallow. He sniffed the air. "What stinks?"

Louisa felt a flicker of pity, quickly snuffed out by hot indignation. She spoke to him like she was explaining something to the kids: "Our pipes are filled with brightly colored plastic, so the toilet is overflowing. I've got to go. You'll need to call a plumber."

"Fine."

Louisa detected annoyance in his tone—as if he had any grounds to be annoyed. Her anger flared.

When she and the kids were nearly out the door, Louisa deliberately affected the cheery sing-song of children's TV: "Kiddos, say bye to Dada."

Phoebe and Finn both wrapped their perfect little arms around their father. Louisa watched Nathan hug them back, breathing in their hair in the same way she always did, staring at them with what she could only describe as pure love. Her heart ached. But the ache was cut through with a flicker of sadness: how long had it been since Nathan had looked at her that way? But Jesus, there was no time for such thoughts—she was already late.

After the chaos of buckles and straps to wrangle her kids into their car seats, then the same maddening process in reverse five minutes later at daycare drop-off, Louisa was finally on her way to River Mill High. She felt as if she'd already worked a full day.

The sight of the red brick behemoth sometimes filled her with dread or fear or anxiety, or all three. Today, she felt nothing but relief. She was good at her job as vice principal of the big suburban public school, the most sought-after one in the region. Her main complaint was her boss, Dr. Poolehauzer, a fool of a principal who'd been hired last year. But the student body was the best you could hope for, so the job was gratifying more often than not. Louisa's days were utterly consuming and intense, with hundreds of people relying on her, which meant that while she was in the building it was impossible to maintain any semblance of an inner monologue about her personal life. For the duration of the school day, it would be as if the sentence "I want a divorce" had never even been uttered.

CHAPTER 3
Nathan

Nathan's head was pounding, and waves of nausea rippled through him as the close-talking plumber told him the toilet would cost five hundred bucks to fix. A rip-off. If Louisa were there she would've negotiated the fee in half, and Nathan could imagine her patronizing tone when he'd tell her how much he paid. But Nathan simply wrote out the check, thinking, *Who cares? It's fine.* He felt desperate for the man and his bad breath to get out.

In the kitchen, he encountered a sink crowded with dishes and a table strewn with bowls half-full of congealing cereal and milk. He opened the fridge to discover that they were out of OJ—of course. Still, *Who cares? It's fine.* Ahead of Nathan was a three-hour faculty meeting on policy changes for the upcoming semester, plus it looked like he was going to be late. Russell Low, the blowhard department chair, would probably chew him out in front of everyone. *Who cares? It's fine.*

All this drudgery felt almost like a video game, a series of moves Nathan was watching on a screen as he occasionally pressed a button to direct the action. Because he'd finally told Louisa the truth: he wanted out. Soon it would be "game over" and Nathan could get up, get out, and move on with his life.

Nathan hadn't meant to blurt out the D-word on his birthday at Giorgio's in front of an audience. He hadn't wanted to humiliate Louisa—in fact, he hoped to cause her the least pain possible with this rupture. He had enormous respect for the mother of his children and his partner of more than fifteen years. Love, too. Nathan still loved Louisa. He just wasn't *in love* with her anymore. That's how he'd been intending to break the news to her, explaining gently and sincerely—in private—that his heart was no longer in their marriage, so it wasn't fair to either of them to keep pretending it was. Only, he'd been trying to conjure the courage for the conversation for several weeks now, without success. So, no wonder it came out like it did, during the birthday dinner tradition that perfectly symbolized all Nathan had come to resent about his current life: always the same place, the same people, the conversation practically identical to the one they'd been carrying on for a decade. Enough already!

The video game simulation continued: commute, glare from his boss, weak department coffee, endless meeting. Nathan played along without complaint. *Who cares? It's fine.* Because he knew what was coming next: skulking away to the abandoned office he'd discovered in the building's basement.

Once there, Nathan checked his phone: "On my way, baby."

The text felt like a song in his soul. His heart's pounding was a bird beating its wings, ready to soar. Nathan knew he was no poet (he could imagine Louisa's raised eyebrows if he ever voiced such snippets aloud), but he didn't care; the clichés were sincerely felt, so what could be wrong with that?

A moment later, she flew through the door: Mona, his Mona!

Nathan observed with awe as she flitted about, unloading a series of bags and her coat—a man's puffer left behind at a friend's party, apparently—then hoisting herself up on the desk, pushing aside Nathan's briefcase with her ass.

She was beautiful, with her delicate body, big eyes, and tumble of jet-black hair. But those weren't the first things that had attracted Nathan to Mona. Rather, it was how she moved through the world, confidently and lightly, with eyes wide open, as if only good things could happen—as if the more experiences she had, the better life would be. Even when Mona got a C on Nathan's first exam, she'd shown up to office hours with an easy smile and reported with a shrug, "I've been too focused on my professor to concentrate on the material, so this is no surprise at all." It *had* been a surprise when she'd leaned across the desk and kissed him. Nathan had hesitated just a moment before kissing her back, feeling happier than he'd felt in ages. Yes, Mona was young. She was twenty-one. And Nathan, he reminded himself, was *forty*.

But he didn't feel forty, whatever that was supposed to feel like. Mona's optimism was infectious. Only when Nathan spent time with her and noticed her sunny outlook did he realize how cynical he'd become; if he had to pinpoint it, he'd say it was sometime around when he realized that he'd never again sleep through the night, and that he'd wake most mornings to discover that he'd disappointed his wife in some new way or another. As someone who dealt in hard numbers, Nathan knew that being with Mona wasn't actually turning back time. But it sure as hell felt like it.

"Do I get a hello?" Nathan felt greedy for her.

Mona set her dark eyes on him, batting her eyelashes, which she knew drove him mad. "Is someone feeling neglected?" She hopped off the desk and scurried over, planting her body in Nathan's lap. She smelled like lilacs, and Nathan felt fizzy. Longing crawled like a creature under the surface of his skin.

"Hello, old man." Mona's cherry lips met his, and as he ran his fingers along her silky skin, she made little purring sounds. He thought he might faint from happiness. How had this perfect woman chosen him? "I got you something for your birthday."

She reached into her bag and pulled out a lavender box, presenting him with a chocolate cupcake. She stabbed a candle in the frosting, brought a lighter to the wick, and then she sang. It was the first time Nathan had heard her singing voice; it was low and glorious. By the third verse—"Happy Birthday, dear Nate!"—she'd pulled off her sweater and released her hair from its twist so that it hung artfully over her perky little tits. Nathan memorized the image. Mona delivered a dollop of chocolate to his nose. "Now, make a wish."

Nathan's mind was white noise as he blew out the candle. All his wishes had already come true.

CHAPTER 4
Louisa

As usual, Louisa was one of the last people left at the school. She'd felt her phone buzzing in her pocket throughout the day, but only now did she have a moment to catch up on correspondence—and to remember that she wasn't just vice principal of River Mill High, but also a person with a life, or (her breath caught in her throat) whatever was left of it. She scrolled through the barrage of texts. Mateo's was simple: "Hope you're doing okay." Amy wrote, "Thinking of you. Call me if you want to talk. ♥." Louisa didn't get misty-eyed until she got to Mickey's third or fourth message: "Sending hugs." "Lean on me!" "Call whenever. I'm here." "Love you, Lou." "Happy hour? Drinks on me." "Earth to Lou—ARE YOU ALIVE AND WELL, OR AT LEAST ALIVE??"

Smiling, Louisa texted her friend back a single check mark. She felt void of words, and still had no explanation for what was going on with her husband.

One thing she knew was that Nathan was on daycare pickup (she texted him a reminder, out of habit). Still, on any other day, Louisa would race home to snatch a few minutes with her kids before their seven-thirty bedtime. But today, she lingered at school to catch up on paperwork, until a knock revealed Abe Jones in her doorframe. He looked nervous, tugging on his dopey tie made of famous news headlines: "Lincoln Shot!" "Prohibition Ends!" "Hitler Dead!" "Nixon Resigns!" "Man on the Moon!" "Obama Triumphs!" "Trump in Chief!" It gave Louisa whiplash to see history summed up and jammed together like that.

"Hey, Jones," she said. Abe stepped into her office and pulled her into a hug. For the first time today, Louisa's eyes welled up. She'd avoided walking by her friend's classroom. She knew the moment she laid eyes on Abe, a witness to Nathan's declaration last night, her façade of a competent professional would crack. She might actually collapse into a heap on the linoleum floor. Now she went limp, letting herself be supported by Abe's strong arms. It occurred to her how tired she was, and her incipient tears gave way to full-on weeping until her mind went blank and she forgot why she was crying. All the while Abe patted her on the back, offering soothing encouragements like "It's okay" and "I know." When she was done, Abe handed her a tissue.

"Stairwell F?" he asked. Louisa nodded.

They set out toward the musty stairwell that probably hadn't been cleaned since the school was built half a century earlier. Stairwell F led nowhere—except, the two of them had discovered years ago, to the roof. They'd been sneaking up there ever since. Louisa never grew tired of the moment when the door creaked open and revealed that rectangle of sky, maybe a cloud's lazy drift.

The roof was cushy underfoot, and the frigid air was cleansing. Louisa felt her cheeks jolt to alertness then go numb. Abe handed her his vape pen. She inhaled deeply—it was marijuana, not tobacco. Abe laughed at her surprise. "I figured you could use it. So, tell me, Bauer, how has the last day been?"

"Just grand. Peachy." Louisa shrugged and took another hit. "This morning was the usual chaos. Finn discovered that dumping his Legos in the toilet would flood the bathroom, which didn't really leave time for Nathan and me to discuss the state of our marriage."

"Well, whatever happens, you're lucky to have those crazy kids."

"Right," she said. "I have so many Lego-related disasters to look forward to. That's one reason not to pitch myself over the edge into the river." Louisa usually appreciated that this view included a sliver of sparkling water.

"Don't joke about that. Plus, the river's like a quarter-mile away. And even if you managed to hurl yourself that far, it'll be frozen solid at least till March."

"Thanks for poking holes in my plan, Jones."

"That's what I'm here for."

"You know, Nathan was the first person to take me to the river."

"Oh yeah?"

"We went cliff-jumping." Louisa had been living in River Mill for nearly a year, having no idea there was an actual river there. "We'd just started dating, so I didn't tell him I was scared of heights."

Abe smiled, indulging her nostalgia. Louisa remembered every moment of that afternoon— the warm summer sun on her skin, the water's surface winking, jewel-like, Nathan surfacing and shaking like a dog, then scaling the cliff, long limbs all flexed muscle, more monkey than human. He'd eventually convinced her to jump. Louisa expected freefall to feel like bundled terror rising in her stomach, but when she sprang away from the ground, she discovered it was surprisingly freeing; the plunge into the water prickled her whole body with pleasure. Nathan came up from behind to wrap his arms around her, then they made love right there on the river bank. Afterward, Louisa lay back on the warm rock face, squinting up at the sun.

That's when she realized she was in love.

She didn't share any of this with Abe now. Instead, she said, "I taught Nathan to back-float that afternoon." That had happened, too. Nathan had told her he couldn't, but Louisa had insisted he could. She instructed him to inhale deeply, and as his stomach puffed out, she reached a hand under the small of his back to readjust his center, then guided his arms to the side, until his torso skimmed the surface. She told him to make gentle kicks to keep his legs buoyant. Slowly, she removed her hand, and he was floating. "He said I was a genius," she recounted to Abe. "He told me I should become a teacher. I'd honestly never considered it before then." Louisa thought of Nathan's beautiful tanned body sprawled out on the rock that day, his skin pressed against hers. It felt like a hundred years ago.

"Bauer, are you all right?"

The words startled her. Louisa felt her knees go weak, and she carefully backed away from the roof's edge.

"I need to go home." Whatever that word meant now.

CHAPTER 5

Louisa and Nathan

"I met someone else."

"Okay."

The kids were fed, bathed, and in bed. Louisa had dropped her skirt suit in the hamper, shedding her workday like a shiver, and was now in sweats. Nathan had poured her a glass of wine. At least he was chivalrous before bashing her over the head with his revelation. Every cell in her body was silently screaming, but Louisa pretended to be cool and calm as she waited for him to continue.

"I didn't mean for it to happen. I wasn't looking to meet someone. She just appeared—*she* actually pursued *me*—then one thing led to another."

Louisa watched her husband sweat as he rattled off the most hackneyed of explanations. She could tell he sensed he was going astray, so he started again.

"Listen, I love you, Louisa. I'll always love you. I love Phoebe and Finn. But all this"—he made a sweeping gesture, which Louisa guessed was meant to encompass their life—"the routines and the kid-friendly meals, the cleaning up messes, the bickering and the half-assed apologies, until it's the same thing all over again—"

Louisa couldn't keep listening. It was like her brain was protecting the rest of her by tuning him out—his wholesale indictment of everything that added up to their life together, his news that he'd found something better and was leveling up. She tuned back in to hear, "Even the easy stuff has started to feel hard. I'm sorry, but I just can't do it anymore."

Louisa scoffed. "It's hard! You can't do it anymore!" She heard the hysterical quality to her voice, but so what? Nathan sounded like one of her students throwing a pity party about a failed essay, crumpling up the pages to chuck in the trash.

"You know," he said, "this is part of what I mean, how you've started acting like I'm this big moron and you're the expert. There's only so much of that a guy can take. I need a fresh start."

Louisa seethed. Nathan was taking the fact that she did far more than her fair share of running the household, and turning it around to blame on her. He needed a fresh start! Who did he think he was? "Newsflash, Nathan, you're a grown man with children! You don't get to have a fresh start."

It was infuriating how he waited patiently to make sure she was finished before speaking. "I know I'm a father, Louisa. I'm not going to ditch the kids. I'm not some kind of monster."

"Right. You're just ditching me, and breaking up our family."

"Honestly, Lou, I sort of thought you'd be relieved to hear I was leaving. Lately, you haven't seemed so happy to have me around."

He was unbelievable, Louisa thought, as if *she'd* pushed *him* into the arms of another woman. "Well, I'm certainly not happy right now. Who is this someone you met, anyway?"

"She's from the university. Her name is Desdemona. Mona for short."

Louisa choked out a laugh. "That's a joke, right? Who on earth would name their child after a Shakespearean heroine who's basically a doormat for her raving-mad husband until he murders her?" She'd taught *Othello* back in the day; she was always frustrated by Desdemona's stupid loyalty in the face of Othello's paranoid fits. "Let me guess, she's a professor of poetry, specializing in Romanticism."

Nathan cleared his throat. He'd been dreading this part in particular. "Close. She's studying English."

"A grad student!"

Nathan didn't know if she'd misunderstood him on purpose, if she was trying to make this as hard on him as possible. "Undergrad," he mumbled.

"Oh, I see," Louisa shouted, "you're leaving me for a teenager!" It was so ridiculous, it was funny. She began cackling. She could feel the veins bulging on her neck, and she guessed it made her look haggard—the opposite of her husband's new girlfriend, probably. Louisa was surrounded by teenagers all day, every day, and to her mind, there was nothing like hanging out with young people to make a person feel old. But clearly Nathan didn't share this opinion.

"She's a senior," Nathan said, "and mature for her age."

Louisa had no words. Maybe Nathan was intentionally saying all the worst things in order to convince her to want out, too. Then a terrible thought bubbled up inside of her. No, it couldn't be true. But she had to ask: "Please tell me this girl is not your student."

Nathan looked like she'd slapped him, as if Louisa was the one at fault here. "I told you, Lou, *she* seduced me. I would never have pursued her."

"No, this isn't happening." It couldn't be. A shiver traveled down Louisa's spine.

Nathan crossed his arms. "Do I need to remind you that you were my teenage student when we met?"

"You were my T.A.! I was nearly nineteen, and you were twenty-two!" Louisa winced at the shriek in her voice. "You weren't married with kids!" She couldn't help adding, "You didn't have crow's feet and age spots!"

"Well, Mona isn't my student anymore."

"Couldn't you lose your job over this?"

Nathan waved a dismissive hand. "It's consensual. She's of age. I've seen colleagues get away with a hell of a lot worse. Anyway, we've been careful."

Louisa rolled her eyes. What stupidity. And he was mumbling like a child—no wonder he'd fallen for his student. Louisa thought about how sometimes in the middle of the night she found Nathan watching infomercials for hair replacement therapy; he'd tried to hide it when he once requested a brochure. She wondered if Desdemona was privy to this habit of her boyfriend's.

Louisa mulled over Nathan's little speech, how he was sick of their routines, and needed to break away from it all. But wasn't it obvious that the only reason he didn't have boring routines with this new person was simply because they hadn't been together long enough to establish any? Louisa had purposely not asked how long they'd been "dating"; she decidedly did not want the play-by-play of her husband's betrayal. And Nathan had accused her of treating him like an idiot, like that was wrong, but what could be more idiotic than his hitching himself to someone half his age in order to—*what?*—wind back time, or prop himself up and feel virile again? Her husband was living in a fantasy world. But whatever, it was his life. The days when Louisa believed that being in love meant a melding of two into one were long gone. Nathan was free to deceive himself as much as he liked, to chase after whatever dream he wanted. Louisa wasn't going to stand there and beg him to want the life they had together—to want her.

"So, what's your plan, then?"

Was Nathan imagining it, or was Louisa actually accepting what he was telling her? Maybe it would be this easy, this *amicable,* as they said. Maybe they could part ways as naturally as they'd come together—sunrise, sunset. Nathan's mind wandered to watching Mona performing sun salutations on the woven rug at the foot of her bed, her petite body like a wave transitioning from one pose to the next. She'd recently gotten certified as a yoga instructor, and Nathan felt proud of her for pursuing her dream.

Louisa cleared her throat. Nathan urged himself to focus. "I'll move out. I suppose I'll crash with Mona until I find my own place."

"You suppose?" Her tone dripped with mockery, as her eyebrows shot up. "It sounds like you haven't really thought this through. Does this Desdemona have roommates? Does her student apartment have a spare room suitable for two toddlers? Or will you be moving a couple of cribs into the dorms? Has Mona even met the kids—wait, don't answer that." Louisa didn't know which response would be worse. "Have you thought about how you'll tell them about—"

"Louisa, stop, please. Enough." Nathan's voice was gruffer than he'd intended. He took a breath. "I'll figure it out, okay?"

But obviously he knew Louisa was not okay. Nor was she content to let him figure out his own plan in his own way. This was what Nathan had grown to resent most about his wife—her belittling and micromanaging, her treating him like he was one of her hapless employees or checked-out students, instead of her husband, her equal. He sometimes wondered if Louisa even liked him anymore; the thought made him sad. "You know, you didn't used to be this way."

"What way, Nathan?" Louisa set her mouth so that little wrinkles appeared around her lips; Nathan felt ashamed for noticing. "You made a good point earlier—I was a teenager when we started dating. Then, guess what? I grew up. I think the problem here is that apparently you never did."

Nathan had no response. Maybe Louisa was right and maybe she was wrong. Nathan wasn't sure what "growing up" really meant, although he guessed Louisa had a clear idea of it in her own mind. Either way, Nathan knew he didn't want to fight with her anymore.

"I'll sleep on the couch tonight. I'll get up with the kids in the morning. I know you must be exhausted."

Only when he said it did Louisa realize it was true. She felt so tired that she couldn't think of another thing to add to this terrible conversation. And when Nathan reached out to hug her, she let it happen. She let herself be comforted by the man she'd thought of as home for the last eighteen years. He walked her to their bed—or was it just hers now?—kissed her on the cheek, and left.

CHAPTER 6

Amy's Birthday

Their reservation was always for eight p.m. It was a compromise, between the educators, Louisa and Abe, who would've preferred earlier, and the corporate ones, Amy and Mateo, who would've preferred later. Mickey and Nathan didn't figure into the calculation, since their hours were all over the place—she was happy with whatever; he complained no matter what. Amy did her best work late in the day: She basically sleep-walked until noon, woke up to the world after lunch, and finally hit her stride around three or four p.m. It was one of the many things she feared about motherhood, how she'd be forced to transform into a morning person, up and at 'em, ready to prepare bottles and construct block towers at seven or six or even five a.m.

The texts began around six-thirty: Abe reminding her about the dinner, Mickey reassuring her that it was perfectly acceptable to unchain herself from her desk after sundown, Mateo asking how late she planned to arrive to her own birthday dinner and what kind of excuse he should invent for her (never mind that he was often later than she was).

Whatever, screw them all and all their jokes about Amy living and breathing her job. Amy happened to like her work, and she couldn't help that she had a lot to do. What she didn't like was that her birthday happened to fall just a couple of weeks after Nathan's. This had been convenient a decade ago: After their first-ever birthday dinner at Giorgio's, which had been a set-up for Amy and Abe, Abe had casually mentioned that since they'd all had such a great time, maybe they should reconvene at the restaurant later in the month for Amy's birthday. On a first date, it felt like a big deal to be making plans two weeks out. But now, just a fortnight after Nathan had dropped his divorce bombshell at the table, Amy wasn't exactly anxious to get the gang back together again. When Amy asked Mickey how many people she'd made the reservation for, Mickey replied, an edge to her voice, "Six, of course."

"Surprise!" Abe popped into her office, a dozen roses in hand. "Happy birthday, Ames!" He was so full of joy, her husband, that Amy, immersed in code just a minute before, let the feeling be contagious.

"I wasn't expecting you." She kept her voice neutral. "Hi."

Abe kissed her and held out the bouquet. The fact that Amy

would now have to find a vase was a flicker in her head before Abe pulled one out of his bag, along with a bottle of water and that little packet of flower food that only the likes of Abe ever bothered using. There was no denying it: even though Amy didn't care about flowers, and was annoyed to have her workday cut short, she had the sweetest husband.

"I came to whisk you away for a surprise pre-dinner drink."

"That wasn't the plan," she replied.

"Hence the surprise part! I know you hate to step away from your computer. But I see a vodka soda with your name on it. Your work will still be here tomorrow."

Amy's husband knew her well, and he was right. What would her life be like without him occasionally reminding her that things like happy hour and runs by the river could be just as gratifying as constructing clear code? Or, maybe not just as gratifying, but supplementary in a net-positive way. Abe was her warm, openhearted teddy bear, a complement to Amy's cool breezes and sharp edges.

It was cute when Abe, who wasn't a big drinker, clinked his Sprite against her vodka soda in cheers. "Happy birthday, my perfect wife," he said. Amy blushed. "Do you remember your birthday two years ago?"

"Of course," she said. "Giorgio's, like always."

"And?" Abe planted a kiss on her neck, prompting her memory.

"Oh, right." Flushed with wine, Amy had felt uncharacteristically bold that night. When their friends encouraged her to shout out a wish, Abe winked and she'd gone for it, voicing what she knew was running through her husband's head: "I wish for a baby." That night, for the first time, Abe didn't use a condom. He'd been so giddy with hope and potential, wearing his goofy grin all the way through to the end, it had both touched and embarrassed Amy. She recalled his warm hand on her belly afterward, the tenderness of it, imagining what might already be brewing beneath. So much had happened since then—or, put another way, so much *hadn't* happened. "That feels like a century ago."

Abe frowned. He still placed his hand on Amy's belly every time afterward, but these days the gesture made her cringe. "Well, two years is a long time. And although I remain optimistic, I wonder if you might reconsider other options." He was speaking gently, but Amy could tell he'd rehearsed for this.

She, too, aimed to be gentle but firm: "Abe, come on, it's my birthday."

"Honey, I know." For a moment it seemed like he was going to drop it, but the way the napkin was turning to fringe between his fingers made Amy realize he was just getting started. "It's just, you're not getting any younger."

Amy made no effort to hide her offense, and she could see Abe immediately regretting his words. She knew how much her husband yearned to have a child—he'd told her so on their very first date, a decade ago at Giorgio's—and he didn't know how to talk about this any better than she did. "*We're* not getting any younger, I meant. But with IUI or IVF..." His voice trailed off.

They'd been over this again and again, ever since that grim appointment with the fertility specialist, Abe bringing it up at the most inopportune times, Amy never wanting to discuss it. She thought about her officemate, Anika, who'd confided in her through four failed rounds of IUI and another two of IVF. She'd described her hot flashes and mood swings in intricate detail, had lifted up her shirt to reveal the apricot-sized bruises across her stomach from the daily injections. She'd explained how the whole venture made her and her wife feel like failures, plus disgusted to have sunk such large sums of money into the procedures instead of say, donating it to a worthy cause or buying a car or spending it on anything else at all. Even without Anika's cautionary tales, Amy had known from the start that she'd never be up for fertility treatments. It disgusted her, honestly, the lengths people went to pass along their own genes when there were so many children out there in need of good parents—children like the one Amy herself had been. Not to mention that these treatments upped your chances of having twins or multiples, the idea of which—no offense to Louisa and Nathan—horrified Amy.

"Abe, I've told you that stuff just isn't for me."

"Okay, okay." He held up his hands in defense. This is what Amy hated, how these discussions pitted the two of them against each other. "So, can we talk about adoption, then?"

"Um."

Adoption wasn't so simple either, and Amy had a hard time articulating her feelings about it to Abe. She was grateful she'd been adopted, plucked from a life of poverty in rural China, passed from the arms of a teenage girl to the loving, capable adults who became her parents and raised her with every comfort and opportunity in suburban New Jersey. Her mother, Adele, had given up a successful veterinarian practice to spend her days shuffling Amy around to school and her myriad extracurriculars. And yet, Amy also couldn't help wondering if her birth mother ever thought of her, if she still considered Amy her child, if she loved her. A part of Amy had always wondered (even as another part felt ashamed to even entertain the thought), if she hadn't been ripped away from every blood relative and adopted, might she have been better off in some fundamental, ineffable way?

Throughout her childhood, Amy had always felt a little alone. She grew up in a place where not a single other face looked like hers, where she was forever the outlier among a sea of whiteness. Her parents had always insisted they didn't see her differences, that it didn't matter, because they loved her just the same as they'd love a biological (i.e., white) child. Amy tried not to blame them for these views—when she was growing up, a "colorblind" attitude had been considered the best way to approach a transracial adoption. But she also believed it explained her loneliness, at least partly. If her parents couldn't see her differences, as they claimed, then they weren't really seeing her. Even as a small child, Amy had known that this stuff mattered. Especially because the rest of the world certainly could see her differences—and made sure to let her know of it in a million different ways.

In college, Amy finally had had Asian classmates. But she'd felt too awkward to join the Chinese Culture Club or partake in the Lunar New Year celebrations. She never even dated an Asian guy. Even now, Amy felt a little uneasy about the fact that her husband and most of her friends were white.

Abe touched her knee. "Ames, think of all the love we have to give. Think of all we could do for a child, and all a child could do for us."

"Mm-hm." But Amy was thinking about something else: Could she be responsible for doing what had been done to her to another baby, summoning them to come fill a void in her and Abe's lives? That was another thing about being adopted: Amy knew that before she arrived in her parents' life, they'd tried for years to have a baby; Amy, they always insisted, was their miracle. It's why Adele had opted to be a stay-at-home-mom, so gung-ho was she about finally having a child (although Amy caught occasional glimpses of her mother's regret at the choice to abandon her career). It was a lot of pressure to put on a kid.

Abe pressed a flyer into Amy's hand; of course he'd done the research. Opening it was like looking in a mirror: boys and girls with big black eyes and little puffs of dark hair stared back at her. Amy felt her heart open to this one pudgy girl; she wanted to reach through the flyer and cuddle her. Noticing the shift—Abe noticed everything—

he took his wife's hand. He is such a good man, Amy thought. He would be an amazing father. And if they adopted from China, their baby would have a mother who looked like her. Amy could do things differently than her parents had.

Amy felt a welling up inside that was big and scary; it was all too much. She turned away from the little girl's gaze and handed the brochure back to Abe. "I have to think about it more."

Abe refolded the brochure wordlessly. He'd said his piece and he knew Amy's need to mull. He stood up and grasped her hand. "Okay, time for dinner."

"All right." It would be a relief. Despite how the last dinner had ended, Amy was looking forward to it: the familiar setting and the same spread of comforting food, their best friends, the evening they'd experienced so many times she could probably script it all out in her head ahead of time, like a rerun of a favorite TV show.

———

At ten past eight, Mickey and Mateo sat presiding over an otherwise empty table. Mickey had handed off the cake to the waitress and Mateo had put in the wine order. Now there was nothing to do but wait.

"Did Mel show you her essay?" Mateo tore into his third slice of bread. "An A-minus from Ms. Gordon, a notoriously tough grader." Mickey made a noise of acknowledgment, but seemed to barely hear him; she was kneading her forearms. "The Cold War one, remember? Mel was glued to that documentary about the Berlin Wall, begging us to send her there for spring break."

"Oh, right," Mickey said. Mateo was looking at her like she was lost in outer space, but she just wasn't in the mood to discuss their daughter's schoolwork. No, she was thinking about her best friend. Louisa had called yesterday and made every excuse to skip the dinner—she was behind at work, couldn't get a sitter, had nothing to wear—but Mickey pressed her to come out. Louisa had already bailed on every plan they'd made in the last two weeks, not sharing a single detail about what was going on with her and Nathan, and Mickey believed she needed to spend time with people who loved her. Plus, it would be like a curse to bail on their birthday tradition. She told Louisa that if anyone were to skip it, it should be Nathan, though Louisa had claimed Nathan insisted on joining them.

Mateo went on, "Mel's developing a real passion for history. We should nurture it with visits to museums and historical sites."

"Can we talk about this another time?" Mickey said, as nicely as possible. Her husband was always doing this, filling every silence with discussion of their daughter.

"Okay. What would you like to talk about, my dear?"

Ignoring his facetious tone, Mickey nestled her head into his shoulder. She'd been chatting with people at the gym all day long; what she wanted right now was a break, to sit in silence and take in the calming music and the aroma of freshly baked bread and the scene that felt like home.

"Hi, sorry, sorry," Abe said, guiding Amy by the hand as they arrived at the table. He delivered kisses to Mickey's cheeks. "Our lateness is on me this time."

Amy waved hello, noticing the empty seats. It seemed like a bad omen, and not just because of Nathan's announcement the last time around.

Abe placed the ceremonial crown on his wife's head, kissing her on the forehead.

"Do I really have to wear this?" Amy felt there was something pathetic about a childless woman of nearly forty wearing a crown made of pink construction paper.

"It's tradition," said Mickey, ending the discussion.

The bottles of Pinot Noir appeared, followed by the olives and bruschetta and burrata. The group dug in, hoping to be comforted by the tastes and textures they loved and relied upon. But the strongest presence at the table were the absent parties.

It was nearly eight-thirty when the two of them—first Nathan, then Louisa—slid into their spots. They were holding martinis, which they must've gotten at the bar. No one drank martinis at the birthday dinners; everyone stuck to wine. The sight of the couple with their untraditional drinks rendered the rest of the group mute.

Nathan broke the silence: "Hi, hello. We're here. Happy birthday, Amy. Let's get this party started."

He grabbed Louisa's hand—the other two couples noticed, and they all breathed a sigh of relief. Maybe they were all okay, and their group would remain intact. Maybe Nathan's announcement at his birthday a couple of weeks ago had been a blip of uncertainty, a pop of panic followed by a return to sober reality. Probably by now everything had returned to normal. Nathan clinked his glass against Louisa's, and took a sloshing gulp; Louisa ingested a polite sip. They all seemed to be holding out for her to say something, too—a jokey quip or a reassuring comment so they could return to their regular rhythm.

But Louisa didn't comply. Instead, she turned to Abe and asked him about a school matter. Okay, so maybe she wasn't ready to make any heartening proclamations to the group, but look at how fine she seemed, sitting there talking about midterm report cards. Surely she wouldn't be able to focus on something so mundane if her marriage were crumbling.

And so, with these inner justifications and reassurances, the group relaxed, settling into their conversational do-si-do, pairing off, coming back together, and forming new pairs. Nathan and Mateo swapped news of their old grad school friends over lasagna and chicken parmigiana. Amy and Mickey discussed triathlon training as they partook of spaghetti carbonara and chicken marsala. Louisa and Abe kept up the River Mill High chatter over cacio e pepe. Everyone topped off their wine, sharing predictions of the snowstorm headed their way that weekend. Then they split off again, Amy and Mateo gossiping about layoffs at their old firm, Louisa apologizing to Mickey for their broken plans, Abe asking after Nathan's kids and Nathan asking after Abe's students, everyone sampling Caprese salad and mushroom risotto. More wine, a round of toasts, everyone reaching for seconds and thirds until forks scraped plates. More wine still. The six diners continued on with this dance, forming every pairing permutation.

Well, except for one.

When Nathan finally turned to Louisa, his vision was a little blurred, and her cheeks were flushed. They'd both overdone it with the wine, not to mention the martinis. They'd agreed to fill in their friends on what was going on with them; after Nathan's performance at the last birthday dinner, Louisa felt they owed everyone an explanation (Nathan didn't think they owed anyone anything, but he'd kept his mouth shut on this point).

But now Louisa was having second thoughts. It was Amy's birthday, after all, and everyone seemed to be enjoying themselves. Why spoil it? For the last hour, Louisa had successfully managed to pack the mess of her life into a little box and relegate it to the far recesses of her mind, and—look!—here she was enjoying herself. Even her husband, though they'd exchanged not a word since sitting down, felt like the familiar presence by Louisa's side for all these years. Sure, it was mostly an act, but not entirely. After all, how many times over the years had she been annoyed about something Nathan had done that day but still laughed genuinely at his jokes at dinner? It was possible to be both angry and amused, frustrated and joyful—people contained multitudes.

That was part of why this situation felt so confusing: because here Louisa was sitting beside her husband at a Giorgio's birthday dinner, the most normal thing in the world. She had to keep reminding herself that things *weren't* normal, that although the ground beneath her felt solid, it had in fact turned to quicksand.

"Hey," she said, turning to Nathan, intending to suggest that they keep mum.

But Nathan misunderstood—he thought she was giving him the go-ahead, so he clinked his fork against his glass. "Ahem, hi everyone, greetings."

Louisa was already uncomfortable. Why was he acting like he was presenting at a sales conference?

"I know our last dinner ended on a bit of a cliffhanger."

Louisa had a strong desire to bolt. Mickey flashed her a reassuring smile, which weirdly also felt like a command to keep her butt firmly planted in its seat.

"We wanted to let you know what's going on with us."

Up until this moment, Amy hadn't been feeling much of anything about the fact that it was her birthday. But now she experienced a welling up of anxiety. Somehow these dinners had morphed into occasions for everyone to lay their cards on the table, to mark their aging with brutal honesty about their hopes and dreams along with their failures and disappointments. Amy couldn't imagine feeling so at ease to behave that way, and she wondered if others felt pressured into opening up more than they wanted to. Nathan was trembling, and Louisa seemed to be working hard to appear fine. Amy wanted to reassure them, to give them a pass. Everyone deserved privacy, even from their closest friends. The words burst out: "You guys don't have to share anything if you don't want to."

Relief flooded Louisa's face. "It's Amy's birthday," she said, "so let's defer to her. She doesn't deserve to have her celebration hijacked by our couples' therapy." She laughed nervously.

"Oh, no," Amy said, "I don't care about my birthday." She didn't want them to think that's what she'd meant, that she was a diva about her big day.

"It sounds like Nathan has something he wants to share," Mickey said. She believed in honesty and communication; she believed in catharsis. Louisa tried to stare her down, but Mickey wouldn't meet her eye. Abe's smile was full of sympathy. Mateo looked down at his plate; he was staying out of it.

Nathan cleared his throat. "Louisa and I have spent a long time together. We have the gift of so many shared experiences, supporting each other's careers, and making two beautiful children together."

Louisa felt her body go weak. If he mentioned their kids by name, she thought she might lose it. Mickey's hand was a surprise around her own; her friend must've swapped seats with Mateo without her noticing.

Nathan inhaled audibly. "But I've decided this life is no longer the right fit for me."

Louisa hoped he might leave it at that, or at least move on to logistics, his plan to move out soon. She didn't have anything to add. She wanted to return to pretending, at least for the remainder of the night, that everything was fine.

But when she looked up from the table she saw that every one of her friends looked devastated. Not only devastated, but scared. *Why?* Louisa wanted to shake them. *He's not leaving you, he's leaving me; he's not rejecting the life he built with you, he's rejecting the life he built with me. This isn't about any of the rest of you!*

Maybe they simply needed more details to grasp what was really happening here. So, Louisa slammed her hands on the table, startling the group from their sad stupor. Plates rattled and wine sloshed out of glasses. "Nathan has been feeling unhappy with our relationship. He met a young woman named Desdemona while she was a student in his class. *She* seduced *him.*" At this, she directed an exaggerated nod to Nathan, giving herself credit for relating the facts as he'd laid them out for her. "And they fell in love." This she extrapolated. But surely they must be in love for Nathan to blow up his life over her. "Nathan will be moving out as soon as he finds an apartment. In the meantime, we are coexisting in our home, and at this dinner."

Mateo smirked, and Mickey shot him a vicious look. "I'm sorry, bro," he said, "but you *fell in love with your student?* Really? You're going to throw away your whole life and put your job at risk for a few hot hookups?"

"You're certainly making a lot of assumptions," Mickey retorted, before realizing with horror that she sounded like she was defending Nathan. She was categorically on Louisa's side.

Amy felt panicked; how had her birthday dinner descended into this? She glared desperately at her husband, and was grateful to find him gearing up to intercede. Abe was forever the peacemaker. "All right, guys. I don't think it's wise for us to sit here and hash this out like it's some kind of a debate. This is between Louisa and Nathan—"

"It's all right, I get it," said Nathan, slurring his words a bit. "Matty's skepticism is legit. I know how it sounds, and it doesn't help that Mona is so young. You're right that Louisa and I have had a bit of a slump in the bedroom."

Louisa's outrage was stronger than her humiliation, and she made no attempt to control the volume or shrillness of her voice: "We have two-year-olds, for god's sake! How many parents of twin toddlers do you know with steamy sex lives? After a day of attending to the non-stop needs and whims of the kids, plus, you know, doing my actual job, I barely have enough energy to brush my teeth." She looked to Mickey and Mateo. "You guys must remember how exhausting it was to parent a little kid?"

"Try parenting a teenager," Mateo said. Everyone ignored him.

"So, your sex life was the main issue?" Mickey sounded genuinely curious, before remembering herself and narrowing her eyes again at Nathan.

"Well, there's a lot more to a relationship than what happens in bed." Mateo sounded like he was talking to Mickey more than Nathan.

What was going on here, Louisa wondered; how had they gotten so far off track? She guessed her friends were trying to be supportive, but she couldn't believe her love life was the current topic of discussion. She blinked hard, like she could snap herself awake from this nightmare. No such luck.

Nathan soldiered on: "Look, Louisa and I want different things. I love our kids more than life itself, but I can't spend every weekend attending sing-alongs and cutting up chicken cutlets and cleaning Goldfish crumbs out of the car seats after every goddamn ride."

"Sounds pretty great to me," Abe mumbled. Amy squeezed his hand, as her mouth remained agape. Never in a million years would she voice aloud to a group the comments they were all rattling off so casually.

"It *is* great," Nathan said, nearly yelling. "Of course it's great, but it's not enough. Louisa may think it is—plus, she's so much better at all that stuff than I am. But I want to go out dancing all night, I want to get lost in foreign cities, I want to—"

"Fuck a twenty-year-old," said Mickey.

"Twenty-one, but yes, actually. Sue me, so what if I do?"

Amy was wondering if Nathan had ever gone out dancing all night. She couldn't even picture him dancing. Had he danced at her and Abe's wedding?

"Everyone has fantasies," Mateo said. "Everyone wants things that are out of reach, especially during a stage of life when—"

Nathan interrupted, sounding impatient: "But I *can* have those things. That's my point." He looked at Louisa with a "back me up here" look, clearly out of deeply ingrained habit. Louisa's look was like a knife, and he realized his error.

Louisa could feel everyone looking at her, expecting a response. Her heart was a drum in her ears, her jaw a vice. When she finally spoke, it was very quiet: "Actually, Nathan, you don't have the faintest idea of what I want." She stood up and scraped her chair out from under the table. "Find your own way home. Or better yet, don't."

Mickey chased after her out to the parking lot, where Louisa waved her off. "Sorry, but I just want to be alone."

"I love you," Mickey called out, shivering without a coat. But Louisa had already disappeared into the darkness.

Back at the table, everyone had sobered up and waiters were stationed all around. It looked like a funeral procession that happened to feature a cake, their rendition of "Happy Birthday" a dirge.

"Make a wish. Shout it out." Mickey felt like she had to say it, out of tradition, but she pronounced the words without enthusiasm.

Amy could only manage a shallow breath. "I wish for all of us to be happy." Lame, maybe, but true. Also, impossible-seeming. It took Amy a handful of blows to extinguish the candles.

All five of them sat there contemplating their own happiness. No one made a move for the cake.

"Does anyone even want any?" Mickey asked. No response. "All right, box it up, please."

Kimmy the waitress carted away the cake, untouched save for the thirty-eight candle holes. Whatever, Mickey thought, Amy could take it into work tomorrow, or she and Abe could stay up all night gorging on it. Anything to wrap up this disaster of an evening and send everyone on their way.

Mateo signaled to Mickey from across the table, and she could tell what he was asking just from the slant of his chin. All she wanted was to get away from the guy causing her best friend such pain, but Mickey was also a good wife and a hopeless empath. She nodded back.

"Okay, you piece of shit," Mateo told Nathan. "You're sleeping on our couch tonight. Come on."

"Thanks, man."

"Well," Abe said, "This has been interesting." He shrugged Amy's coat over her shoulders, then put on his own. "See everyone here in a couple of months, same place, same time. Your turn next, Mickey."

"Great." It felt anything but.

CHAPTER 7

Abe and Amy

Amy was staring out the car window, and it was driving Abe nuts that he could only see the back of her head. She hadn't said a word since they'd left the restaurant.

"How's the heat, too high?" Abe fiddled with the vents.

"It's fine."

"Should I put on some music?"

"That's all right." She still didn't move her head.

"Okay." Abe felt the tension building. Maybe Amy could sit here in silence like this, but he couldn't handle it. "Look, Ames, I know what you're thinking."

"You do?" She finally turned to face him, her beautiful round face with the high cheekbones, her obsidian eyes. Abe's knuckles relaxed against the steering wheel.

"You're wondering if that's going to happen to us when we become parents. The rut of routines, the crappy sex life, the feeling trapped, the cheating." Abe didn't even like to say the last word aloud. It all sounded so foreign to him, but then so did fatherhood, the idea of a tiny creature who would come to live in their home and be theirs to care for and love.

Amy laughed, and Abe stiffened again. What was so funny? "I know you would never cheat on me," she said, still smiling.

True, Abe would never even contemplate cheating. And with a student? He shuddered at the thought. Abe loved the kids in his classes, but they were *kids*. He knew Nathan's students were a little older than his own, but still. After a day at school, Abe craved nothing more than adult company; he craved his wife.

But Amy had misunderstood him. Abe himself had always been happy with routine and structure, content with his little habits and small daily successes; what Nathan had described as so intolerable sounded just fine to Abe. And who really cared if their sex life took a hit for a while as they adjusted to parenthood? Whereas Amy was different. She worked like a maniac, yes, but when she finally gave herself a break, she was as apt to go whitewater rafting as she was to get a tattoo on a whim—she had a little peony on her ankle from a trip to Niagara Falls a few years ago. Abe wondered if motherhood would leave his wife restless and unhappy. She was thirty-eight today, which Abe could hardly believe; she still got carded sometimes, and despite her understated way of moving through the world, she was frequently the object of men's gazes. Whereas Abe was three years younger, and women rarely flirted with him.

"Actually, I was thinking about you," he ventured, a little embarrassed.

"Oh Abe," she said, "you know I hold myself to way too high of a standard to ever cheat. Walking around carrying all that guilt and shame—I could never bear it."

"Okay." It wasn't exactly what he'd hoped to hear, but at least it was honest. "And what about all the other stuff? The drudgery, the wiping of asses, the feeling trapped?"

Amy shrugged. "We could just outsource what we don't want to do. Hire a housekeeper and a nanny, get take-out every night."

Abe laughed, and Amy joined in. He assumed she was joking, but it wasn't such a bad idea: outsourcing the hard work of parenting. The first birthday gift Amy had given Abe was a bimonthly house-cleaning service. When they'd started dating, Amy was shocked to learn that Abe still cleaned his own toilet. He'd reminded her that a teacher didn't have the same disposable income as a computer engineer at a financial firm. With Amy's salary, Abe had since gotten used to all the ways money could smooth over the rough edges of life. He felt a moment of guilt, knowing that Louisa and Nathan were still living on so much less—no wonder Nathan felt so stressed.

"Okay," ventured Abe, "so if you aren't worried about parenthood potentially ruining our marriage, what *were* you thinking at dinner?"

"I was thinking, let's do it."

"Do what?"

"Let's adopt a baby." Amy said it casually, like she was suggesting they go to the movies.

"Really?"

"Yeah." Amy couldn't quite believe what she was saying, but the evening had really shaken her. Louisa and Nathan had experienced a massive breakdown in communication—in understanding each other's needs and wants. Whereas Amy had known from the start how badly Abe wanted a child. So what if she herself remained ambivalent? She was so sick of her own waffling. Plenty of women felt ambivalent about the prospect of motherhood before they became mothers, then they got over it and fell in love with their children. Amy assumed she would, too.

She realized Abe was still looking at her expectantly. She cleared her throat: "When I was listening to Nathan and Louisa, all I could think was, that's so not us. Right? I mean, we've been trying and failing to have a baby for two years now. That's a lot of failure, especially for someone like me, who could hardly tolerate an A-minus in school. Whenever we've struggled, we turn to each other for comfort—we don't attack or flee. I feel closer to you now than I did that night two years ago, when we came home from my birthday dinner, me all boozy and you ready to knock me up."

Amy remembered how giddy Abe had been, so high on hope, cavalierly tossing out the condoms and leaping into bed with her. Since then, that fizzy anticipation had been replaced by something more substantial—Amy's certainty that she was married to a solid man who would stick by her side, no matter what. "If we can make it through that, we can make it through anything. Don't you think?" They were such a strong team, and if anyone could help a child navigate such a complicated world, it was the two of them.

Abe wanted to gun the gas to maximum speed, but he settled for banging his palm against the dashboard. "All right, Mama, let's adopt ourselves a baby!"

Amy's face bloomed into a smile, then wilted slightly: "But just one, okay? No twins." As confident as Amy felt in her relationship, as much as she knew that she and Abe could figure out a better way to parent than the version that had apparently broken Louisa and Nathan, she remembered visiting the new family of four shortly after they'd returned home from the hospital: Every time Finn had stopped crying, Phoebe took it as her cue to start; and just after Phoebe was changed into a fresh diaper, it was Finn's turn for a blowout. It was like the twins had spent their time in the womb hatching a plan to cause as much chaos as possible. Their parents were no match for their collusion.

"No twins, deal," said Abe.

Later that night, Abe didn't place his hand on Amy's belly or flash her that hopeful smile. Amy felt a bit nostalgic for the gestures, but mostly in the way you do after finally breaking a bad habit. The more powerful feeling was relief—no longer would she be the receptacle for a failing project; no longer would she have to think of herself as a machine with faulty parts. She fell asleep meditating on the fact that her body would become her own again. Meanwhile, Abe lay beside her dreaming of the tiny body that would soon find its way into their lives.

CHAPTER 8

Nathan

Louisa always got up first, then set up the French press with the perfect ratio of grounds to boiling water. That's the first thing Nathan thought of when he woke up on his friends' couch, instinctively sniffing the air for Italian roast, his temples throbbing. But just as he was registering the loss of this morning routine, he rejected it with a scoff. If his feelings toward his wife were wrapped up in something so mundane as morning coffee, clearly his marriage had devolved past saving. For Mona, he would've leapt out of bed at dawn and prepared some intricate Starbucks-style drink with extra foam and a shot of vanilla hyacinth whatever—and she would've expressed sincere appreciation. When was the last time Louisa had appreciated anything Nathan did? *I told you so,* he wanted to declare, as if he were in a debate. Nathan knew he was being ridiculous. But he couldn't help feeling defensive, after his friends had put him on trial last night at dinner. As if it was unheard of in the history of humankind that a spouse might choose to leave a marriage.

Nathan peeled himself upright and headed to the kitchen, where he found Mickey and Mateo's teenage daughter at the table. Now he would have to play the good houseguest, earning his keep with sunny conversation. He tried to remember whether Melody played a winter sport that he could ask about.

"Wow," the girl said, twirling a pencil between her fingers. "I guess the power of positive thinking is real. Here I was racing to finish my calc problem set, which I understand not at all, and who shows up but a math professor."

"Hey, Melody. Nice to see you, too. I'll need an infusion of caffeine before I can face any numbers."

"I'd be fine if this was about numbers. But did you know the more advanced math gets, the less it's about actual numbers? You never reach your limit, you just approach it. You're never calculating something directly, you're only calculating change. Any actual numbers are infinitely small so that you start to go insane wondering if they're even real at all. Nothing's what it is, it's all derivative. What kind of crap is that? It's maddening. To think I actually used to like math."

Nathan couldn't help but laugh. He'd forgotten how much he liked Melody. "You might just have the makings of a mathematician in you. You remind me of me at your age."

Nathan endured Melody giving him the once-over, knowing what she must be seeing: bleary eyes, hair pointed every which way, rumpled clothes. He did not cut an aspirational figure.

"I'm going to be a historian," she said. "I want to understand the real world."

Good luck with that, Nathan thought sarcastically, but he said it straight: "Good luck with that."

"Anyway, I'll get you coffee, then you can finish my homework. Deal?"

"I'll get myself the coffee, then I'll help you finish your own homework."

Melody groaned. "Fine."

Sitting with the girl before her problem set, Nathan got drawn in, as he always did with numbers (the page was filled with them, despite Melody's rant). It was a relief to retreat into the abstract, to be drawing slopes on graphs and manipulating functions and working with unknowns on crisp white paper. He became utterly absorbed, so that he didn't notice Mickey until she cleared her throat.

Her hands on hips and anxious glances at Melody made Nathan feel accused. Did Mickey seriously think he would hit on her daughter? Just to clarify that no, he wouldn't, he sat up straight and screeched his chair a few inches away from Melody's.

Mickey redirected her attention to her daughter, but the disapproving stance remained. "Your ride leaves in five. You were supposed to finish your homework last night."

"I had a premonition that a math professor would appear in the morning, so I waited."

Nathan was impressed with Melody's vocabulary, and he saw Mickey register that, then twist up her mouth in annoyance. "Well, please get moving." As an afterthought, she addressed Nathan. "I left a towel for you. Mateo can drive you home."

"Thanks, Mickey. I appreciate your hospitality."

Mickey snorted. "Don't get comfortable. This was a one-time thing."

"Mom's on Team Louisa," Melody said, deadpan.

"Ah," Nathan said, surprised that the girl knew the situation. "And whose team are you on?"

"I need more information to make a well-informed decision. I've mostly heard Louisa's side, via Mom, but I imagine you have your own story. Although, is it true that your girlfriend is my age?"

"What? No!" After months of keeping their relationship hidden, it was a shock for Nathan to hear the daughter of his friends inquire so casually about Mona.

Mickey laughed, he assumed at his expense. "Come on, that's enough interrogation for seven a.m. We're gonna be late."

Nathan was left alone in a kitchen where the loudest noise was the hum of the refrigerator and the biggest mess the brown ring of his coffee mug on the granite—a respite from the usual toddler-filled chaos of his mornings. One wipe of a paper towel and the place was spotless. He would've liked to hit pause to hibernate in this quiet, clean space a bit longer. Alas, the day beckoned.

CHAPTER 9

Mickey

Mickey was pissed off. *One, two, three, four reps.* Pissed that a man could up and abandon his family, pissed that he could put his physical pleasure above all and screw everything else, screw every*one* else. Because who would be left to pick up the pieces? Louisa, that's who—the woman, the mother. Pissed that she, Mickey, had been pressured into hosting this man, making up their pull-out couch like she was running a freaking Airbnb. She slid off the bench press to add another set of ten-pound discs to each side of the bar. She was pissed that this man had cozied up to her daughter this morning to help her with work that she likely didn't even need help with. *Five, six, seven, eight reps,* then yet another set of ten-pound discs. Mel was probably just being polite and trying to make the man feel smart and useful. Because that was the fate of women, to put their own needs behind the needs of men, and to make men feel needed, too. Mickey was now benching nearly her whole bodyweight, fueled by anger, bending and flexing her arms and grunting with such vigor that she'd attracted an observer.

"Holy shit, Mickey Mouse, look at you go."

At the sound of the familiar rasp, Mickey's anger evaporated—along with her super-human strength. She splayed out her arms and caught her breath, then let her eyes drift up and drink in the sight: Keisha. She was peering down at Mickey, face slick with sweat and curls pulled back by a wide red headband.

"What are you doing here on a Wednesday?" For as long as Mickey had known Keisha, Wednesdays had been her rest days.

"Change of plans, thought I'd squeeze in a run." Keisha often spoke in fragments, not wasting a word. Mickey found her brevity refreshing. "Care to join?"

"I wish, but my front desk girl called out."

Keisha raised her eyebrows. Mickey knew she needed to find more reliable employees; she was the first to admit that she had a weakness for a pretty face in an interview. Mateo once commented that her gym was straight out of a rom-com movie—everyone working there looked like a Hollywood actor version of a gym employee.

"Find me after," Mickey said. "We can stretch together before I pick up Mel."

"Cool. Doing hills today—wish me luck."

"Luck!" Not that Keisha needed it, Mickey thought as she watched her friend head to the treadmills, calves as taut as if she were wearing sky-high heels, ass looking like...well, she wasn't going to go down that route. Since Keisha had recently broken up with her long-term partner, Leah, she'd been training even harder, and the results showed.

Mickey had Keisha to thank for this whole enterprise. Back when she was bouncing around from gym to gym as a personal trainer, she'd met Keisha on the triathlon circuit and they'd bonded over their fierce competitiveness. Mickey would spend half their bike rides complaining about the subpar facilities she encountered when meeting clients, so Keisha suggested she open her own spot. Keisha knew about starting a business. She'd been a corporate lawyer until she got sick of the old boys' club vibe, then had opened up her own boutique firm; being in charge of her schedule meant she could carve out plenty of time for training. Only when Keisha made the suggestion did Mickey realize that she already had a clear vision for her gym: women-only, body-positive, professional but welcoming, with a clean, simple design; the soundtrack would be singer-song-writers and indie rock, none of that top-forty remix crap. Someone brand new to exercise should feel as comfortable as a semi-pro athlete. She would call the place FleXX. When she pitched the idea to Mateo, he was more than supportive. The startup he'd helped launch had just gone public, and he agreed this was the perfect use of their small windfall (the house renovations could wait). Keisha agreed to invest, too, as a silent partner. So, Mickey went for it. FleXX was up and running the week of her thirtieth birthday. Keisha stayed by Mickey's side cheering her on as the place grew and grew. Eight years later, it was now a local hot spot with a waiting list; Mickey limited memberships, so FleXX wouldn't turn into a place where you had to wait twenty minutes for a machine.

Mickey scanned the space she'd created. There were so many women's bodies—toned and fleshy, broad and petite, curvy and boyish, and everything in between, all beautiful. Mickey felt grateful. She made a conscious effort to cultivate her gratitude so that it expanded inside of her and pushed out the bad vibes (this was the kind of thing she did now that she'd started attending FleXX's yoga classes). She made a note to encourage Louisa to return to this cocoon of femininity; it would do her good, and Mel could babysit the kids. But contaminating Mickey's good vibes was another flash of anger at Nathan—the prick!—whose bullshit adjunct professor gig allowed him plenty of time to go jogging post-twins, while Louisa had barely had time to sleep, never mind work out. It had been over a year since her friend had visited FleXX.

Mickey grabbed a set of free weights for triceps extensions when she caught sight of Keisha running: her lovely long back, her powerful arms pumping. She must've sensed Mickey watching because she turned to wave without breaking her stride.

Mickey hooked a left into the locker room, ostensibly to monitor the towel supply. While there, she figured she might as well check on the toilet paper. Oh, maybe she had to pee, too. But when she locked herself in the leftmost stall and tugged down her yoga pants, Mickey stopped deluding herself about why she was in there. It was her go-to: picturing Keisha's confident gait as she ran toward her and then tackled her in a sweaty embrace. They were here in the locker room, under the showers, spandex stripped off, soaping up and running their fingers through each other's hair, down to their sudsy-slick skin. Keisha's body was at once soft and firm pressed up against her, and—

The flush from the next stall startled Mickey. She gasped, then held her breath. She was no idiot—she knew her gym had earned a reputation where it wasn't unheard of to enter the locker room and hear panting from a stall (SexyFleXXy and Lady Tinder were among its tamer nicknames). But Mickey was the owner, and a goddamned professional. She yanked up her pants, exited the stall, and washed her hands, thinking, *I've gotta stop doing this.*

CHAPTER 10
Louisa

Well, this is inconvenient, thought Louisa, ushering the girl—no, *woman,* she corrected herself—to her new classroom. Kendra Grant was a maternity leave fill-in who didn't look old enough to have graduated college, although if Dr. Poolehauzer had hired her, she must've at least had her degree. Which meant Nathan's girlfriend was even younger. Then again, Louisa had seen her boss around attractive women—alternately tongue-tied and inappropriately flirtatious. She could picture him in the interview, transfixed by this bright-eyed, big-breasted siren, hiring her on the spot no matter her qualifications.

Louisa willed herself to focus on the orientation—to review the schedule and class rosters—and to stop thinking about Mona. She would keep her personal problems separate from work. She would be a mentor to Ms. Grant in the same way she was to any other new teacher.

"That should do it," she concluded. "If you have any questions, you know where to find me."

"Thanks a million," Ms. Grant said. "I'm so excited to be surrounded by such brilliant colleagues, everyone so committed to educating the next generation. I only hope that I can add to that effort in some small way."

"Great." Louisa felt embarrassed by the woman's little speech. "Good luck with day one. Remember, it'll get easier."

Back in her office, she beelined to her chocolate stash and tore into a KitKat. It was a relief to be away from Kendra Grant, from her dewy skin and also her unabashed earnestness. Louisa wondered if that's what Nathan liked about Mona, in contrast to his wife. Louisa hadn't always been so jaded. She'd been a college freshman when she met Nathan. He was her T.A. in Statistics (even English majors had to take one math class). It was unlike Louisa to visit office hours, but she was a mediocre math student and attended Nathan's faithfully, enjoying his attention—and yes, attracted to his lanky, boyish looks. Again and again, Nathan explained the problems that flummoxed her, always patient, always kind. He was working toward his doctorate, and when Louisa asked about his studies, his eyes lit up. He explained about stochastic processes, specifically something called Markov chains, the probability of a next step dependent only on its current spot, never where it had been before. Louisa liked the sound of that, and of Nathan's voice explaining it. She liked the idea of his mind preoccupied by these mysterious abstractions.

After the final exam, when Louisa had gone to thank Nathan (she'd been grateful to eke out a B-minus), she ended up asking him out for ice cream. The invite flew out of her mouth. Nathan hesitated before he agreed, which Louisa appreciated; he wasn't the type to prey on his students.

It felt comfortable strolling together through campus, neither one having to slow down their long-legged stride. Nathan was easy to talk to; he listened and asked follow-up questions, which felt important to Louisa. Plus, he was funny, showing a goofier side than he had in class or in his office. In the ice cream shop, he decisively ordered a scoop of vanilla while Louisa deliberated before picking mint chip. After eating their cones, Nathan reached into his briefcase and pulled out Snakes and Ladders. Louisa was too intrigued to find it strange that he'd been carrying around a board game all afternoon.

"I had that game as a kid," she said.

"Me too," Nathan said, looking shy. "Whenever my parents got into it with each other, my brother would bring me to the basement to play board games. He liked the ones that required skill and strategy, but I preferred Snakes and Ladders. I liked experiencing the occasional delight of a ladder or shock of a snake. It felt nice to give up control like that, like riding a wave." Nathan seemed a little embarrassed as he set up the game. "But that's not why I brought it here."

He began explaining his research, how Snakes and Ladders was a Markov chain: Depending on the roll of the die, Louisa's piece had an equal probability of moving to one of six squares. The next move was determined only by the piece's current position and the roll, not by any of its previous moves. History didn't count—it didn't matter how her piece had gotten to its current square, only where it would go from there.

Nathan went on to draw matrices and discuss stochastic probabilities, then to explain applications of his research, like modeling weather patterns and the stock market. But Louisa was stuck on the first idea, that history didn't matter. "It's like the ultimate living in the now," she said, and Nathan laughed.

He clarified that his research wasn't about human behavior, but Louisa still found it an intriguing possibility that "memoryless" chains might apply to people. That a person's thoughts and actions didn't have to be weighed down by their history. That it was possible to sever the past from the present, to shrug off all that baggage and make a clean break. It made Louisa wonder if she might leave her past in the past—a lonesome childhood spent mostly with babysitters—and create a future with this man, moment by moment.

Remembering this now made Louisa feel queasy—*she* was now the past for Nathan, *she* was the baggage, the one being shrugged off in favor of fresh, new possibilities. She wondered if Nathan had related that same Snakes-and-Ladders-in-the-basement tale while courting Mona. She questioned whether he'd even played the game as a kid.

Three sharp raps on the door made Louisa jump in her cheap office chair, which creaked in commiseration. Abe's head appeared in her door frame. "They've been paging you over the loudspeaker. Are you okay? Do you need me to cover?"

The look of concern in her friend's eyes, like she was a fragile egg, shook Louisa out of her reminiscence. "I'm fine. Sorry, I—" She almost said she'd been on an important call, but there was no sense in lying to Abe, who wouldn't care anyway. She crumpled the candy wrapper into the trash. "I just needed a minute to collect myself. Where am I needed?"

"Boys' bathroom, first floor, sorry to say."

"Fabulous."

The moment Louisa opened her office door, the smell slithered into her nostrils: rotten eggs plus the cafeteria on veggie loaf day combined with the boys' locker room after a game. As she trekked to the source of the stench, the path grew more pungent. It seemed like a terrible metaphor for her life at the moment. Descending the stairs through the slumping march of adolescents, Louisa began skipping every other stair, flew around the banister, then *smack*—bone against bone. She wheeled around, bringing a palm to her bruised jaw, and spotted a pair of seniors detaching their mouths from one another like suction cups. Deep in their hookup haze, they barely seemed to register the bump. Louisa fixed them with a disapproving look, then flew down another flight. The odor grew thicker, the crowd thinner— only a few burnouts too out of it to register that they might as well be stewing in a sewer.

Principal Poolehauzer had beaten Louisa to the bathroom, and was now standing by the door in a faux-casual pose, acting as if the air were infused with tulips, and pointedly not gloating over how on top of the school's goings-on he was compared to his deputy. "Ms. Bauer," he remarked blithely, "someone appears to have played a practical joke." *No shit,* Louisa wanted to reply. "The custodian's on his way, but I need you to investigate."

Louisa couldn't help thinking that the previous principal would never have sent her on such a demeaning mission; Patricia Brown, her former boss, had been a leader and a mentor to Louisa. She'd retired a year ago, and Louisa still couldn't understand why the superintendent had replaced her with a buffoon like Poolehauzer. Still, the man was her boss. "I'm on it, Dr. P."

Ignoring her humiliation, she leaned into the grimy void of the boys' bathroom and yelled, "Warning, vice principal entering in ten seconds. One, two, three..." Meanwhile, Poolehauzer started to whistle a jaunty tune.

At the count of ten, Louisa barged in. She quickly discovered the stink bomb, then released the antidote, a silly honking contraption whose efficacy was partial at best. For the next five hours, the first floor would be swirling with hydrogen sulfide and ammonia and scented with stale flatulence, on top of its usual *eau de reek* of teenage sweat and cafeteria food.

Next, Louisa was supposed to search for the perp. She could anticipate her boss' overblown urgency: "Did you uncover any evidence?" as if this were *CSI: High School*. As if the stink bomber might have dropped his Student ID card or etched into the wall, "You'll never catch me!" so they could conduct a handwriting analysis and DNA test. Reluctantly, Louisa scoured the tile floor and then began on the stalls, holding her breath all the while.

Ducking her head into the middle stall, she stopped short. She ingested a gulp of oxygen before she could remember not to. She dropped onto the seat, despite the germs, and studied the drawing of the woman on the stall wall. She looked familiar, rendered in that anime style that transforms every female into a porn star—curves barely contained by a low-cut wrap dress, shapely legs teetering on stilettos, face dominated by big bedroom eyes and framed by long, loose waves. It took Louisa a moment to register the caption emerging from the pouty lips. It read, "GRANT ME COCK!" Beneath the words, a less talented artist had added a crude drawing of an ejaculating penis. *Ah, right: Ms. Grant. Mildly clever, if it weren't so gross.*

Louisa sat in the stall, transfixed. Just three hours into Kendra Grant's stint at River Mill, a couple of students had already found the time and initiative to vandalize school property in order to publicly express their lust-slash-misogyny toward their new teacher. They might have been worried about whether she was a tough grader, or anxious to impress her with their intelligence, but no: they were thinking about sex. Because that's apparently what was on everyone's mind all the time. Louisa thought about sex, too, but not constantly.

She and Nathan used to have more sex—and good sex, too. In those heady early years, they had each other's schedules memorized so when they both had a free hour, they'd triangulate their positions on campus to determine the closest meeting spot: his apartment, her dorm, or his office. Back then, Louisa was the one urging Nathan to loosen up and have a little fun—his office had a lock on the door, after all. Her favorite thing was to straddle him in his big upholstered arm- chair. Her verve and spontaneity seemed like a big part of why Nathan had fallen for her, and not just in bed: Louisa pushed Nathan to attend poetry readings and try new foods and sign up for a charity hula-hoop-athon (in the end he'd waited on the sidelines holding her purse, but still, he'd shown up). Plus, she was game to play stu- dent to his professor, always intent to learn whatever he had to teach her, which she knew turned him on. As for Louisa, she loved Nathan's steadiness and attention. He always listened and was there for her when she needed him. She hadn't had enough of that before.

But Louisa had been so young. Over time, she'd grown into a sturdier version of herself. She was happy to settle into a more reli- able rhythm, to feel less needy and less ruled by the immediate needs of the body, and to have a thing or two to teach Nathan, too, instead of it always being the other way around. For a long time, this shift in balance worked. They'd gotten married, built a home.

When they'd finally gotten around to having kids, after putting it off, then Nathan mourning his parents, then another year of trying, the reversal was complete: Louisa took quickly to mother- hood, to understanding and fulfilling her babies' needs, which were basic but relentless. It wasn't that it was easy. But she was good at it, and she felt confident in her role. Whereas Nathan was now the one flailing around, unsure of his every move. Louisa found herself cemented in the teacher role, instructing her husband about how to feed the twins and burp them and hold one each in the crook of each arm to soothe them when they both wailed at once.

How did she know all this stuff? Nathan would ask her. Sometimes with awe, but other times with an edge, like he was accusing her of studying some secret textbook behind his back only to get a leg up and make him feel stupid. Louisa found this side of Nathan unattrac- tive, his anxiety about not being an expert, his need to make little digs at her about her competence. She'd assumed that as an aca- demic he'd be a lifelong learner, always curious, forever open to new knowledge. But it became clear to Louisa that this mindset didn't apply to early parenthood for Nathan. So, yes, sometimes she lost her patience, snapped at him or rolled her eyes. But she'd never stopped loving him—she couldn't believe he thought she might be relieved to find out he was leaving her.

As for the sex, though, Nathan had seemed just as overwhelmed as she'd felt in that first year. Louisa assumed they were on the same page about desire taking a backseat to basic needs like sleep and sustenance. As the kids had emerged from infancy and—finally, miraculously!—started sleeping through the night, Louisa and Nathan had eased back into a bedroom routine. *Routine*—Louisa caught herself. It was exactly what Nathan had bemoaned in his breakup soliloquy.

And apparently now he'd found himself a new student. He could once again be the wise mentor guiding and shaping his young girl-friend's half-formed self. Or maybe it really was all about the sex, enjoying the taut body of a twenty-one-year-old over that of a thirty-six-year-old whose stomach was still squishy from pregnancy and whose breasts had been ravaged by nursing. Or perhaps there was more to it than youth and sex, and Nathan was more than a tired cliché—who knew? Louisa could drive herself crazy guessing at all the reasons. Still, no matter the specifics, no matter that the girl had come on to him first, or so he claimed, there was no denying that the circumstances were despicable: Nathan was in a position of power over her, and nearly twice her age, not to mention the fact that he had a wife and kids at home. Louisa could scream. She did scream.

"Ms. Bauer?" Her boss' voice echoed through the bathroom. "Have you fallen in?"

Louisa snapped back to the present, to the middle stall in the boys' bathroom where she sat slumped over the toilet. She resisted the quicksand musing about how she'd ended up here. "I'm coming."

She drew in a sharp breath, stood up, and straightened her skirt. In the tinny mirror above the sinks she checked her teeth for food, before exiting the bathroom to deliver her report in as even-keeled a voice as she could manage. She comforted herself with the knowledge that every step back to her office meant it would smell a little bit less like shit.

CHAPTER 11

Mateo

Mateo was like a student driver, hands at ten and two on the wheel, eyes glued to the road, no distracting radio, all nerves.

He glanced at the passenger seat, where Nathan looked a little nervous, too. "Where to—home?" he asked, the last word catching in his throat. He wasn't sure if the house Louisa and the kids lived in still qualified as Nathan's home.

"Nah, man, I've got to get to campus. Can you drop me off at Numbers HQ?"

"Sure, if I can remember the way."

Numbers HQ was what they'd called the math department building, Cedar Hall, back in grad school. That felt like ancient history to Mateo. But Nathan still spent his days toiling away in those crumbling classrooms.

"I can't get over that you bought a Tesla," Nathan said, running his palm along the dash. "What's it like driving this bad boy? Maybe I'll spring for one, too, after my '95 Nissan Ultima finally kicks the bucket. Then my midlife crisis will be complete."

Mateo laughed along with his friend, thinking but not saying that splurging on a car he couldn't afford would be a far wiser way to shake up his life than breaking up his family. Nathan was still laughing, and Mateo wondered if he thought this whole thing was a joke. "In my dreams. You should see my bank account."

Mateo didn't take the bait. He'd offered Nathan a position at his first company all those years ago, and Nathan had turned him down, optimistic that a university tenure-track position was just around the corner; in reality, he'd spent over a decade toiling as an adjunct, securing a job as a full-time lecturer just this year. The two men had taken different paths, and Mateo felt no need to apologize for his success. He only wished Nathan wouldn't put himself down so frequently; he was a talented mathematician, but academia could be a tough and poorly compensated road.

As he wound through north campus, relying on muscle memory to lead him to Cedar Hall, Mateo was struck by how familiar it all felt, the whole scene frozen in time since he'd marched at graduation, shoulders heavy with doctoral robes. He could almost trick himself that he and Nathan were headed to the canteen for coffees before joining the T.A. pool in the front row of Professor Ji's Calculus I survey. But one look at his friend's tired mien reminded Mateo that they were not in fact contemporaries with the young crossing the paths around them. Mateo had fared better physically—living with Mickey whipped you into shape practically by osmosis—but there was still no denying the march of time. Hell, Mateo's own daughter would be walking among a crowd like this at some yet-to-be-determined campus mere months from now (the thought squeezed on Mateo's heart).

"It's like someone's staging a remake of our past," Mateo ventured. "Same set, different characters."

"Well, a few of the characters are the same."

There it was again, Nathan's self-critical tone. "But you still love teaching, right?"

"Some days, yeah. Others, I flash forward decades from now, and there I am, still standing at the lectern of Cedar Hall Seven, talking at bored freshman about permutations and combinations as they calculate the probability that they'll stay awake till the end of the hour."

It was a line, Mateo was sure. Still, what a bleak image Nathan painted of his future. No wonder he was bucking against the routine of his home life, when his work felt so routine, too. Mateo, who'd spent the past decade launching start-ups—watching a few soar while a couple crashed and burned—always felt grateful to return home at the end of the day. After long, intense, often volatile hours, all he wanted was the familiarity of Mickey and Mel, their cozy little unit. Nothing about the three of them felt routine; Mel was always growing and changing, and so were he and Mickey: she with her gym and the latest race she was training for, he with whatever new business venture. So, they were forever readjusting to accommodate shifting circumstances. That was what it meant to be a family. Mateo felt his breath catch again, anticipating the loss of his daughter, and the adjustment that would entail.

"Do you have time for a coffee," Nathan asked, "to prolong the memory tour?"

Mateo had hoped to squeeze in a run before his ten o'clock board meeting, but coffee was the least he could do for his friend. "Sure, buddy. The canteen?"

"Nah, let's avoid the lines. I've got one of those Keurig deals in my office."

The prospect of this hang was growing even less appealing—Mateo had no interest in crowding into Nathan's hovel of an office to drink crappy K-cup coffee. But again, his friend clearly needed him.

They sat nursing their coffees before Mateo got up the nerve to ask, "So, do you want to talk about it?"

"*It* being what, my relationship status?"

"Sure, if you want to put it like that. Whatever's on your mind. If you need an outlet..." Mateo's voice trailed off. He knew how to talk to wealthy investors and he could improvise a motivational speech to a room full of employees, but he didn't know the first thing about this kind of talk.

"Well, I admit I had an ulterior motive for asking you to coffee. Mona hasn't met any of my friends, and I really want you to get to know her. She's so wonderful—"

"The girl is coming here, now?!" Mateo modulated his volume. "You're serious?"

"She's not a *girl*, Matty. But yes."

So, he'd been tricked, and now he was cornered. It was one thing for Nathan to crash on his couch, but quite another for him to force his mistress on him. It was typical Nathan, pulling this childish nonsense. How was Mateo supposed to act, and what would he tell Mickey?

"There she is now!" Nathan sounded giddy. Mateo followed his friend's gaze to the doorway.

Her smile radiated across the office, growing brighter as she walked in and closed the door. Mateo couldn't quite believe that Nathan was the object of this smile. His friend was attractive enough—before Louisa, he'd always had plenty of dates—but now he was pushing middle age. And here was this very young woman, seemingly resisting the urge to leap onto Nathan's lap; she stopped short, hoisting herself up on the desk instead. Had Nathan even considered the fact that his office only had two chairs? The look on his face—boyish, gob-smacked—made Mateo feel like an intruder on their private moment.

"You must be Mateo," she said. "Professor Bauer here told me I'd think you were cute." She winked, and Mateo felt deeply uneasy. Was she seriously joking about the fact that she'd been Nathan's student, and flirting with him, too? When Mateo met with young female employees, he always kept the door ajar.

She held out a hand, leaving Mateo no choice but to shake it. Besides the high-wattage smile, Mona seemed unremarkable to him. Medium height, long black hair, and when she shrugged off her jacket, she appeared shrunken in her oversized sweater. She looked nothing like Louisa, who was tall and full-figured, her wavy brown hair more of a statement piece than any specific style. It seemed like

Nathan had made a point to find the physical opposite of his wife. "I'm Desdemona."

The usual socially acceptable responses, like, *I've heard so much about you* or, *So nice to meet you* did not apply. "Hi," Mateo stuttered.

Nathan took over: "Matty and I first met in this very building." *When we were grad students and you were an infant,* Mateo thought. "We've been friends ever since."

The couple grinned at each other idiotically. "I almost forgot," Mona said, "I brought a treat. Nate and I adore the raspberry croissants from the canteen."

Nate! Mateo wasn't sure how much of this he could take. He shuffled through various topics, like her favorite class or her post-college plans—the types of questions he'd ask Mel's friends—but he couldn't muster the energy for it. And he couldn't ask what he really wanted to know, which was how on earth did the two of them think this relationship was a good idea? "Actually, I've got to run to a meeting," he said. "Raincheck on the croissant."

He pointedly ignored Nathan's look of disappointment. *He* wasn't an asshole for fleeing; *Nathan* was the asshole for springing this upon him.

"I'll walk you out," Nathan said. Down the hall, he added, "Please give her a chance."

Mateo felt impatient. "Dude, you should be careful. I don't think the university is going to like this situation any more than your wife does." Nathan bristled at the mention of Louisa. "Look, I'm just trying to help. I suspect your thinking may be a little clouded at the moment."

Nathan made a lame effort to puff up his chest. "On the contrary, my thinking is clearer than it's been in years."

"Whatever you say." Mateo patted his friend on the back. "Good luck."

He couldn't move fast enough, away from campus and back toward his life.

CHAPTER 12
Nathan

Nathan returned to his office, feeling deflated. Now that everything was out in the open, he was eager to introduce Mona around. He'd thought if his friends could just meet her, they'd understand. But he'd forgotten that Mateo could be kind of uptight. Plus, he supposed his sneak-attack approach had been misguided.

"It's going to take time," Mona told him, cradling her arms around his neck. The fact that she met his moping with comfort lifted his spirits. With Louisa, any negative feeling he expressed was regarded as a personal inconvenience or didn't register at all. (Nathan reminded himself that he didn't have to keep making these comparisons, building his case to legitimize leaving Louisa; still, old habits die hard.) "These people have known you as a married man for years and years. Louisa is their friend. Change is hard, for everyone."

"Change is feeling pretty good to me right now." Nathan tilted his head into Mona's palm.

"Sure, but you're the one who chose this change. And it messes up the dynamic of your little group. Mateo's reaction is about himself, not you. He'll come around—love will win out." Mona kissed him gently. This woman made him feel so seen, and in such a flattering light.

"What would I do without you?" Nathan blurted out a version of this sentiment every time he was with her.

"Here's my suggestion," Mona said. "Try to approach this whole transition with a beginner's mind."

"Excuse me?"

"Meaning, with openness and curiosity, like you do when you're trying something new. When you're an expert, or you think you are, you're full of preconceived notions; you've already decided what to expect. But a beginner has fresh eyes. Living your life that way lets you embrace the unknown, and opens yourself up to all sorts of possibilities."

Nathan thought about it. "Okay, I'm into that."

Mona tore off a piece of the croissant. "Here, try eating this with a beginner's mind."

Nathan held it up to his face and inspected it like it was a foreign object. It was close to weightless, with flecks of turbinado sugar sparkling like crystals on its surface. It smelled of raspberry and butter, and when he bit into it, the flakes melted on his tongue, surprising him with bursts of tart and sweet. It was maybe the best thing he had ever tasted. "Fuck. What is that, magic?"

"No, silly, it's Buddhism. We studied it in yoga training. A teacher I had described beginner's mind as like temporarily turning off your memory. Without a memory, you're free to be fully present, moment by moment by moment."

Nathan grinned—the connections between Mona and himself truly amazed him: "You know, memorylessness was a major concept in my graduate work."

"How so?"

"I studied Markov chains." Nathan reached for a napkin and began drawing a chart. "So, you have a set of finite states that you move between, and the probability of moving to each other state depends only on the probability associated with the current state. Like, say we're talking about the weather, and the states are sunny and rainy." As Nathan filled out the chart, he explained how tomorrow's forecast depends only on today's. So, you start in one state—say, sunny—and you look at the probability of the forecast following a sunny day. Maybe two-thirds of the time you get another sunny day and one-third rain. After a rainy day, say you have half sunny days and half rainy ones. Nathan added loops, arrows, and percentages to his sketch. "You can set up a chain of steps to predict the weather, with the probability of each next state determined only by the current state. The chain is memoryless." Of course, it wasn't really this simple, he noted—there was air pressure and other factors that affected the weather, and more states than sunny and rainy—but it was just a demo. "So, just because it's been raining for a week doesn't mean it'll keep raining. There's an equal chance it'll be rainy or sunny, no matter what came before today's rain." Nathan winked at Mona.

It had been a while since Nathan had thought about his dissertation. He'd been drawn to Markov chains because they made such intuitive sense to him: if this was happening, then this or that or that other thing could happen next. In life, most of what people did made little rational sense, acting randomly, on whims and feelings—Nathan included. The world's irrationality is why he'd found math so enticing—the numbers always added up; there were always solutions to the problems. Although the more advanced his studies, the more he discovered that the vast majority of math was about the unknown (as Melody had alluded to that very morning). Nathan remembered the satisfaction of learning to create the Markov chain models, sequencing step by step, calculating predictions. For him, the study of probability seemed to bridge the gap between the known and the unknown. He'd been in the thick of that work when he met Louisa, and now he felt a strong wave of déjà vu—ironic, considering he was talking about a concept where memory was irrelevant. He'd explained his research to Louisa on their first date—he'd liked her so much, and been so nervous—and the way she'd tracked him with wide eyes, nodding eagerly, had made him feel whole and good. Remembering their bond was like the return of feeling to a limb, the sharp jabs of pins and needles. Nathan pushed the memory away.

"Anyway, what was I saying?"

"You were talking about the weather," Mona reminded him, as if he'd been making empty small talk. Still, her smile nudged a matching one onto his face. "How if you let go of your expectations, you can embrace today's sun or rain."

"Uh, sort of." It was a creative interpretation, Nathan would give her that.

Bemusement twinkled in Mona's eyes. "There you go again with your mathematic myopia. Your marked-off chains—"

"*Markov* chains. Andrey Markov was a renowned Russian mathematician."

"I'm sure he was a very smart old white man. My point is, you're talking about a situation with a limited number of outcomes, and a fixed chance of which one will occur. But beginner's mind blows that out of the water, because it's about endless possibility. Not just sunny or rainy—it might be a triple-rainbow sky with neon lightning and thunder like a stadium of bass drums. See what I mean?"

"I think," Nathan said. "Although the beauty of Markov chains is that you can use them to make predictions with a degree of accuracy. They allow you to take a notion that's so vast and unknowable—the future—and map a kind of order onto it."

Mona shrugged. "I suppose I just don't see the value in that. Why try to wrangle something as exquisite and full of potential as the future and shrink it into a structure dictated by equations or whatever?"

Nathan laughed. "Well, I've certainly never thought of it that way."

"Plus, you claim your Markov chains are memoryless, but aren't the probabilities of each next state derived from past data? Like with the weather, aren't you using what happened before to figure out that it's sunny two-thirds of the time after a sunny day?

That doesn't sound so memoryless to me."

"Huh, fair point." Nathan was impressed. He wrapped Mona's hands in his own. "Oh, I love you, Mona."

"So, speaking of moving on to new states, I was perusing Zillow and there are some really cute one-bedrooms just west of campus." Mona whipped out her phone and clicked through photos, bright, wide-angle shots that made the spaces look deceptively big and airy. "And I was thinking, since I'll be spending so much time there, and since Gretchen and her girlfriend treat me like a third wheel at my own place anyway, what if I just moved in with you from the get-go? We'd save money, too."

"Really?" Nathan felt giddy. "Pinch me, I must be dreaming."

Mona's laugh was always so big and uninhibited. She was someone who expected her life to be full of delight and success; she believed things would work out for her, so they did. "It'll be fun, like playing house!"

As Mona launched into specs like square footage and closet space, Nathan let it wash over him. "Although we'll need a two-bedroom," he said, "for Finn and Phoebe."

Nathan might've imagined it: Mona's slight stiffening before she rolled out her shoulders. "Will your ex be okay with that? I'd think it would be disorienting for the kids to have to shuffle back and forth between two homes."

"Well, they're my kids, too." Nathan felt a pang, thinking of his children, so small and innocent. It was going to be hard to tell them that he was moving out.

"Maybe they could stay in the home they've always known and you could go visit them there? That's a common arrangement, right?"

Nathan took a deep breath. Recently when he'd broached the possibility of Mona meeting Finn and Phoebe, she'd deflected, saying she wouldn't want them to think she was trying to replace their mother or feel confused about who she was. That would've made sense when they were still under wraps, but why now? Nathan felt the least he could do for his kids, given that he was breaking up their family, was be open with them about what was going on. Sure, they were only two, but Nathan was constantly surprised by how much they understood. Plus, he knew that they would love Mona, and that she would grow to love them, too. But Nathan understood that it was a lot for her. It was one thing for her to gush about the kids she babysat, quite another for her to hang out with the children of her boyfriend. It was like what Mona herself had said about Mateo getting used to their new situation: probably she just needed time.

"Well, a second bedroom would be nice in any case," he said. "For the twins, or as an office, or your yoga studio."

"Sure. In the meantime, you can't stay at the house, right? Do you want to crash at my place?"

"What about Gretchen?" Nathan had met Mona's roommate only once in passing. He thought she'd scowled at him, but when he related this to Mona, she claimed he was being paranoid, that Gretchen couldn't care less who Mona was sleeping with.

Mona shrugged. "Don't worry about her."

"All right. This weekend, then. I'll bring over some things."

"Cool." Mona checked her phone. "You have class."

It amazed Nathan that it all sounded so casual. This was really happening.

Outside, the ice had thawed to slush, and the snow was falling heavy and wet. Nathan was pulling on his hood when Mona poked him in the side. "Beginner's mind, remember?" She tilted her face to the sky, and caught a flake on her tongue.

But when Nathan looked up, a flake fell right in his eye, half-blinding him. He blinked wildly, and Mona laughed. "I think you can tell a lot about a person based on how comfortable they are with the elements, like whether they open their umbrella at the first raindrop or choose to feel the rain on their skin for a while."

"Huh." Nathan considered where he fell on this spectrum.

After they parted ways, he tried Mona's approach of succumbing to the snow—he moved at his normal pace, sans hood, whistling as he walked. He imagined the gentle landing of each snowflake on his head. For a moment he felt at one with the world, and congratulated himself for the feeling. His mind wandered to a field blanketed in snow, tumbling into it with Mona, rolling around until they were both shivering with satisfaction.

When one of his students interrupted his lecture to ask why he was soaked, Nathan responded by asking why the boy was so dry, and the whole class tittered. Nathan always earned a handful of fans each semester, but he pictured becoming one of those professors whom all the students raved about in their course evaluations. It was a new chapter for him, and he welcomed it with a beginner's mind.

CHAPTER 13

Mona

Mona had an hour to kill before her noon vinyasa class, so she decided to take a meandering path from Cedar Hall to the studio. The snowfall was fluffy and storybook-like, and the brisk walk felt good, Mona's muscles happy with the effort. She concentrated on her breath, each puff out a visible mist that kept her focused. Despite the friction with Mateo, Mona felt at peace about the morning: Nate had been so proud to show her off to his friend, then he spoke with such passion about his research, then they'd agreed to move in together. What had begun as a gauzy, sparkly tryst was growing into something solid and sweet. Mona loved this kind of change, so organic and beautiful—it made her whole body brighten with energy.

Her phone jingled, "Mom" flashing up on the screen. "Hi Mom."

"Hi dear. How's school?" Mona heard her mother's faint slurp, and could picture her precise position: seated at the kitchen table in the house where Mona had grown up, peering out the picture window to the bird feeder in the yard, palm cupping a mug of milky English Breakfast.

"Good, fine. I'm teaching back-to-back yoga before Anthro later."

"So busy! Please don't overstrain yourself."

"I never do," Mona said, annoyance slipping into her tone.

"Have you followed up with the orthopedist you found last semester?"

"Not yet. But I feel good. The yoga really helps."

"Hm, okay." This was the extent of disapproval her mother expressed about Mona's commitment to yoga, but it was clear she would've preferred her daughter to lean on western medicine to manage the vestigial pain of her childhood scoliosis. Mona often regretted asking her parents to pony up the three thousand bucks for her yoga teacher training.

"Anything else going on? Any big plans this weekend?"

"Not much. Just studying and seeing some friends. How about you and Dad?"

"Oh, you know us. I'll do my walks and my crocheting, and he'll be parked in front of the 76ers."

The familiar summary made Mona feel claustrophobic and a little sad. "Enjoy, Mom. I've got to run."

"Okay, dear. Take care of yourself. I love you."

Mona said goodbye and clicked off her phone with relief. She felt a spike of glee, thinking, *I have Nate to take care of me now.* Not that she'd told her parents about him; they'd never understand.

Before she met Nate, Mona had been coasting along the undergrad experience, attending class, going to parties, hooking up with this or that guy, studying yoga, taking the bus back to Philly once or twice a semester to see her parents. It was all fine, all predictable, all regularly reinforced to her as the way things were supposed to be. This was the life of a college student. This was normal.

And yet, Mona's body had started to tell a different story—an all-too-familiar one. Her lower back began a low moan, and sudden moves could cause it to seize up in spasm. At night, she'd awaken to sharp jabs in her spine and a stiffness in her right hip. None of it felt as bad as it'd been when Mona was a pre-teen, when she'd stood in the doctor's office, hips uneven and ribs jutting to one side. Scoliosis, the doctor diagnosed. Mona spent years wearing a brace, stiff and itchy, removing it only to shower. She avoided sitting for long stretches. The treatment had worked, gradually reducing the curve of her spine, and by freshman year of high school, she got the sign-off to toss the brace. Still, the pain never fully receded. Mona believed it wasn't just being physically sedentary that wreaked havoc on her body; spiritual sedentariness did it, too. She observed that the pain always returned at times when she was stuck in her life, in need of a change. Like her senior year of high school, when she was on the verge of heading to Penn State along with half her graduating class. Last minute, she'd decided to go to school in Massachusetts instead, and the pain faded.

This time around, Mona had resisted the message of the pain—at least, at first. She liked college, she was fine. She tried adjusting her diet, drinking less, sleeping more. But still, her body complained. Reluctantly, she got a referral to an orthopedist and scheduled an appointment for a Wednesday afternoon, after her first statistics lecture. When Mona walked into that class, her back was in knots, her hip aching. By the time she walked out, everything had started to ease. She never made it to the doctor.

It had been her professor. Dr. Bauer. *Nate.* From the moment Mona had laid eyes on him, she'd felt a fierce attraction, and it distracted her from her pain. He was a dynamic lecturer; with every gesture, she felt like there were strings connecting their two bodies. The feeling grew stronger over the course of the class, and it shifted something in Mona: her physical discomfort gave way to longing. She heard little of what the professor said, but she was finely attuned to his passion for the subject matter. Only as he was wrapping up did Mona dare raise her hand to ask a question. When he turned to call on her, it was like the sun shone down upon her; she felt illuminated. And she was certain the connection ran both ways.

So, yes, they fell in love. But Mona didn't believe that's what had healed her. Rather, it was the change, the jolt from her routine. She'd been in a rut—spiritually sedentary—and the cure was to try something new, with new people in new places. Nate, she soon discovered, had been in a rut, too. Mona wasn't thrilled to learn that he was married with children. But it wasn't a deal-breaker, either; he was so clearly unhappy in his life, feeling inadequate and undervalued in his family role, whereas he seemed to come alive with Mona. Plus, he was an attentive and enthusiastic caretaker. All she had to do was grimace and he'd be behind her, massaging the knots out of her back. When she expressed her gratitude, Nate insisted he was the lucky one. It was all very sexy. Mona wasn't sure if she believed in fate, but something about the two of them felt destined, how they'd come together and helped each other transform.

"Slut!"

Mona snapped back to her surroundings and jerked her head around. The defiant look on the boy's face told her she'd heard him correctly. She recognized him. He'd been in Nate's stats class with her, one of those guys who liked to hear the sound of his voice as he pontificated about this or that obvious point before a captive audience. For a moment she felt too stunned to react. Like, was he really addressing her? Who even used "slut" as a slur anymore? But no one else was there on the path. Usually Mona was good at tuning out other people's judgments of her, especially when she knew they didn't capture the truth of the situation. But the direct confrontation, and the disgust plain on the boy's face, rattled her. She sped up her pace, ignoring the wobble in the knees, until she was running.

CHAPTER 14

Mateo

When Mateo mentioned as a matter of course that he'd met Nathan's girlfriend, the bar of soap catapulted from Mickey's wet hands onto the tiles.

"You *what?!* Tell me everything!"

Mateo retrieved the soap. They were standing under the twin showerheads, their nightly ritual. "She was fine. Friendly, a little nervous, or maybe that was just me. Pretty, I guess."

He stood under the water and closed his eyes as shampoo suds ran down his face. The waterfall showerheads were probably the best investment they'd made in their home. No matter what happened during his day, Mateo could look forward to rinsing it all away in the most luxurious way, the next best thing to a personal masseuse.

"That's it?"

Mateo opened his eyes to see his wife up in his face, looking impatient. "Come on, babe, you've got to give me more than that. For starters, what does she look like?"

"Um." Mateo racked his brain, but mostly he remembered his own discomfort, and his good friend acting like a fool, a googly-eyed puppy-dog. "She's got long hair. Average height, skinny. Big eyes. She wore a big sweater. Oh, and bracelets, I think."

Mickey flicked water at him. "You may as well be describing a mugger you barely got a glimpse of. Was it that traumatic?"

"I guess I wasn't so focused on her looks."

Mickey muttered "No shit." Just audibly enough that she could pretend it was under her breath while knowing full well that Mateo could hear.

"Look, the whole scenario made me squirm," he said. "Nathan ambushed me. He made me think the two of us were having coffee, then suddenly Mona was there, batting her eyes at him and asking me if I wanted to split a croissant. The two of them acted like of course I'd be delighted to meet the young woman Nathan was leaving his wife for. She's very young, that I can confirm. But I wasn't focused on the size of her breasts or whatever."

Mickey's eyeroll wounded Mateo. "I would think you'd be happy to have a husband who's not some sleazy creep always checking out other women."

"Noticing what other people looked like wouldn't make you a

sleazy creep," Mickey said. "It's about appreciating beauty in the world. It's about being in touch with your pleasure."

"Uh huh."

This was familiar territory. When Mateo starting running companies, with lots of young female employees, he'd consciously tuned down the part of himself that detected attractiveness and attraction during business hours. It wasn't that hard. He'd explained to Mickey that it was like putting on a pair of corrective lenses. He knew it made him a better leader, and partly explained why he employed a much higher percentage of women than most tech firms. They felt comfortable working for him. It was a point of pride for Mateo. Recently, when the torrent of #metoo stories poured out, Mateo was both shocked and not shocked; he wondered why more powerful men hadn't taken the same tack, whereas Mickey had acted dismissive of Mateo's strategy. She was a boss, too, she'd say, and that didn't prevent her from enjoying the view of her fellow human beings. But it was different for her: she was a woman, and she ran a gym, where half the job was noting clients' progress, which included praising their bodies. Mateo's approach worked for him, in spite of what his wife thought.

Mickey glided into Mateo's half of the shower, edging him partway out of the water. She kissed his neck, adding a touch of teeth. "Do you think this is how Mona kisses?"

The half of his body exposed to the air prickled with goosebumps, which annoyed Mateo. The whole point of having double showerheads was to prevent this usual pitfall of joint showering.

Mickey grabbed his butt with cold hands. "Do you think this is how she touches Nathan?"

"Hey, quit it." Mateo turned off the water and stepped out to grab a towel.

Mickey was on his tail. "I was just playing around." She sat her sopping wet body onto the bed—on Mateo's side. "You should lighten up."

"Forgive me if I don't find it funny that Nathan left his wife for a little nookie with his student, whatever he claims his reasons to be. I'm surprised you're being so cavalier, given that it's your best friend he's left in the lurch." A puddle was forming around Mickey on the comforter, and it took restraint for Mateo not to suggest that she grab a towel.

"Oh, come on," she said. "You and I both know this isn't about how much I care about Louisa." Mateo tensed up. "Look at you, staying ten feet away as I sit here naked on our bed, my tits staring you in the face, my pussy practically begging you to come say hi."

"You don't have to be vulgar, Mick."

"What's vulgar? I'm your wife. Admit it, when Nathan was going on about how ho-hum everything had become, weren't you thinking about us?"

Mateo scoffed. "Actually, yes. I was thinking about how sad it was that he felt that way about his marriage and how much I value ours. I was thinking how stupid it seemed to throw away his wonderful life in favor of the thrill of some silly fling."

"Why, because sex isn't important?"

"Don't twist my words," he replied. "That's not what I said."

Mickey finally pulled on a shirt. "Well, here's what I was thinking. Oh, they barely have sex, and Nathan couldn't take it anymore."

Mateo assumed his wife didn't really think the breakup was as simple as that. "You mean, *we* barely have sex, and *you* can't take it anymore."

They fell into a silence, and Mateo waited, half-terrified, for Mickey to announce that she, too, wanted a divorce.

Finally, she sighed. "Don't you think it's sad that we take a shower together every night and I can't remember the last time it led to more than that?"

"Well, I can. It was when you confiscated that joint from Mel's purse." Mateo's spirits lifted at the memory.

Micky brightened. "Oh my god, and we hotboxed the bathroom. See, that was fun! Don't you want to have more fun like that? That was weeks ago."

Mateo shrugged. "Sure." But what he didn't say was that he always had fun with Mickey, no matter what they were doing; he only wished she felt the same about him.

He squeezed his wife's hand. He admired everything about it, the oval calluses borne of weight-lifting, the nails painted electric blue, the pretty freckles that had accumulated over time; he kissed his favorite constellation of them at the base of her thumb. He knew what his wife wanted. In the tender gesture of brushing the pads of her fingers against his cheek, Mateo could feel her hope and desire tempered by the urge to manage her expectations. He didn't want to disappoint her. He hated feeling like a disappointment. But the fact was, Mickey had always wanted it more than he had, at least since their early years. And Mateo didn't like to be pushed into something he wasn't in the mood for. They'd managed it together over time— until a year or so ago, when Mickey's sex drive had skyrocketed just as Mateo's took a nosedive.

"I love you," he told his wife. Then he pulled on his pajamas, and drew back the comforter; luckily, the sheets were dry.

"I love you, too," she said back. It was easy to read defeat in the slouch of her spine, disappointment in the slump of her scapula as she, too, pulled on her pajamas. Mateo turned away and switched off the light.

CHAPTER 15
Louisa

High school was a strange place to be on Valentine's Day, the hallways strewn with lollipop wrappers and construction paper cutouts, kids clutching single roses like trophies and chowing down on fistfuls of chalky pastel hearts in class. There was a frenetic energy in the air that seemed more about the stirrings of hormones in overdrive than the stirrings of the heart. The occasional drama over the identity of a secret admirer was more whodunit than romance, with girls clustered into excited packs to swap clues.

Still, thought Louisa, it was possible that all of this *was* love—what did she know, anyway? When was the last time she'd fashioned a heart out of pink tissue paper or given or received a bouquet of flowers or a box of chocolates? It seemed possible that she'd once done these things, though her memory was fuzzy. It made her wonder if she would ever know love again.

It had been two weeks since Nathan had moved out.

Abe appeared in her office doorway. "I knew I'd find you here, thinking deep thoughts, or nursing a hangover, or both."

Louisa frowned, not in the mood for her friend's observations. Since Nathan had left, she'd been making her way through quite a bit of wine each night.

"Anyway, top of the morning, boss."

"I've told you not to call me that. What's that?" She pointed to the bag in Abe's hand. "It smells like chocolate."

"Bingo. A Boston crème donut, for you."

"Ooh, fork it over. I assume Cupid sent you on a pity mission, but I don't even care. A moment ago, my breakfast plan was foraging my desk for a granola bar."

"I've also got this." Abe held out a small wrapped cube. "It's from Amy and Mickey. I was issued strict orders not to peek inside, and also to pass along the note that Dr. Poolehauzer might enjoy watching you open it."

"I'll take that under advisement." Louisa perused a card containing Mickey's tiny print: "Fuck Nathan. Fuck yourself instead."

"So, a vibrator?"

"I assume so." Abe shifted from foot to foot.

"Want to partake?" She waited a beat, enjoying watching Abe fidget. "I mean, in the donut?"

Abe raised his eyebrows. "Nah, that's for you to enjoy on your own." He paused. "The donut, I mean."

Louisa bit off a hunk, letting the viscous fake-cream ooze onto her cheek. Abe played along. "You've got a little, um..." He indicated the edge of his mouth.

"What?" Louisa played dumb.

This was what happened when you spent all your time with high school kids; sometimes you turned into them. Their antics were interrupted by a knock on the door. Louisa wiped her mouth in time for Ms. Spinoza, the principal's assistant, to barge in. "Your class observation schedule, Ms. Bauer."

"Thanks." Last year, Poolehauzer had gotten wind of Louisa tipping off teachers about when she'd be coming for their graded observations; so now he left her in the dark until the last minute. Louisa glanced at the sheet, then gave a quick shake of the head to an expectant Abe: he was in the clear. He mouthed, "Phew," waved, and was gone. First period was in three minutes, and Louisa was assigned to observe Kendra Grant.

Slipping into the back of the classroom, Louisa had no expectations. The newest hire had started less than a month ago, and although the students were decently behaved overall, they were still teenagers, meaning they could suss out vulnerability like a sixth sense. Anything might happen. Still, Louisa was surprised at what was being said by the student presenter.

"I'm a bitch, I'm a ho, I'm a ladyboss, you know. Dig my lyrics, dig my flow, neon red and it glows. I'm the tops, I'm first-class, got the titties, got the ass. I may never please the mass, I'll blow through the ceiling glass."

The girl wore a wide grin, clearly thrilled to be reciting these words in class. Louisa recognized the lyrics, from that rap song that played on repeat on Hot 97. The artist—Carrie something?—would probably be horrified to hear her lyrics recited in such a lackluster way.

"It's about identity," said the girl's co-presenter, consulting her notes, looking less comfortable than her partner. "Shari P isn't just one thing. She's a bitch and a ho, but she's also a ladyboss who plans to blow through the ceiling glass, which is a reference to the glass ceiling, which is a metaphor for the barrier women face in trying to advance as much as men." The girl smiled with satisfaction at her analysis.

This was one reason Louisa liked spending time around teenagers—despite the jaded exterior so many of them shrugged on like a sweatshirt, underneath they were usually earnest, eager to do well in a presentation.

Dr. Poolehauzer entered the room just as the girl tapped at a laptop and the PowerPoint behind them flicked to a still of the music video: Shari P in a bustier, hot pants, and platform stilettoes, ass center-screen as she knelt on her knees before a man in a suit.

"Wowzer" slipped out of Louisa's mouth.

"Good morning, class," the principal stuttered. "Would someone care to fill me in on the context here?"

"Girls?" Ms. Grant, unruffled, indicated the pair at the front of the class.

The first girl spoke again, slightly less confidently than before. "Ms. Grant said to analyze a text we love, in honor of Valentine's Day. We picked 'Hashtag I Am.'"

The other girl chimed in with "Shari's a bitch and a ho, but also a ladyboss, you know. She doesn't need a man. She loves herself. It's an inspiring message for Valentine's Day."

Dr. P glared at Louisa, like this was somehow her fault. Then he homed in on Ms. Grant. "Not exactly school-appropriate, is it?"

Louisa was tongue-tied. She wanted to pipe up in Ms. Grant's defense, but she also didn't want to defy her boss in public; Poolehauzer was ultra-sensitive, and she knew from experience that any perceived slight would get taken out on her later. She was saved by a hand shooting up from the back of the room.

"I want to address the principal's question." The girl brushed uneven bangs off her face. Her hair was dyed a shade of red not found in nature; Louisa wondered if the color would suit her own complexion. "My classmates spoke of Shari P's aspirations to break the glass ceiling, to shatter the gender inequities that plague our world. I'd say that's appropriate for school, considering our society's institutional misogyny and our sexist pig of a president who's been rolling back the rights of women and every other marginalized group, returning us to the glory days of 1960, or more like 1860. But actually, Shari P's message strikes me as darker than my classmates' interpretation. She says she'll 'blow through the ceiling glass,' and there she is, positioned to perform oral sex on a man who appears to be her boss—because that's how women succeed, right? By sucking co—"

"Thank you, Ro," Ms. Grant said, clearly stifling a grin; Louisa herself was doing the same. Half the room was giggling, and the other half had jaws dropped.

Louisa sensed the anger roiling beneath Dr. P's cool façade. She suspected her boss was the type who wished women would quit being such nags about things like equal pay and workplace discrimination, believing if they'd just redirect that energy into their jobs then they'd probably do as well as men. Louisa sometimes had to stop herself from speculating about whether Dr. P had helped elect the current president; no good could come of that line of thought.

The principal cleared his throat with attempted authority. "Well, using the sexist slurs I've heard here today doesn't exactly help the feminist cause, does it?" He looked smug, until he realized the room was not swayed, at which point he narrowed his eyes at the teacher. "You're new here, Ms. Grant, so you may not realize that we don't tolerate lewdness at River Mill. Consider this your warning. Good day."

He eyed Louisa, like he expected her to accompany him dutifully out the door. She indicated her clipboard: she had to stay for her evaluation. It felt like a small victory.

When Dr. P was out of sight, Ms. Grant shimmied her shoulders, like she was shaking him off, then passed out half-slips of paper to the class. "Now it's my turn. I brought in a poem I love."

Louisa followed along as Ms. Grant read aloud, "Call the roller of big cigars,/ The muscular one, and bid him whip/ In kitchen cups concupiscent curds." At the stanza's final line, Ms. Grant urged everyone to join in, and their voices formed a chorus: "The only emperor is the emperor of ice-cream."

"Okay," the teacher said, "we've got a muscular man whipping up ice cream. What comes to mind when you think ice cream?"

The students shouted out their answers: dessert, fun, delicious, being a kid.

"Pleasure," said one boy, and a couple of girls tittered. He was the kind of boy Louisa would've pined after as a teenager: tall and gangly, with a mess of sandy curls and big brown eyes. "If the only emperor is the emperor of ice cream, it's saying pleasure rules."

"Bingo," Ms. Grant replied. "It's the strongest motivator, the underpinning to any worthwhile pursuit, a necessary ingredient in every recipe: pleasure. At least, that's what Wallace Stevens seems to think. How about you guys?"

The kids squirmed in their seats. Louisa's mind went to the obscene drawing of Ms. Grant in the boys' bathroom. Was the artist in the room now? A big kid smirked, "What's with the horny feet?"

Ms. Grant nodded and read the lines: "If her horny feet protrude, they come/ To show how cold she is, and dumb." She explained that here, "horny" meant calloused, and "dumb" meant mute.

"So, the woman's dead?"

"Right," she said. "It's her wake, and meanwhile someone's making ice cream in the next room. And there's that line again: 'The only emperor is the emperor of ice cream.'"

Louisa couldn't help piping up: "Despite all the terrible stuff going on, we still eat ice cream. It's sweet, then it melts, and there's death on the other side of the door. So, eat dessert now, because soon you'll die."

A few kids laughed. Ms. Grant beamed. "Yes, precisely. Thank you, Ms. Bauer."

This was what learning was supposed to be, thought Louisa. So much of education was soulless, prosaic, pitifully deficient—but learning could be a pleasure, just like ice cream. Louisa glanced down at her clipboard, and marked "excellent" on every measure for the new teacher.

The lesson returned to Louisa at the end of the day, when she exhaled the last breath of the building's canned air and inhaled her first breath of the fresh version outside—a pleasure. The moment flipped a switch inside her. She shook off her armor of authority, and just as fast, the weariness set in.

All day Louisa had craved solitude—just a few minutes of no one complaining or demanding things of her—and now here she was, finally alone, and free. It should have been a pleasure. But as Louisa watched the sun bleed into peach streaks across the horizon, she felt a pang in the pit of her stomach, and a shadowy memory of Nathan along with it. There was nothing lonelier than watching a sunset alone—on Valentine's Day, no less.

As the sky dimmed to dark, Louisa walked to her car, reminding herself that she had plenty of pleasures in her life: ice cream and wine, yes, but also being with friends and feeling her toddlers' downy cheeks against her own. This last one she would get to experience in mere minutes, when she picked them up from daycare.

Ever since she and Nathan had sat Phoebe and Finn down and explained as simply as they could that he would be going away for a while, Louisa had been lax about the kids' bedtimes. They'd grown needier, understandably, clinging to Louisa in the evenings, asking for just one more song (then another), just one more book (then another). Louisa indulged the requests, trying to compensate for their missing father, and too tired to push back. Plus, reading them story after story was something she could do; on her own, she was worried about all the things she *wouldn't* be able to do for them.

Now in fresh PJs and still damp from their baths, the twins piled into Louisa's bed with her, where they all cuddled and sang "You Are My Sunshine" three times through. They fell asleep tucked into their mother's sides, and she carried them to their cribs. It was pleasure, utter and pure. It was enough.

And yet. When Louisa lay back down in bed, it felt cavernous and lonely. Was it sagging in a new way, mourning its former occupant? It was a ridiculous thought. Louisa knew she was the one in mourning, not the bed. She'd been the one to insist on a king. It was right after she'd earned her first paycheck as vice principal. Before that, they'd been surviving on a double, but just barely, since Nathan thrashed around in his sleep. It was a delight to upgrade to the oversized mattress—a pleasure. Now Louisa wished she had a single, no extra space to mock her solitude. Pleasure could be found everywhere, but there was a certain well that could only be filled up one way.

Sex. It was one of Nathan's gripes, not just in his revelation that he wanted to leave her, but for longer than Louisa cared to admit. She felt like a fool. She was angry, but whether at Nathan or herself or something more amorphous she couldn't tell. She remembered in the months after the twins were born, how her husband had tried to hide his disappointment when she'd kept putting him off in bed. Eventually he no longer hid his frustration; he would mope around like a petulant child, and Louisa would fume at his selfishness and insensitivity. But Louisa also recalled more recent nights, when Nathan had reached for her, and she'd turned away, touched-out from the kids, snapping, was he kidding after the day she'd had. She'd feel her husband's despondency emanating from across the bed, and stew in her own guilt, thinking, well, maybe tomorrow. Now there wouldn't be any more tomorrows with Nathan. It was just her, alone in her big, empty bed.

Well, Louisa thought with a sigh, she was nothing if not practical. She may not have a lover, but she had friends who'd bestowed a gift upon her that morning, and she could give pleasure to herself. The vibrator was purple glass, sleek and feminine. As Louisa lay back, she pictured Shari P from the video, and murmured the lyrics: "I'm a bitch, I'm a ho, I'm a ladyboss you know." Afterward, she sighed with resignation and wished herself a Happy Valentine's Day.

CHAPTER 16
Nathan

Nathan told himself he didn't care that the realtor assumed Mona was his daughter, and that she felt the need to reassure them of what a safe area it was, even for female students coming home late at night from the library—then winked at Mona, like dear old Dad didn't need to know that "library" was just code. All that mattered to Nathan was that the apartment was just right: not too far from campus, not too expensive, and though technically a one-bedroom, the walk-in closet looked big enough to fit a couple of mini-cribs. He and Mona would finally have a home of their own.

The lease signing felt like foreplay. Passing the pen back and forth was like electricity passing between their fingers. Each marking of initials here and signature there felt like official, notarized confirmation that their love was for real. Nathan examined his initials nuzzled up next to Mona's on a line acknowledging that they wouldn't install a washer-dryer: NRB and DRG.

"What's your middle name?" he asked. It was exciting that there was still so much of Mona to get to know.

"Ray."

"No way!" he gasped with delight. "Mine, too."

Mona kissed his nose. "You're cute, you know that?"

"Kismet," said the realtor, in the flattest tone possible. By now she'd figured out that Nathan was not in fact Mona's father, and she'd turned off her charm. No matter—she couldn't put a damper on Nathan's good mood.

"Are you named after my uncle Ray, too?" he asked. Good, he was making Mona laugh. "Or, let me guess, a ray of sunshine?"

"Ray was my mother's maiden name."

"Of course." The mention of Mona's mother made Nathan go quiet. He'd heard Mona take her mother's Sunday morning calls, then step outside to talk. But she never talked about her parents to him, except to say that they were conservative and wouldn't like the idea of her moving in with any boyfriend, much less an older one who'd been her professor. Her private life was private, she said, none of her parents' business. Nathan hadn't protested—who was he to meddle? Especially when he wasn't sure how he would've explained Mona to his own parents, had they still been living. Nathan hadn't been tight with his folks—after growing up, he'd rarely returned home—but he'd loved them and knew they'd loved him, too, in their way. They both died in Nathan's thirty-fifth year: his mother from breast cancer, then his father six months later from prostate cancer (by the time he'd finally gone to the doctor, it was too far along). Nathan and Louisa had recently started talking about having a child, but after that ordeal—Nathan flying out to San Luis Obispo twice a month to help with his parents' care—they'd put pregnancy on the backburner. Louisa had been the one to suggest holding off, and Nathan was grateful she'd recognized what he himself hadn't: how much he needed a breather. Well, that was all a long time ago now.

"One more signature for each of you, then we're all set."

The realtor snatched up the paperwork before Nathan could examine their two signatures side by side: Desdemona Ray Gill and Nathan Ray Bauer. Mona took his face between her palms and kissed him with a loud smack. "Hey, roomie," she said. "Let's go celebrate."

"Tacos and margaritas?" he suggested. They'd never gone out to dinner before, but the realtor's office was a couple towns over from River Mill, far from where the people they knew hung out; Nathan had spotted a Mexican joint a few doors down.

"Bueno." Mona linked her arm in Nathan's. "By the way, have I told you that I'm a nightmare to live with?"

"Um, I just watched you initial a line about how you'd wake me up each morning with a BJ and welcome me home each night with a stiff drink."

"Ha! More like, I watched you initial a line saying you were cool with my leaving my stuff everywhere and never lifting a finger to cook or clean."

"So, I'm moving in with another toddler?"

"Pretty much."

Nathan did his best to mirror Mona's playful look, but he felt a twist of unease in his belly. Although he'd been joking, officially moving in with Mona meant officially moving out of his family home—the home that was strewn all over with Phoebe and Finn's things, but that also included Phoebe and Finn. What would it mean to become a permanent part-time father? A day without his children was a vacation; several days without them was like a jail sentence.

"Yoo-hoo. Where'd you go?"

"Nowhere." Nathan squeezed Mona's hand. "I'm right here with you."

But when they were seated, Nathan couldn't focus; the words on the menu swam before his eyes. He was about to suggest that Mona order for both of them, when he heard a familiar voice.

"Nathan Bauer, hello."

He looked up to see his colleague Lydia Wexler standing beside the booth. She was wearing her standard uniform of gray slacks and a faded floral shirt—she must've owned a dozen of each. Nathan had always suspected that Lydia disliked him, and considered him inferior for having failed to secure a tenure-track position. Lydia, who'd set a department record for youngest professor to earn tenure, lived and breathed her job. Nathan had never once seen her outside of Cedar Hall, and here they were so far from campus. He was surprised to learn that she also frequented restaurants, or at least was frequenting this one restaurant on this one occasion—a very ill-timed occasion, as far as Nathan was concerned. He scratched the back of his neck, discovered it wet with sweat.

"Hi, Lydia."

Lydia was clearly waiting to be introduced to Nathan's companion, but he and Mona hadn't yet discussed how they would present themselves now that Mona was no longer his student. Nathan's mouth went dry.

Mona saved him by extending a hand. "Hello, I'm Mona."

"Mona was my student," Nathan blurted out, before he could stop himself. Mona blinked at him, slack-jawed. "I promised a taco dinner to the top scorer on the stats final, and Mona aced it."

No one said anything for what felt like a minute, an hour, a day. Mona eventually broke the silence with, "I studied really hard."

Lydia narrowed her eyes at Nathan. He almost wanted to yell, "Just kidding, we're fucking! We're totally fucking and we're moving in together, too!" Instead, he said, "Bribery is a great motivator," followed by a limp laugh.

"You're joking," Lydia said, but not as a question. Nathan nodded, at a loss for how else to respond. Why was she still standing there?

"Well, it's been good running into you," he said. "Enjoy your dinner. I hear this place makes a mean margarita. Highly recommended! Five stars!" He'd turned into a goddamn Yelp review. What a fool he was.

Lydia gave a thumbs-up—with what undertones, Nathan couldn't tell—and walked off.

Nathan wanted so much to dismiss the interaction as small talk with a colleague. He wanted to move on to discussing whether they should order their own margaritas frozen or on the rocks. But Mona was staring at her plate. "Should we leave?"

"I thought we were celebrating," he said lamely.

"Right. My stellar grades."

Neither of them laughed, and the weight of what had just happened hung over the table.

"I'm sorry," he said. "I panicked."

Mona's eyes shone with compassion. It was one of the dozens of reasons Nathan adored her—for how fast she forgave. "I love you," he said.

She leaned across the table. "Screw this place. Let's get takeout and eat it on the floor of our new apartment. We'll have a picnic, stark-fucking-naked, and you can lick salsa off my tits. You game?"

Nathan was already up and out the door.

CHAPTER 17

Louisa

When Louisa entered the principal's office, Chad Mack, the dean of students, was already seated, reaching over their boss' desk, clasping Dr. P's hand as the principal shook it heartily. He glanced at Louisa accusingly, like, *Where have you been?* despite the fact that she was at most three minutes late. Chad Mack was generally incompetent at his job, but he was always punctual, and one of his two main hobbies was to point out his punctuality to Louisa (the other was to gun for her position in a way that was obvious to everyone except their oblivious boss).

Dr. P continued pumping Chad's hand without acknowledging Louisa's presence. "A long, strong handshake projects power and confidence."

"I can feel that," Chad said. He wore an expensive suit and tie, always the best dressed at the school. Louisa often wondered if that's why Poolehauzer kept him around, if he thought it reflected well upon himself to be flanked by someone so stylish. *Appearances count for a lot!* Poolehauzer sometimes lectured Louisa. Her work wardrobe consisted of various nondescript blouses and skirts, reflecting exactly the requisite effort, and nothing more; Louisa had neither the time nor the patience to shop. Plus, she was skeptical of people who dressed too well, believing they were usually overcompensating for something.

The handshake persisted. Louisa wasn't even the one whose hand was being shaken and she wanted to squirm away in discomfort. "With grip, you want to go harder than people expect, but not break any bones."

"Though that would really show 'em who's boss, huh?" Chad chuckled. "Give a guy a death-grip handshake and word would spread fast about your prowess."

"Not a bad point, Mack Attack."

Louisa cleared her throat. It was already four-ten. Although Dr. P had called them in for what he claimed would be a "quickie," these afternoon meetings had a way of stretching out past sundown, Poolehauzer holding them hostage as he held forth on such diverse topics as his recent adventures in home-brewing, overrated Caribbean resorts versus the hidden gems, and the lifechanging power of a Canada Goose parka. Today, Louisa had to be out of there

74

by five on the dot to pick up her kids. "You called us in for a meeting?"

"Oh, hello there, Ms. Bauer." Dr. Poolehauzer finally retracted his hand. He leaned back in what Louisa thought of as his throne, a plush, upholstered number with scrolled arms and a high arched back, the only decent chair in the building.

"Hi. So, the meeting?"

"Right. Testing, testing, one two three." Dr. P tapped at a pretend microphone, then paused for effect. "As you know, state tests will be administered in two short months, and word on Main Street is that they're much tougher than last year's." Louisa straightened her posture—testing had become a necessary evil in education, and she'd long since given up fighting its inevitability. "So, let's hope this year's crop of kiddos are super-geniuses ... at least when it comes to bubbling in multiple-choice problems, am I right?"

"Right!" Chad, loyal yes-man, nodded like a marionette. Louisa imagined him at the ready for the principal's command to stand, fetch, or collate.

The two men waited for Louisa's echo. "Right," she mumbled. She was always resisting forming her part of this unified front; although she'd been on the administration for several years now, Louisa still thought of herself as a teacher at heart.

"All righty." Poolehauzer flung a loafered foot up onto his desk, revealing a sliver of pasty leg. He picked up a pamphlet, cleared his throat, and began reading. "This year, for River Mill High to be deemed competent, the Department of Education has set the following goal for our student body: a five percent increase from last year's test results, across all grades and assessments."

Louisa took a big, nervous breath. "That's a big uptick. What happens if we don't reach the goal?" She feared she already knew the answer.

"Oh, the usual. Reduced funding, probationary status, et cetera, et cetera. We'll probably only have the budget to keep one of you two." Dr. P gestured in the direction of Louisa and Chad, and laughed like he was kidding. Only he didn't say, "Just kidding." Instead, he turned to his computer and began a rapid-fire burst of typing. Louisa's brain became a wind tunnel as she stared straight ahead, avoiding eye contact with her colleague who, despite being kind of a dunce, was beloved by their boss. Plus, Chad Mack had started at River Mill a year before she had, and seniority counted at the school.

Poolehauzer shrugged. "Relax, we'll be fine. The students will just step it up, simple as that."

"Failure is not an option," Chad added, adopting what he'd once described to Louisa as his "optimal thinking" stance: butt on edge of seat, torso tilted forward. "We have every incentive to make sure the students do well on these tests."

"Should we discuss a plan?" Louisa cracked her notebook and clicked open her pen.

Poolehauzer stretched his arms in the air. "Nah. I trust you, Ms. Bauer, to figure out all the nuts and bolts. Amping up test prep, that kind of thing. I'm positive you'll come up with a plan for success."

Was her boss being serious or sarcastic? Louisa sometimes wondered whether Poolehauzer was firing on all cylinders, or if perhaps a person had to be a little crazy to take the job of principal of a public high school in this day and age. His broad smile revealed a fleck of something spinach-like wedged between two molars, making him look a little deranged.

"Moving on," he said. "The student surveys from first semester revealed stress scores through the roof. Mr. Mack has suggested that the solution might lie in a new field called social and emotional learning." Louisa marveled at her boss deeming social and emotional learning a "new" field, not to mention the fact that she'd been trying for years to get the school to adopt an SEL curriculum. As Dr. P mansplained about TED Talks and mindfulness apps, Louisa kept an anxious eye on the clock. It was now ten minutes to five, and the meeting didn't seem anywhere close to finished.

When it became clear that Chad Mack would be spearheading the SEL initiative, Louisa excused herself. In the hall, she pulled up her text message thread with Nathan, and reluctantly began composing: "I'm stuck in a meeting. I know it's my night, but can you do pick-up?" She pressed send, hating to need him, and then stared at her screen. No sign of typing, no response, nothing. Nathan was useless, as usual.

Back in the principal's office, Louisa's colleagues were taking a snack break. "Try one, Ms. Bauer." Dr. P held out a Tupperware of cookies that looked like they belonged on a magazine cover. "Vanessa whipped up a batch of her famous hazelnut tartlets. These babies won the bakeoff at our block party."

"My god, this is the best thing I've ever eaten," Chad said, and for once, Louisa agreed with him. The mingling of butter and sugar on her tongue made her want to cry.

"That wife of mine is the tops." Dr. P picked up the framed photo of his family: he and Vanessa and their four tow-headed sons, everyone in chambray shirts and white linen shorts, on a beach somewhere at sunset. All six of them were smiling at the camera, eyes open, looking like they were happy to be there. The photo was positioned outward on Dr. P's desk, so visitors were forced to gaze upon his charming family. Louisa found this aggressive.

Dr. P replaced the frame. "With four wild boys and everything else going on, I don't know how Vanessa does all she does."

Louisa bit her tongue. *She doesn't work, and she has a nanny and a housekeeper at her beck and call, that's how.* Vanessa Poolehauzer was rumored to have a bottomless family trust. Louisa had met her twice, at the annual River Mill benefit, and both times she'd approached the interactions optimistically, thinking surely they'd find common conversational ground: They were both mothers, and Louisa was second-in-command to the woman's husband. But Louisa left both encounters feeling diminished, like Vanessa considered her some hapless pet whose job was a quirky affectation.

"Ms. Bauer, I'll have Vanessa send you the recipe."

How could Dr. P possibly think Louisa had time to bake? And why wouldn't he ask his wife to send the recipe to Chad, too? But it was easier to be gracious. "Great, thanks."

She glanced at her phone—still no word from Nathan. "I hate to break up this cookie klatch, but I've got to go pick up my kids."

"Gotcha." Dr. P nodded in commiseration. "There's nothing tougher than being a working parent. The Mackster and I will hang back and hammer out an anti-stress game plan, and you can play catch-up later, Ms. Bauer. Unless you've got somewhere else to be, Mr. Mack?"

"Of course not." Because he was a single man with no responsibilities outside of work. Because he would've happily dragged in a sleeping bag to camp out in the principal's office if it meant more face time with the boss. Well, screw both of them.

"A tartlet for the road, Ms. Bauer?" Dr. P shook the Tupperware in her direction.

"Why not?" She grabbed three, then raced out, praying she'd hit all green lights on her drive.

Five hours later, Louisa's phone finally beeped. Nathan's reply: "Sorry, didn't see this earlier. I was signing a lease. So, good news: I'll have a place for the kids to come visit soon." Louisa stared at the text for a good minute and a half as a soup of anger and sadness churned inside of her.

Her phone beeped again: an email from Vanessa Poolehauzer, subject "Hope you enjoy making these as much as I do!" with the hazelnut tartlet recipe pasted into the body. Louisa scrolled down, counting sixteen ingredients, including one that she didn't know how to pronounce. The preparation time was two hours, twenty minutes, plus chilling.

"Looking forward to it!" she replied, then copied and pasted the same note to Nathan.

CHAPTER 18
Amy

"The grocery store, the coffee shop, the park." The speaker sat directly across from Amy in the circle of metal folding chairs, so he seemed to be talking just to her. It was intense. "Everywhere I go, babies and kids, kids and babies. You think you'd finally get a break at an upscale restaurant at nine p.m. You think you'd be safe. But there they are—the pregnant women mocking you with their big bellies and smug smiles and tiny sips of wine. All you wanted was a twenty-dollar plate of pasta, and instead you're surrounded, held hostage by other women's fecundity."

Fecundity, Amy repeated in her head, shifting in her chair. *That's not a word you hear every day.* Why say "fecundity" instead of "fertility," she wondered? Was it for the drama? Or maybe for variation, so sick was this woman probably of talking and thinking about the more commonplace synonym, and its ugly counterpart: infertility. No one talked about infecundity.

Another woman chimed in, "How about Take Your Daughter to Work Day? At least the workplace should be an adults-only zone. But you have to be a good sport as all these adorable kids come in and say cute things about the decorations in your cubicle. This year, my manager asked me to organize an art project for them. An art project!"

Amy also would've been annoyed if she'd been asked to transform into an elementary school teacher at the office. But she happened to like Take Your Daughter to Work Day. There were always a couple of girls fascinated by Amy's work who asked smart, curious questions, and it heartened Amy to think of them growing up to become formidable forces in their chosen fields.

A man spoke next: "My office looks out onto a playground, so I tend to keep the shades drawn. On sunny days, my colleagues look at me like I'm a freak."

The guy did sort of look like a vampire, pale and long-faced, so Amy could see where his coworkers were coming from. She took a furtive survey of the group—everyone kind-eyed, nodding sympathetically. It made her want to scream. They could've been at a support group for pedophiles instead of people struggling with infertility. It was interesting how much these two groups had in common, actually, that twinned longing and loathing, the stigma and

79

secrecy, all the energy it took to get through the day. Amy knew how offensive this observation was. She filed it away to share later with Mickey, probably the only person who'd laugh.

Amy tuned back in to realize the speaker was her husband. "The birthday parties are what get me. My friend has twins, and for their second birthday, they had all these lawn games in their backyard: mini basketball hoops and ring tosses. The kids were so excited. Then the ice cream truck showed up, and forget it, they lost their freaking minds. My friend's son burst into tears, he didn't know what to do with so much emotion. Like, what do you even do with that?"

A muffled sob emerged from Abe's throat. Amy reached for his hand as he went on, "I love those kids like they're my own—I held them in the hospital when they were five-pound preemies; I was in the room when they took their first steps." He paused and locked eyes with Amy. She welled up with love for him and realized what a mistake it had been to beg off these meetings for so long, forcing Abe to attend on his own. As little as she identified with the group, her husband needed her here. "I just want my kids to grow up with my friends' kids, you know? I wanted my own kids to be at that party, too."

Another woman picked up the thread. She described the call from her sister saying she was pregnant, and how she'd tried to tamp down the part of her that felt her own sadness and loss alongside her sister's joy, and the guilt and shame that followed.

Amy glanced at her husband, who was listening with his whole body, every inch of his being empathetic to this woman's complex emotional landscape. That must've provided at least a modicum a comfort. What a decent man Abe was. Amy squeezed his hand.

It was now the leader's turn to speak, to issue blithe sympathies and pat reassurances. Amy did not like this woman, with her flowy Eileen Fisher ensemble, her pitying eyes, and her insistence on remaining a blank slate even as she urged everyone else to spill their most intimate feelings. Had she too experienced infertility, and if so, had she gone on to have a child? Or did she birth a brood of ten kids, easy-peasy? Or had she never been interested in motherhood in the first place? She didn't say.

Amy knew she wasn't being fair. But she'd always found the whole therapy and self-help genre embarrassing, even as she knew other people (generally white people, it seemed) found real solace in it. Clichés didn't sound like clichés when they applied directly to your situation. These groups really did meet in church basements and serve weak coffee and stale cookies, but that didn't mean the people who sat around in a circle had feelings that were any less real or raw.

That was the other thing—the intensity of the feelings. The longing for a child oozed from these people's pores, and it made Amy squirm, highlighting the fact that she didn't share the feeling. She felt curious, cautiously open. But longing? No.

"I'm going to the ladies," she whispered to Abe. In the bathroom, she sat on the toilet long after she'd finished peeing. She, too, had attended Phoebe and Finn's second birthday party, but she remembered it differently than Abe. Sure, some of the kids had been delighted for some of the time, but there were also plenty of tantrums and meltdowns. And while half of the parents (including Louisa) looked weary with the effort of orchestrating the kids' fun and games, the other half (including Nathan) had retreated inside to drink Bloody Marys. It made Amy wonder if those were the only two options for parents of young kids: overextended or absentee. She remembered Abe as a kind of hero that day, throwing himself into the fray to teach the kids how to dribble soccer balls. Meanwhile, Amy herself hovered awkwardly at the edges, aware of being the only woman there not attached to a child. Finally, Mickey and Mateo showed up (their daughter was too old for ring tosses and ice cream sundaes), and Amy was thrilled when Mickey suggested they duck around the corner to smoke a joint. It was the best part of Amy's day, giggling with her friend behind the fence as they blew birthday horns at each other.

"Yoo-hoo." Abe's voice was followed by knocks on the bathroom door.

"I'll be out in a minute," Amy called out.

"No, let me in." It was a whisper, spoken (if Amy weren't mistaken) in a mischievous tone. She reached for the door of the single stall.

"Hi," Abe said.

"Hi."

"I feel like we're double agents, with our big fat secret," he said. "Do you think we should tell the group?"

"That's up to you, honey." Amy didn't say that this group was for him, not her. Or that she didn't get why he wanted to keep coming to these meetings after they'd visited an adoption agency and had an appointment in their calendar to fill out the application.

Abe shook his hands as he paced between the sink and the hand-dryer. "I don't know. It feels like a betrayal, like we're abandoning them all in their struggle. Is that ridiculous?"

"No." *Yes.* Amy didn't know why Abe felt such allegiance to these people, but more than that, she didn't know why their infertility felt so intrinsic to his identity. For Amy, it was a raincloud that sometimes appeared over their heads; often it didn't bother her at all. Her feelings about adoption were complicated, but no part of her felt that it would be a betrayal to anyone. In fact, at one point in the meeting, she'd felt tempted to shout out, "Have none of you heard of adoption? Why don't you get over your egotistic obsession with passing along your DNA and go find an existing child who needs parents?!"

Amy put a hand on her husband's shoulder. "Why don't you think about it more? There's no need to decide now, or share today if you're not sure. It also seems pretty off-topic to what everyone else is talking about in there."

"It's just, there was this couple that used to come, Rashid and Alicia. At some point, I realized it'd been weeks since they'd participated, then it became obvious that Alicia was pregnant. When someone finally asked her, she confessed she'd formed such a bond with everyone and hadn't been sure how to say goodbye."

"Okay." It sounded like a hopeful story to Amy. People could move on from here. They could get lucky or get help from science or lean on faith or whatever, then be swept along to the next room full of strangers with something in common: the waiting room at the OB office or a prenatal Pilates studio. But Amy was no longer surprised when she and Abe interpreted the same situation in starkly different ways. It was an aspect of her relationship that she found by turns intriguing and irritating, being married to someone with such a different outlook on life. "I'm sure they didn't mean to hurt anyone by keeping it a secret," she said. "It was probably hard for them to share their happiness in that room."

"True. And I'm so happy we're taking this next step. We're going to be parents!"

"Yes," Amy said, trying to mimic her husband's joy. "Plus, I can't imagine anyone will begrudge us our news. Anyone can decide to adopt."

"Well, not anyone."

"I know, I know. It costs a ton of money, and you've got to jump through all the hoops and pass all the tests. But still."

What she meant was, adoption was a process with a series of concrete steps that you could research and plan for. It didn't require the magical "miracle of life" ingredient that the people in that room would've killed to get their hands on.

"Also," Abe said gently, "your partner has to agree to it. But it's not just that. I've been trying to convince you to get on board with this for nearly a year. Now that you have, I guess I have to face my own ambivalence about it, you know? Giving up on the idea of having a biological child." Amy's heart began pounding. "I feel like an asshole saying that, especially given your history. But I always pictured our kid having your beautiful eyes and my nerdy interest in World War II."

Amy surprised herself by feeling sympathetic: "They can still share your interest in war history. They'll just be spared your crooked nose." She kissed the tip of it.

"But also your high cheekbones." He kissed them one by one.

"Abe, I'm glad you're telling me this stuff. And I get it."

More than he knew. Amy had been mourning her birth parents her whole life, the people she imagined would look like reflections of herself and feel just as familiar. And now both she and Abe were mourning the loss of that potential in their future child. She knew the desire for a biological link was natural, and deeply rooted, the want to look at your family and see your features reflected on their faces (despite her urge to lash out at the group earlier for expressing just this desire). Amy had known this in her bones for as long as she'd known herself, even as she also knew that her adoptive parents loved her deeply. It filled her with emotion to realize that Abe, despite all their differences, understood this, too.

Amy's desire for her husband welled up inside of her, making her feel fully, deliciously present in her body. She reached for him, and then they were peeling off one another's clothes, turning to each other like they always did when they were overwhelmed with feeling—happiness, sadness, anger, or otherwise. They weren't the types to go at it in a single-stall bathroom of a church basement, but there they were, Amy leaning into the tile wall as Abe held her by the hips from behind. The location neither excited Amy nor grossed her out. For them, it was never about the place; it was always about the two of them together.

CHAPTER 19

Abe

Abe was taking himself on a tour of his home, like he was a visitor at a museum. He took it all in, trying to see all the stuff he'd long ago stopped seeing. The living room furniture was tasteful, if a little worn; the couch was big and comfy, perfect for sprawling, or—maybe he'd point this out?—for a family to pile onto for movie night. The coffee table was all sharp edges, but surely they weren't expected to have the place childproofed already, right? The framed pictures on the wall were a combination of black-and-white prints from that summer Abe had gotten into photography (see, he had healthy hobbies!), posters of concerts he and Amy had attended (they were a couple who had fun together!), and an eclectic array of prints from their various international trips (they had means! they were interested in other cultures!).

But another glance around had Abe second-guessing himself: the hodgepodge of wall decorations had no uniform style. Did that convey that *they* were all over the place, and therefore unfit to guide a tiny being into personhood? Abe knew he was overthinking this. And yet, the caseworker had told them, you want to paint a clear picture of who you are, and you want your home to reflect that picture.

Onto his office. It was a mess, but the kind of mess where Abe knew the whereabouts of everything he needed: stacks of homework to grade, lesson ideas, folders for National Honor Society activities. To Abe, his office told a story of a teacher who cared about his students, and valued history and education. Surely these were qualities of a good father, too. Feeling confident, Abe straightened out a pile of papers.

Then he reconsidered: Did the office actually give the impression that Abe was a workaholic, and that his priorities were skewed? Abe cleared off his desk so that it was a sleek slab, the desk of a man with a calm, uncluttered head, a man who had plenty of room in his life for a family.

But damnit, this was ridiculous. The caseworker had said just to be themselves, and Abe didn't have a child yet, so they couldn't expect him to be acting like a father already. Surely other prospective adoptive parents didn't have full nurseries set up, their houses strewn with toys to signal their fitness for the job. Like, *Look, our home is just as much of a disaster as our friends whose reproductive organs are in proper working order! Bring on the baby!* No, that was just creepy. Abe replaced his school stuff on his desk, but tidied it up a bit just to be safe.

He headed to the kitchen, which was clean and bright, with a sink, a dishwasher, a table, and a fridge. What the hell else was a kitchen supposed to have? Well, Abe would've liked marble countertops, and Amy wished for pull-out shelves in the pantry. But a kid could survive without such amenities. Abe laughed. Look, he could laugh at himself! But when he opened the fridge, his assurance plummeted again: There was a six-pack of Sam Adams, pad thai leftovers, some leather-skinned Granny Smiths, and a door's worth of condiments. The freezer was no better: a package of chicken breasts, a pint of ice cream, and a veritable tundra of freezer burn. *Damn,* Abe thought, *our fridge makes us look like college kids.*

Abe sighed and cracked open a Sam Adams, took a sip, then exclaimed "Shit" and emptied the rest down the drain. Beer on his breath would certainly be a mark against him; he could almost hear himself protesting that he rarely drank. He deposited the can at the bottom of their recycling, under a bunch of pastel La Croix. He sat down at the table, anxious for the home visit to be over before it had even started.

Six p.m. The social worker was supposed to arrive at six-thirty. Abe had reminded Amy of the appointment last night and then again this morning, plus it was in their shared Google calendar. She'd promised she'd be home in time. There was no reason to worry.

Abe drummed his fingers on the table, worried. He opened another beer—he'd sip this one slowly. He could have a beer after work and still be a decent man—a decent dad. This was all so preposterous. He and Amy were good people, with good jobs and a good home, and they'd be good parents, too. What did they have to prove? They really could just be themselves. Abe felt exasperated and angry. How many people had to get their home approved by a stranger before they could become parents? Well, why not go through the list?

For starters, not Louisa and Nathan. They'd seemed on shaky ground for a while, if Abe was honest about it, Louisa frequently griping about Nathan's shortcomings, the two of them bickering about petty things. And now they were throwing in the towel just a couple of years into parenthood, shattering the kids' stability for their own selfish reasons. Okay, for Nathan's selfish reasons. But actually, Abe did think Louisa could be harsh on Nathan, and if they weren't sleeping together, then that was a concern, too. And no wonder they fought about money. Hadn't it been irresponsible to have kids when they still had substantial student loans and no savings? They couldn't have known they would have twins, and be on the hook for double daycare tuition and double everything else, but still—you had to prepare for such things. Abe loved his friends, and he felt for Louisa in particular. But he also felt a bit judgmental of how they hadn't put in the proper effort to preserve their marriage and by extension their family. Meanwhile, other people would've killed to have what they had.

Then there was Mickey and Mateo. Melody had come by accident—*by accident!* Mickey had barely earned her degree when she got pregnant, and Mateo was still in grad school; neither one of them had a W2 or a savings account to present to a caseworker. Melody was a toddler when Abe first met her parents, and their home would not have passed an adoption agency inspection, not by a long shot. Mickey and Mateo threw epic parties, during which Melody was passed from person to person like a hot potato until finally falling asleep in someone's lap; eventually it occurred to Mickey to transfer her daughter to the crib. Abe never doubted that Melody was loved by her parents. Plus, she'd had her village: In those days, Louisa was over there several evenings a week building block towers and reading with the girl; Nathan taught her to count to a hundred by age two, and she basically became the mascot of Mateo's math department. But Mickey and Mateo were in their early twenties then, still kids themselves. It had taken them years to get their footing, to even think about things like balanced meals and bedtime routines.

Speaking of children having children, what about Abe's student last year, poor Ella Macintyre? Just a sophomore, she'd tried hiding her belly well into her second trimester, until she abruptly dropped out of school over spring break. She'd had atrocious spelling and used sparkly gel pens with feathers on the end—and *she* was now a mother? Abe actually cared a lot about Ella and, after some digging, had found out she'd taken the GED and had a healthy baby son named Brayden.

Abe knew his bitterness wasn't really about these other parents. It was about the fact that only the people whose reproductive parts were defective had to endure a professional coming over to scrutinize their life to decide whether or not they were fit to have a child—and to pay an exorbitant fee for the privilege. Oh, Abe understood; of course he did. No one would want to hand over their offspring, whom they couldn't raise for any number of reasons, to just anyone. You had to find decent, loving people with enough resources and a good home. Vetting was essential. But that didn't mean it wasn't humiliating for the ones being vetted.

Where on earth was Amy?

It was six twenty-five when Abe finally heard a car pull up outside. But when he went to the front window, he saw it wasn't his wife's Prius; it was an unfamiliar Subaru Forester. Damnit. Showing up early was probably a social worker power move.

Abe shot his wife a text: "Where are you?!" then threw open the door and tried out a few stances before settling on one arm leaned against the doorframe and the other waving: he was casual, welcoming, the man of the house. He expected an unsmiling middle-aged lady in a cheap suit, but the woman who stepped out of her car was younger than he was, and wearing jeans. She smiled as she introduced herself. "I'm Julia Jimenez."

"Abe Jones." What should he say about Amy? That she had an emergency and had to run out? That she was sick in bed? That he had no idea where she was, and that her absence not only looked bad to Julia Jimenez but also made Abe question her commitment to this process and, more than that, sunk him into a pit of despair, given that she knew how important this was to him? *Whoa.* He had to get a grip.

"Amy, my wife, is stuck at work. She should be here soon." Abe knew it was the truth. Plus, he was a terrible liar.

"It's fine. I'm early—a bad habit of mine. It unnerves people." She said it in such a friendly tone, and Abe's laugh was full of relief. He heard himself exclaim how cold it was outside, then ask Julia about her drive: weather and route talk, *so lame.* But he didn't know how this worked; was she waiting for a tour?

At six thirty-three, Amy swooped in, arms full of groceries. She greeted Abe with a peck on the mouth (not their usual deep kiss after a day apart). She shook Julia Jimenez's hand, apologized for running late—"The traffic on the Pike was murder"—and invited her into the kitchen for snacks.

It was like a party, Amy the perfect host. She set out a full spread: a wheel of Brie and two kinds of crackers, grapes, dried apricots, and crunchy rice rollers. She dug right in, grabbing a rice roller and chatting about how she'd discovered them in Boston's Chinatown and now they were her mainstay. She cracked open a seltzer, tossed a can to Abe, and asked Julia if she preferred lemon or pamplemousse. "So, how does this whole thing work?" she asked, popping an apricot into her mouth and widening her eyes like she was downright thrilled to have her home inspected for acceptability.

Abe knew it was an act. Usually when Amy came home from

work, she holed up in the basement or the bath to decompress for half an hour. Early on in their relationship, Abe had tried to join her. But she'd made it clear that she needed the alone time. And she was never this chatty, never someone to smear a hunk of Brie onto a cracker and lick the remains off her thumb. Abe stood back, entertained and amazed. So, this was his wife's idea of a good mother—laden with groceries, a casual snacker, light-hearted and inviting as she led Julia Jimenez around their house. Abe tagged along, impressed at his own life reflected back at him, everything painted in rosy hues of warmth and love. What had he been so worried about? Julia Jimenez or anyone would be able to see that he and Amy were perfect candidates to adopt.

After the social worker left, Abe pulled his wife in for a hug. He sung her praises, trading off compliments with little kisses.

"Thanks. I think it went well, too." Now her voice sounded drained, and she wasn't returning his kisses. "I'm heading upstairs. It's been a long day."

"All right, honey." Abe figured he'd give her some time by herself, then go join her. But when he cracked the bedroom door, he found his wife asleep, snoring lightly. He draped a blanket over her, kissed her on the forehead, and went back downstairs to watch TV and polish off the Brie.

CHAPTER 20

Mickey

Mickey tapped Mel on the calf as they passed in opposite directions in neighboring pool lanes. Another half-lane to the wall, breathing every third stroke, flip turn, then the half-lane back until she'd meet her daughter once again in the middle—Mickey's favorite moment of each lap. Fifty taps down, fifty more to go. They were swimming 2,500 yards today, Mel taking it easier than Mickey to maintain the same pace. The girl's swim season was over, and this year, her last on her high school team, was the first one when her times had bested her mother's. At every meet, Mickey had gone hoarse from cheering, she was so proud of Mel, especially when she anchored the team's two-hundred-yard relay. At the final meet, Mickey had cried as she hugged her dripping-wet daughter after her last race.

This was what motherhood was all about, Mickey knew: teaching your daughter to stay afloat, then nurturing her as she learned her strokes and grew strong and elegant, cutting through the water; watching as each day she became less of you and more of herself, until one day she surpassed you altogether. Motherhood was connecting with your child (tap fifty-one) and then letting her go. Sometimes Mel tapped back, and Mickey grinned wildly, letting her mouth fill with chlorinated water.

There were nicer pools in town, but Mickey had a soft spot for the YMCA. When she was pregnant with Mel, she'd taken a parenting class here. She was normally a DIY person, but for maybe the first time in her life, Mickey had found herself petrified at the task that lay ahead: raising a human. She was twenty-one years old at the time, and no one in her life had kids. Her own parents had barely been parents to her while she was growing up; Mickey had come along as the opposite kind of surprise, a late-in-life baby after they'd nearly finished raising three sons. They'd been so close to home-free, and while not exactly taking this out on their daughter, they'd kept Mickey at an arm's length throughout her childhood. The moment she was off to college, they'd packed up the house and moved abroad, back to the English countryside where Mickey's mother had grown up. When Mel was born and Mickey suggested her parents fly back to meet their granddaughter, they'd rattled off a litany of excuses preventing them from traveling. They hadn't met

Mel until she was nearly two years old.

In parenting class, Mickey had learned about healthy attachment, how a child who felt emotionally and physically bonded to a parent had the sense of security needed to venture out in the world, to take risks and form healthy relationships. Mickey took this seriously—it was her main focus through Mel's infancy. And as the girl began to toddle and then run around, Mickey marveled at how the research bore out: At a party, Mel usually threw herself into unfamiliar situations with new kids, then returned occasionally to rest her head in her mother's lap and receive a kiss, then ran off again. Mickey knew she wasn't perfect, but she never doubted that she was a good mother.

It felt the same now, Mel swimming toward Mickey and then away, toward and away. In a few short months, she'd be off swimming in another pool, perhaps all the way on the west coast. Or maybe she'd decide she didn't want to swim at all in college. Mateo had hoped Mel would apply to local schools (there were so many wonderful options right here in western Mass!), but Mickey felt proud of her daughter for wanting to venture so far away. Mel was so brave, so big-spirited. Tap one hundred, *done*.

They swam to opposite ends of the pool and hopped out. Pulling off her goggles and freeing her ponytail from her cap, Mickey hopped from foot to foot to release the water from her ear canals. By the time she turned around to find her daughter, she spotted her in conversation with the lifeguard, a teenage boy who looked like he'd been working out to fill out his skinny frame. Mel's hip jutted subtly to the side, and her sentences were punctuated with laughter as she ran her fingers through her wet hair. Clearly, Mel had inherited her mother's ability to flirt. And the boy looked like he was enjoying it, too, spinning his whistle around his finger one way and then the other (had every lifeguard in the history of lifeguarding performed this move?). Mickey couldn't help her smile; it was a pleasure to see her daughter so poised and confident, so full of life.

"Boo." A hip bump, and the familiar smell of vanilla and spice (and everything nice), with base notes of chlorine. Mickey knew this was Keisha's usual swimming time. She stole a glance at her friend in a Speedo. "Mel and lifeguard boy, huh?"

"Apparently," said Mickey. "I wish you'd brought popcorn—what a show. There's nothing like teen romance."

Keisha laughed. "First, since when do you eat popcorn?"

"Metaphorical popcorn. Second?"

"You've gotta be the only mother who enjoys watching her

teenage daughter lust after a boy, and vice versa. You know what they're thinking about, right? Not butterflies and rainbows."

"Come on, it's fun to see Mel in touch with her own pleasure. When are we more alive than when we want?" Mickey performed a few quad stretches. "It's no secret I run a sex-positive household. Mel knows we keep condoms right in the medicine cabinet next to the Band-aids. They're available to one and all." She made a sweeping gesture that made Keisha smirk.

"Thanks, but condoms are the last thing I need." Keisha claimed she'd never slept with a man. She'd been with her partner, Leah, for as long as Mickey had known her—until they broke up a couple months ago. Mickey was dying to know if she'd dated anyone since, but Keisha wouldn't say. "Anyway, it's hot in here. The cold water calls. Later, Mickey Mouse." She kissed Mickey on the cheek before hopping in.

Mickey glanced once more at Mel, guessing that her daughter's sensations mirrored her own, the same flutters in her stomach. Then she made for the locker room. Her daughter deserved some privacy.

Later, prepping a stir fry, Mel slicing carrots and Mickey chopping an onion, Mel turned to her mom to ask, "So, aren't you going to ask me about the lifeguard?"

"I figured you'd tell me if you wanted to." This was Mickey's secret to getting Mel to open up: she never pushed; she always let her daughter talk on her own terms and timeline. Sometimes she felt more like a big sister than a mother to Mel.

"His name is Bryce, and he's a senior at River Mill. But don't you dare ask Louisa about him!"

Mickey held up her hands in defense. "Fine, I'll just ask Abe then." Mel pelted a carrot coin at her mom. "Hey, I'm already dealing with enough vegetable-induced trauma over here." Mickey indicated the pile of chopped onion and the tears streaming down her face.

"Anyway, we've been texting, and we're going to the movies on Friday."

"A Friday night date! How exciting!" Mickey lifted her daughter and spun her around. Mel was giggling, half a carrot still in hand, looking delighted even as she insisted it was no big deal and not really a date.

"I know you love your veggies, but this is a lot of enthusiasm even for you two." Mateo stood in the kitchen doorway. Mickey, caught up in her giddiness, flitted over and kissed him on the lips.

"Our beautiful daughter has a date on Friday night with a boy with an exceptionally cute butt."

"Mom!"

"What? It's true. I saw for myself. Good hair, too. It does that impressive swoopy thing."

Mateo stiffened. "Who is this guy?"

"He's a lifeguard at the Y," Mickey said. "So, we know he knows CPR and the Heimlich."

"Let's hope he doesn't need to demonstrate either of those skills," Mateo said. "Well, I'd like to meet him before you go out, and please be home by midnight."

"Or what, my chariot will turn into a pumpkin?" Mel asked.

Mickey laughed; Mateo didn't.

"Or your dad will turn into a basket case," Mickey said, then refocused on her daughter. "So, what will you wear? You can borrow my teardrop earrings if you want. They're good luck!"

"Thanks, Mom."

Mickey's phone lit up with Louisa, so she handed off her chef's knife to Mateo and ducked into the other room.

Louisa's voice was in her ear. "Did you get the email?"

"What? I haven't checked."

"Nathan sent out a mass email with his new address. Apparently he decided the right move was to BCC me along with everyone else."

"Wow, what a dick." Mickey wondered if Nathan was intentionally being awful or just thoughtless. "Did you Google-Earth it?"

"Of course, and I found the real estate listing, too. It's in a little complex on the other side of the river, ugly as can be. There's wall-to-wall carpeting, and what looks like faux-wood paneling."

"What an asshole." The response didn't make sense, but this was how Mickey felt she had to punctuate these types of conversations with Louisa. Acting indignant, together, made both of them feel better, or at least it made Mickey feel better and she hoped it did the same for Louisa. If nothing else, she was relieved her friend was confiding in her.

"Anyway," said Louisa, "I regret my digging, because now I have a precise setting in mind as I imagine him and Mona fucking all over the damned place, getting carpet burn on their knees."

"Ouch."

"We did that—made love in every room of this house the first week we moved in. God, that feels like another century."

"Lou, you've got to stop torturing yourself. If you're feeling frustrated, remember your little Valentine's Day present."

It was stupid advice—Mickey knew Louisa didn't want to sleep with Nathan; she just didn't want him to be sleeping with someone else. But Mickey was suddenly distracted, thinking, when was the last time she and Mateo had had sex outside of the bedroom, or in any kind of interesting position? She pushed the question away to tune back in to her friend.

"It's a good thing the kids are asleep and I can't afford a babysitter, because otherwise I'd be doing a drive-by of his place right now."

"I'll babysit for you anytime, Lou, although I don't support this particular mission."

"Should I send them a housewarming gift? Maybe a big box of condoms, because if Nathan gets that girl pregnant, I will scream myself mute."

"Sure. I'll go halfsies with you. I'll drive it over and leave it on their porch, save you a trip."

"Deal. Oh, that's Phoebe calling."

"Okay. But Louisa?"

"Yeah?"

"Nathan is a dick, and you're the bee's knees, and I love you."

"I love you, too."

After they hung up, Mickey held the phone for a while, silently cursing Nathan. It occurred to her that maybe her disgust with him was about more than his betrayal of Louisa. Maybe it was also about his brazenly doing what Mickey would've never dared to do: namely, turning his life upside-down just to chase his pleasure. Maybe Mickey was jealous. As much as Nathan's selfishness repulsed her, if she was honest with herself, a part of her was in awe of it. Particularly when her own husband seemed to work so hard to minimize her sexuality, to convey that her desire just wasn't that important, to insist that if she could just focus on the good stuff they had instead of demanding more, then everything would be fine. Once, after Mateo had reluctantly given in to her prodding, right in the middle of things he declared, "This is bordering on nonconsensual, you know." At the time, Mickey had laughed in disbelief, thinking he had to be joking. But she'd never forgotten the comment; it had cut her and left a scar. Mateo had no clue how wounding his lack of interest was. He could claim again and again that it was him, not her—his sex drive had simply waned in recent years—but it wasn't a matter of him or her, it was a matter of *them*.

And now he was acting like an old-fashioned sitcom dad with Melody, so edgy over her interest in a boy. He didn't used to be so uptight. He'd always been such a supportive father, enthusiastic about all of Mel's projects and whims. But apparently that didn't extend to her desire to date this new guy.

As they were getting ready for bed, Mateo returned to their earlier conversation: "Before, when you wished Mel luck, what was the luck for exactly? That she'll get laid on her date?" He seemed primed for a fight.

"Whoa, easy. I was wishing that it would go well, that Mel would have a good time."

Mateo's scoff pushed Mickey to continue. "If that good time includes kissing or more with this boy, cool. Mel is smart, she knows how to handle herself. I'll give her a safe sex refresher on her way out if it'll make you feel better." This last comment was intentionally provocative, but whatever, Mickey was annoyed at the confrontation.

"Very reassuring, Mick. You know, you're incredible. You *want* our teenage daughter to be sleeping with boys, don't you?"

"Newsflash: it's not about what I want, it's about what she wants. Mel is our daughter, but she's also nearly grown up, whether you like it or not. She's not going to tamp down her sexuality just because you want her to."

Mateo sat on the bed and got very quiet. When he eventually spoke, it was through clenched teeth. "Who are we talking about here, Mick?"

Mickey countered her husband's hush with volume, practically shouting, "Me, we're talking about me, okay?" Her heart was banging around in her chest, and she wished she could pull it out and cradle it in her hands.

"You know what I realized today?" Her words gathered like a flood, and she could hardly believe she was letting them all pour out. "I'm envious of Nathan. For letting himself feel his feelings powerfully enough to pursue them. I guess that's a guy thing, being perfectly comfortable listening to your wants and needs and not letting anyone else convince you that they're not okay or too much. But I call bullshit, because that should just be an everyone thing."

Mickey had started off fueled by rage, but now she felt her jaw unclench and her shoulders soften. She realized she was speaking from a place of pain. She slumped down next to Mateo so their thighs touched. "You know that saying about how the opposite of love isn't hate, it's indifference? I have so much desire, and lately, it's been ignored in this marriage. "

"Mick, I love you." Mateo's voice cracked. All anger seemed to have drained out of him, too.

"I know you do, and I love you, too. But it makes me so sad that you don't see how much it hurts me that you barely touch me. That

I have to beg, and still, four times out of five, I'm rebuffed. It's humiliating."

Mateo reached for her hands. "I do see that, Mickey. I see you. I don't want to reject you—it's about my body, growing older, whatever. I don't have the same, you know, fire as you. I want you to have what you want, but I just don't think I can give it to you."

Other women might've been devastated to hear this from their husbands. But not Mickey, not in this moment. Instead, Mateo's words, "I want you to have what you want," piqued something inside of her, something that she realized had been percolating for some time. She squeezed Mateo's hands. She was all nerves, but she couldn't help it, the words were going to burst right out of her. "I have an idea."

"Okay." What was that look on his face? Mickey wasn't sure, but she decided to read it as curious, open-minded.

She took a breath. "What would you say about opening up our marriage?"

"You mean like ...."

"Sleeping with other people," she said. "Just sex, no relationships."

"Just sex, no relationships," he repeated, like he was trying to take it in.

Mickey's heart was racing. Since Mateo didn't immediately reject the idea, she went on, brimming with bravery. "We'd be honest with each other, communicating through all of it, with everything out in the open. Maybe it would take some of the pressure off of us to fulfill each other's every need. We could just give it a shot."

"Hm." Mateo looked down at his hands. "I've never considered this."

Mickey felt on a roll. "It isn't just about me getting off. I honestly believe that it would benefit you, too. It might embarrass you to hear it, but I like the idea of you with another woman." Mickey wasn't really sure this was true. She was making it up as she went along, trying to foster a spirit of expansiveness and experimentation between them. "It could turn over a new erotic leaf for you, to venture out like this."

Mateo was bobbing his head, not quite encouraging Mickey to continue, but still not stopping her either. "We're about to enter a new chapter in our lives," she said, "being on our own, just the two of us. I want us to do everything we can to stay connected. Maybe it sounds strange that introducing new people into the mix might strengthen things between us, but I think it makes a funny kind of sense. I mean, Jesus, we've been together eighteen years. Our relationship is a full-blown grown-up: it can vote! It can buy cigarettes!"

Mateo interjected, "It can't buy cigarettes until it's twenty-one."

"Fine, but I bet it can at least find a way to get a vape pen." There, she'd made him smile. "Anyway, no wonder things are feeling a little stale. I don't put that all on you. I'm incredibly attracted to you, but you must know I'm attracted to other people, too. All the freaking time."

Mateo looked ready to speak, so Mickey shut up. "Well," he said, glancing at his feet, "I don't want to end up abandoned like Louisa."

They were both silent. Mickey didn't reassure him, didn't say, *I would never*. It was hard to wait out the silence, tempting to downplay things to spare his feelings. But Mickey had been doing that in ways both explicit and implicit for over a year: *It's not a big deal, it's okay, maybe you'll be up for it tomorrow*. All to preserve her husband's ego, all in the hopes that if he just felt man enough, things between them would improve. Well, enough of that. It was time for a new strategy. It was time to consider her own feelings, too.

"I don't know, Mick," he said finally. "This is a lot to take in. Can I mull it over?"

It wasn't a no! "Of course," she exclaimed. "Take whatever time you need."

"All right. I guess I'll sleep on it."

"Excellent idea." Mickey risked a smile; she was rewarded when Mateo mirrored it.

"Well, uh, good night."

"I love you," she said, kissing him on the cheek.

"I love you, too."

They retreated to their respective sides of the bed. Mickey drew her knees up to her chest, feeling hopeful as she drifted to sleep.

The sky was already lightening when she was roused from a deep sleep. "Mick, are you awake?"

"Mm-hm." She turned over to find her husband propped up on an elbow, looking wide awake.

"You know, I sometimes think about that first night we met," he said.

Mickey sat up. "Cleo and me at that party. We asked you to join us."

"Right." Was Mickey imagining it, or was there a glint in Mateo's eye? "I never took you up on that invitation."

She laughed. "Right? That kind of thing might be fun for us."

He shrugged. "Or it might blow up in our faces."

"It might, but I think it's worth a try."

"Obviously we'd need to talk logistics."

"Obviously," Mickey repeated. Logistics were her husband's comfort zone. How many complex sets of logistics had he coordinated at the companies he'd set up?

"Okay," Mateo said.

"Okay?" Mickey asked.

"Let's try it."

Mickey was astounded: Her husband—*Mateo*—was agreeing to rethink the fundamental terms of their marriage. She felt a surge of optimism in her belly, and farther down.

"I'll push my luck," she said. "Would you like to, uh, get busy before passing out?"

"It's five a.m.," Mateo said. "Raincheck for two hours from now?"

"Sure, it's a date."

See, they were making progress already! Mateo settled onto his pillow, and when his breathing became deep and rhythmic, Mickey reached into her pajama shorts. For once, she didn't think about Keisha, or the guy in the next car who'd met her eyes at the intersection, or the crossing guard outside Mel's school, or one of a dozen other regular players in her fantasies. Instead, she pictured herself with her husband, slow and passionate like it had been in the early days.

CHAPTER 21

Louisa

The apartment was nicer than it had looked in Louisa's online snooping. Pretty red brick, decent-sized windows, a little garden out front. Louisa was reluctant to admit that it reminded her of where Nathan had been living when they first met, the three-bedroom he'd shared with Mateo and another guy in grad school housing. That had been a happy spot.

"Dada!"

"Dada!"

"Going to Dada!"

Phoebe and Finn had kept up this high-pitched call-and-response all morning, no matter how many times Louisa asked them to cut it out. Only when she pulled over during the trip across town to rest her cheek against the steering wheel did they go momentarily quiet. How was she possibly going to make it through the next twenty-four hours?

"Mama okay?" Phoebe had asked from the backseat.

"I'm fine, sweetheart," she'd said, blinking away tears and shifting back to drive. "Who's excited to see Dada?"

Both kids cheered and launched back into their duet, as under her breath Louisa said, "Well, I'm not."

Now parked outside Nathan's new home, Louisa couldn't bring herself to budge. It'd been one thing to hand the kids over for afternoon visits with their father. But now they'd be spending the night with him, which meant Louisa would be spending the night without them, alone. She'd felt bitter when Nathan hadn't tried to see his kids more often, then indignant when he finally pushed for a whole weekend. She would've liked to put him off for a while, relishing the idea of Nathan missing his children. Shouldn't he have to suffer a little bit, too, or was that entirely Louisa's burden to bear? But she couldn't deny her kids the opportunity to spend time with their father. So, here she was, being a good sport, sending her precious hearts off to a sleepover in a strange place with Nathan and his new, barely-legal girlfriend.

Louisa sighed dramatically, and exited the car with shoulders slumped, like she was a child being summoned to face a punishment. She unbuckled Phoebe and Finn, and the three of them approached the building, her progeny surrounding her like bodyguards, their small hands tucked into hers.

Two knocks to the canary-yellow door. Louisa wiped her feet on the welcome mat, trying to smear as much dirt as possible onto the cursive "Home is Where the Heart Is!"

"Why are there flowers in shoes?" Phoebe asked, pointing to the pair of red rain boots filled with daffodils.

"I don't know, sweetie. Pinterest, probably." Louisa had no patience for whimsical home decoration.

"Coming!" The unfamiliar voice made Louisa tense up once again. She'd been too proud to request that Mona not be present when she dropped off the kids; she'd just prayed for Nathan to intuit that courtesy on his own. But no such luck. When the door swung open, Louisa was struck by how she stood facing her physical opposite: Mona had sleek, ink-black hair where Louisa's was big and wavy and light brown; Mona had enormous dark eyes in contrast to Louisa's squinty gray eyes; and Mona was petite and narrow-shouldered (though not child-like, thank god) where Louisa was tall and broad. And while Louisa had spent an hour that morning fretting over her outfit before landing on a thin cashmere sweater and her dark "boyfriend" jeans (the mortifying name was not lost on her, but alas, they flattered her butt), Mona appeared to still be in her pajamas: stretchy pants and a worn t-shirt. It occurred to Louisa how comfortable someone had to be in their own skin to look like a slob when first meeting the woman whose husband they'd stolen. Either that or Mona simply didn't give a shit.

"Hi guys!" Mona's voice was veneered with enthusiasm. "Come in, come in! Slow morning, we're just getting up."

It was noon. Louisa did the math: Phoebe and Finn had started wailing for her at five forty-five, and she'd felt proud to have fended them off until six; six hours had passed since then. Also, *we're* just getting up—*we*, meaning Mona and Nathan had only recently been in bed together. Where *was* Nathan, anyway? Was he really such a coward to be hiding, leaving his lover to fend for herself? Pathetic.

"Louisa, I'm Mona." She held out a hand. Louisa shook it limply, disregarding all of Dr. Poolehauzer's advice about power shakes. "I've heard so much about you. It's so nice to finally meet you."

Seriously? Louisa thought. *Would you have preferred to meet me while you were sneaking around with my husband and I was at home wrestling my kids into their bath?*

"And these guys, too." Mona waved maniacally at Phoebe and Finn, making it clear she'd spent little time around small children. The kids clutched at their mother's sides.

For the first time, Louisa found herself considering Mona's perspective. She wondered why the young woman had chosen to get mixed up in this mess. Sure, it was a common fantasy to fool around with your professor. But to turn an illicit little fling into a to-do list of adult obligations—meeting your boyfriend's ex, hosting his kids for sleepovers—made Louisa wonder if things had spun out of control and Mona was now in a position she'd never intended to be in, and if she was in denial about her distress as some kind of coping mechanism. It made Louisa want to help, like she would a student in trouble. It made her furious at Nathan all over again.

"Where's Dada?" Phoebe whispered.

"Dada!" Finn shouted.

"Nate!" Mona called out. *Nate?*

A door off the living room creaked open, and Louisa's heart caught in her throat. It was Nathan, her Nathan, his hair tousled in that particular Nathan morning way, his long, lean frame on full display as he lifted his arms in a stretch. He was wearing the flannel pajamas and slippers she'd gotten him for his birthday a few years back.

But he didn't even look at her, which made Louisa feel like she'd been gut-punched. Instead, he crouched down and held out his arms. "Hi kiddos!"

At least his excitement at seeing his children seemed genuine. Louisa watched the twins fly into his arms, devouring their father's attention like starving people before a feast—the implication being that Louisa had been starving them. It was too heartbreaking. She had to look away.

Finally, he turned to her. "Hello, Louisa. Thank you for bringing them over."

So formal. Louisa forced her lips to turn upward into a semblance of a smile.

"Got pops, Dada?" Finn asked.

"I sure do." Nathan pulled a pair of lollipops from his pocket. "Give Mona a hug hello, then you each can have one."

Louisa was outraged. She'd given her kids candy on Halloween and at their birthday parties, but apparently Nathan had now decided it was fine not only to hand them lollipops any old time, but also to wield them as bribes. At least the kids hesitated before caving.

As Mona hugged Louisa's children, her thin shirt pulled across her chest, revealing that she was wearing no bra over what looked to be perky B-cups. *Oh, screw her.* Louisa couldn't believe that moments ago she'd been feeling bad for this husband-stealing minx. Honestly, how could her own boobs compete? Not only had they been subjected to gravity for a decade and a half longer than Mona's, they'd also spent nine months growing to fill with milk, then a year nurturing two world-class sucklers. It wasn't a fair fight. Nothing about this was fair.

"Nate's making meatless sloppy joes for lunch," Mona said. Louisa glanced at Nathan and read the flicker of panic as he anticipated his girlfriend's next remark. "Would you like to join us?"

Louisa chuckled to herself at the idea of them trying to get the twins to eat textured soy protein or whatever, then trying to clean them up after a lunch that literally included "sloppy" in its name—correction: at Mona trying to clean them up. Nathan would most certainly find some urgent task to attend to in the other room.

"Thanks, but I've got to—" but she was ushered inside before she could finish her sentence. She could admit to herself that she was curious: about the décor and everything else about this new life Nathan was building for himself. Did her husband neglect his dirty dishes here, too, or had he learned to clean up after himself? Louisa wondered where everything had come from, too, the couch and coffee table and art on the wall. Had it all been Mona's, or did the two of them buy these things together? And how much of it was purchased with money earned by Louisa? She and Nathan had been putting off sorting out their finances, the joint bank accounts and credit cards and even their will. The thought of those conversations exhausted her.

As Nathan escaped to the kitchen, and the kids settled onto the rug with their lollipops, Mona invited Louisa to sit. "Feels good to take a load off, huh? I can't even imagine how depleted you must feel, what with the kids and the big job. How's your semester going?"

"Oh, you know, ups and downs. The highs are high, the lows are low, but I'm in it for the students, of course." Louisa was babbling. This was ludicrous. Why was she still here? She could feel her children eyeing her, perplexed, too.

Mona was nodding intently. "Personally, I'm trying to soak it all in for my last few months. I've always loved school. It's crazy to think this is the end of the line for me."

Jesus, read the room! Louisa was speechless. How could Mona speak so casually, flaunting the fact that she was still in college? Had she no shame that she was little more than half Nathan's age, and talking to his ex and the mother of his children? Is this why Nathan liked her, for her utter lack of awareness that maybe he interpreted as confidence?

Mona called back to the kitchen, "Nate, can you grab juice for the kiddos and check on the coffee?"

First lollipops and now juice? Louisa bit her tongue—she would not come off as a shrew; she would not give Nathan that satisfaction. She'd had to restrain herself from packing meals for the kids, and she'd restrain herself again now.

"I'll be decadent—cream and lots of sugar." Mona smiled triumphantly, as if Louisa needed confirmation that she possessed the miracle metabolism of youth. "Louisa, how do you take yours?"

"Black."

Nathan knew that, although he nodded from the doorway as if it were new information, then obediently went to fetch the coffee. Who was this version of her husband? Early in their relationship, Nathan had talked almost non-stop. He'd once confided in her his worry that he'd run out of time before he could share all he had to tell her. Gradually, though, he'd grown more taciturn. Louisa had assumed it was because he'd mellowed out; but lately, she wondered if he'd actually succeeded in sharing all he had to say to her, and that was that.

He wordlessly handed her a mug now. It was clear he had no idea how to act around her and his new paramour. Not that Louisa knew either. Looking at Nathan, she felt an almost intolerable mix of fury, nostalgia, pity, and (yes, unfortunately) love.

"Thanks," she said. He nodded soberly.

"Nate, we were just talking about how much I'm going to miss school when I graduate."

Louisa swore she detected a smirk on Nathan's face, at Mona's expense. It was just a flicker, but she chose to take it as an acknowledgment that his girlfriend, while so young and perky-titted, also seemed clueless that saying such a thing in front of present company was wildly inappropriate.

Louisa was done with whatever this was. "I need to get going." The sentence was like a signal, drawing her children to her, the two of them climbing onto her lap and grasping at whatever part of her body they could access. Finn was whimpering, trying not to cry, and Phoebe whispered, "Mama, stay." It made Louisa ache. She couldn't bear another minute of it. She eased their small, warm bodies off of her.

"I packed their PJs and clothes and diapers for Finn, plus the bath toys and the stuffed penguins, and I wrote out their schedules, in case you forgot. They nap at two, go down for the night at seven-thirty, and um, what am I forgetting?"

Louisa heard the tremor in her voice. She felt a surge through her body, like she was about to do something dangerous and grossly irresponsible. Like she was flinging herself over a cliff, abandoning her children to fend for themselves, when they were so young, so incapable of advocating for themselves, so subject to cheap bribery! The hurricane of emotion reminded Louisa of those early postpartum days, with hormones gone haywire and every feeling cranked up to eleven. "Goodbye, my loves."

She didn't mean to catch Nathan's eye, to let him see the water pooling in her eyes. He smiled wanly. "We'll be fine, Lou. And you will, too."

She swallowed hard, thinking, how dare he use the pet name he'd used for her once upon a time ... during tender moments, when they made up after a fight, in bed. Louisa handed off the two tiny backpacks, then gathered Phoebe and Finn into one last embrace. They both clutched at her, and she clutched back. Finally, she gathered up the courage to peel off their limbs, and to get up and walk out.

She yearned for the safety of her car, where she could sink into her sorrow and have herself a good cry. But Mona was on her tail, calling out, "Louisa, please wait," as she stepped off the curb.

Louisa was too polite to ignore her. She turned to face her, blinking away tears.

"Look," said Mona, "it may not seem like it, but Nate is really trying. He wants this to be amicable, and so do I."

"Uh huh." *Amicable*—a word only ever used in the context of a break-up. Louisa was tempted to say, *Well, how about what I want? Doesn't anyone care about that?* Of course, what she wanted in the moment was to scram. She inhaled deeply. "I'll be back at ten tomorrow morning. Please tell Nathan to have the kids ready to go."

"Sure thing. It's been so great to meet you." Mona leaned in for a hug, and Louisa was too stunned to intercept it. "Be well."

"You, too," Louisa said. What an absurd joke. What a nightmare.

———

"I survived ... barely," she texted Mickey when she finally made it into her car. Her friend responded with a string of hearts and an invitation to talk if she wanted.

Louisa peeled off. Ten minutes later she was pushing a cart through the frozen food aisle of the MegaMart, feeling anesthetized by the freezers' chill, not unpleasantly. She avoided eye contact with the other shoppers: the young man with the stacks of microwave meals, the middle-aged woman with the makings of a salad plus a half-gallon of ice cream, the couple with the baguette and brie who looked on the verge of tearing off each other's clothes. It was so exposing, seeing everyone's groceries on display.

Only when Louisa passed a woman whose cart contents matched her own almost exactly—bananas, apple sauce, mac-n-cheese, Cheerios—did she realize how exposed she was, too. Although, there was one significant difference: while the other cart contained a baby, with a toddler shuffling along at its side, Louisa was alone. She watched the other woman search Louisa's vicinity for children, a knowing smile hovering at the edges of her lips—until she failed to find any, averted her gaze, and passed by; maybe she thought Louisa was one of those weird adults who'd never graduated from kids' food.

Louisa's heart lurched at the absence of Finn and Phoebe. She considered it like a parable: Was a mother still a mother without her children? Suddenly, she couldn't stand the sight of all the food she fed to her kids; she abandoned the cart. At the end of the aisle was a display of Goldfish crackers, Finn's favorite snack. Hardly realizing what she was doing, Louisa reached for a bag and tucked it inside her purse, then made for the exit.

Her plan had been to spend the day compiling a test-prep proposal for Poolehauzer, maybe followed by some trashy TV, Chinese take-out, and a couple glasses of wine, then to bed by ten. Louisa didn't know she was driving to the movie theater until she arrived. She bought a ticket to whatever was playing, then sat through the flickering images, barely registering the story unfolding before her eyes. She stuffed handful after handful of Goldfish into her mouth, chewing the crackers into a cheesy mush, until she was left holding an empty package and her lap was decorated with orange crumbs. She didn't know if the movie was just starting or about to end; all she knew was that she couldn't stay one minute longer.

Out in the lobby, she thought of stepping into another theater. She thought of returning to Nathan's, telling him she simply could not handle this arrangement, then retrieving her kids, and kissing them all over their precious little faces until she felt whole again. She thought of immersing herself in her work through the night and all the way until pickup time. She thought of Googling "Desdemona Ray Gill" (she'd spotted her full name on a folder in the den) to torture herself with whatever she found. But to formulate and follow through on any plan required energy and decisiveness, which Louisa lacked at the moment. So, she simply stood there, paralyzed, hollowed out, watching theater-goers come and go and listening to the pop, pop, pop of the popcorn.

CHAPTER 22
Louisa

Mickey and Amy showed up just as the light began leeching from the sky. The golden hour, Louisa had once thought of this time, back when it meant an easing of the day's pressures and relaxing into the evening. The witching hour, she'd later come to think of it, when the kids were babies, the period when they totally lost it, just as Louisa needed them to get with the program of dinner, bath, and bed.

"It's happy hour!" Mickey declared, traipsing into Louisa's living room. She tossed Louisa a can of Stella, and Amy followed up with a bag of Fritos, Louisa's favorite.

"Happy hour," Louisa repeated, holding up her beer. "Look at me, so friggin' happy."

She plunked down between her friends on the couch, her right butt cheek catching on something sharp—a Lego, she guessed, before reaching to confirm the suspicion. She took in the room with its tornado of toys. She thought momentarily about tidying up, or at least apologizing for the state of things, but she let it go, knowing neither friend would judge her or care. In fact, Amy reached for the xylophone and mallet balancing on the arm of the couch and improvised a plucky tune.

"Hey, that's pretty good," Louisa said.

"I was forced to play piano for like a decade, so."

"Be honest, Lou," said Mickey, kicking away a gathering of Fisher-Price people. "All those nights you've spent hunched over a bathtub, attacking toddler tangles while getting completely soaked, haven't you sometimes wished for this? For your kids to disappear—poof!— so you could enjoy a relaxing evening with your friends?"

Louisa stiffened. "What are you implying? Like, be careful what you wish for?"

"No, dummy!" Mickey said. "I'm saying that when your wishes come true, even in sort of a fucked-up way, how about try to enjoy it a little?"

Amy laughed. "Wise words. You should write a parenting advice book."

For Louisa, this back-and-forth had defined her experience as a mother: the animal need to be nestled up as close as possible to her children and to breathe in their intoxicating scents, shot through with the occasional overwhelming desire to escape. And yet, inevitably, the moment she got free of them, she'd find herself whipping out her phone to scroll through photos of their delicious little faces. Of course Louisa wanted a relaxing evening with her friends; and also of course a house empty of her children made her feel empty in the pit of herself. That both were true was totally maddening.

"Earth to Lou." Mickey chucked a stuffed shark at her. It thudded into her rib and came to life, wagging its tail and belting out the repetitive lyrics of "Baby Shark."

Amy looked horrified. "What on earth?"

"You seriously don't know this song?" It amazed Louisa how parents and non-parents sometimes lived on separate planets. "I'm envious of your ignorance. That earworm has topped the toddler charts for like a year."

As the stuffie moved onto the Papa Shark verse, Amy listened skeptically. "Man, kids are inscrutable."

"I wonder what mine are up to," said Louisa, pressing "off" on the shark's fin. "I hope they're giving Mona hell. Or I guess I hope they're perfectly fine. I don't know." She couldn't explain it, the stew of conflicting emotions battling it out in her heart and gut.

Mickey turned to her. "How did the drop-off go?"

Louisa was trying to decide whether to start with the fact that Mona had had no qualms opening the door at noon wearing pajamas or the wrenching regret Louisa had felt driving away all alone. But then she noticed her friends' pitched-forward postures, and their expectant, almost hungry faces. Louisa knew that they were here for her; but she saw that they were also here for the story: to hear her outrage and self-pity and heartbreak, all the titillating details to be relished vicariously while feeling grateful none of it was happening to them. Sure, they'd experienced these emotions before, including in their own respective relationships—but certainly not to this degree, and certainly not with such wrenching consequences. That was the reassurance her friends wanted. Louisa's situation would cast their own in stark contrast: They weren't so bad off, they weren't getting divorced, they were just fine.

Suddenly, she was in no mood to share. She shoved a fistful of Fritos in her mouth. "I'm just trying to stay positive and move forward," she said.

From the way Mickey and Amy exchanged looks, she knew how unconvincing she sounded. But at least they had the grace not to call her out on it.

"I have an idea," said Amy. "Let's gather up Nathan's stuff and toss it out the window."

Mickey laughed. "What are you, seventeen? That sounds like a move Mel and her friends would pull."

"Plus, who do you think would end up cleaning it all up?" Louisa didn't admit that Nathan had already cleared out all his stuff, down to his stock of extra razor cartridges and his extensive book collection.

"Jeez, I was just brainstorming."

Louisa touched Amy's shoulder. "Not in a million years could I imagine you tossing Abe's things out the window."

Amy's face turned to stone, and Louisa knew she'd said the wrong thing. In fact, that was precisely the point: Amy had suggested an action that she herself would never take, so it followed that her marriage would never deteriorate to the point where such an action would become necessary. Apparently, it was out of bounds for Louisa to compare her own broken marriage to her friend's intact one. Louisa was getting a crash course in all the unspoken rules of separation, and it was sapping what little energy she had left. She loved her friends, but maybe it would've been better to spend the evening alone.

"Well," Amy said, "talk to me after we have a kid, maybe." A joke, again putting a protective moat between her own marriage—childless, and therefore free of problems—and Louisa's—trampled over by toddlers.

"Oh, it wasn't the kids, not really," Louisa said, feeling irritable. Again, she sensed the anxious shifting in her friends' seats, their ears perking up. They wanted to hear about a rupture, some specific, dramatic event Louisa could point to that had landed her in this spot, while they themselves resided safely elsewhere. Perhaps it was also verboten of Louisa to suggest that the stuff that tore her and Nathan apart had existed even when things were good between them; how they'd grown a little lax about nurturing the relationship; how routines had slid into ruts; how there was day-to-day tension over big stuff, like their mismatched career ambitions, and little stuff, like chores. It was all a matter of scale and intensity: at one point the good had outweighed the bad, until the balance tipped and it didn't. And yes, some of the problems between Nathan and her might also be problems in her friends' marriages, too. But Louisa didn't feel like delving into all of that, so she just said, "I mean, Nathan fell in love with another woman."

Both her friends seemed to relax, which irked Louisa.

"I have an idea." Mickey grabbed Louisa's phone and manipulated a bunch of buttons before passing it back. "There, now you're signed up for Tinder. Why should Nathan have all the fun?"

Louisa considered her screen a little warily, as Mickey and Amy peered over her shoulders. All three of them had been coupled up for at least a decade, so the dating revolution via phone app had passed them by. Even the homepage looked intimidating. When it became clear that Louisa wasn't going to act, her friends did it for her, their fingers coming at her from both sides, swiping left and right and left again. Louisa watched the flashing images, barely registering each man before it was replaced by the next—this one with a beard, that one with a bare chest, a baseball cap, glasses, a dog, a pair of skis, a scenic view, another dog, another beard. It was dizzying. She could see how this might become addictive, and how some people swore it off entirely.

Mickey swiped right at a muscleman type atop a motorcycle. "I'd love to see you straddle that thing."

Louisa rolled her eyes, feeling relieved to have moved past her relationship failures and onto this silliness.

Amy swiped left at three guys in a row. "It's odd how similar this is to scrolling through kids up for adoption "

"Wait, what?" Louisa snatched up her phone and clicked it dark.

Amy spoke quietly. "It's an option Abe and I are exploring."

"Amy, wow," Louisa said. "I'm so happy to hear that." She was excited for her friend, plus happy to relinquish the spotlight.

Mickey squeezed Amy's arm. "How amazing that you'll be able to share your own experience being adopted with your adopted kid."

"Yeah." There was an awkward silence as they waited for Amy to say more—the friends hardly ever talked about her adoption. "Anyway, it's very early stages. We haven't even heard the results of our home visit."

Louisa again surveyed the wreckage of her living room, and pictured the contrast of Abe and Amy's pristine home. "I have a feeling you did just fine. You'll let us know if you need a character reference, right?"

Amy was blushing. "I actually brought over the forms."

Louisa's phone badooped, and a message popped up. Mickey clicked on the bubble and yelped.

"Oh my god," Amy said.

Louisa stared. There it was, up close and personal, so clear it could've been featured in an anatomy textbook: the male sex organ. It was semi-hard and curved slightly to the left, the balls tucked unassumingly beneath and sprouting a smattering of fine brown hairs.

Louisa examined the image for so long that its creep factor gave way to absurdity and eventually to a kind of whimsical sweetness. She giggled.

"Your first dick pic," said Mickey.

"What a rite of passage," said Louisa.

"Cheers," said Amy, and they all clinked their drinks.

Louisa tossed her phone aside. "Blech."

"You could grow to like them, you know," Mickey said. Louisa raised an eyebrow. "Fine, maybe not. Anyway, plenty of guys open on a subtler note, and you might actually be interested in meeting some of them."

"And how would you know?" Amy asked playfully.

Mickey cleared her throat. "Actually, I have news, too. Mateo and I have decided to open up our marriage."

"Excuse me?" said Louisa. "Please explain." A part of her was stunned, but another part was surprised at the fact that it had taken them so long. Mickey and Mateo were one of the happiest couples Louisa knew, but Mickey had never seemed cut out for monogamy. She collected crushes like other people collected stamps or vinyl records.

"I second that," said Amy.

"Well, it's pretty simple. We've been together a long time. We're great partners, but it's a lot of pressure to expect each other to fulfill all of one another's needs. So, we're trying a new tack."

"By needs, you mean sex?" Louisa asked.

"Pretty much." Mickey shrugged.

"Wait," Amy said. "You think it's too much to expect your partner to fulfill your sexual needs?"

Mickey looked tongue-tied. The naiveté of the question made Louisa realize she'd never heard Amy open up about her own love life. She'd always assumed that was either because she was closer to Abe, or because Amy wasn't big on divulging such intimacies. But now she wondered if perhaps Amy and Abe had some very kinky situation going on or if they still went at it like teenagers. Maybe they were that rare long-term couple who successfully fulfilled all of each other's needs.

"What I want to know," she asked Mickey, "is why now, after two decades together?"

"Well, Mel's off to school soon, so we'll be empty nesters. We figured it's a good time to shake things up, turn over a new leaf, whatever other clichés."

"Uh huh." Louisa suspected there was more to the story, and that

Mickey was too gracious to admit that Louisa and Nathan had been a cautionary tale. Their separation had been a wake-up call—other couples better clean up their acts, lest the divorce boogeyman come for them, too.

But she didn't push it. "So, maybe we'll both find ourselves dates for next weekend, and we can pick out a baby for Amy while we're at it."

As they scrolled through faces on her phone—men, then women, and eventually babies—for brief stretches Louisa felt hopeful, about all the possibilities, all the people out there who, like her, were looking for something they lacked. Until the collective neediness overwhelmed her—the loneliness of all these strangers—and she had to swipe to the two faces she knew and loved best: chubby, smiling, with pale gray eyes identical to her own.

But before she had a chance to give in to her weepiness, the two faces sitting beside her pried her phone from her fingers and reminded her of a different need: to eat. The three of them moved to the kitchen, where they divided and conquered to make a meal. Louisa was so relieved to have her hands occupied that chopping onions didn't even make her cry.

CHAPTER 23

Nathan

Nathan read and re-read the same bullet points, not absorbing their meaning. He'd written the lecture notes just last semester, but they seemed like a time capsule from a different eon. A time when he was still sharing a bed with Louisa, living under the same roof as his children, and when Desdemona Gill was just a name among dozens on his roster. It was this very lecture, on categorical versus quantitative variables, during which Mona had raised her hand and asked a question; he didn't remember what, because he'd found her gravelly voice so distracting.

That was the beginning.

Nathan knew it was a cliché, but it hadn't felt that way. Before the next class, Mona appeared at his lectern with a lidded cup from the department canteen. "Matcha latte, my treat," she said. He guessed he looked skeptical, because she added, "It's both anti-inflammatory and delicious." Nathan tried it, and was pleasantly surprised. Was she flirting with him, or just one of those particularly deferent students? Nathan tried not to notice her body, but he couldn't help observing her fingers kneading a spot on her lower back. He indicated the front row and said, "Top-secret intel: they just replaced those seats with the fancy ergonomic kind." Was he flirting with her, or just being helpful? Nathan didn't dare probe his motives. For the next ninety minutes, Mona sat front and center, sipping her latte, tracking his every move. Nathan flipped through his slides on autopilot, his head all white noise.

And now a full cycle of classes had passed and here Nathan was, happy, despite not being able to concentrate on his work (it was fine, he knew the material cold), still high on the weekend of playing house with Mona and the kids. That's how it had felt—like play. The dance party and the pizza dinner and the towers they'd built up and knocked down. At one point, Nathan had collapsed onto the couch in blissful exhaustion while Mona unrolled three yoga mats and led the kids in sun salutations. Watching the three people he loved sit cross-legged and sing a call-and-response chant, Nathan thought, *This is what it was all for, this is it right here.* There was the frenzied bedtime routine, followed by the reward of his children snoring sweetly, and closing the door on their day. Then Mona turned to him and said, "Now what?"

He'd laughed—it was so obvious: "Now we zone out to mindless TV and revel in our accomplishment of surviving the day."

But that hadn't satisfied Mona. "It's kind of sexy, being trapped here at home, like it's a snowstorm." As she crawled toward him on the couch, Nathan remembered all the times he'd despaired at having to swap one kind of life for another: the one where he and Louisa connected and laughed and made spontaneous love for the one where his wonderful, energetic kids also left him irritable and beat by eight p.m. Nathan began massaging Mona's back, which led to her kissing him and easing off his shirt, and Nathan had a revelation that he'd been wrong: He *could* have it all, the kids and the lover, the family life and the passion. It was all right here in front of him.

"Nathan?"

Startled, Nathan looked up from his lecture notes to see Russell Low, the department head, standing in the doorframe of his office. He instinctively sat up straighter. Had he missed some meeting? Russell never popped by just to chat. "Hey, man. How can I help you?"

Russell's exhale made a little puff sound, which Nathan took as a bad omen. "I'm just going to come right out and say it. There's been a complaint filed about inappropriate behavior between you and a student. The disciplinary committee has been notified and they're launching an investigation."

Nathan attempted to act normal. He tried swallowing, but his mouth was cotton, his tongue a useless appendage. He shuffled his notes, the gesture of a competent professor. He almost asked who had filed the complaint, but it was obvious: Lydia Wexler, to whom Nathan had stupidly recommended the margarita at the Mexican restaurant. He'd consciously excised that evening from his head.

Russell was waiting for a response, but Nathan didn't know what to say. It's not like he hadn't considered the possibility of getting in trouble. But his relationship with Mona was consensual, she was twenty-one, and they'd been discreet back when she was his student. Nathan had all his class records, and could prove that he hadn't treated her preferentially; his T.A.s did the grading, anyway. Mona had raised the question of whether their entanglement could cause him professional problems, but Nathan had brushed off the concern. He'd known colleagues who'd gotten involved with students, and the university had turned a blind eye. And yet, Nathan understood that the cultural tide had turned. And he'd never consulted the official wording of his employment contract. Which meant he didn't have the tools to defend himself now.

"So, what will happen?" he asked Russell, feeling slow, and sounding it, too.

He saw the flash of disappointment cross Russell's face. His boss had probably been hoping Nathan would dismiss the accusation as absurd and present some incontrovertible piece of evidence to squash it. That would've made Russell's life a lot easier. "It depends on what the committee finds. For now, you teach, you grade, you attend to your departmental duties. You keep your head down. When the investigation is complete—well, we'll cross that bridge when we come to it."

"All right."

Was Russell married or in a relationship? Was he straight, gay, asexual? In a moment like this, Nathan wished he could appeal to the man's humanity. But he had no clue about the private life of his department head. He was scared to even smile, like it might indicate that he wasn't taking this seriously.

"Listen, the committee will do its thing. But ..." Russell was struggling to get it out—maybe a rebuke or a word of consolation or advice. Nathan didn't know. It occurred to him that maybe his boss actually liked him. "Just, is it true that you're living with her, that your names are on a lease together?"

Nathan felt stupid as he choked out the word, "Yes." But what was the implication, that at least if he was going to shack up with his student, he should've kept her name off the lease? Was he going to be punished for keeping things above-board, and for refusing to admit that he had something to hide? Well, Nathan could play that game: "We didn't start seeing each other until the semester ended, until she was no longer my student."

Russell looked frozen in the entrance of the office. Nathan wanted to keep defending himself. To explain how he wasn't some predatory professor who threatened his most vulnerable students, coercing them into bed and then sending them away with unfulfilled promises and tattered self-esteem. Nathan had known men like that, and he, too, found them repugnant. He wanted to tell Russell that he and Mona were different: *she'd* pursued *him*, they'd fallen in *love*, he'd left his *wife* for her. And yes, they were living together, creating a home and hosting his kids for sleepovers. It was all on the up and up! Reminding himself of these facts—the one and only truth of the situation—calmed Nathan. Yes, the university had a responsibility to do their due diligence and pursue a complaint, but this would all get straightened out in time.

"Thanks for stopping by," he told Russell.

The department chair nodded, and was gone.

Turning back to his lecture notes, Nathan now concentrated with a ferocious intensity. His thoughts and feelings fell away, replaced by numbers, controllable variables, and reason.

CHAPTER 24

Abe's Birthday

It was Amy's way of decompressing at the end of the day, letting a ticker-tape of statistics scan by in the background of her brain: She'd slept six fitful hours last night, rising an hour early to get a jump-start on work so she could bang out eleven hours before racing home at seven to get ready. She rated her day's productivity an eight out of ten, and her mood a six. It was forty degrees out, and a three-mile drive from their home to Giorgio's, which would take twelve minutes right now in rush hour, but seven minutes after dinner on the way home. Abe was thirty-five today, three years and three months younger than she was, and it would always be this way; he'd never catch up. Amy's love for her husband was incalculable, and always would be. She was on day fifteen of her cycle: peak ovulation.

Knowing the day of her cycle had become as automatic as knowing the day of the week. Peak ovulation usually meant peak anxiety for Amy. But, it hit her with a jolt of joy: it no longer mattered. She was again free to go about her days oblivious to her eggs' journey through her reproductive system; she could become one of those careless women who ruin a pair of panties every month when—*oops, is it that time already?* (not that Amy would ever be so careless). Amy felt flush with freedom, along with a powerful wave of lust. She gazed over at Abe driving, his strong hands gripping the wheel, and she wanted to pounce. She flashed back to another drive to Giorgio's, eight or nine years ago: They weren't yet living together, so Abe had picked her up in his 1996 Toyota Tercel (RIP), and Amy announced she had a little gift for him. Abe had never even heard the term "road head," but his flushed objections lasted only about ten seconds.

This time Amy didn't say a word before leaning over her husband's lap and unzipping his fly. Abe lifted his thighs a few inches, but otherwise gave no acknowledgment of anything out of the ordinary occurring. His hands remained on the wheel at ten and two. She heard him inhale, sigh, and tick on the turn signal, then she sensed the car edging around a corner as her cheek pressed up against his inner thigh.

Amy felt like she was in high school, when every sexual encounter was illicit, covert, and included a certain degree of discomfort. Though as the seatbelt latch dug into her hip and her neck cramped, she was reminded that her middle-aged body was not cut out for this maneuver. When she was a teenager, there'd always been the specter of potential pregnancy looming over the pleasure, the warnings of her parents and health teachers about how if she was going to do adult things then she better take adult responsibility for her actions, *or else!* It was one reason Amy had claimed to prefer giving blowjobs to her high school boyfriend over "going all the way"—it meant she could push from her mind the terrifying visions of getting pregnant, dropping out of school, and working some sad minimum-wage job, her life over before it even began.

Was that why Amy had felt so scared when she and Abe began trying to get pregnant? Was it just a hangover from those long-ago days? Had her body internalized the teenage whatever-you-do-don't-get-pregnant warning and that's why the conception never took root? That was ridiculous, Amy knew. Yet here she was, going down on Abe, and despite the contortions she was performing, once again she felt freed from all the baggage that came with sex. Amy was giving pleasure to her husband—pure pleasure, no strings attached. Luckily, it was when they were stopped at a light that she heard the guttural noises indicating he was close. When he finished, she felt content. All those sperm—a hundred million or more would never travel through her fallopian tubes, never make it near her eggs, and it was totally fine. It didn't matter!

Amy sat up and returned to her side of the car with a small smile. "Happy birthday, honey."

When Abe grasped her hand, she could feel his pulse racing. "I nearly drove us off the road."

"Well, that would've been dramatic." She knew Abe was the person least likely to get in an accident while getting fellated at the wheel; he'd used his goddamn turn signal, after all. "Where are we, anyway?" she asked. It was a residential street, and none of the houses looked familiar.

"I have no idea." They both laughed.

"I love you," Amy said. How lovely it was to be lost with her husband on his birthday, in an unfamiliar place with the person most familiar in the world. Amy wanted to suggest that they skip the group dinner, and go somewhere new instead, just the two of them—but she knew Abe was wholeheartedly committed to the Giorgio's tradition. So, they sat for a moment, observing a couple pass by with a stroller, a dog dart across a yard, and a man drag garbage bins out to the curb, the two of them side by side.

Mateo was a wreck. He nearly ran a red, then he idled too long after the light changed and got aggressively beeped at, then he cut off a truck, causing the driver to unleash an impressive soliloquy of expletives.

"Oh, screw you, too," Mickey barked out the window, flipping double birds. Conflict like this energized her. Her eyes gleamed as she turned back to her husband. "Mateo, you maniac, what is up with you?"

"Sorry, I'm a little distracted. I'm okay."

Was he okay? It had been three weeks since Mateo had found himself in an open marriage, since he and his wife had sat across from each other at their kitchen table and laid out all the ground rules. Mateo had suggested "don't ask, don't tell." If ignorance wasn't bliss exactly, at least it wasn't humiliation and envy and who knows how the hell he'd feel knowing some other person had been comingling with his wife, their bare skin creating friction and heat. But Mickey had convinced him that the way to stay connected was to keep it all open—including their lines of communication. Mateo understood, sort of. So, the official policy was "ask if you want, tell if you're asked." Of course, Mateo did not plan on asking. Instead, every time Mickey left the house, he paced around, unable to be still as he wondered if she was out having sanctioned extramarital relations. Even Mel had noticed something was off, saying, "You're freaking me out, Dad. Please chill." But Mateo could only relax after Mickey returned, fifteen minutes or a half hour later with a CVS bag or a pile of mail from FleXX. He assumed this was just a bumpy transition period; in time, he would grow comfortable with the new arrangement.

Mickey, however, did plan on asking. "What's going on? Please tell me." She poked him in the ribs.

"Hey, I'm driving."

"Did you and some alluring coworker slip out to a motel for your lunch hour?"

"Very funny." When Mickey jabbed him in the side again, Mateo grabbed her finger and squeezed.

"Hey! Oh come on, tell me."

Her persistence was wearing him down, and the truth was, after his wife had prodded him to open his eyes to the many members of the opposite sex he encountered each day, Mateo had started to notice new feelings. He couldn't believe what he was about to share. "Well, there was this one woman."

Mickey whistled. "Now we're talking."

Mateo felt emboldened. "I went to reception this morning to grab some guys for a meeting, and she was sitting there. Legs crossed, hands in her lap, totally cool. Not even looking at her phone. She flashed me this thousand-watt smile, like I was exactly the person she wished to see. I introduced myself, and when she shook my hand, it was like there were sparks. It sounds stupid, I know—"

"No." Mickey took his hand, and Mateo marveled at the simultaneous sameness and difference of the two gestures: Both women had strong grips and soft skin, yet Mickey's was familiar and comforting whereas the mystery woman's had been exciting and new. "Go on."

He shrugged. "That was it. I didn't even find out her name. My colleague appeared and whisked her off to his office, and I headed into my meeting."

Mateo's heart was pounding, like the morning's exhilaration had been bottled up and was now finally being released into the car.

"I'm proud of you, baby." Micky leaned in for a kiss and tousled his hair. "I'm so glad you're tuning into your desire, and—holy shit!" She threw her body on top of his, bumping the steering wheel and sending them veering nearly into the next lane.

"Calm down, Mick." Mateo righted the car. "What the hell was that?"

"Look to your left. That's Abe, right?" Mateo glanced to the left lane, and indeed, there was Abe in his Honda Civic. "Do you see what's happening?"

He looked more closely and realized Abe looked like a zombie, eyes at half-mast, head lolling against the headrest. "Where is Amy?"

Mickey shrieked and pointed. And there she was: Mateo's former colleague, bent over Abe, head buried between his legs. "Wow," Mateo said, the most coherent thought he could conjure. As Mateo got in the right turn lane—Giorgio's was a block east—Abe continued straight.

"Wow," Mateo repeated. Abe, the most straight-laced guy he knew, treated to a blowjob on the way to dinner with friends; you just never knew with people.

In recent past, whenever Mateo and his wife witnessed a public display of affection, he'd try to ignore it and tamp down the pungent concoction of sadness and shame that bubbled up inside of him. Mateo hated feeling out of sync with his wife. He didn't want to deny the woman he loved what she wanted. But just because her wants were louder than his, did that mean they were more important? Mateo had turned this question over in his head so many times over the last year that it had frayed at its edges.

But this incident felt different. Mickey was laughing so hard she snorted, and it was contagious. There they were, the two of them filled with delight at the absurdity—or maybe just the existence—of people's desire, and the things they did to the objects of their desire. Mateo guessed Mickey would bring up what she'd glimpsed at dinner, but for him, he was just glad to have experienced it together with his wife. He felt closer to her than he had in a while.

———

Louisa opened her front door and stood face to face with a face she knew as well as her own: heart-shaped and freckled with dimples, soft hazel eyes, framed by strawberry-blonde waves. It was the spitting image of Mickey during their first years of friendship, and it made Louisa want to crack open a couple of beers and spill her heart about her intriguing new math T.A. Except, Louisa was thirty-six not eighteen, that math T.A. was now the husband who'd left her, and she was staring at Mickey's daughter, not Mickey.

"Can I, uh, come in?" Melody asked.

"Sure, sure." Louisa didn't know how long she'd stood frozen in the doorframe, transported back two decades. She snapped out of it and handed Melody the baby monitor, then delivered her spiel about waiting ten minutes before going in if the kids woke up, which Mel tolerated though she'd heard it a dozen times before. Louisa led her back to the kitchen to finish clearing the twins' dinner. "Do people tell you that you look like your mother?"

Mel rolled her eyes. "All the friggin' time."

"It's a compliment. Your mom is a babe."

"Come on."

"Should I change the subject? Let's see. Any word from colleges? How's your dating life?"

"Excuse me, but how's *your* dating life?" Mel opened the cupboard, grabbed a bag of chips, and dug in. She'd been raised to consider this her second home, and Louisa loved how comfortable she was here. "Are you bringing a plus-one tonight?"

"Very funny. See, you are just like your mother. No, I am minus a plus-one. First in a long list of reasons, because Nathan will be in attendance, too."

Melody gasped. "What? Why? I'm sorry but this is all his fault. Plus, it's Abe's birthday, who's more your friend, right? So why do you have to play all nicey-nice with Nathan?"

"It isn't that simple."

"Seems pretty simple to me." Mel shrugged, and Louisa was

reminded that she was a teenager. Among teenagers, who was right mattered most. For Louisa, one of the most disappointing lessons of adulthood had been discovering that fairness counted for very little in most situations. Louisa had created children with a man who no longer wanted to be with her so, like it or not, they were stuck in each other's lives. And it wouldn't help to pretend that that wasn't the case. Abe had offered to ask Nathan to skip the birthday dinner. He'd suggested it casually, like it would be no big deal to break the tradition of all six of them at the table for the first time in over a decade. More than the potential discomfort of spending an evening at dinner with her ex, it broke Louisa's heart to imagine breaking up their sextet. So, while she sort of hoped Nathan would be gracious enough to opt out, Louisa couldn't bring herself to be the one to prompt it. That said, there was no way they were expanding the group to seven— Louisa had made it clear to Abe to convey to the group (Nathan) that the reservation was for six only (no Mona). In fact, perhaps Nathan would ask Mona to babysit (yeah, right).

"Well, I think you're brave. I'm in awe of you." Mel sounded like a sage adult, then erased the impression by stuffing her mouth full of chips and adding, "I can't believe that motherfucker left you."

"Mel!"

Bits of chip flew from her mouth as she laughed. "What? Would you prefer 'asshole,' or 'dickwad'? There are plenty of apt descriptors to choose from. Though I did con him into doing my homework a while ago."

Louisa shook her head. "Should I be entrusting my kids to you?"

"I dunno, should you? Why don't *you* skip the dinner and stay home with me? We can order pizza and eat ice cream and I'll tell you all my boy drama to make you feel better about yours. What do you say?"

Mel flashed her teeth, and Louisa felt enticed. She could skip an evening that she assumed would be almost fine at best, disastrous at worst. She could change out of her itchy wool dress, put on her flannel PJs, and veg out in front of bad reality TV with Mel. It was crazy how the girl had transformed, from the little kid Louisa hosted for sleepovers and had to spend an hour soothing to bed into this incredible, confident almost-adult. Mickey had done an amazing job with Mel, despite being barely an adult when the girl was born. It occurred to Louisa how hard it would be to say goodbye to Mel when she left for college.

Their phones beeped in harmony, as identical messages graced their screens: "Mel, did you make it to Lou's? Lou, are you on your way? ♥♥♥." Mickey. As if she knew Louisa would be tempted to bail in favor of an evening at home with her daughter.

"Yes, ma'am, Mel's here, and my ETA is T minus 10 minutes," Louisa typed back.

"I may regret this," Louisa said to Mel. "Wish me luck."

"Luck." She ushered Louisa out the door into the frigid air. Massachusetts hadn't gotten the memo that spring had sprung. "Have fun!"

Abe was always sentimental on his birthday, but today he was filled with even more feeling than usual. He wanted to give a speech, but every time he raised his glass, someone would tell him to hold off until the whole group arrived. Louisa appeared at the same time as the appetizers. She looked around the table and her gaze stopped at the one empty seat—Nathan's. She plucked a bruschetta straight from the waiter's tray, clearly trying to exude breeziness. She kissed Abe hello, and said hi to the others.

Everyone was sneaking glances at their watches and phones, but no one voiced it aloud: When would Nathan show? Would he show at all? By eight-twenty, empty appetizer dishes whisked away, Abe decided he'd waited long enough. It was Nathan's loss to show up so late and miss the man of honor's speech.

"Attention, attention," he said, clinking fork against glass. Mickey and Louisa grumbled but with smiles on their faces: they were used to Abe's long-winded sentimentality. "I just want to take a moment to thank you guys for joining me for my birthday. I can't tell you how grateful I am for all of my friends, for this good food and wine, for remaining healthy for another trip around the sun, and most of all for my perfect wife, Amy, and for the opportunity to be with her and build a life together."

Mickey coughed, adding half-under her breath, "And for fellatio." Mateo gave her a warning look, and Amy turned red.

"Excuse me?" Abe said.

"I think you heard me," she said, a twinkle in her eye.

Louisa looked from person to person, searching for answers. She giggled, feeling drunk on half a glass of wine and the fact that so far Nathan was a no-show. "Someone tell me what's going on."

"I won't deny it," Abe said. "My wife gave me a blowjob on the drive over here. So what? I don't know if you guys know this, but when two people love each other very much—"

Amy pelted a piece of bread at him.

"Mateo and I can corroborate," said Mickey. "We were witnesses from the next lane." Amy turned redder. "So, was that a special birthday treat or a regular occurrence?"

"No one has to answer that," Mateo said.

"Either way," Mickey said, "color me impressed."

Louisa was on board with not putting people on the spot about their sex lives, but she was also disappointed not to hear the answer to Mickey's question. Her curiosity was piqued: Exactly how frequently was her colleague who favored history-themed accessories getting BJs on the go?

When her own love life had dwindled after the twins were born, Louisa assumed she and Nathan fell somewhere on the normal spectrum of long-term couples; maybe they were closer to one end than the other, but she figured most marriages eventually experienced a waning of bedroom activity. Frequent, frenetic sex was for the young and newly coupled; over time, that gave way to the comfort of closeness and the steadiness of building a life together. When Nathan had pushed her to reup their intimacy, Louisa had accused him of pining away for a fantasy. Until he could unburden her of her work load, and the bottomless needs of the fifteen-pound barnacles who believed her body was an extension of their own, plus the money stress, and the personal grooming required just to get by as a woman, not to mention the relentless rotation of errands and housework that he didn't seem so inclined to pitch in with—until Nathan could wave a magic wand and change the fundamental reality of a middle-class working mother, Louisa was simply not going to endure all she endured in a day and then shake off her exhaustion and—*tada!*— transform into a sex kitten come ten p.m. She was only human. She thought this was the norm. But obviously she'd been wrong—obviously she knew nothing—because her very reasonable argument had driven her husband into the arms of a college student. And apparently everyone else was getting so much nookie that they couldn't even wait until they'd parked the car to rip each other's pants off.

The waitress leaned over their table, delivering a plate of burrata. "On me, but don't tell."

"Kimmy!" Mickey stood up. "Make a muscle. Everyone, check out this bicep, sculpted at FleXX, since you started coming, what, three months ago?"

The waitress flexed and kissed her own upper arm. "Thanks to Mickey here, I feel like Xena the Warrior Princess."

"Oh stop. You did all the work. I just cheered you on."

"So, what's up with you guys? What are you chatting about?"

"Blowjobs," Mickey deadpanned.

"She's not even kidding, unfortunately," Abe said. "I was expressing my gratitude to all my friends here, when I was so rudely interrupted by Mickey's foul mouth. What I was going to say is how for the first time in years, I don't feel despair at getting older. I know it's likely still a long path ahead before Amy and I meet our child, but we're finally on that path, moving toward our family. I feel so grateful that adoption is an option, and that it's one we have the means to pursue."

Mateo had stopped listening. He was eyeing Mickey eyeing this Kimmy, dewy-skinned and long-limbed and probably closer in age to his daughter than to him. Mickey heaped a slab of burrata onto a hunk of bread, then took a bite, closing her eyes and moaning. It was foreplay. Or afterplay. Some kind of play going on between his wife and someone who wasn't him. Mateo tried to catch Mickey's eye, but she was focused on licking her fingers.

"Excuse me," he said, though no one seemed to notice when he stood. He needed a break. At the bar, he decided he wanted the opposite of a drink—something to flush all the alcohol from his system and return him to himself. He ordered a seltzer with lime, then claimed a stool.

A few minutes later, he heard Amy's familiar voice beside him: "I'll have what he's having."

"Seltzer?" asked the bartender.

"Oh, never mind. Vodka soda, please." She nudged Mateo. "Hey, friend."

"Hi." He gestured to the stool on his right.

"If I sit down, do you promise not to hit on me?" Mateo looked like a deer in headlights—Amy was sometimes astounded that he led multimillion-dollar negotiations. "Relax. Mickey told us about your new little arrangement. She's leaning into it hard, huh?"

"I guess so." Mateo sipped at his seltzer.

"And what about you?"

"Am I leaning into it? No, I'm more going with the flow. What's that expression? 'Happy wife, happy life.'"

"I've never heard that one." Amy tried to think of the equivalent for "happy husband," but nothing seemed to rhyme with "husband." *Bludgeon?*

"What's up with you?" he asked. "Besides your eventful ride over here, I mean."

She sighed. "You guys will be ribbing us about that for quite some time, I guess. Sometimes I wonder if celebrating our birthdays in the same way over and over again has kept us all stunted. Like, maybe how you spend your birthday says something about how the coming year will go, and we're all stuck on repeat."

"There are worse ways to celebrate a birthday than surrounded by friends."

"So, why'd you escape to the bar then?" she asked.

"Touché. Well, Abe seems pretty optimistic about your future."

"Sure." Amy felt a twinge in her gut.

"Is that why you sought refuge with me? Too much speechifying, too much special occasioning?"

"Bingo."

"You think that's why Nathan bailed?" he asked.

Amy shrugged. She was glad Nathan hadn't showed up. She found it sort of sad how hard Louisa was working to keep their separation on good terms, so everyone could remain friends. It was one thing to put on a happy face for their kids, but she wished Louisa felt more comfortable falling apart a little in front of her friends, getting angry, announcing what she needed. Though maybe Amy wasn't one to talk.

"I'm worried," said Mateo. "I'm going to text him."

"Text who?"

Mateo looked at her like she'd been replaced by a replica. "Nathan."

"Oh right." Amy sort of did feel like a replica of herself. As she'd listened to Abe's speech, she had to keep reminding herself that he was talking about her, about their life and their future. "I'm a little spacy tonight."

"I'm happy for you guys, about the adoption thing."

"Yeah, it's exciting." Amy forced her eyes wide. She clinked the ice cubes against her glass, motioning to the bartender for a refill.

"It's normal to be scared," Mateo said. "When I found out Mickey was pregnant, man, I was terrified."

"But you guys were still in school. You'd just started dating. And it was an accident."

"Yes, yes, and yes," he laughed. "Though truthfully, I don't think I ever would've had the courage to choose to be a dad. So, it was a gift that it happened anyway. The point is, I think every prospective parent is scared, even if you've spent years hoping and planning for it. You'd be nuts not to be. You have no idea what you're in for. Every platitude is true. It's the most amazing ride, and it really does go by in a flash. All the worries—whether you'll be good enough, how you'll fit everything into a day, how you'll shoulder the massive responsibility of raising a human, it all just sort of works itself out."

"Easy for you to say when you're staring down the finish line," Amy said. "I bet you don't even remember the early years, all the muck Louisa's steeped in now."

"It's true, it's all a blissful blur. Though believe me, the muck doesn't go away. I'd happily trade teenage muck for toddler muck."

Amy felt suddenly claustrophobic in this conversation. "Let's get back to the group."

Mateo didn't miss a beat. "Unless you want to rendezvous in my car? I'll just text Mickey that I'm ducking out for some quick head."

"It really turns me on when a guy's flirting includes saying he'll check in with his wife."

"I'm so glad the beta-test went well. Now I'm ready to launch my flirting strategy into the wider world of women."

"This is why Mickey opened up your marriage, huh? Because she knew you'd never actually convince another woman to sleep with you."

They were still joking around when they returned to the table and found Kimmy leaning into Mateo's chair, totally integrated into the group. Mateo sat down in Nathan's empty seat at the other end of the table and tried to focus on Abe's story. It was the one about his student whose pocket started smoking in the middle of his presentation; apparently his vape pen had gotten activated. The rest of them had heard it before, but Kimmy was rapt. "I have so many questions," she said. "If only I didn't have half a dozen other tables to attend to."

"Has anyone heard from Nathan?" Mateo asked. It was like he'd said something vulgar, the way everyone craned their necks. "I texted him, but no reply. I'm kind of concerned."

"Oh please," Mickey said. "He just came to his senses and decided to keep his distance."

Mateo turned to Louisa, who shrugged. "I'm not my ex's keeper."

"Well, it's getting pretty late," Mateo said. "Should we move on to cake? Kimmy, would you please bring it out?"

"Sure thing!" The waitress began gathering up the dinner plates. Mateo saw that some were still half-full of food, and he hoped people weren't still eating. He felt like a prick for rushing things along, but whatever, it was a school night for Mel; she shouldn't be out babysitting so late anyway.

Something about a cake on a tray, illuminated by three dozen candles (one for good luck), brought out the childlike awe in all of them. They followed its path to the table, watched as it was placed before Abe, and took a break from their own thoughts to join him in what they assumed he was wishing for.

Louisa remembered her visits to Abe's classroom, observing how inventive and playful he was with his students; he would be an incredible father. Mickey considered how patiently Abe had sat with Mel to help her with her college applications. Mateo thought of the times Abe had come over for dinner and ended up repairing a leaky faucet or helping to construct a bookshelf; he was always so generous. Amy squeezed her husband's hand, believing he deserved everything his heart desired, wishing for it all to come true for him.

Abe filled his lungs with air and looked around at the smiling faces of his favorite people. He felt so warmed by love and friendship that for a moment he forgot about the wish so powerful that it had become a part of himself. Instead, as he snuffed out the candles in one big exhale, he wished that the group would keep up this birthday tradition forever.

CHAPTER 25

Mickey

When Mickey was nervous, she performed Kegels—a habit she'd never broken since giving birth seventeen years earlier. Mateo was driving, nodding along to talk news in that way that meant he wasn't really listening. The mood in the car was opposite of the drive to dinner. Mickey cracked the window, but still the tension hung in the air. She flicked off the radio.

"Are we going to talk about it?" she asked.

"What, your burgeoning romance with Kimmy the waitress, or your flaunting it in front of all our friends?"

"Whoa." Mickey had been surprised at how readily Mateo had agreed to their new martial arrangement, but at the same time, he was often full of surprises. That was part of the fun of being with him. Like earlier, when he'd shared his crush on that office visitor. So, Mickey had thought it was fair game to flaunt her own little crush. She wanted to explain. "I assumed—"

He cut her off, "That's your first problem, assuming."

She was taken aback. "Okay."

"Listen, I thought I was agreeing to the possibility that you might seek out some side action—discreetly, on your own time. Not center stage before an audience of me and our oldest friends. I'm still getting used to all this, you know?"

"I know," she said. "I'm sorry. I actually thought you'd prefer to have things out in the open. Like, to keep you involved."

"That didn't feel like I was involved. That felt like I'd been kicked out in the cold and was peering in through a grimy window. Kimmy literally took my seat at the table."

Mickey rested her hand on Mateo's shoulder, and felt knots under her palm. "Are you saying you'd like to be involved?"

Mateo shrugged her off, but at least he was smiling. "Listen, I can turn around and drop you back at Giorgio's if you want to continue what you started."

Mickey decided to play along. "Well, Kimmy's shift doesn't end until eleven."

"How inconvenient." Mateo was quiet for a moment. "I've gotta say, when I've fantasized about you with other women, I never thought about logistics, like having to wait for someone's shift to end."

"Back up, what'd you say?"

"You heard me."

"Care to pull over?"

"We're two minutes from home."

Yes, Mickey thought, where their daughter would soon be plopping onto the couch and convincing her father to join her for a *Rick and Morty* marathon. "Pull over."

So, he did. The street was still, the sidewalks empty, just a few rectangles of light peeking out from an otherwise dark row of houses. Mickey usually hated this aspect of their town, how everything shut down by ten p.m. But really, who knew what was going on behind all those bland exteriors? Who knew what could happen in a parked car on the side of a road late at night?

Mickey moved her mouth an inch from Mateo's ear. "Kimmy needs help taking off her uniform, so she sneaks me back to the staff room." She undid his seatbelt and pulled him into the back seat, improvising: "We close the door. We're alone. I unbutton Kimmy's shirt. There's a constellation tattooed across her ribs. I kiss each star, until my tongue finds her bra. Black lace. I reach around to unhook it." She began peeling off Mateo's clothing, then he hers. As she went on imagining the encounter aloud—kissing Kimmy's neck, shoulder, and breasts—Mateo acted out each move she described.

It felt easy, natural, and Mateo started narrating, too: "I go looking for you. I find you in the staff room, naked, straddling our waitress, her hands on your tits. She leans down to lick your nipples, making little circles with her tongue. You're arching your back, saying, 'I want you so bad.' I'm watching you from the doorway, touching myself. You turn to notice me, beckon me over. You reach for my fly and guide my lips onto Kimmy's lips."

"I want you so bad," Mickey said, lying back as best as she could in the car.

"Me too," Mateo said, making his way down her body with his mouth.

When he and Mickey first got together, Mateo's 1982 Volvo station wagon had been their default spot. Back then, he'd had multiple roommates and paper-thin walls—and sometimes no wall at all: at a party, someone had drunkenly punched through the drywall from Nathan's room to Mateo's, after which the guys would throw a ball back and forth through the hole. Meanwhile, Mickey was an R.A. in a freshman dorm and preferred that her charges not witness the comings and goings of a romantic partner. Hence, all the coupling in the car. They'd be out at night and Mickey would say, "I need to grab something from the trunk," or Mateo would invent a destination to drive to, and off they'd go. The car was well-stocked with a blanket, tissues, mints, water, and a comb. Louisa and Nathan were privy to their friends' backseat activities, and it was a running joke that when the four of them had plans, Louisa insisted they take her car, not Mateo's.

When they finished tonight in the backseat of the Tesla, Mickey could've used a bottle of water. A quick search of her surroundings turned up calculus worksheets, strawberry lip balm, and a balled-up Chipotle bag—their backseat was still young-adult territory, but the young adult was now Mickey's daughter, not herself.

Despite the lack of hydration, Mickey felt blissful, catching her breath, thighs sticky against the leather seats. "That was a throwback, huh?"

"Seriously." Mateo pulled on his boxers, then slouched back and hooked his thumb under Mickey's bra strap. "Maybe that's been our problem lately, not enough car action."

"We're always saying we don't spend enough time in our cars, you know?"

Mateo laughed. Halfway to the front seat, Mickey wiggled her butt in the air and wheeled around to smirk at Mateo. He grabbed her by the hips to pull her back next to him, starting things up again. Kissing her husband, Mickey thought about the irony that it'd taken opening up their relationship for them to finally start having sex again. And not just any sex, but fun sex, surprising sex, the kind they hadn't had for years. Life was funny.

This time was slow and tender. As she and her husband moved against each other, Mickey didn't conjure up an imaginary third; even in her head, it was just the two of them. Until, that is, the sound of Mickey's cell phone took her out of the moment. As soon as the vibrations stopped, they started up again—three times.

"Hold on," she said, reaching into the front seat to grope around for her phone. The info on the screen was so alarming—eight missed calls from Louisa since they'd parted ways half an hour ago—that Mickey lost hold of the phone and it slid under the seat. Was it something about Mel? Or the twins? Or Louisa herself? The buzzing began again, and Mickey lunged forward as if her life depended on it.

She grabbed the device just in time. "Lou, what's wrong?"

CHAPTER 26
Nathan

Nathan had meant to go to the dinner. He'd been starting to go cross-eyed from working, so he pushed aside the papers and fluttered his eyes closed, focusing on the flow of air in and out of his body. He imagined Mona's gentle prompts to inhale and exhale. Until Mona taught him about mindfulness, Nathan had dismissed the idea of breath as medicine. But she'd insisted it really helped her with her back pain: The point wasn't to cure your ailments; rather, it was to tune in to them, to be exactly where you were with whatever was going on, and that would turn into its own kind of remedy. Nathan got it now. As soon as he'd started paying attention to his thoughts, he realized he spent nearly all his time lost in the past or worrying about the future. He was daydreaming through his present, and missing it as a result. *Be present.* Now, whenever his jaw got tense or his knees nervous, Mona gave him a little tap and whispered those words: *Be present.* It was such a beautiful, simple thing.

He and Mona began their days in a pair of chairs by the window. Meditation sounded too woo-woo to Nathan, so he called it breathing. Lately, during their morning sessions, Nathan would feel his entire body quivering with nerves; it was ever since his department head's confrontation. Adrenaline raced through his veins. He yearned to push away the discomfort, to wriggle out of his skin. But he resisted these impulses, knowing they wouldn't serve him. Instead he stayed with his body, breathing. The anxiety didn't go away, but acknowledging it—honoring the feelings, as Mona would say—succeeded in making it less intense. Nathan experienced the air cycling in and out of his nose, his chest rising and falling, and he felt he would be okay.

When the timer on Mona's phone went off with its tinny tune, it was like a Pavlovian bell: Nathan would reach for her and pull her onto his lap. This was the best part. He felt wide-awake to the world, and to the sensations on the surface of his skin and beneath. As he and Mona communed, Nathan felt more alive than he had in years. If he could have, he would've burrowed down into these mornings and nestled inside them forever.

But, as Mona was fond of saying, life was change; nothing was permanent. Eventually she'd throw open the shades and crack the windows to breathe in the morning chill. Mona took her time selecting her day's outfit, taking pleasure in how she presented herself to the world. Nathan would linger in bed, watching his girlfriend like it was performance art, putting off his own preparation for the day. Mona once mentioned that she knew transitions were tough for him, and it was like a revelation, illuminating something that had always lurked inside of him: yes, it was true, he found transitions difficult. As a kid, he'd thrown epic tantrums when it was time to leave a preferred activity, to the point where his parents threatened to leave him at home if he couldn't control himself; it wasn't so much that he'd grown out of that behavior as that he'd learned to cut out the kicking and crying part. Nathan could still throw an epic tantrum—on the inside. Mona told him the breathing would help, and it did.

But today was especially rough. Nathan had back-to-back classes through the afternoon, the thought of which turned his eyelids to lead. But that was nothing compared to the anticipation of the faculty meeting happening in a few minutes, which would be his first encounter with his boss since a week ago. After all that, Giorgio's. Nathan knew Louisa hoped he'd bail on the dinner, or at least he knew she *thought* she hoped that—but Nathan believed another part of his ex craved normalcy and consistency. And nothing was more normal than their friend group at a Giorgio's birthday dinner. Nathan had done so much to disrupt their lives that he felt he owed it to Louisa to keep up this tradition, to show up and play his part in their party of six. Plus, who was he kidding? Nathan wanted normalcy, too. His new life was big and exciting, but sometimes it gave him whiplash to consider how much had changed in the past few months. It would be comforting to slip back into an old routine of his friends and their well-worn jokes and stories, so long as he knew he could slip back out of it again at the end of the night.

But there was no slipping out of anything at the moment. The faculty meeting loomed, and Nathan felt a bit frantic, inhaling and exhaling, trying (in vain) to stay in the moment.

"Nathan, hey, can I steal you for a sec?"

Nathan's eyes popped open. Russell Low leaned over him, a file folder in hand. "Is it meeting time? Sorry, I lost track of time."

Russell gave no reassuring smile or nod. "Let's, uh, head to my office."

That slight hesitation, the furrowed brow—Nathan already knew. Still, he obediently stood and followed his boss down the hall.

Russell settled into his armchair. "Well, the disciplinary committee's investigation concluded that you were involved in an inappropriate relationship with a student. Given your status at the university"—meaning, non-tenured, and not even on the tenure track—"you don't have much recourse. You're being let go, effective immediately. You have until midnight to clear out your office, and your faculty email address will be deactivated next week. Professor Wexler will take over your classes for the remainder of the semester."

Nathan couldn't help but laugh; how fitting that Lydia Wexler, who'd put all of this in motion, would also be replacing him at the lectern. "Let me guess," Nathan said, "no severance, no grace period for my health insurance, no letter of recommendation."

Russell looked at his lap.

"Fan-flipping-tastic. You know, I've given my whole professional life to this place. Five years earning my Ph.D., over a decade toiling as an adjunct, working my ass off to get good student reviews and my byline on papers, and attending all those stilted faculty functions to suck up to the pompous gatekeepers"—he indicated Russell—"all to finally get anointed as a full-time lecturer, whoop-de-doo. After all that, it disappears in an instant." He couldn't stop talking. "And why? Because a young woman and I fell in love?" It didn't add up for Nathan; it didn't compute.

"No," said Russell calmly, "because you are a faculty member and you engaged in a romantic relationship with a student, which is verboten. It's spelled out very clearly in the university handbook."

"Thanks, Russ, old pal. I've always appreciated your pedantic bullshit. It's been nice knowing you." He shook the man's hand and was gone.

Some period of time later, Nathan found himself wandering around the campus green, unsure of where to go. Should he call someone—Mona, or Louisa? He tried to ground himself, but he couldn't feel his own legs, never mind the breath entering and leaving his body.

Without planning it, he found himself in a liquor store, then back on campus, in the office that was still his for the next several hours. His feet were kicked up on the desk, his mug was full and sloshing. Full again, and again, and again. Then everything was empty, including his trash can, which Martin the custodian had just come by to collect. Martin asked if Nathan was all right. Nathan offered him a drink, but when he held up the bottle he saw that it was empty, too. Oops. Nathan laughed until he felt a gush of saliva fill his mouth. He leaned over the trashcan and hurled. He apologized to Martin—or said something approximating an apology. He couldn't remember Martin's response. That would be his last interaction with the custodian, he realized as he stumbled down the hall. Shame piled upon shame.

It wasn't out of responsibility that Nathan hailed himself a cab—he just forgot where he'd parked his car. He gave the driver his address, and he woke to see his house through the window. His home. The color with the quirky name that he and Louisa had picked out at Sherman-Williams all those years ago: *Maybe Mulberry*. It had made them laugh, because was it mulberry or wasn't it? They'd bought dozens of cans, then Nathan spent a summer doing the paint job himself, standing on the rickety ladder, building up his lats and calves and all the weird muscles he'd never flexed while teaching seminars on statistics. For once, he'd felt like he was accomplishing something concrete, that at the end of each day he could see incontestable evidence of his progress; it had been incredibly satisfying. There was the lawn, still scraggly despite all his efforts with sod and fertilizer and whatever the Home Depot guys threw at him. And there were the stupid flower beds he'd finally planted after Louisa had nagged him about it for months. Look at them now: he admitted it, they looked nice.

Nathan handed a wad of cash to the driver and stumbled up to the porch, which was littered with kid stuff. The toys they favored lately were by the door: Finn's yellow scooter and Phoebe's purple one, the strider bikes, a couple of soccer balls. At the back of the porch was the museum of discarded stuff, all those bright pusher toys the kids used when they were first learning to walk, including the one that played "Welcome to the Learning Farm!" an earworm so powerful that he and Louisa would wake up in the middle of the night and croon it to each other. Feeling nostalgic, Nathan almost turned on the toy to hear it again.

He had a key, but something deep in his gut told him to ring the bell.

The door swung open, and there she stood, wearing the Shakespeare nightgown she'd gotten from her faculty Secret Santa a couple years ago, her posture perfect, her curls pulled into the messy bun she favored while washing up. She was beautiful, Nathan's wife. He looked down, locking eyes with an agonized Macbeth spanning her hip, the pajama cotton now pilled.

"Hi, I'm home."

CHAPTER 27

Louisa

Louisa was flossing, which was something she'd started doing ever since that student enrichment assembly she'd been roped into emceeing. Something the speaker said had struck her: "Create opportunities for small successes in your life, and celebrate them." What a good idea! Louisa was so used to holding herself to impossible standards, then beating herself up when she didn't meet them. But flossing took forty-five seconds and made Louisa feel briefly like a goddamned goddess. She was just getting into her molars when the doorbell rang.

She knew who it was. Because really, who else would be dropping by at eleven p.m.—an Amazon delivery guy? Plus, there had to be some explanation for his bailing on dinner. Which is why she didn't even bother to toss the string of floss, never mind throw on a robe.

Nathan stood in the doorframe and greeted her like he had a thousand times before. And for a moment Louisa was tricked, warped back in time. Like she could just let him in, and they'd sit on the couch with a bowl of popcorn reviewing their respective evenings, him sharing whatever adventures he'd had out in the world, her relating the various adorable and/or infuriating things the kids had done before bedtime. Then they'd realize it was way too late and stumble to bed, Nathan's arms wrapped around Louisa's waist as they both slept the sleep of the dead—i.e., the sleep of parents of toddlers.

But, no. Louisa shook off the fantasy and saw how wasted Nathan was: his body wavered like a weeping willow, his skin was sallow and sweaty.

"Are you okay?"

"Of course, yeah." She could smell the whiskey on his breath. "I'm fine, I'm fine. Do you have any water?"

On the one hand, Louisa knew how stupid it would be to try to talk to Nathan while he was in this state. On the other, something was clearly wrong, and it felt crucial to find out what. It took ten minutes of roundabout nonsense for her to get it out of him: the university had found out about him and Mona, and he'd been ousted.

Right. An inevitable outcome. As soon as Nathan told her he'd fallen for a student, Louisa had been waiting for the other shoe to drop. And yet, he'd acted like she was being melodramatic, that Mona was of age, that it was all consensual, blah blah blah. So, Louisa had stopped thinking about it; there was so much else on her mind. But now her original conviction returned to her, and she felt the opposite of surprise.

She watched Nathan slouched on the couch, gulping water then setting the glass down too hard on the coffee table. Thirty seconds later he was snoring, his neck looking like it had been snapped in half. Louisa wedged a pillow under his head. She felt pity, and also relief. Because guess what? This—Nathan, his firing, all of it—wasn't Louisa's mess to deal with.

Out of principle, Louisa hadn't saved Mona's number on her phone. But she found it without much trouble, buried in an email exchange with Nathan over the kids' sleepover arrangements.

"Hello?" Mona sounded like she'd been sleeping.

"Hi, it's Louisa. Sorry to call so late, but Nathan showed up on my doorstop, pretty drunk."

"Oh!" So much concern was contained in the one syllable that, for the first time, Louisa realized Mona must be in love with her husband. It was a jab to her gut, distracting Louisa before it occurred to her that Mona had no idea what happened. Probably as far as she knew, Nathan had spent the night with everyone at Giorgio's.

"He's all right—he's asleep. But I would prefer that he's not here in the morning when the kids wake up."

"Okay, I'll be there in ten."

"Thanks."

She'd been straightforward and clear. Only when she hung up did Louisa start to freak out. Her husband's girlfriend was on her way over, to her house, invited by her! What the fuck?

She called Mickey. She called her again, and again, and again. No way was her friend asleep—she regularly stayed up past two a.m. doing the books for the gym with some ancient Jane Fonda video on in the background. Her idea of relaxing. So, why wasn't she picking up?

Finally, she did. "Lou, what's wrong?"

"I was flossing my teeth, then Nathan showed up and he got fired and now he's passed out on my couch and Mona is coming over and—"

"Whoa, slow down."

Mickey made her back up and go through exactly what had happened. It worked to calm her down and help her process.

"Keep it short and sweet," Mickey advised. "There's no need for a heart-to-heart. Be polite, but let her handle it. Remember, this isn't on you. Say goodbye, kiss the kids, then go to bed."

"You're right. Good advice. Yes." Louisa was nodding. She'd follow these steps and she'd be fine. Louisa saw headlights in her driveway. "She's here."

"I love you. You can do it. Stay strong."

Louisa wasn't sure what to say in greeting, but when she opened the door, she discovered there was no need; Mona rushed past her right to Nathan. She crouched in front of him, cradled him in her arms, and began murmuring who-knows-what in his ear. Look at that: He was snoring like a steam train, his pores screaming booze, and he'd wandered back to his old house with his ex, and still Mona offered nothing but TLC. She must've really loved him. Louisa felt like she was invading an intimate moment, despite it occurring in her own living room.

Eventually, Mona turned to her. "Do you know what happened?" Louisa squirmed. She hated to be the messenger. "Please tell me."

"He said he was fired. Because of your, um, relationship."

"Right." Mona sounded resigned. "It's this whole 'Me Too' thing. Now a man can't look at a woman sideways without being indicted for it."

"Well, that's not exactly accurate. Nathan was your professor. You don't see how that could be perceived as problematic?" Louisa couldn't believe she was having this conversation.

"This relationship has been totally consensual from day one. Come on, you know Nathan—he wasn't on some power trip, and I wasn't under some silly spell. The narrative of our relationship being problematic casts me as a helpless victim, totally erasing my agency and personhood. Frankly, it's insulting. And implying this situation is in the same category with actual sexual predators cheapens the whole cause."

"Okay." The girl had some points, but Louisa wasn't convinced. No one was accusing Nathan of being Harvey Weinstein. But a man didn't have to be Harvey Weinstein to be in the wrong when it came to relationships with women. It wasn't so black-and-white.

"All I'm saying is that it isn't so black-and-white."

Louisa coughed out a laugh. "Well, on that point, we agree."

They were quiet for a moment before Mona spoke again. "Listen, even though I don't believe our relationship is a crime, I also know it wasn't victimless. I didn't intend to break up a family. And I'm sorry."

Louisa's voice caught in her throat, so she didn't find out what would've come out in response: *Thank you* or *fuck you* seemed equally likely. It felt inconceivable that her husband's mistress was standing in her living room apologizing to her, as her husband lay beside them, passed out and oblivious.

Nathan made a guttural noise and Mona grabbed his hand. "Poor guy. Let's get you home."

Louisa helped her lift him. They each took a side, tucking their heads under his armpits and shuffle-dragging him out to Mona's car. Louisa took some satisfaction in hearing Mona grunt with the effort—she couldn't have been very strong—but still, for a moment, it felt like they were a team. Louisa watched as Mona buckled Nathan's seatbelt and brushed his hair back from his face. She looked to Louisa like a grownup woman who happened to be in love with her husband. In a moment, the two of them would be gone, taking with them Nathan's drunken career flameout—good riddance.

Louisa felt a flash of magnanimity. "Listen," she said to Mona, as she closed the passenger-side door. "You seem like a nice person. I wish you and Nathan luck, truly."

Before Louisa knew it, she was enveloped in a tight embrace. Then Mona got into the driver's seat and Louisa watched them drive off, feeling punchy with freedom. In her pajamas and boots, she skipped across the damp lawn back to the door.

In bed, she sprawled out like a starfish and decided to spend not a single moment more worrying about Nathan's fiasco, which had nothing to do with her and wasn't her problem.

Until the morning, when she sprung out of sleep, sat up ramrod straight, and thought, *Fuck me. This has* everything *to do with me. This is* absolutely *my problem.*

Nathan had lost his job, which meant he'd lost his paychecks—the ones that funded a chunk of their rent and the kids' daycare and the bazillion other expenses that came with housing, clothing, feeding, and entertaining themselves and their children. When Louisa had asked how Nathan planned to pay for his new apartment on top of all his other expenses, he'd told her not to worry, that it didn't concern her. She'd pressed and said that actually it concerned her very much, and Nathan admitted that Mona was teaching yoga and also he had savings. *Ah*—meaning the small inheritance from his parents that Nathan had claimed would be funneled to a college fund for the kids. Apparently now it would be a lovers' lair fund. Absurd. And this had been back when Nathan was still earning regular paychecks.

So, what would they do now? Surely Nathan would be barred from teaching at any other university, or even a high school; he'd never be hired to work with kids again. And what else did his prestigious Ph.D. in mathematics qualify him to do? A big fat nothing. Would he lean on his new partner who was a couple months shy of a college degree to support him and his two children?

Louisa spilled all of these worries the next morning to Abe.

"Holy shit," Abe kept saying, like some wind-up doll with only one phrase at its disposal.

"I know," Louisa kept answering.

"And Bauer, have you signed divorce papers yet?"

"No, we haven't figured out the details."

Abe nodded warily.

"What?"

"It's just, you've always been the main breadwinner. And now that Nathan's out of a job, without much of a shot at gainful employment in the near future ...."

"Oh no." She knew where he was going with this.

"Oh yes, unfortunately. Nathan could demand child support *and* alimony."

Louisa banged a fist on her desk. "What the hell, you know? It's like, I'm the one who busted my ass to support our family when Nathan was whiling away his time as an adjunct, teaching a couple of classes a semester. Now I'm the one who gets punished?"

"I don't think anyone has ever described divorce as fair. But who knows, maybe Nathan won't push for it. Mona's into yoga, right? Maybe she'll persuade him to be all Zen so he won't try to screw you out of all your money."

"Mona is a child." All of Louisa's generous feelings from the night before had shriveled up. It was a consolation to indulge briefly in schadenfreude, imagining the pending state of Nathan's relationship. "I'm sure she'll be thrilled to see her broke, middle-aged boyfriend moping around the apartment, which they'll soon be evicted from. That sounds very sexy."

"Very."

"Anyway, I imagine she'll be happy for any money Nathan can squeeze out of me." Louisa dropped her head onto Abe's shoulder. "Oh Abe."

Despite everything, Louisa was grateful to talk like this to her friend, to simply be heard. Mickey had texted her twice already that morning, asking about the Mona encounter and how she was doing, but Louisa hadn't yet responded. Mickey was a problem-solver, and she'd immediately want to make a plan—or worse, offer to lend her money. Louisa knew it was a privilege to have people in her life who wouldn't let her starve (and she knew it was an exaggeration to imagine she might starve), but she refused to be anyone's charity case. And goddamnit, if it weren't for Nathan and his irresponsibility, his immaturity, his letting himself be led around by his dick, she wouldn't be in this stupid position to begin with!

"Ms. Bauer?"

Fucking Chad Mack, poking his nosy little nose into her office. "Good morning, Mack."

"Our testing meeting started five minutes ago. Dr. Poolehauzer and I were waiting for you, but I decided to hunt you down so as to not waste any more time. I figured you might be in here chatting with your buddy."

"My fault," said Abe. "I had a very important student matter to discuss with Ms. Bauer."

"Oh?" The dean's ears perked up at the potential for gossip.

"Highly confidential. Very sensitive. The type of issue that only Ms. Bauer could handle." Louisa watched Chad register the dig before shaking it off.

"All right, well. She has other responsibilities, which are being sharked."

"Sharked?"

"That's what I said."

"Right," said Abe, his voice laced with amusement. "I'll leave you two to it. I don't want to shark any of my own responsibilities."

Abe's performance for Chad cheered Louisa up. She squeezed her friend's arm on the way out, and he whispered, "It'll be okay, I promise."

⁓

For the length of the hallway, Chad Mack stayed one step ahead of Louisa. She sometimes found herself wondering what had happened to the dean to make him this way—how bad he was bullied in his own high school years, maybe—but still she felt little sympathy for her arch-nemesis.

In the principal's office, Dr. P was pitched forward in his chair as if ready to dive into a body of water. Before Louisa even sat down, he barked, "Test prep! Gimme an update!"

Louisa froze. She'd been meaning to think about test prep, to devise a plan and start implementing it. But there were only so many hours in the day, only so many thoughts she could hold in her head, only so much stress she could shoulder. Their previous conversation on testing came flooding back to Louisa—the required five percent increase across all student scores, the reduced funding if they didn't meet the mark, her job on the line—and she understood why she'd pushed it from her mind.

"Earth to Ms. Bauer. Where do we stand on test prep?"

She would simply have to fake it. "Um, the new test prep books are on order, and the teachers are supposed to be executing the new curriculum once per week. I've heard some anecdotal feedback that students are making progress, and the teachers feel—"

Poolehauzer held up a hand to stop her. "Supposed to ... anecdotal feedback ... the teachers feel ..." His voice was mocking. "No, I want data, Ms. Bauer! Quantitative data!"

"Hard numbers," Chad added, making Louisa want to throttle him.

"I have an idea," Dr. P said. "Let's block off the three days before April break. We'll do a trial run of the tests for every student in every subject, to see whether we're on target to bring up the scores." He held up his hand again, anticipating Louisa's objection that it was too much too soon. "Ms. Bauer, I trust that you'll figure out the arrangements, organize a committee or a squad or what-have-you. Okay? Okay." He clapped his hands. "Deputies, disperse!" He shooed them out of his office.

Louisa had a to-do list a mile long, and out of the corner of her eye she spotted mousy Meredith Pritchett making a beeline for her—as usual, the world history teacher appeared primed with grievances. Louisa ducked out of sight, trotted toward Stairwell F, and jogged up the three flights. When she reached the roof, she was panting. Her heart clanged against her chest. She rested her palms on her knees and gulped in the fresh air, for ten seconds, twenty, thirty. Finally, she stretched to her full height, willed her body to take up as much space as possible, and let out a howl like the world had never heard before.

CHAPTER 28

Mickey

Mickey hated barre, and she never did things she hated, yet here she was performing a million hairpin lifts, curtsy dips, and toe circles until she thought her left leg might fall off. But these maddening little movements that went on forever were all the rage among Mickey's clientele, so she'd brought in an instructor, one of those high-school queen-bee types with a high ponytail and a bubble butt. Mickey made a point of occasionally participating in all of FleXX's classes. They'd moved on to pretzel, palms planted and legs twisted at two right angles, back leg lifting up an inch, down an inch, ad nauseum. "Flex your glutes! Fire up your seat!"

"Butt," Mickey muttered under her breath, her tiny rebellion: Every time the instructor said "seat," she replied with "butt," because that's what the woman meant, and let's call a spade a spade, shall we? From the next mat over, Keisha shot her a warning look, like Mickey was going to get them both in trouble. And okay, fine, that was the real reason Mickey was here in the studio tormenting her *butt* via interminable micro-movements: she'd spotted Keisha's name on the sign-up sheet. Ever since she and Mateo had gone at it in the car on the way home from Abe's birthday dinner, Mickey had felt charged up, ready to make her next move.

They switched sides, left arms on the bar, facing right, which was the view Mickey had been holding out for: Keisha's glutes, Keisha's seat (butt), Keisha's muscles flexing up, up, up, up. They were balancing on their left tippy-toes, with right legs lifted parallel to the floor performing tiny circles. Mickey's mouth was inches from Keisha's ear. As their legs got shaky, their perches more precarious, she began a low chant of "Baby Got Back," but with slightly altered lyrics: "Oh my god, Becky, look at her seat." Keisha's shoulders shook with silent laughter, and when Mickey whispered, "I like big seats and I cannot lie," Keisha toppled over. She shook her head at Mickey, who looked the other way, keeping a straight face. She was the boss, after all.

⟶

Mickey was accustomed to abrupt goodbyes with Keisha. Being with her was like a building up of pressure, and there always came the time when she felt if she spent another moment in the woman's presence, she'd either explode or be forced to find a release—so she fled. Keisha seemed to understand. "Till next time, Mickey Mouse," she'd say, smiling. Keisha knew her power and reveled in it. It was one of her most attractive qualities.

This time, though, Mickey lingered. After barre class, they made their way slowly up the stairs, each step like a jab to Mickey's sore glutes. "Want to stick around to stretch?"

"Stretch our seats?" Keisha smirked.

"We can do it in my office. I'm staying late anyway to do the books. Mateo is out on a date." This just came out. Mateo wasn't out on a date. But he could've been—and who knew, maybe he was. All air seemed to have exited the stairwell, as Keisha waited.

Mickey's mouth was dry. "We've, um, decided to make our marriage more fluid, more ... open."

"Open?"

"Yes."

"Interesting."

"Uh-huh."

It was like they'd regressed to primitive versions of themselves, vocabulary stripped down to just the essentials. Primitive needs, primitive feelings.

It was both similar to and different from how Mickey had always imagined it would be with Keisha. They were in the gym, sweaty in their post-workout clothes, though they weren't in the locker room, which was busy with other clients (Mickey had never considered this in her fantasies).

Keisha came around to Mickey's side of the desk. "I've been taking this deep-tissue massage class. I can show you some of my moves ..." They both laughed—at the cheesiness of the line, and out of nerves, and excitement. "I'm sorry. I haven't been with anyone since Leah. I'm just ...."

"It's okay," Mickey said. "A massage sounds lovely."

Mickey lay down onto her belly, and Keisha began on her shoulders and moved inch by inch down her spine. Every spot she touched lit up and tingled, like Mickey's skin was electric. As her hands dipped past Mickey's lower back, Mickey felt suddenly shy—she told herself it was her seat being rubbed, not her butt, certainly not her ass. She took deliberate breaths, stifling her sighs.

Keisha applied pressure with her palms until Mickey felt a series of gentle releases. Still, she was nervous to give herself over to the experience. "Just let go," Keisha urged her, which finally did the trick. By the time Keisha reached to turn her onto her back, Mickey was utterly relaxed, her limbs like jelly.

It was such delicious pleasure to have this powerful woman looming over her, manipulating her body like a ragdoll. Mickey let herself delight in what was coming. And then it was happening: Keisha's pillowy lips pressed against her own, as her body slid on top of her, toasty-warm.

The sensations were all new, yet the newness was also like a portal back in time. To college—when Mickey had hooked up with new people all the time, a constant discovery, a non-stop adventure. Back then, every possibility seemed open to her. It was a miracle she'd gotten a scholarship to transport her away from her middle-of-nowhere upbringing and her distant parents. She'd been excited from day one, sitting in her dorm room poring over the course catalog, in awe at the hundreds of pages of classes, then going out to her first college party, meeting dozens of people, all inherently more interesting than the people she'd known her whole life back home. For years following that first night, Mickey stayed up late and woke up early; she could never get enough of her new life. And unlike in her hometown, where she'd earned a reputation as "too much," in college she collected friends like spare change: everyone was attracted to her glow; everyone wanted her to shine it upon them. As a college student, Mickey had felt abundant, brimming over with joy.

She hadn't been looking to meet a partner. And on paper, Mateo couldn't have been more different from someone Mickey imagined she'd fall in love with: He was a math nerd, with no fashion sense, and he'd never heard of any of the books or movies Mickey read and watched. Plus, he was inexperienced; he'd been with just two other women, including the on-and-off high-school girlfriend he'd held onto for half of college.

Yet, when Mickey first laid eyes on Mateo at that grad school party, she could tell his body was chiseled under the ill-fitting button-down (he strength-trained to de-stress). She saw a spark in his eyes. And he was kind to her. It was lust, if not love, at first sight. She'd woken up alone the morning after what she assumed would be a one-night thing. But when Mickey went to her computer, she found the monitor filled with Mateo's goofy grin. Then the mouth started moving—lips parting and pressing together, on repeat—as a mechanical voice announced, "Good morning, Mickey! I had an early morning class. Can I see you again?" It was the dorkiest, sweetest thing—a math major's idea of a love letter.

Immediately, she summoned Louisa to her room to show her the message, and Louisa promptly called Nathan (whom she'd recently started seeing) to get the dirt on Mateo; they were in the same Ph.D. program, and roommates. Mickey moved into Mateo's apartment a few weeks later, and never looked back. She'd always been impulsive, and it just felt right. Three months later, she was pregnant; another three months, and she had her diploma in hand; three months after that, they were married at town hall; three more months, and she was cradling her beautiful little Melody in her arms.

Mickey had been amazed to discover that the fullness she'd felt from experiencing so much—switching her major four times, sleeping her way through the soccer teams (both men's and women's), and saying yes to every party, every lecture, every two a.m. skinny-dip-and-diner run—could all be replaced by just two people. With Mateo and Melody, she was fulfilled. Her world hadn't shrunk; rather, her instant family had grown to become her world. And—this surprised no one more than Mickey herself—it made her happy.

Of course, she was also miserable and overwhelmed and exhausted. She couldn't count the number of times she decided she couldn't take it anymore and dropped off baby Mel with Louisa, saying blithely, "I'll be back, eventually." Then she'd peel away at double the speed limit, desperate for a life that was like the rest of her friends' lives: wide open, with no real responsibility, and certainly no husband or baby.

But those feelings never lasted. After a good dose of driving in peaceful silence (plus a nap in the backseat), Mickey would feel her breasts fill with milk, which would remind her of the fullness of her life, and she'd return to pick up her daughter and take her home to her father. After putting Mel down for the evening, more often than not Mickey and Mateo would have passionate reunion sex.

As Mel grew from an extension of Mickey into her own little self, Mickey discovered other areas to pour her energy into. The running and biking, the swimming, and then the gym. And supporting Mateo as he grew and sold off his companies. The years skipped by. Mel grew taller and more herself. The gym and the businesses thrived. The house became their home, and then so did a bigger house. Mickey's body got stronger as she made a name for herself on the triathlon circuit. Mickey and Mateo matured into their marriage, their love growing roots and flourishing. The sex became less frequent, with Mateo not always in the mood anymore, but it was a slow taper. All the while, the passage of time was punctuated by the birthday dinners with their friends.

It was enough—more than enough—for years and years. And then it wasn't. Nothing appeared so different. But what had elevated Mickey's life and infused it all with color and vibrancy had been the passion at the core of her marriage. And lately, it had withered. Not to mention that her daughter—her heart—was about to leave home. So, for the first time in nearly two decades, Mickey found herself missing the person she'd been back in college, optimistic and adventurous and full of potential.

She'd known she had to find a way back to who she wanted to be. And not in a crazy, burn-it-all-down way (like, ahem, certain husbands of certain friends she knew). Because although Mickey might've yearned for a younger version of herself, she was not in denial about being a grown woman. So, here she was, feeling open, and expansive, and practically electric with possibility and excitement. It was something. It was a start.

"Hi." Keisha kissed her shoulder. "That was nice."

"It sure was." They were lying prone on adjoining yoga mats, like a post-coital savasana. Mickey was spent and content. And also a little high on endorphins and pheromones and whatever else was emanating from the woman beside her. She was buzzing. She was about to ask if Keisha felt it, too, when she realized that yes, she must've felt it, because the buzzing was coming from Mickey's phone, which Keisha was holding out to her.

It was a text from Mel: "I'M IN! UCLA BABY, HERE I COME!"

A yelp escaped Mickey's mouth as she sat up. She felt thrilled and a little forlorn. Her daughter had achieved her big dream—and California was three thousand miles away.

Keisha sat up, too. "Is everything okay?"

"Yes, fine, fine. Mel got into UCLA."

"Oh, fantastic!" Keisha pumped her arm.

Suddenly, this situation felt odd and a little awkward, being here with Keisha, naked on the floor of her office. Mickey was fast about getting dressed, anxious to get back to her little family. She pecked Keisha on the cheek. "This was fun. I've got to go home."

She couldn't wait to hug her daughter and share how proud she was.

CHAPTER 29

Mateo

Did Mateo want to meet Nathan for a drink? No. Did he want to catch up? No. Did he want to hear all the ways Nathan had screwed up his life, rattled off in a self-pitying monologue as if Nathan himself hadn't been the agent of the screw-up? No. But Mateo had agreed to meet Nathan out of a vague principle of enduring friendship and brotherhood. And now Nathan was late—*unbelievable*. Mateo had left the office promptly at seven to meet his buddy, as a favor; meanwhile, Nathan had no job and no excuse.

When Nathan finally walked in at eight, he looked even more disheveled than usual. He clapped Mateo on the back in greeting—no apology—and ordered an IPA. Mateo didn't know if Nathan knew that he already knew what had happened. He waited for Nathan to bring it up. But instead, his buddy started shooting the shit about the Red Sox and their slow start, and whether or not their bats were going to wake up. "We should get out to a game this spring. Remember how we used to do that?"

"Yeah, man," said Mateo. "It's been a long time."

"Bleachers or die." Nathan raised a fist.

Mateo surprised himself at his nostalgia. "Back when we were writing our dissertations, it was the only way I could get you to shower and leave your reeking hovel of a room. I'd wave those Sox tickets in front of your face, and you'd bolt up. Worked like a charm. Meanwhile I was looking for any excuse to escape my work."

"Well, Matty, I was a harder worker than you." Nathan said it like a joke, but it had been true once upon a time. Back in grad school, Nathan had been more committed and disciplined. Ironically, the reward for all that hard work had been a decade of collecting pennies as an adjunct. Whereas Mateo, who'd abandoned academia out of restlessness, had found work that earned him a small fortune. Now he worked sixty-hour weeks, and Nathan not at all.

"Anyway," said Nathan, "I'm free whenever. Name a date and I'll grab us tickets. You can thank me with beer."

"Sure." Mateo thought this would be Nathan's opening: his schedule was now open and he hoped to be treated to beer, and Mateo braced himself for the woe-is-me saga to start. But Nathan didn't go there. He stayed in reminiscence mode, taking them back to their days of T.A.-ing and cramming for exams. What were clearly sharp memories for Nathan all felt a bit fuzzy around the edges for Mateo. The carefree vibe Nathan was describing didn't sound familiar; Mateo had had a newborn at the time, but the joy of the period came back to him in a powerful rush.

"We should do this more often," Mateo found himself saying. He'd been dreading the evening beforehand, but his worries turned out to be unfounded. He was having a good time, in the way he and Nathan used to before Nathan had blown up his life, forcing everyone else to deal with the repercussions. Mateo was relaxed. He was laughing. And he couldn't help noticing the pretty brunette at the end of the bar who kept catching his eye and flipping her hair in a way that made Mateo shift in his seat.

"I was thinking the same thing," Nathan said. "Cheers."

In the bathroom, Mateo gave himself a pep talk. He wasn't doing anything wrong. Not only that, nothing had even happened. It wasn't a betrayal to smile at a pretty woman, to signal that he was interested and—this is what gave him the tightness in his throat—available. He slid the ring off his finger and slipped it into his pocket. Mateo didn't plan to lie about being married, but he knew single women often looked for a ring as a sign that a man was off-limits. He was just giving himself a chance. Staring at his reflection in the mirror, Mateo told himself, "You got this."

But he really had no idea what he was doing. He assumed a wink would be cheesy, and any physical contact might be overstepping. So, as he passed the woman at the bar, he waved. When he returned to his stool, Nathan was agape. "Did you just wave to that woman?"

"I did."

"With what end in mind?"

"Sexual intercourse," Mateo deadpanned. "What can I say, Nathan? You're rubbing off on me."

He hoped Nathan would let it go, but he pressed on. "In the two decades I've known you, I've never seen you wave to a woman like that. Tell me what's going on."

He sighed. "I'm now in an open marriage."

Nathan snorted, looking half-thrilled and half-horrified. "You? Since when has getting it on with women other than your wife ever been something you wanted?"

"Well, it was Mickey's idea."

"Obviously it was Mickey's idea! I can see *her* in an open marriage—sleeping around and keeping it strictly business, wham, bam, thank you, ma'am. *You,* on the other hand." Nathan shook his head. "You think you can sleep with a woman and keep your feelings out of it?"

Mateo was about to object, like who said anything about keeping feelings out of it, but Nathan anticipated his response. "Or I'm sorry, by 'open' did you mean you're open to side *relationships*? This is going to be a ringing success. Good luck, man." He laughed in a way that felt unkind.

Mateo was irritated. He didn't come here to be denigrated by his friend, to have a delicate new situation picked apart—by Nathan, of all people. "Thank you for your opinion, but I don't think you're really in a position to be doling out marital advice. Next, are you going to share your plans for my company, seeing as how your career is progressing so swimmingly?"

Nathan's face drained of color, and Mateo felt like a dick.

Nathan hung his head. "I was hoping to spend a few hours not thinking about what a sorry loser I am. But sure, let's delve into it."

"I'm sorry," Mateo stammered. "I'm sure it's complicated, and—"

"Stop, it's fine. I mean, it's not fine, but you don't have to do that. Listen, I'm sorry for earlier. I love you, Matty, but I'm not feeling this anymore." Nathan gestured to the bartender. "Get that woman over there a drink, say it's on this guy." He dropped a twenty-dollar bill on the bar, clapped Mateo on the back, and was gone.

The next few moments Mateo saw like a series of snapshots: the bartender's hands jiggling the martini shaker, the V-shaped glass filling with liquid, slender fingers clutching the stem, the woman sliding several seats down to take Nathan's spot next to Mateo.

"Thanks for this," she said, plucking an olive off of its spear and popping it into her mouth. "I'm Olivia."

"Matt." The single syllable felt odd in his mouth. He was either Mateo or Matty, never Matt. He realized he was expected to say more. "What do you do for work, Olivia?"

"I'm a horticulturist." She could probably read the question on his face. "I design gardens—like flower arrangements en masse, for the grounds of museums and other institutions." Her eyes were the color of milk chocolate, and her smile made her freckles pop. Mateo wondered if she noticed that he worked out.

"I once tried to grow tomatoes in my yard," he said, "but the squirrels got to them."

"I could help with that. There are these cages, this hot pepper spray, all kinds of things you could try. Next time, call me. You'll have plump, juicy tomatoes in no time."

"You're on."

What was going on here? The single people Mateo knew had led him to believe that the last decade-plus of flirtation all happened online, through apps and filtered selfies and suggestive texts. But apparently it also still happened in the way Mateo remembered it, through meaningless conversation and wry facial expressions and leaning close enough to catch a whiff of one another's scent. Oh, and alcohol. Mateo decided to go for it: "Care for a tequila shot?"

"Oh sure. If Thursday night is for anything, it's shots."

Before he knew it, they were singing along to that Taylor Swift song "You need to calm down." It was the kind of ubiquitous hit Mickey would never allow in her gym, the kind Mateo secretly enjoyed. He thought maybe this was the moment to reveal that he was married but open—but how? He leaned in to Olivia's ear, figuring he'd wing it with an explanation; but just then, she turned her head and kissed him. Just a peck. He hesitated for a moment, then kissed her back. She went deeper, practically enveloping him with her mouth, and Mateo was all in. When she cradled his face, her fingers were surprisingly rough. "Sorry, gardening hands," she said, her tongue an inch from his mouth. He wanted to reply, *Um, could you please run those calloused fingers all down my body?* But he was shy.

The more they kissed, the more ravenous Mateo felt. For a flash, he thought of Nathan with defiance—if only his friend could see him now. He came up for air long enough to ask, "Should we go back to your place?" He felt a little creepy, asking to accompany a woman he barely knew to her home. But before he could backtrack and apologize, Olivia was grabbing her coat.

The cold air was a slap to Mateo's face, a wake-up call. He felt a surge of panic. Who was this stranger holding his hand, whose head barely reached his shoulders despite her heels, who was leaning into him and suggesting they get a cab considering all the drinks? The drinks, the drinks ... it seemed like another person had been the one back at the bar boozing and flirting with this person whose last name he didn't even know. Mateo felt stone-cold sober. He was about to say so, when he felt the vibrations of a text in his pocket.

"I'M IN! UCLA BABY, HERE I COME!"

Melody! His daughter had gotten into her top pick for college, which was all the way on the other side of the country. Mateo felt a pang distinct from all the pangs he'd been feeling for the past hour: he was proud, heartbroken, overjoyed. His Mel!

He turned to Olivia. "I'm so sorry, but I need a raincheck. My daughter just got into college, and I've got to go congratulate her in person. I can drop you home or call you a cab."

"You have a daughter old enough to go to college?"

"Her name's Mel. Also, I'm married. But we're open. I would never cheat on Mickey. That's my wife. So, if you want to get together another time, or—"

"Forget it." She was already walking away, and Mateo thought he heard her mutter "asshole." Was he an asshole for being honest about his relationship status, and for wanting to go hug his college-bound daughter? Mateo didn't know, but he was sort of relieved Mel had given him an out. He wasn't sure he would've been able to go through with it.

He sped the whole way home, so excited to see the look on his daughter's face, to tell her how proud of her he was.

CHAPTER 30

Mickey and Mateo

They pulled into the driveway one right after the other. They bolted out of their cars, and Mateo gathered Mickey into a hug.

"She did it," he said.

"She did it, and we did it," Mickey replied. "We're quite the team." When he drew back, he saw the tears in her eyes and wiped them away.

"The best team," he said.

Inside, they called out to Mel. They were met by silence.

It occurred to them simultaneously that they had the scent of other people in their hair and on their skin.

"It's been a long day," said Mickey. "Let's hit the shower, then we can celebrate."

"I was going to say the same. Ice cream sundaes?"

"And we can pop some bubbly, treat the girl to a glass."

But Mel's room was empty. Mateo texted her, and she wrote back that she was out with her friends, obviously.

Mickey laughed. "We both assumed she'd been sitting at home waiting for us. Man, I feel a hundred years old."

"Oh, come on, you're my hot, sexy wife." Mateo tugged her toward him again, and detected something musky. He wondered if she could smell Olivia on him, and if it might actually be a turn-on.

Under the twin showerheads, washing off their respective evenings, Mateo said, "We could have another kid, you know. People our age still have babies."

"Right when we're almost home-free? Sorry, that ship has sailed."

Mateo hadn't really been serious—the idea just popped into his head, one possibility in a life that suddenly seemed full of them. But when Mickey rejected it out of hand, he felt a surge of nostalgia for the baby years, Mel at her mother's breast, the onesies and the bottles, the cuddles and the tantrums.

"Oh, come on." He joined his wife under her stream. "Let's make ourselves a baby."

Mickey was on the pill—had been for years, but it was fun to fantasize. They kept up the act until they were both satisfied.

When Mel came home a couple of hours later, she found her parents asleep on the living room couch, limbs pretzeled together.

"Ew, guys."

Her voice startled both of them awake. Mickey leapt up and embraced her daughter. "Mel, the star, the college co-ed!"

Mateo wrapped his arms around the two of them. "We knew you could do it."

They attacked their daughter with kisses, until she wriggled away. "I get it, you guys love me. Okay, enough!"

Mickey held up her hands in defense. "Okay, enough."

"You know we're never going to let you leave us, right?" Mateo said.

Mel rolled her eyes and headed for the stairs, but it was obvious that she was smiling.

Mickey called after her, "You reek of alcohol, young lady."

Mel didn't even look back as she raised her middle finger.

"What a lovely girl," Mateo said, beaming ironically at his wife.

"The loveliest." Mickey dropped her head onto his shoulder, and they retired up to bed.

CHAPTER 31

Amy

"High, high, higher."

Amy's arms were starting to ache from pushing Phoebe on the swing. While Finn was content with Abe's half-hearted shoves on the next swing over, his sister could not be satisfied. Amy made a valiant effort to arc the girl farther up into the air, vaguely worrying she might propel the swing vertical and send Phoebe plummeting to the concrete. Actual parents all must know whether that kind of thing was possible.

"Together, both same!" Finn was thrilled to be moving back and forth in sync with his sister. Amy remembered from her own childhood that this turn of events meant you were destined to marry and have each other's babies. She recalled one boy who, when he'd been caught in synch with Amy, screamed in disgust, made the slant-eyed gesture, and leapt off the swing; mortified, Amy had avoided the swings forever after. But Phoebe was nonplussed; she wanted to go higher still. Amy pushed with all her might and the girl went soaring.

How little it took to get these kids squealing with glee. Amy couldn't recall the last time she felt such simple satisfaction. Their delight was contagious, but Amy stifled her smile when she caught Abe watching her, wearing his meaningful look. He kept doing that: Every time she started having fun with the kids, he'd draw attention to it and spoil it for her. She wanted to tell him to quit it, but didn't want to ruin the mood.

"Who's up for the slide?" Amy hollered, arms pulsing with fatigue.

The twins ran like maniacs to the play structure, and of course, one tripped. Phoebe landed hard, palms to the concrete. At first, there was that long, calm-before-the-storm moment when the girl's face scrunched up silently. Amy wished to pause time and flee before the inevitable crying came. But she was the grown-up, the one in charge. As overjoyed as Phoebe had been two minutes earlier, now she was wailing in misery. Was this what it was to parent a toddler? A rollercoaster of emotion, always moments from the next big drop? They'd only been babysitting for an hour, and Amy was already spent.

But here was Phoebe, sobs now subdued, extending her arms to Amy. Amy opened her own arms and the girl clung for comfort. The crying turned to blubbering and finally a sigh. Then Phoebe lifted her head from Amy's chest and blinked up at her, cheeks tear-stained. "I'm okay," she announced. Ten seconds later, she was off and running to join her brother on the slide.

Huh. Who knew with these funny little creatures? Amy barked out a laugh. Abe caught her eye, and there was that annoying look again. She averted her gaze.

Amy and Abe stood observing the kids' loop: they scaled the steps, jumped twice at the top, slid down, and ran back to the steps, on repeat. Amy didn't know whether she was supposed to intervene to discipline Finn when he cut off another boy in line or to spot Phoebe when she seemed on the verge of falling.

She looked around at the other adults, presumably all parents plus a few gray-haired, hunched-over ones who must've been grand-parents. Almost everyone was white, save one other Asian woman and a Black couple. They all seemed at home here. Most seemed to know each other, too, calling out greetings as they spotted a new arrival. They gathered in little pockets of conversation, chatting easily while their kids played. They all knew how to do this.

No one addressed Amy or even smiled in her direction. It made her feel awkward, like she was wearing a sign that read "non-parent." She was returned to her childhood isolation, always aware of her dif-ference. No one spoke to Abe either, which made Amy feel even more alone, like they were two outcasts banded together. But Abe didn't seem to mind; he was whistling in appreciation of Phoebe's success-ful jump off a step. Amy wondered if her husband had ever felt uncomfortable in his skin or surroundings.

"I'll be right back," she said, and headed to the bathroom. She didn't really have to pee. She just needed a breather from the scene. When she squatted on the toilet, she found herself murmuring a prayer before pulling down her pants. But nope, her panties were still clear. Her period always came like clockwork, and now she was two weeks late. She felt a queasy twisting in her gut.

This was a thing, apparently, or at least an urban legend. People had talked about it in the infertility group, how a friend or a sister-in-law or a friend of a friend had started the adoption process and then, *boom!*, they were pregnant. Something about taking the pres-sure off being the key to making it happen, like how people always said you'd find love when you stopped looking for it. Well, Amy called bullshit. That was just another way for society to make women feel bad for knowing what they wanted and working to achieve it. Then again, Amy and Abe had stopped tracking her cycle down to the hour and their sex life had felt easier as a result—less goal-oriented. Amy hugged herself and tried to intuit some kind of sign. She didn't *feel* pregnant. Then again, she had no idea what pregnancy would feel like, despite all she'd read. She pulled up her pants, washed her hands, and returned to the playground, anxious to forget about the last five minutes.

She found Abe lifting the twins one by one to the water fountain. When it was Phoebe's turn, she stuck her fingers in the water and sprayed Abe, giggling hysterically. Abe flicked the water back at Phoebe, and soon they were all laughing. Throwing herself back into this would be a good distraction, Amy hoped. She ran up to the group, lifted Finn in the air, and yelled, "Who wants pizza?"

CHAPTER 32
Louisa

Louisa needed to spend her Sunday organizing the logistics of the state practice tests. She assumed she could drop the kids off with Nathan. But when she called to set up a plan, he said he was sorry but he and Mona had a weekend yoga retreat. No offer to cancel, and Louisa couldn't bring herself to ask. So, when Abe generously offered to help with the tests, Louisa asked if he might help with childcare instead. Before she'd finished her sentence, he answered, "Absolutely, you can count on Amy and me." Louisa had the best friends.

Sundays had always looked like this, in a way. From her first year of teaching, Louisa had spent half her weekend hunched over a cup of coffee plus student papers and lesson plans. Once she was caffeinated and in the zone, she could work for hours without break. Nathan would check in on her occasionally, bringing a snack or reminding her to stretch her legs. Sometimes he'd sit with her, along with his own students' papers or a paperback. When she'd finally declare her work done, the two of them would go out for a drink and a few rounds of Boggle, then grab tacos on their way home. They kept it up after having kids, only the drinks and Boggle happened in their living room and the tacos were ordered in. Louisa knew lots of people spent their Sundays brunching or binge-watching TV, but she hadn't known anything different than this ritual. It was cozy and predictable, and made her feel both productive and protected.

Louisa still spent her Sundays working, at least when she could get childcare or during the kids' naps, but it didn't have the same homey feel. No one came to check in on her or keep her company. She had to make her own snacks and remind herself to take breaks. She still finished the day with a drink and tacos, but you couldn't play Boggle by yourself. It made Louisa feel sorry for herself.

Having finished the spreadsheet assigning kids and proctors to classrooms for their tests, Louisa went to prepare a plate of nachos—the ultimate self-pity food. As she ate, she reminded herself that her situation wasn't so dire. She still had cheese melted over chips, after all. Where Nathan was, such indulgences were likely verboten in favor of steamed vegetables and quinoa (never mind that he had a young and energetic girlfriend to indulge in, too). A blob of cheese dropped onto Louisa's phone. It illuminated the screen and revealed a text from DanTheMan78, a guy she must've swiped right on in her dating app. "Happy Sunday ... hows it going??"

A pointless ellipsis. No apostrophe. The stupid double question mark that had become trendy for some reason. And yet, here was someone checking in on her, curious about how she was. Louisa revisited DanTheMan78's profile and found kind eyes and good teeth. Oh, what the hell, she'd write back. "Dandy. Eating nachos, working." She thought for a moment, then erased "working," and added "Hungry?" She cringed at herself, but pressed send as if on a dare.

His response popped up almost immediately. "Starving. Tho Ive got more of a sweet tooth."

Louisa was grinning. This was so silly. It was probably the kind of thing River Mill students texted each other all day long under their desks, albeit with more explicit language. But what was she supposed to do? You didn't grow out of flirting and into something more mature and dignified—or maybe some people did, but Louisa didn't know the first thing about those advanced tactics. Dating, alas, was the great leveler. She was pondering whether she was really up for diving back into it, when DanTheMan78 texted, "Drinks this week?"

Before she could second-guess herself, she typed, "My ex has the kids on Thursday," then erased it and typed, "Thursday?"

"Its a date!!" he replied.

It was a date. *Holy shit.*

———

Finn and Phoebe stormed through the front door, pounced onto the couch, and burrowed into both sides of their mother, where they talked over each other to catch her up on their big day out with Uncle Abe and Aunt Amy. Louisa caught snippets: playground, pizza, something about a dog with a cone around its neck, and the revelation that Amy's underwear had purple polka-dots.

Amy sunk into the armchair across from Louisa. "It's true. Phoebe was very curious."

"I'll take your word for it. You look like you could use a drink."

"Yes, please."

But Louisa's kids had her pegged to the couch cushion. "Abe, would you grab the cabernet and some glasses?"

"Sure. Or how about I handle bedtime for these two monsters, and you two handle drinks?"

Louisa felt a swell of love for Abe. "You, my friend, are an angel sent from heaven."

He fluttered his arms like wings. "Come on, kiddos, let's get your butts upstairs." The mention of butts sent Finn into hysterics. "Two books each and if you're super-duper-good you can pick out a third. Go on, kiss your mom goodnight."

Sloppy kisses landed on Louisa's cheeks, then she watched her kids chase Abe up the stairs. She turned to Amy. "He's a natural."

"I know."

Her tone surprised Louisa: stark, a little sad. Louisa was closer to Abe than Amy; Abe was one of her oldest friends, and they'd come up together as teachers. She'd always felt that put some distance between her and Amy, to be so tight with her husband. Although if Amy had once felt threatened by Louisa, surely that must've disappeared in the wake of her recent life implosion. Seriously, she was sitting there in stained sweatpants and a River Mill class t-shirt so old that the seniors it honored were already well into their twenties. She touched Amy's forearm. "Are you okay?" She could tell Amy was going to reply with a routine "Of course," so she intercepted it, "I mean, really? What's going on with you?"

Amy swallowed hard. "Can I ask you a question?"

"Sure. Anything."

"How did you know you wanted to be a mother?"

"Wow, that's a toughie. Well, I guess I went from barely thinking about it to thinking about it more and more. But by then, some other stuff was going on"—Louisa thought of Nathan mourning his parents—"and it took a while to make it happen."

"Were you scared when you were pregnant? Were you worried you'd made a mistake?"

"Sure. I think every pregnant woman—and, uh, every prospective mother" (Louisa was aware that Amy's path to parenthood wouldn't match her own) "feels that way some of the time. There's really no way to prepare for what's coming."

"Right!" Amy grew animated. "That's what seems so crazy to me. You can't know what it's like to be a parent before you do it, and then there's no turning back. It's like the only decision in life where you can't change your mind and reverse course. With everything else, you can try it and if it's not for you, you can say 'never mind' and move on—to another career, place to live, relationship. Sorry."

"It's fine."

"But with a kid you're stuck—and with this impossibly giant task of raising a human being."

Louisa had never considered parenthood that way. "I think it's really responsible of you to be thinking about all of this now.

I guarantee you many people don't. Nathan and I talked about what a big change it would be, but that was about it. And look at Mickey and Mateo. Parenthood hit them out of nowhere, and here they are, alive to tell the tale."

"Yeah." But Amy didn't sound convinced. "It's just, lately when I think about it, it's too—I don't know ..." She drifted off.

Louisa wondered if her friend was seeking a different kind of assurance. "Listen, I know how much Abe wants to be a father. He's been talking about it since we were basically kids ourselves. And I know as his wife, you're supposed to be so grateful to have a husband like him, such great dad material and so enthusiastic about it. But it's a lot of pressure."

"It sure is." Amy was looking at her like a sad puppy.

Louisa felt she was voicing something Amy needed to hear, so she kept going. "You know, you don't have to want a baby. Who ever said that everyone should want the same things, that all women should want to have babies? That's ludicrous. I know you've already jumped through so many hoops for the adoption, so maybe it feels like it's too late to turn back. But it's not."

Amy shook her head, and tears started streaming down her face.

"Amy, listen to me. Abe loves you and he will understand."

Just then Abe appeared in the room. "I'll understand what?"

Amy looked like she'd been caught. She wiped away her tears. Louisa jumped in with, "That your wife isn't ready to go home. She needs some girl time with me tonight. Right?" Amy's nod was barely detectible. "I'll call her a car later."

Abe seemed skeptical, but Louisa shot him a look like, please, go along with this.

Abe kissed his wife delicately on both cheeks. Louisa loved how much Abe loved Amy, even if she couldn't help thinking that Nathan had never once kissed her like that. "You sure, honey? You must be wiped after today, and we've got work tomorrow. Bauer, your kids are gems, but they're also a handful."

Again, Louisa answered on Amy's behalf. "It's the parent second-wind syndrome. Whenever I spend a full day with my kids, at about four p.m. I'm swearing up and down I'll be in bed by nine. But when they finally go to bed, all I want is time to myself, so I end up staying up till midnight doing who knows what."

Abe still appeared concerned, but he gave in. "All right. I love you, Ames. Love you too, Bauer." Amy blew him kisses as Louisa shooed him out the door.

She hoped they'd pick up right where they left off, that Amy would share more about her ambivalence about the adoption, and her fears about motherhood. Louisa had never heard her friend open up like this before, and she thought it would be good for her. She was also genuinely curious about how being adopted herself would affect Amy's feelings about adopting.

But instead, Amy suggested they watch a movie. Louisa let her pick, and they ended up watching that kooky old comedy *Overboard*, which Louisa hadn't seen in years. She was enjoying it until the story specifics came back to her, that Shelley Long's character gets amnesia and ends up duped into mothering a pack of boys. Had Amy remembered the plot when she picked the movie, and what was she thinking now? But a glance at Louisa's side revealed that Amy had drifted off; she was sleeping soundly. She didn't even wake up when Louisa cried her way through the sappy ending.

It was the second time in two weeks a visitor had passed out on Louisa's couch, but unlike with Nathan, it felt nice to have Amy there, to not be the only adult on the premises. It was like hosting a grown-up sleepover.

As Louisa draped a blanket over her friend, she had an idea: she found the letter of recommendation she'd written for the adoption agency, printed out a copy, and tucked it into Amy's purse.

CHAPTER 33
Mona

Mona made eye contact with each person who entered the studio, reassuring them with her gaze that she would accept them for whoever they were, wherever they were in this moment. For the next ninety minutes, they would all be here together sharing an experience, which she considered sacred. Each new face met Mona's welcome with their own openhearted greeting. This was the value of a retreat: the freshness, the opportunity to shake things up. In fact, that's what Mona planned to focus on during her Dharma talk. When everyone had settled into sukhasana poses, open palms resting on crossed legs, Mona straightened her spine and began.

"It's human nature to crave consistency and cling to stability, to find comfort in routine." She listened to her voice echoing through the room. "Most of us believe we need these things. And yet, once we've got them, we often sense that something's still missing. Personally, when everything feels too easy and familiar to me, I start to feel it as aches and pains in my body. I think of them like little red flags warning me to make a change. Like when you've been sitting for too long and your foot falls asleep. You've got to get up and move!

"Because consider this possibility: maybe we don't actually know what serves us. Maybe what we need isn't what we think we need. Is it possible that the things we claim we want—familiarity, stability—come from a place of fear rather than desire? And what is there to be scared of? Well, fear of loneliness, for one. And fear of who we are if we're not surrounded by our routine cast of characters and settings and stuff, all of the things that we believe define us. But, instead of giving in to that fear, what if we conjured up the courage to face it? What if we opened our hearts and challenged ourselves to break out of our routines, to shake off the familiar, to explore new possibilities and people and ways of being? What if we embraced our inner strength and had faith in our resilience that's far more powerful than we even know?"

She paused. "Everyone please close your eyes and imagine it: What might your new story be, where might you go, who might you become?"

Mona counted her inhales and exhales as she pictured her own story: her autopilot college life disrupted by the pain in her back, followed by her encounter with Nate that changed everything. Now they'd arrived at a new crossroads: Nate had lost his job and Mona was on the brink of graduating. And once again her body was alerting her that something wasn't right. Perched on her blanket stack, Mona pondered the questions she'd asked of the yogis: *What might her new story be? Where might she go? Who might she become?* She didn't have answers at the moment, which was an intriguing place to be. She was full of potential, open to all paths.

She inhaled deeply and addressed the group. "I promise you, a freer, more expansive, more beautiful version of yourself is possible. Now, please join me in three oms."

The room filled with voices, and Mona felt the sounds vibrate through her bones long after they'd gone quiet. She'd been studying yoga for years, but it was Nate who'd encouraged her to apply to teach here, at her first retreat; when she'd been accepted, she basked in the pride beaming from his smile. For the next hour and a half, Mona gave instructions and watched the bodies blossom and flow. She weaved in and out of the rows, placing a hand here and redirecting a limb there, feeling the heat between herself and the person she was touching. It was like magic—how Mona would sit alone scribbling asanas in her notebook, then she'd voice the scribbles aloud in class and they'd transform into this beautiful cascade of movement.

This was yoga.

Mona sealed the practice just as she'd started it, making eye contact with everyone present. The people seemed changed: calmer or more joyful or just different, ninety minutes removed from whoever they'd been when they walked in. Mona herself felt a little lighter, too.

Five minutes after class, just one person was left in the back, a man taking his time to roll up his mat. Mona was gathering her things, thinking ahead to lunch with Nate, followed by a walking mindfulness seminar, then two more vinyasa classes to teach in the afternoon. She was caught off guard when the man appeared inches from her face.

"You," he spat, so close she could smell the coffee on his breath. All the muscles she'd just spent ninety minutes loosening tensed up. "I could've sworn I knew you, but I didn't figure out how until halfway through that bullshit speech about breaking up routines."

Mona searched his face and realized she recognized him, too: he'd been a staple of the campus party circuit back when she, too, was on that scene. They'd never had a conversation, and she was surprised by the nasal whine of his voice.

"Breaking up families is more like it. Your powers of rationalization are quite impressive. You ruined my favorite professor's life, and you're sitting around bragging about it like you solved some big life mystery. Totally shameless."

Before Mona could respond, he was through the door, yelling "Namaste" back at her. Mona took a breath. She knew this was how some people saw her. She'd been told so, and in much harsher terms: she'd be walking across campus, minding her own business, when suddenly she'd be hit by a "homewrecker bitch" or "dirty ho," flung from the mouths of women as often as men. She would always experience a moment of surprise—like, were they really spewing those insults at *her*? Then she'd do her best to let it go. She never told Nate, or anyone else.

Even more confounding were the looks of pity. These all came from women. The ones who believed Mona had been seduced by a powerful older man and pressured into a relationship against her will. Even some of her friends reacted like she'd been taken advantage of when she finally revealed the identity of her mystery boyfriend; she'd stopped hanging out with them. It made her furious. She wasn't some poor, helpless victim. Even the thought of it was offensive to all the real victims out there.

Yes, technically Nate had left his wife to be with her, but that was his choice. And Mona believed that if it hadn't been her, it would've been someone else. Strong, happy marriages weren't vulnerable to the lure of "the other woman." And just because Mona was younger than Nate and happened to have taken his class didn't mean she was some naïve child without agency or will; she was twenty-one years old, a full-blown adult. She'd fallen in love with her eyes wide open.

Sure, their situation was complicated. It was messy. There was hurt and loss and a hell of a lot to coordinate, with two little kids in the picture. But change was always hard, and Mona believed growth wasn't possible without growing pains. Despite it all, she and Nate had found a good thing. And although she knew his ex was going through a lot, when Mona had gone to her house that night to collect a passed-out, post-getting-canned Nate, Louisa had seemed relieved to be rid of him. Nate had suggested as much before—that Louisa was likely over the marriage, too, but just hadn't gotten up the courage to call it quits. Mona had nearly blurted to her that night, "See? Isn't this better for everyone?" though she hadn't wanted to come off as flippant.

Mona herself had grown up in a stable two-parent home, the kind everyone was always holding up as the gold standard; and it had been miserable. Her parents, still together today, were the definition of routine. It never would've occurred to them to consider whether they were actually happy together, just as it never would've occurred to them to try a toothpaste different from the Crest they'd been using for decades. They lived their lives on autopilot, which was no life at all, if you asked Mona. Life was change; evolution was key to growth.

Mona was still pondering all this as she walked back to the studio apartment that was hers and Nate's for the weekend. She set aside the unpleasant encounter, and focused on how she was feeling strong from the yoga and clear-headed from the crisp spring air. The sun was out, and she was optimistic about the day, excited for lunch with her beau.

Until, that is, she entered their studio and was hit by its staleness. The only light came from the glow of a laptop screen, which illuminated Nate's grimace. He was still in the clothes he'd slept in, and when Mona leaned down to kiss him, it was clear he hadn't yet brushed his teeth.

"Hey," she said.

Nate didn't look up. "I might as well be blasting my résumé into a black hole. I applied to something like thirty jobs this week, and guess how many I've heard back from? Zero."

"I'm sorry, babe." Mona plopped onto the bed, feeling deflated. She'd imagined this retreat would be a literal retreat from Nate's unemployment, a break from this very conversation. She'd hoped Nate would get motivated to join the sunrise joggers, or attend the morning tea and Buddhism lecture. But no, he'd stayed in one spot, stewing. She knew he wouldn't ask about her yoga class; he was clearly too deep in his own head. Well, Mona could help with that, at least. She gave a little tug to the elastic of his boxers.

Nate brushed her off. "Sorry, Mona, I'm not in the mood."

The words stung. He'd never not been in the mood before.

He stood up and started pacing. "I'm trying to keep up on it all—our rent and my share of the house, plus daycare for the kids. But the truth is, I can't make the numbers work. So, I met with a divorce lawyer—"

"Wait, what?" Mona's jaw tightened. "I thought you guys were planning to do mediation."

"We were. But it's a whole other story now that I've lost my job. Considering the circumstances, the lawyer thought I could get a good chunk of alimony, and maybe child support, too."

"Hold on, so Louisa would be paying *you*? Even though you're the one who left, and the kids are still living mostly with her?"

Nate shot her a harsh look, like, *whose side are you on?* then looked away, maybe in shame. "Not *paying* me. Providing me with what I need to live."

"Okay." Though Mona didn't really get the distinction. She didn't even want to participate in this conversation; she probably shouldn't have opened her mouth. She hadn't really believed in marriage before dating Nate, but now she felt even more convinced: the proceedings that went along with ending one were truly ugly. She thought about Louisa, getting served divorce papers that demanded she pay up. It made Mona cringe, regardless of the fact that she loved the guy who planned to serve the papers.

You ruined my professor's life. The words returned to her, an echo in her head. "If this is just about money, I can get another job and pitch in more with our rent. My semester is so light, and I'll be graduating soon anyway."

It was like Nate barely heard her. "I'm not trying to be a dick here. It's just, Louisa is the one earning money. Meanwhile, I've had that opportunity taken away from me. I'm out of options. I just don't know what to do." He dropped his head into his hands and groaned, like he could barely take his own despicableness. "Man, I've fucked everything up, haven't I?"

Mona watched her boyfriend start to cry, shoulders heaving. He looked like a little boy, and she felt pity, followed by tenderness. She placed a hand on the back of his neck. She believed in the healing power of touch; it had worked so well for her. But Nate flinched: he didn't want her comfort. She considered what he'd said, that he'd fucked *everything* up—did everything include her? Mona felt helpless and flimsy, in way over her head. For the first time, she felt the decades gaping between Nate and her.

They clearly both needed a reset. So, she kissed the top of Nate's head and told him she'd catch up with him later. Then she left for lunch, looking forward to conversation that would not involve words like "divorce lawyer" and "alimony." A little guiltily, she forced her boyfriend from her mind, and soon found herself daydreaming of a faraway place—palm trees, sunshine, the soothing sounds of the ocean's rhythm.

CHAPTER 34

Amy

Lately, Amy had been waking up feeling like there were too many hours in the day ahead of her. By the time she got to the office she was ready to crawl back into bed. She spent her mornings meandering around the internet, falling for clickbait, then losing interest as soon as each new tab loaded.

Inevitably, she'd find herself at the adoption site. Their profile had been posted last week. Half the time she'd scroll right past it, then have to backtrack, because the photo, which Abe had hired a photographer to shoot, looked nothing like them. Amy had wanted to use one of the dozens of snapshots they'd taken on their vacations: she and Abe bathed in Greece's golden hour light, the whitewashed landscape of Oia glittering behind them; or the two of them huddled on a dusty Kenyan road mere feet from a herd of zebras; or, if Abe felt an international image was too flashy, the shot of them at the peak of local Mount Greylock, faces glowing, surrounded by the foggy purple vista. In all those pictures, Amy felt like the true version of herself, as cheesy as that sounded. Travel always did that to her: Amy felt most at ease when everything around her was different and new. Plus, in the photos, Abe's and her love was as obvious as if it'd been flashing in neon letters.

But Abe had a very particular idea of how to project their prospective parenthood: the two of them in turtleneck sweaters, lounging in a strategically chaste embrace on the back patio, "To show that there's room between us for a child!" Abe explained. Amy knew this vision was borne out of Abe's deep longing to be a father, and really, an hour-long photo shoot wasn't much to ask of her. If this was what he needed, then Amy was on board. But it'd been a raw, freezing day, and looking at the photo now, Amy swore she could see the blue sheen lurking under the subtle rose lipstick Abe had encouraged her to wear; her smile was strained. The pose looked like what it was: posed, with Amy leaning awkwardly into Abe's shoulder, her hands placed stiffly on his knee, as he held her in a weird show of wholesomeness. The staginess gave her a strange unease. *Blech*—she closed out of the tab.

"Amy? Got a moment?" Her manager.

Amy guessed what he wanted to talk to her about as she followed him back to his office. Her mind hummed with white noise as he stated the obvious: Her work was slipping, riddled with bugs, and she'd missed her last couple of deadlines. It was the nicest version of this kind of conversation, filled with earnest inquiries about whether something was going on, and how might he help. Amy was honest if vague, saying she'd been distracted by a personal matter. She apologized, swore to do better, and promised she'd come see him if she kept struggling. When he shook her hand, she almost started crying.

Back at her desk, Amy bloomed with shame. Her excellence at work lay at the core of her sense of self. If she no longer had that, what did she have?

Amy felt a rare impulse to call her mother. Adele usually phoned her once a week, on her way home from the animal shelter where she volunteered on Sundays, and they spent a breezy ten minutes catching each other up on their lives. A recent addition was Adele asking delicately about their progress with the adoption. Amy would put her off politely, not just because she didn't feel like discussing it, but also because she sensed her mother asked mostly as a way to share how it'd been for her back when she'd adopted Amy. Even if this was simply Adele's way of trying to connect, it made Amy feel like her own very different experience was somehow lesser than or wrong. It was easier to just not talk about it.

Amy rarely initiated phone calls with her mother, and never in the middle of a workday, which is probably why Adele answered with an alarmed, "Sweetie, is something wrong?" But rather than responding that yes, something *was* wrong, as Amy had planned to do when dialing, the question caused Amy to clam up and snap back with an irritable "Everything's fine, Mom. I was just calling to say hi." She did eventually share that she'd been feeling a little distracted at work.

"That's to be expected, dear. When your dad and I were waiting to get matched with you, I couldn't keep a thought in my head. Abe sent me your profile, by the way—it looks great."

"You don't think the picture is a little odd?" Surely anyone who knew Amy would detect its phoniness.

"Oh, I don't know." Amy could hear amusement in Adele's voice. "It's typical over-achieving Abe, trying to look like Father of the Year. In the ad your dad and I put together, we described ourselves as 'outdoorsy types.' When have you ever seen me enjoying the outdoors? I think I wrote that I loved to cook—ha! You present yourselves however you think would be most appealing to birth moms. You do whatever you can to be a parent."

Amy imagined her birth mother, intrigued by the idea of adoptive parents who would take her daughter out biking and camping. Amy felt a blip of joy realizing that maybe she'd inherited her love of hiking genetically; it certainly didn't come from the people who'd raised her. She'd also never seen her mother turn on the stove. In fact, Adele grumbled every time she was forced to assemble a sandwich; Amy had taken over making her own school lunch by age six.

Adele sighed. "Oh Amy, you're always so hard on yourself. It's fine to have other things on your mind besides your job for a while. Try to give yourself a break."

"Okay, Mom." It was actually what Amy needed to hear. She hung up feeling a little better. But then she thought about how here she was, nearly forty years old and still seeking reassurance from her mother. She didn't know if she was up for that kind of commitment: four decades or more of caring for a child of her own. *Try to give yourself a break,* she reminded herself.

It had become a habit for Amy to take out Louisa's letter of recommendation whenever she needed a self-esteem boost. She re-read her friend's kind words: "Amy is the hardest worker I've ever met. She has a super-human ability to push through challenges and persevere ... everything Amy does is deliberate and purposeful. She's so strong and sure of herself." Who were these words describing? Surely not her. "Amy is kind and caring, always attuned to the needs of others, and generous in every sense. All of these qualities will make her a wonderful mother."

Tearing up a little, Amy re-folded the letter and returned it to her purse.

Her coworkers started filtering out of the office at five-thirty. That was usually Amy's signal to put her head down and grind out another couple of hours; evening was her most productive time. But today, she decided to take her mother's advice. She checked the schedule for FleXX before shutting down her computer: Mickey was always encouraging her to drop by for a class, or "to get your sedentary ass moving," as she put it so delicately. Amy could make it just in time for Jenny Lewis Power Hour, whatever that was.

She texted Mickey that she was coming for the class; her friend replied, "Great! Mel and I will join, too!"

An hour later, Amy was in the thick of it: lunging and squat-jumping and swinging kettlebells to and fro. Man, was she bad at this. Every other move, the instructor appeared at her side to adjust her form. Amy wasn't used to being bad at things. But she also wasn't used to being surrounded by women of all different types—of race, body type, age, and style—and their enthusiastic cheers and claps.

Mickey and her daughter were positioned on either side of her, rewarding her with high-fives after each set of mountain-climbers and (modified) pushups. Melody was a mini-Mickey, in looks and mannerisms and ability to perform dozens of mountain-climbers and (non-modified) pushups.

Wouldn't it be interesting, Amy thought idly, to gaze at your child and see a version of your own face gazing back, to see the results of your genetic code copied onto another person? She'd never had that with her own parents, of course, and she'd let go of that fantasy when her own path to parenthood veered toward adoption. But now, who knew? When Melody and Mickey laughed, the sound was identical, like the ringing of a bell, clear and strong.

It felt good to be breathing hard and exerting herself. The class ended with a plank contest. A team player, Amy participated, though her arms began trembling within seconds and she dropped out. Soon, more and more of the class did, too. As time ticked by, only two plankers remained: Mickey and the woman to her left. They were clearly friends, and they began heckling each other. The woman reached out to try to collapse Mickey's elbow, and Mickey countered by tickling the woman's waist. Two minutes in, then two and a half, and they were both still going strong. Finally, at the three-minute mark, Mickey collapsed to her belly with a groan. The other woman jumped up and pumped her fist.

"All right, Keisha!" Melody shouted.

"Did you let me win?" the woman—Keisha—demanded of Mickey.

"No way, babe. You beat me, fair and square."

Keisha flexed her impressive bicep. "Kiss it."

"Make me." Mickey delivered a tap to Keisha's butt, then scooted out of reach

Ah, thought Amy, *so they're sleeping together.* The sexual charge between them was as obvious as the fatigue settling into Amy's muscles. She glanced at Melody, who was oblivious. She wondered if Mateo knew. For the hundredth time, Amy marveled at the fact that Mickey and Mateo had ended up together; this pairing with Keisha made so much more sense: Mickey with a fellow superwoman.

People lingered after class. It was like happy hour, only with more spandex, and sports drinks instead of booze. Amy was proud of Mickey for having fostered such a friendly, inclusive vibe at her gym, even if she herself was in no mood to mingle. She spotted a boy's face pressed up against the glass of the front door, just as Melody ran outside and dragged him inside.

"No boys allowed," Mickey chastised as she pulled the kid into a hug. "Amy, meet Bryce, Mel's paramour and the only male-identifying person allowed past these doors."

"What about Mateo?" Amy asked.

"Eh, depends on the day," Mickey said. "So, what are you two up to tonight?"

Melody deadpanned, "Shooting up heroin, shoplifting fireworks, maybe getting myself knocked up down by the lake."

"Cool, cool, have fun." Mickey mussed her daughter's hair. "Just be home by ten. It's a school night."

"Bye, Mom."

Bryce waved, and they were gone.

Keisha sighed. "Man, I remember when that girl played with dolls and Play-Doh. Don't know how you handle raising a human. It's too much."

"It's certainly not for everyone," Mickey said. "You, for example, would be a terrible mother."

She was looking at Keisha, and the two of them burst into laughter. But Amy felt a wave of nausea. Suddenly aware of her third-wheel status, she excused herself. Mickey's words remained reverberating around her head.

CHAPTER 35

Louisa

Louisa was flying high. The school had made it through the third day of practice tests with no major hitches. And the kids were with Nathan tonight. So, instead of the usual mad dash to pick them up and hustle them through till bedtime, she made her way home leisurely, poured herself a glass of wine, and spent a relaxing hour preparing for her date. She rescued a red wrap dress from the back of her closet. She'd last worn it pre-motherhood, but dared to venture it suited her even better now, what with her augmented hips and breasts. A swipe of matching lipstick, a quick floofing up of her hair, and she was ready. Or, as ready as she was ever going to be.

It was one of the first warm evenings of spring, so on a whim, Louisa retrieved her bike from the garage. It creaked and squeaked from lack of use, but Louisa didn't mind. Pumping her legs, with the wind in her hair, she felt pretty and carefree. She was enjoying the ride so much that she briefly managed to forget she was headed to the first "first date" she'd been on in nearly two decades. By the time she arrived at the restaurant, exactly on time, it was too late to feel nervous.

DanTheMan78 already had a booth. He stood up and introduced himself as Daniel, offering a hearty handshake. He was shorter than Louisa had expected—an inch or two less than she was—but once she got over that, she was able to take in how attractive he was. Full head of dark wavy hair going salt-and-pepper at the temples; big green eyes; broad, muscular shoulders; and a sexy smile. Louisa was overcome by a powerful mix of desire and terror. She felt competing impulses to throw herself on top of this man and to flee.

"Louisa, hi. Well, you are breathtaking."

Louisa guessed she was supposed to find the line cheesy, but no one had ever called her "breathtaking" before, and DanTheMan78—er, Daniel—sounded genuine. She could barely hear over the pounding of her heartbeat. A deflection of the compliment was on the tip of her tongue, but she swallowed it. She decided to be brave and confident and easygoing. She slid into the booth beside (not across from) Daniel, and said, "Thank you." The whole right side of her body was now touching the whole left side of his body, which to Louisa seemed as outlandish as if they'd found themselves on Mars. And yet, she smiled as if it were the most natural thing in the world.

She felt a little like herself and a little like she was playing a part. She was having fun.

Here's what Louisa learned over the course of two drinks and appetizers: Daniel was originally from Maryland, he'd lived in New York and Chicago, then he'd moved to New England for a job five years ago. He worked in finance, but didn't plan to bore Louisa with the details of his job. He was impressed by Louisa's work, and believed educators were, hands down, the hardest-working people— saints, basically. He'd been married briefly in his twenties but had no children; he adored his nieces. He asked precisely the right number of questions about Louisa's separation (two) before changing the subject to ask about the best place Louisa had traveled (Argentina). He was an incredible kisser.

They didn't stick around for dinner. Daniel lifted Louisa's bike into the trunk of his car—"That is so hot that you biked here," he said—and she climbed into his passenger seat to be whisked away to his condo.

She was giddy with nerves but trying to play it cool. Another version of Louisa might've been wary of sleeping with a man on a first date, but this version was all for it. Leading up to tonight, she might've hoped she'd feel a connection with her date that would be the start of something. But after sliding into the booth next to Daniel and getting a whiff of his musky scent, Louisa realized that the last thing she wanted was to slip back into any semblance of a relationship. How much more freeing it was to make the date itself the main event, with no pressure or expectations for more. Daniel said he hadn't read a book in years, but who cared? Louisa saw absolutely no reason that she shouldn't have sex with him within the hour.

Daniel had clearly been versed in the language of consent. Louisa had attended a River Mill assembly on the subject and found the whole thing inspiring but also mystifying: were you really supposed to ask permission during every step of a hookup? Wouldn't that make the whole thing incredibly awkward? Louisa had left the assembly feeling old and out of touch. But Daniel proved that it wasn't how Louisa had imagined it. It was comforting to stay in the moment, checking in with herself again and again that yes, she did want him to take off her dress, then her bra, then her underwear. Yes, she did want to press her body against his, and kiss him and be kissed. Yes, she did want to be with someone new for the first time in eighteen years.

Eventually the gentle questions and nods tapered off and the two of them were just in it, a pair of bodies moving together. Louisa felt like she'd stepped out of herself and into a shiny new skin. She wasn't a mother or a wife or an administrator or a friend. She was a sexy woman having sex with a sexy man. The thought made her giggle, it was so ridiculous. She felt like a teenager. For a flash she thought of Nathan, how this escape is what he must've found with Mona; so, fine, okay, she got it. Daniel made a noise that Louisa assumed meant he was close, so she let herself go, too. She was left buzzing and glowing. Daniel wrapped his arms around her, and Louisa felt she'd fallen into a fantasy. She let herself fall farther, until she slipped into a deep, restful sleep.

Reality came roaring back at dawn. Louisa's body needed no alarm clock to jolt awake at five forty-five. She took a couple of moments to admire the beautiful naked body of the sleeping man beside her, and to congratulate herself on a mission accomplished. Then she got up and got dressed, humming happily. But when she went outside, she found the trunk of Daniel's car ajar, with nothing inside. Her bike was gone.

The magic of the previous night vanished. *Stupid, stupid,* she berated herself. This was what Louisa got for letting her guard down and allowing herself a night of fun. She took a twelve-hour break from her life and was punished for it. A goddamned stolen bike. Which, by the way, had been expensive—a gift to herself after completing her first year as vice principal—and which she now couldn't afford to replace.

She texted Daniel to alert him of the break-in (he was likely still sleeping), then pulled up the Lyft app and found a car willing to chauffeur her home for sixteen bucks. Reluctantly, she ordered the ride. It wasn't even six a.m. and already she was spending senseless money. *Stupid.* She simply didn't have the wiggle room in her life to be human and err. Louisa sighed, cursing her shitty circumstances. Going forward, she would simply have to be perfect.

CHAPTER 36

Louisa

At least everyone would be in a good mood today, Louisa reasoned. It was the Friday before spring break, the practice tests had wrapped up, and Louisa had organized a teacher appreciation breakfast before school to thank everyone for being good sports about the interruption to their classes. To shake off the frustrations of the early morning, she threw herself into the set-up, hauling huge urns of coffee across the cafeteria and arranging bagel trays at the long table up front.

Abe arrived a few minutes early bearing a big box of pastries, and Louisa realized she was ravenous; the last thing she'd eaten was a couple of spring rolls with Daniel at the restaurant last night, which felt like a week ago. "You're my savior," she told Abe, tearing into a blueberry scone. "Stairwell F later?"

"Sure, sixth period." Abe squeezed her arm, then left to join the other members of his department, who were just trickling in. Louisa understood Abe's tendency to play down their friendship in front of other teachers; she was their boss, after all.

But Louisa was forever fighting the boss persona, always trying to distance herself from the rest of the administration—Poolehauzer and Chad Mack, the dynamic duo—and align herself with the teachers, to let them know she was still one of them at heart. She smiled warmly as the faculty streamed in, offering chipper greetings as they collected their coffee and bagels. They arranged themselves around the tables, chatting with vigor, enjoying the rare treat of socializing with fellow adults in the building. Standing by the buffet, Louisa watched them a little longingly, feeling abandoned at her post. She took a second pastry.

Poolehauzer had a knack for showing up to school events just when all the work had wrapped up. When he finally sauntered in, Louisa had just cleaned up the last of the stray coffee stirrers and balled-up napkins. "Grab me a coffee, will you? Milk and sugar, por favor."

It was just because she was right next to the urn, Louisa told herself. If Chad Mack had been standing here, Dr. P would've asked the same thing of him. Speaking of which, where was the dean? "Is Chad on his way?"

"Mr. Mack is just finishing running the practice tests through the scanners." Poolehauzer indicated the coffee stirrers, and Louisa handed him one. "He'll be down momentarily with the results."

"The results, already?" A foreboding pressure materialized in Louisa's chest.

"You know Mr. Mack, always the go-getter. He pulled an all-nighter to get it done." Louisa resisted rolling her eyes. "With the whole faculty here now, it's a great opportunity to share the data and fill them in on next steps for test prep."

The pressure spread up Louisa's throat. "I was thinking we'd give them a break," she said. "Let them enjoy their week off before diving back into the testing stuff. This is a teacher appreciation breakfast, after all."

"Ms. Bauer, what better way to show appreciation for our teachers than by giving them the information and tools they need to prepare their students for success?" He said it like it was obvious.

Louisa couldn't let it go. "It's just, we'd never hijack a pep rally to remind students to study for the SATs, you know?"

"*Hijack*, Ms. Bauer?" Dr. P's laugh was mirthless. "There's no need to be so dramatic." He cast an amused glance at Chad Mack, who'd appeared at his side, as if summoned by telepathy.

The dean attempted to mirror his boss' amusement, but Louisa saw through it to his exhaustion: dark bags hung under his eyes. How funny to think that while she'd been communing in bed with a near-stranger, Chad Mack had been in his office, hunched over the Scantron machine feeding in answer sheet after answer sheet. But her amusement was short-lived.

"Bad news, team," said Chad. "Scores are down from last year, one to two percent across all subjects. That's six to seven percent lower than where we need to be."

Both men turned to Louisa—or more accurately, turned *on* her. "This is unacceptable," Poolehauzer said, nostrils flaring. "All curriculum is hereby suspended for test prep intensive."

"But you can't just—"

"Ms. Bauer," he snapped. "Last time I checked, I'm the principal of this school. Mr. Mack, inform the masses."

Chad nodded and approached the microphone. "Attention, esteemed faculty," Louisa heard patched through the speakers. It was the robotic monotone Mack used for public speaking; he must've thought it sounded professional.

"Principal Poolehauzer and the River Mill administration planned this breakfast to express our deepest gratitude and sincerest appreciation for all of you, and for your tireless efforts to prepare our students to achieve their biggest, boldest dreams." If he uttered one more superlative, Louisa would scream. "On that note, we have the results of this week's practice tests. Here to share the numbers along with some important news regarding the lead-up to the real tests next month is our hardworking and diligent vice principal, our very own Ms. Bauer. Give it up for Ms. Bauer!"

Chad's claps into the microphone were like punches to Louisa's eardrums. The teachers joined in with tepid applause, and Chad stepped back from the mic.

Louisa was furious. She fantasized about shooting lasers from her eyeballs into the dean's, but he avoided eye contact, smiling blithely into the middle distance. It was one thing for Mack to make her deliver the bad news, but quite another for him to set her up as if she weren't about to rain on everyone's parade and spring break and future month of teaching. She had no choice but to step up to the mic. She winced at the sound of her inhale reverberating through the cafeteria.

She did her best, sandwiching the test results and the mandate for amped-up test prep between remarks about how much the faculty was valued and well wishes for a restful spring break. But the teachers weren't idiots—they understood the bait-and-switch, how their curriculum was being chucked in favor of multiple-choice sets. A range of emotions flashed across their faces: bitterness, frustration, disdain, worry, and resignation. All of it was directed at Louisa. Somehow these teachers, who knew the brutality of standing before a class of listless or sneering faces, didn't realize that their own expressions were just as obvious to a speaker standing before them— or they simply didn't care. Louisa didn't dare to seek out Abe's face in the crowd.

She handed the microphone back to Chad. He resumed his monotone, assuring the teachers that they'd all receive the test results specific to their subjects, and that detailed test-prep plans would be in their mailboxes when they returned from break. Louisa knew who would be responsible for creating those plans. She excused herself and marched to the faculty bathroom.

She was sitting in a stall, mulling over the phrase, "Don't shoot the messenger," when she heard two sets of footsteps on the tile floor. She immediately recognized the voice of Meredith Pritchett, world history teacher: "The way they talk to us, it's like our idiot president. Make River Mill great again!"

Louisa felt her throat constrict.

"Oh, it wasn't that bad," the other one said, a thin soprano that

Louisa couldn't identify.

"That's just because you're new here." *Ah, right*—Kendra Grant. "You'll see how it is soon enough."

"But isn't state testing just part of the deal?" Kendra asked. "The students didn't do well, so it makes sense that the admins are in panic mode."

Meredith sighed. "All I'm saying is, those people are not on your side—Ms. Bauer especially. At least the men don't pretend they care before stabbing you in the back. Ms. Bauer's really a heartless you-know-what. Watch out for her."

"Huh," Kendra replied. "Well, thanks for the advice."

The taps turned on, drowning out whatever remained of the conversation. Louisa sat there stunned. She'd always been perfectly pleasant to Meredith Pritchett, whom she judged to be an adequate if uninspired teacher. Her comments weren't just mean, they were unfair, plus downright sexist. Louisa flushed twice, hoping the teacher would hear that she'd been overheard and feel chastened. Though a lot of good that would do.

How to avoid slipping into despair? If any of Abe's pastries were left, at least Louisa could soothe her emotions with food. After that, she'd hole up in her office to avoid everyone and everything, the exact behavior expected of a heartless you-know-what. Of course, she knew that within moments either Tweedle Dee or Tweedle Dum-Dum would appear to let her know she'd be spending her spring break on test prep plans for the whole faculty. And she better do a damn good job of it, too.

CHAPTER 37
Louisa

Sixth period, finally. Louisa climbed Stairwell F to the roof, where she found Abe hunched over a thermos and a squat paper cup. "Hey Jones."

"Good afternoon, cumulus cloud." It really was a storybook sky, with big, cottony clouds set against a sheet of turquoise. It always amazed Louisa to escape the school's stale air and fluorescent lighting and discover a beautiful day outside. "How much would you like a latte?" Abe asked. "A little or a lot-tay?"

Louisa rolled her eyes. "The latter."

"I figured." He poured her a cup.

She sat down next to him, pulling her knees up to her chest. "So, how bad was that this morning?" she asked. "A. Par for the course. B. Grading a hundred essays on a Saturday bad. C. The teachers are planning a *coup d'etat*. D. Poolehauzer, Mack, and I will be burned at the stake by eighth period."

Abe snorted in laughter. "Can I plead the fifth?"

"Fine. But believe me, all that nonsense was sprung on me last minute, too. I was just following orders."

Abe raised his eyebrows. "You realize I teach the Nuremberg trials, right? That defense doesn't exactly fly."

"Are you seriously equating me at that assembly with the Nazis?"

"Oh Bauer, I'm just pulling your chain. You are nothing like the Nazis." He patted her arm, mock-comforting.

"Well, I overheard Meredith Pritchett call me a heartless you-know-what in the bathroom."

"A heartless what?"

"I dunno—bitch? Worse? She literally said 'you-know-what.' I guess you're just supposed to know what."

Abe snorted. "That woman has the imagination of a slab of wood. Don't let it get to you."

Louisa wasn't appeased. "I became an administrator to be a voice for the teachers, to do good, you know?" Abe nodded; he'd heard a hundred versions of this from her. "I think of myself as a benevolent boss, not a heartless you-know-what. It wasn't my call to raise expectations on the state tests or to tie school funding to the results. On the one hand, Poolehauzer and Mack consider me this softie pushover, and on the other, the teachers think of me as the enemy."

"That's just how it goes when you're the boss. Happily, you've still got one fan." Abe flashed her his winningest smile.

"I know, Jones, you're the best, blah blah blah." But Louisa couldn't pull herself out of her wallowing. "Remember Take Your Daughter to Work Day last year?"

"Uh, how could I forget?"

Phoebe had just turned one, too young for the official program. Still, Louisa had thought it would be a nice opportunity to be with her baby for the afternoon while also humanizing herself in the eyes of the faculty. She'd imagined Phoebe strapped into the Baby Bjorn, pudgy legs pumping as Louisa bustled around the school and all the teachers cooed at her adorable child. They'd feel so warmed by the image of Louisa as a working mom that they'd revise their view of her, from stern administrator to relatable woman trying to juggle it all.

Of course, that wasn't what happened. In order to drop off Phoebe before his afternoon seminar, Nathan had had to pick her up from daycare in the middle of her nap; on the ride over she'd wailed so much that he'd appeased her with two bananas and a bag of peanut butter puffs. All of this he'd reported to Louisa as he dropped off their seriously cranky daughter, along with a diaper bag that Louisa would later learn had not been restocked with diapers. Louisa knew that her husband disliked visiting her at River Mill; it stressed him out to return to a high school, despite being decades removed from his own teenage years. So, he was out of there before Louisa had a chance to suggest that maybe, given the circumstances, it wasn't the best idea for Phoebe to stay.

As a result, Louisa had spent the next three hours shushing a screaming baby. Then she'd heard a distinctive rumbling, a preview to her daughter bursting force with an epic—and literal—shitstorm. And that was when Louisa discovered the lack of diapers. In a previous era, Nathan's scatterbrain had sometimes charmed her, but that day her resentment soared.

Abe had come to the rescue with a roll of toilet paper and duct tape. Together they'd cleaned things up and jerry-rigged an approximation of a diaper, effective enough for Louisa to transport her daughter home without further incident.

In short, the day had not been a success. Afterward, Louisa knew she was probably imagining that any mention of her children made her colleagues skittish, but still, she stopped talking about Phoebe and Finn at work. She kept her personal and professional lives separate, which hardened her into the stern administrator more than ever.

"On a more pleasant subject, I hope," said Abe now, "tell me about your date. Was it, A. As miserable as test prep"—Louisa smacked his arm—"B. As mediocre as teachers' lounge coffee; C. As pleasant as a period stolen away with me on the roof; or D. As mind-blowing as sixty shades of gray, or whatever it's called?"

Louisa started giggling and couldn't stop.

"D?"

She nodded shyly, feeling her cheeks flush.

"Holy shit, Bauer. Good for you."

"See how effective multiple-choice tests are?"

Abe didn't acknowledge the comment. "So, when are you going to see him again?"

Louisa shrugged. "I think it was a one-time thing. I don't have the bandwidth for anything more than hot, meaningless sex."

"I could use some of that. I mean, not the meaningless part."

This was a surprise—Abe never made digs about his sex life; plus, hadn't he been treated to road head on the way to his recent birthday dinner? But Louisa thought of Amy the previous weekend, curled up on her couch like a child, expressing doubts about having her own child. "Is everything okay with you and Amy?"

"Sure, I guess. She's been in a funk lately. I think it's the adoption stuff; it's hard to be in limbo, just waiting, knowing it might still be a long road ahead. Plus, I think it dredges up stuff from her own childhood. I'm just trying to stay positive and keep spirits up for the both of us. I'm hoping our trip will help."

"Right! Spring break in New York City." Louisa experienced a pang of jealousy, knowing she'd be stuck at home, working. But she wasn't the only one with problems. She turned back to Abe. "It'll be good to get away. You know, navigate the crushing crowds of Times Square, pack yourself like sardines into subway cars, breathe in the Manhattan bouquet of trash and car exhaust—I could go on." She was trying to make him laugh, and it was working.

The period was almost over. Louisa stood up. "Well, I've got about two days' worth of work to do and dozens of dirty looks from teachers to field before picking up my kids in a few hours."

"Sounds fun," Abe said. "I'm going to hide out up here for a bit more before seventh."

"Safe travels, Jones. And good luck with Amy." Louisa kissed Abe's cheek, which was not as well-shaven as it should've been.

"Thanks, Bauer. And chin up—don't let the Meredith Pritchetts of the world get you down."

At this hour, NPR could usually be relied upon to play soft, soothing music, a balm for all the decent people who'd been bombarded by hours' worth of apocalyptic news, in addition to whatever personal trials they'd endured that day. But no such luck tonight, Louisa discovered as she stood over the kitchen sink munching on cheese and crackers. The president was hosting a special press conference, titled, "The State of Our Schools."

Louisa couldn't bring herself to switch it off, though her private rebellion was to pay only partial attention. None of it was anything she hadn't heard before. *Our beautiful children are trapped in failing government schools. Many people are saying they're horribly unprepared for the future. Horribly unprepared. Look, our teachers are lazy losers. It's horrible. Excuse me, they work half-days. They whine about the money. But what many people don't realize is they're too dumb to do anything else. Believe me. They're weak. They don't do a good job. Everyone knows that—it's a disgrace. Excuse me, these are the people we trust our incredible kids to? Wait till you see my plan. You're gonna be happy. It's about accountability, and standards, and testing—a tremendous amount of testing! You're gonna be very happy.*

Louisa clicked it off. Her jaw was clenched so tight it ached. So worked up had she been earlier about her cowardly colleagues throwing her under the bus and all the teachers hating her as a result that she'd forgotten to remember that her job was on the line with the state tests.

Her worries were interrupted by her phone's buzz. A text from DantheMan78: "hey sexy mama. thinking of you and your pretty pussy. up for round 2?"

Louisa flung the phone and watched it clatter to the floor.

"Blech," she muttered. She shook her head, trying to shake off the knowledge that she'd been intimate with a man capable of sending that text. If there weren't two sleeping children upstairs, she would've driven straight to Mickey's and insisted they go out for beers, which Mickey would've upgraded to fancy cocktails. But since Louisa was stuck here—in her house, in her life—she stepped over her phone, filled a mug to the brim with wine, and carried it along with the rest of the bottle up to bed.

CHAPTER 38

Amy

Abe had planned a trip that was like a rom-com montage, and Amy was documenting the whole thing on Instagram: the vintage typewriter and funky drapery in their room at the Ace Hotel; selfies atop each terrace of the Whitney; their Broadway Playbills held up at intermission; the High Line's old rail tracks overgrown with wild-flowers; plates of food as artful as anything they'd seen hanging in museums. Amy's feed was full of her perfect, enviable vacation.

Usually, Amy didn't bother posting, or when she did, she imme-diately felt sort of stupid, thinking, who really cared about what she'd seen and what she thought about it; plus, why should she care how her random collection of followers reacted to it? But the truth was that Amy did care, and she hoped they would, too, and that made her feel stupid all over again. So, in response, she'd delete all her social media apps until the urge hit her again and then she'd redownload them in a maddening loop.

Now Amy was back at it, impulsively pulling out her phone to check her notifications. As each heart or comment popped up, she felt a little hit of happiness, a little jolt of validation. And when the responses eventually trailed off, she'd simply post another picture to restart the feedback stream. The problem was, no matter how many likes and comments she racked up, they seemed to slip through her fingers like sand, leaving her empty-handed.

Everything felt a little like that lately. The sensation of Abe's hand clasping Amy's own, the morning sunlight glinting against the sky-scrapers, the strong coffee with the precise doses of milk and sugar: all of these small joys usually added up to a general feeling of well-being, buoying Amy along through the unpleasant parts of her days. But now she couldn't hold onto any of it.

It wasn't that Amy felt miserable; rather, she felt numb. Their first night, Abe began running kisses up her arm to her neck, hitting on all her sensitive spots. Amy went along with it, remembering how she'd once read that desire could follow arousal, instead of the other way around. This felt good, and so did that, and that, too, and it also felt good to know that she was making Abe feel good. Amy even came—pretty weakly, but not every time could be award-winning. There was usually an afterglow, a period when her skin would stay sort of tingly and the whole world would appear bathed in a gauzy sheen. Amy always felt grateful that Abe was a cuddler. But this time, as they lay on their crisp hotel sheets, Abe cradling her in his arms, Amy felt nothing. Actually, she felt sort of sweaty and claustrophobic. She slipped out of his embrace and went to take a shower.

There were a lot of dinners; there seemed to be more dinners than there were evenings. After snapping photos of her food, Amy would sit across from Abe at this or that restaurant fidgeting her wedding ring and thinking, "We are in New York City, at a restaurant, eating a nice dinner," as if to remind herself. She'd hear the buzz of the ceiling fan and the murmurs of fellow diners, and feel overcome by vertigo. Was this her vacation, her husband, her life?

The more she withdrew, the more Abe tried to engage. The quieter she got, the more animated he grew. Her husband had a bottomless trove of trivia about the sites they visited, insightful opinions about the plays, wry observations of all the people they saw. Any conversational morsel Amy offered up was pounced upon and followed up with a thoughtful question from her husband. Amy felt sick and guilty; she didn't deserve this man. He poured her wine and she swirled it around in her glass, not drinking a drop. That had to mean something, right? That she was taking into consideration the potential bundle of cells in her uterus. Or maybe it was just the nausea. Amy moved her food around her plate, occasionally venturing a bite.

On their last night in New York, they were about to sit down to yet another meal at yet another trendy restaurant, the road from appetizer to dessert looking interminable. "Hey," Amy said, tugging at Abe's sleeve. She wanted to go back to the hotel to sleep, and let her husband enjoy the evening on his own. But she knew such a suggestion would hurt Abe. "Can we skip this, do something casual instead?"

Abe was heading for the door before she even finished her sentence; she'd finally expressed an opinion, and he was eager to please, to make it all better.

They began walking downtown. The fresh air felt good, and Amy wanted to keep moving, hoping that if she stayed in motion, her thoughts and feelings wouldn't catch up to her. They walked from Flatiron to Gramercy to the East Village. The farther south they went, the narrower and grittier the streets became, the younger and more animated the crowds. Amy liked being among so many people. She finally felt like she could breathe.

As a child, Amy had come to the city frequently, on day trips with her parents from New Jersey. They'd often visited the Central Park Zoo, where Amy's mother, Adele, a former veterinarian, held forth about common medical conditions of the different animals; Adele seemed happiest during those afternoons, which always pleased Amy. But despite all those childhood trips, today Amy had only the vaguest idea of the city's geography. It was a grid, she knew, the numbered streets descending south. But once they hit Houston—the equivalent of Zero Street—and ventured into the Lower East Side, Amy was lost. So, it came as a surprise when suddenly she found herself in Chinatown.

Amy couldn't read the signs. The aromas were not familiar. Among the produce stacked into mountains outside storefronts, there were strangely shaped fruits that seemed straight out of Dr. Seuss. But the people—they could've been her sisters and brothers, her parents, her children. Everywhere Amy looked, she saw faces that looked more like her own than her own parents' faces did. They looked back at her, suspecting nothing. It made Amy feel giddy, and like an imposter. A wave of nausea rippled through her.

It was a lot; it was too much. A man standing in a doorway handed Amy a menu and started speaking, but his words hit her ears like dissonant noise. When he beckoned her inside the dumpling shop, Amy realized how hungry she was, and how much she wanted to stand at the little counter slurping soup. Abe was game, as always.

When she ordered in English, Amy swore the face of the woman behind the register hardened slightly. Abe echoed her order, and soon they were sitting before a feast. It was such a relief to have an appetite. Amy ate like she hadn't in a week, stuffing herself with sustenance.

It was after her seventh or eighth dumpling that her body rebelled, forcing her to the tiny bathroom in the back. Everything she'd consumed came rushing back up, barely digested. And then Amy was empty again. She wiped her mouth and stood blinking at the mirror.

A knock on the door accompanied Abe's concerned voice. Amy let him in, and he handed her a ginger ale—who knows how he'd procured it so quickly. "Are you okay?"

Amy didn't even know how to begin to answer. So instead she just blurted it out. "I think I'm pregnant."

CHAPTER 39

Abe

Abe couldn't trust his ears, and Amy refused to repeat herself.

"You heard me," she said, before throwing up again. In the cab back to the hotel, Amy hung her head out the window, as Abe rubbed small circles onto her back. Up in their room, she shed her pants and climbed into bed. Within minutes she was asleep.

Which left Abe alone to process this news, to consider his sleeping wife, who was possibly—*why didn't she know for sure?*—growing their future child inside of her. It felt too good to be true. It felt unreal. Abe had spent the past week on pins and needles, doing all he could to try to lift Amy out of the dumps. It pained him to feel so distant from her and to see her so unhappy, and to not know why or how to help. But Abe wouldn't let himself panic or sink into despair. If he'd learned anything about marriage, it was that the relationship had peaks and valleys, and that partners drifted apart and came together again, and that this, too, shall pass. As frustrating as it felt right now to be shut out, the solution lay in waiting it out. Amy knew he was there when she was ready to open up. Beyond that, what could Abe do?

Well, now she'd opened up, with what turned out to be an obvious explanation for her recent moodiness. New hormones had been coursing through her body for—*how long?* Abe didn't even know how far along she was! He'd read a thousand times that the first trimester of pregnancy left a woman exhausted, sick, and emotional—exactly how Amy had seemed lately. Abe had memorized all the symptoms when they were first trying to conceive, when Amy's every yawn or headache prompted a blip of hope in him. Though he'd long since stopped paying attention. How could he have been so oblivious? Why had he abandoned hope?

As he watched Amy's chest rise and fall in slumber, he thought of a dozen questions. Had she seen her doctor? Had she started taking prenatal vitamins? When could they share the news with family and friends? What did she need from him? How could he support her?

Abe's body pulsed with adrenaline. There was no way he could sleep. He kissed his wife on the forehead and ventured out.

The hotel bar was another universe. Electronic dance music was pumping and all the patrons looked twenty-five, vaguely European, wearing clothes that Abe didn't have the faintest idea where you could buy. He ordered a beer, which cost double what he would've paid at home—this whole vacation was a splurge, but Abe had planned for that; he'd been saving for months. He knew he was paying for the atmosphere, the people-watching, the novel experiences.

"My wife is pregnant." It just came out. Who was he even talking to? The bartender, he supposed. And when the guy didn't hear him the first time, he said it again. "I just found out my wife's pregnant."

"Oh yeah? Cool, man. Congrats."

Abe didn't know what he expected—for the guy to pop open a bottle of Champagne, for a parade to start barreling through the bar, for the sky to fall, or all of the above. Because that's how the news felt to Abe: show-stopping, earth-shattering. Of course, one person's life-changing news was just background noise for most everyone else. It was amazing, thought Abe, how everyone was stomping around the same green earth, but when it came down to it, each individual occupied their own radically different reality. Women got pregnant every day. Yet, for years, Amy had not been among those women. And now she was. Life was incredible.

CHAPTER 40

Amy

The whole ride home, Amy kept trying to summon the courage to talk to her husband. She said she wanted to rest, but she kept peeking her eyes open to steal glances of him behind the wheel, working so hard to contain his joy. The sight of his face, all alight, made her tear up, so she'd clench her eyes closed again.

She was thinking about when they first decided to take the plunge into parenthood—on her birthday two years ago. It had been one of those stretches of intense connection between the two of them, when every conversation left Amy feeling seen and understood, when being with Abe was like attending the best party, when she sometimes couldn't sleep for feeling so lucky to have found her soulmate—it was a period when she used terms like "soulmate." Amy had brimmed over with joy and abundance. It made her want to fulfill each and every desire of her husband's. So, of course she would join him in his vision for their future. Of course she wanted to give him a child.

The doubts had trickled in almost immediately. Amy felt ashamed to recognize yet another way she was different from everyone around her. Her own parents had fought so hard to have a child. Nearly every couple she knew had kids or planned to have them, and the single women in her life talked with worry and grief about the possibility of not meeting a partner in time to reproduce. Men could feel indifferent toward parenthood, it seemed, but what kind of woman didn't want a baby? Amy felt defective, and part of her feared the cause was her early severance from her birth mother (even though she'd met other adopted women who'd happily become mothers). Still, she'd held out hope that she would change her mind, that Abe's excitement and determination would grow contagious. And then, when they'd had problems getting pregnant, that became its own project, a weirdly welcome distraction. Which is probably why Amy let things go on so long without addressing her hesitations with Abe. It was a mortifying realization.

Two hours into the drive, she tried again. "Abe," she said. "I made two different appointments with my OB, and both times I canceled."

Abe was nodding, ever anxious to understand. "You're scared."

"Well, yeah."

"Let's reschedule and we'll go together. I'll be there with you every step of the way."

Amy opened her mouth to speak—to clarify—but words failed her.

Which is how, a week later, she found herself halfway between sitting and lying on an ultrasound bed in a dark room, with Abe at her side, and a technician swirling cold jelly onto her stomach. The transducer moved across her skin like a magic wand, about to proclaim her future. There it was on the screen: a tiny white blob, the beginnings of a baby. Amy hadn't been imagining the whole thing; it was true. She was pregnant.

A whimper emitted from Abe as he squeezed her hand.

"Congrats," said the technician. "You're nine weeks along."

Amy felt the room closing in on her. She struggled to breathe. "Can you give us a moment?"

When the technician left, Abe exclaimed, "Nine weeks, Ames! Do you think it was that time in the bathroom outside the infertility meeting? The irony!"

Amy inhaled as best she could, then came out with it. "I'm not sure I can do this."

He didn't understand; he thought she needed a pep talk. "Sure you can, honey. I know you've been through a lot. I know it's overwhelming. But you're a rock star, you're—"

"That's not what I mean. I'm not sure I want to be a mother, Abe. I'm not sure I want a baby."

Amy glanced again at the photo on the screen: the window into her insides, which now struck her as obscene. She looked away, avoiding Abe's face. A clenching in her belly sent her scurrying to the trash can. Abe tried to comfort her, but the feel of his palm on her back made her queasy all over again. She got dressed slowly, shaky on her legs, then Abe handed her her purse, and she walked out ahead of him.

CHAPTER 41
Mona

It was simple: Nate needed money, so Mona would help. Her friend Kendra told her you could get a substitute teacher license in an afternoon and earn decent money; and Mona happened to be taking all evening classes, so the hours would work. When Kendra mentioned the name of the high school where she was filling in as a long-term sub, Mona's interest was piqued. Ever since she'd picked up a passed-out Nate from his old house, Mona had felt intrigued by Louisa. After they'd dragged him together to Mona's car, Mona had watched as Louisa skipped across the lawn back to the house. Not exactly the behavior of an inflexible nag, which was how Nate had described his wife. Mona had felt an urge to befriend her, which she knew was slightly nuts. Now, especially, when Nate seemed insistent on wringing Louisa dry for every last dollar, Mona thought it would be wise to get involved, to help. How exactly, she wasn't sure yet, but she assumed if she got to know Louisa better, she could figure out a way. Because above all, Mona was a helper.

Mona's first day, she was assigned to fill in for Abe Jones, teaching ninth and twelfth grade social studies. She wrote her new teacher name on the blackboard, then read it aloud: "Ms. Gill." She felt like a fake, a child in her mother's high heels. She'd slipped on the pumps this morning, in hopes of not getting mistaken for a student. She was nervous, but optimistic, too. Was this how Nate felt, she wondered, before a new class? Mona admired his work so much. She took her position at the front of the room, watching the clock tick toward the first bell. She told herself she was ready.

Suddenly, the empty desks were occupied by thirty adolescent bodies, along with their hairdos and complexions and energy. Mona couldn't quite believe the transformation. After everyone settled, all thirty pairs of eyes fixed onto her. The gazes were curious or bored or downright hostile.

Mona felt high on the power: she could tell them to do anything, and maybe they would do it. She caught the eye of a boy in the back who was the spitting image of a guy she'd dated in high school: long and lean, with blonde curls and brown eyes. He affected that cool, slouching stance characteristic of popular high school boys everywhere, and Mona felt the familiar butterflies in her stomach. Her mind wandered to the experience of sitting in Nate's class. It honestly surprised her that teachers and students didn't hook up all the time. Mr. Jones had left a lesson plan. The title made Mona's eyes glaze over—"World History Test Prep"—but she did her best. She reviewed the strategies: the previewing of passages and underlining of key sentences and maintenance of good posture so you didn't keel over and slip into a coma mid-exam (she ad-libbed a bit). Then the kids took turns answering the multiple-choice questions. It was uncanny how Mona felt transported back to high school, watching the creep of the clock hands, feeling as if real life meant anything and everything going on outside these four walls.

When the bell finally rang and everyone got up, it was a shock to see that most of the students towered over her; some of the boys stood a full foot above Mona's petite frame, despite her three-inch heels. Still, they looked at her like she was an authority figure. As they said their goodbyes, they called her Ms. Gill or "Teach," as if this were all perfectly normal.

When Mona walked down the halls, no one questioned her presence. She even ventured to admonish a kid for slamming shut a locker, and the kid flashed her an irritated look, like any student would flash any teacher. It was fun to try on this new identity. Mona thought she could get used to it.

And then she spotted her, from all the way down the hall: tall and broad, with her mass of curls bouncing, totally in her element, a little terrifying. She was navigating the crowded hallway at a pace double that of everyone around her, creating a wake in her path. When she drew closer, Mona saw that she looked exhausted. It was kind of amazing, how she could simultaneously exude such prowess and such fatigue. In contrast, Mona approached every situation like a novice, and tried to bring a bright wakefulness to it. It was a wonder to witness, this photonegative of herself. Mona was still gaping, captivated, when suddenly they stood face to face.

When Louisa noticed her, it caught Mona off guard. The vice principal's eyes doubled in size and she went stock-still. Somehow Mona hadn't thought to prepare for an actual confrontation.

"Hi," she blurted out. Then she charged forward, escaping into the crowd before she could register Louisa's response.

A moment later, she was back in her classroom, heart pounding, when Louisa busted in. "Jones, you will not believe who I just—*oh!*"

"Hi again," said Mona. She was seated behind the desk, trapped. "Mr. Jones is out today. I'm filling in."

Louisa's expression cycled through several contortions, as she seemed to consider the possibilities of what was going on here.

"I'm a sub," Mona said. "Just temporary."

A sly smile spread across Louisa's face, and Mona realized how what she'd said could be interpreted in several ways. She returned the smile, which had the effect of cutting through the tension. Again, she had the feeling, *I like this woman. We could be friends.*

Mona found herself asking Louisa if she wanted to go out for coffee.

Louisa was matter-of-fact. "I don't go out for coffee. My to-do list would give you nightmares. But if you go, can you bring me back a latte, two percent milk?"

"Sugar?"

"Nope."

"Okey-doke."

Louisa vanished, and Mona marveled at the fact that somehow in the past two minutes she'd morphed into her boyfriend's wife's assistant.

CHAPTER 42
Louisa

Still in shock, Louisa texted Nathan "WTF" and added so many question marks and exclamation points that they spilled over to a second line. He responded with a single question mark, which made Louisa seethe. It was typical Nathan to feign ignorance or nonchalance. Like why would Louisa possibly be worked up about his young girlfriend invading her place of work—subbing for Abe, no less! But it soon occurred to Louisa that maybe Nathan had no idea that Mona was at River Mill. Maybe Mona hadn't filled him in on her boyfriend's-wife-job-infiltration mission; the possibility made the girl more interesting to Louisa. It made her wonder about what was going on between Nathan and her. She didn't even pretend not to gloat. "Talk to your girlfriend," she texted back.

It was odd that Abe was out sick. He'd taken maybe three days off in the decade-plus that Louisa had worked with him. Without her friend to escape to the roof with, she felt a little lost. So, she texted Mickey an "SOS." Louisa couldn't remember the last time she'd left the building during a school day. But this was an emergency. Mickey suggested they meet in fifteen minutes under the football bleachers for mugs of kombucha, Mickey's treat. Louisa didn't even check her calendar before agreeing.

Just the sight of her friend made Louisa feel slightly less manic. She nearly galloped across the grass to get to her, sitting in the shade of the risers, a few feet from a gym class; last week during the same class, Louisa had been called out to the field to handle a pair of students who'd pants-ed a classmate; real class-acts, these kids. From her current vantage point, all she could see was a bunch of gangly legs in motion.

Mickey nudged her. "Remember how in college we used to sit on the bleachers to ogle the football players during practice?"

"Ew, is that what you're thinking about?" It amazed Louisa how any adult could have a single erotic thought within fifty yards of a high school; it was the least sexy setting on the planet.

Mickey took a swig of kombucha. "I was just trying to distract you. But maybe we should tackle the Mona situation head-on, come up with a plan. Now that she's here on-site, how can we best mess with her"

"What, so I get fired, too? That's just what Finn and Phoebe need, two unemployed parents. Then Mona can support all five of us on her shiny new substitute-teacher wages."

"That's not a bad idea. You could definitely use a break from all this." Mickey made a sweeping gesture, which seemed to encompass more than the grounds of the high school.

Louisa sighed. "Well, it turns out only one of us can quit our life. Not that I really want to quit my life, but you know what I mean. That's what's so infuriating, that Nathan could walk away from all his responsibilities, and get away with it."

"I can't imagine he's thrilled to have lost his job."

Louisa shot her a look. "Whose side are you on?"

"Sorry, yours, obviously. Well, now that Nathan's not working, he should pitch in more with the kids."

"You're right." Louisa wondered why it hadn't occurred to her to ask that of him, or more pointedly, why it hadn't occurred to *him* to offer. "We haven't set up a system. We just take it week by week. It's stupid, I know, and inevitably means I get stuck doing more. But I guess without a schedule, the whole thing feels less real, less permanent."

Louisa didn't want to admit to Mickey how much she missed Nathan, despite everything. She remembered Mona's words—*I'm a sub, just temporary*—and how they'd stirred up something inside of her. Relief, or maybe hope? She sighed again. It was tiring and tiresome to swing so wildly between extreme emotions.

"Have you guys filled out the paperwork yet?" Mickey asked.

"Paperwork? Oh." Louisa knew a divorce was a unique kind of breakup, one that required notarized documents and lawyers and who knew what else to make it official; she hadn't yet done the research on what exactly it entailed. That had to be significant, that neither one of them had served the other with divorce papers yet. It wasn't like Louisa to blow off logistics.

"Well, there's no rush," said Mickey. "It just might give you some closure."

"Closure, sure."

"Sorry, I don't know why I'm bringing this up now. Anyway, why not tell Nathan to take the kids tonight? To give you a break."

"You're right." Louisa flashed back to her night with Daniel, then shook off the memory. "Speaking of breaks, this one has about run its course."

"May I escort you back inside?"

"So, you can catch a glimpse of the infamous homewrecker?"

Mickey looked mock-aghast. "How dare you accuse me of such a thing? I just want to be a supportive friend."

"I'll see you later."

"This weekend, at Mateo's birthday. You're coming, right?"

Louisa groaned. It had been a relief to have a hiatus from the birthday dinners. Nathan had skipped Abe's celebration, due to extenuating circumstances, but there was no way he'd opt out of his best friend's night.

Just as Louisa was opening her mouth to invent an excuse for why she might not make it, Mickey said, "I'll be a human barrier, preventing you from having to say a single word to Nathan. I promise. We'll have a good time."

"Fine, I guess I'll come."

"All right, I'm off to see if I can find Mel's boyfriend in the halls to mortify him with a hug."

Louisa decided not to ask if she was serious. Back inside the school, she was met with noise and chaos. It looked like a spontaneous pep rally had started up in the corridor only the overarching mood was anger not pep. Students were shouting and clapping and jumping up and down with handmade signs. As Louisa got closer, she could see "S.A.T." on the signs. Closer still, she saw that the kids had reclaimed the acronym to stand for "Students Against Testing." Clever, though it put a lump in Louisa's throat. A chant started up: "River Mill, this ain't cool. Stop the test prep, bring back school." *Uh-oh.*

Louisa scanned the crowd for its ringleaders. It would've been a comfort had it been the nerds: the leaders of the debate club or the National Merit Scholars, the kids for whom an interruption to their classes was obviously an outrage. But when Louisa spotted Jay Robinson, Leo Feit, and Annabelle Smith leading the chants, she felt a pit in her stomach. The trio represented peak popularity of the junior class: They strutted through the hallways with confidence oozing from their clear pores; they huddled together at the center cafeteria table, their conventionally attractive bodies displayed in poses of effortless nonchalance. To fellow classmates, Jay, Leo, and Annabelle were a walking, talking museum exhibit of the best way to be—the *only* way to be. Everyone cared about them; but as popular kids, their signature trait was how little they cared—or seemed to care—about anyone or anything else.

And yet, look at them now: shouting to bring back science labs and poetry reading and all the extracurriculars that had been chucked in favor of test prep. Louisa wanted to admire them for taking up a cause, and using their popularity as a force for change.

But given that they were demanding to change the very policy that Louisa had instituted, a policy that was crucial for the future success of this school as well as for Louisa's job, she very much wanted them to shut their goddamn traps.

Louisa reminded herself that she was in charge. She knew how to make intimidating eye contact and hide any nerves behind a façade of steely resolve. She marched right into the scrum. "You, you, and you," she snapped. "Detention for a week for disturbing the peace. Everyone else, the show's over. Get back to class."

Students scattered, dropping half-eaten snacks and stomping on posters and leaving the corridor a disaster for the poor custodians. Amid the flurry, Louisa spotted Leo and Annabelle conferring with a teacher, who was patting them on the back and collecting their posters. When the crowd thinned, Louisa was shocked to realize that the teacher was Kendra Grant. Had she orchestrated the protest? Another shock: there was Mona, too, chatting with Jay, a grin spread across her pretty face. She must've sensed she was being stared at, because she turned and caught Louisa's eye.

"Louisa." She sounded startled.

"It's Ms. Bauer," Louisa snapped.

"Right, I'm sorry. Ms. Bauer. Listen, we weren't trying to stir up trouble. And I had no idea that you ..." She tried again. "The kids are genuinely upset about all this mindless test prep that's replaced actual learning, and they wanted to channel it into something positive. Kendra and I—er, Ms. Grant and I started talking about the power of civic protest to effect change, and—"

"Enough," Louisa said. "Stop."

Mona stood there chastened, head bowed like a child. An involuntary laugh escaped Louisa's throat; Mona was just so goddamned young. She'd been here a single day and already claimed to know the students' inner hearts, plus had found a way to make Louisa's life even more difficult. It was all so crazy.

"Listen to me," she barked. Mona nodded compliantly. "I'll be here late dealing with the fallout of this mess. So, I'll need you to pick up my children from daycare and deliver them to their father. You can tell him I sent you."

She strode away, stamping muddy footprints into S.A.T. posters in her tracks.

CHAPTER 43
Nathan

After Louisa's outrage invaded his phone, Nathan had reached out to Mona to find out what his ex was so worked up about. But in typical Mona form, she'd replied, "Busy busy, I'll explain later."

So that added another layer of thrumming anxiety onto the anxiety Nathan already felt after hearing the term "irretrievable breakdown of marriage" so many times that it had started to sound like gibberish. The papers his lawyer had finalized listed the divorce as "no-fault." While Louisa could technically contest this, citing Nathan's adultery as grounds for a "fault" divorce, the process was so much more onerous and expensive, and Nathan was betting that Louisa wouldn't be up for all that. Plus, his lawyer assured him, even in the case of a fault divorce, the fact of adultery wouldn't prevent the guilty spouse (Nathan) from receiving alimony and child support if he was otherwise entitled to it. That was a relief to Nathan, even as he simultaneously felt like the world's biggest piece of shit. At least he was making progress: The papers would be ready and served to Louisa within the week.

Nathan was sitting in his makeshift home office, i.e., at the kitchen counter, attempting to focus on the algebra textbook chapter he was editing. He could have done this job back in high school. But ironically, the fact that he found the work so beneath him prevented him from concentrating. He'd taken on the assignment out of desperation, calculating that he could edit a chapter every three hours, resulting in a not-terrible wage of thirty bucks per hour. But he kept getting distracted.

Nathan took a break to text Mateo about his birthday dinner: Now that he and Mona were living together, it was feeling less and less okay to keep excluding her from these things, so could they expand the reservation to seven? Mateo's reply was prompt: "K"; but the single letter left Nathan wondering at the subtext: hostile or hesitant or indifferent? Next, Nathan felt peckish, so he went to fix himself a snack. And on and on went the procrastination.

So there Nathan was, on hour five of editing the same chapter, feeling sorry for himself—*a man with a Ph.D.! a professor!*—now earning minimum wage. It wasn't that this was so new. He'd spent his years as an adjunct wallowing in a similar state of self-pity, when his take-home pay was the equivalent of a part-time cashier at Walgreens.

But at least then he'd been surrounded by fellow over-educated, under-appreciated, and under-paid academics; he'd had a community with which to commiserate. Now he was alone, disgraced, and unable to pay attention to equations that the average eighth grader had mastered.

It was in this state that Nathan was interrupted by the sounds of his children and his girlfriend. The fridge was empty save for a bunch of shriveled grapes and a couple of beers, the apartment was a mess, and Nathan had planned on working through the evening. Was he so out of it that he'd spaced on having the kids tonight? Sometimes Nathan felt a pang of sympathy remembering Louisa's exasperation with his forgetfulness.

"Surprise, surprise," Mona called out. "It's double-trouble twin time!"

Mona flitted about, taking off the kids' jackets and shoes and setting them up with crayons and paper, then informing Nathan breezily that Louisa had asked them last minute to take the children. She plopped a pizza box onto the counter. It would be vegetarian, but still, the aroma made Nathan's mouth water.

"I splurged to celebrate my first day of work."

"First day of work?" he asked.

"I'm substitute teaching at River Mill. Kendra Grant hooked me up with the gig."

Nathan opened his mouth to speak but nothing came out.

The bombshells kept dropping: Mona was filling in for Abe; she'd helped orchestrate a schoolwide protest of a test prep program that had been spearheaded by Louisa.

"Oops," Mona said, shrugging, but there was a twinkle in her eye.

This was the kind of thing Nathan usually adored about her: the mischief she got herself into in the name of a good cause, her irresistible combination of naivete and faux-naivete that allowed her to make things happen when others couldn't or simply wouldn't. Under other circumstances, Nathan might've opened up about his disappointment in Louisa: Fifteen years ago, she would've been the one leading that protest; she'd been the most bright-eyed of idealists. But somewhere along the way she'd transformed into a pragmatic administrator. But at the moment, Nathan felt nothing but irritation with his girlfriend. Mona knew he'd met with a lawyer. The last thing he wanted was to add fuel to the fire of his divorce. His stomach twisted in knots as he worried about the papers heading Louisa's way.

"Aren't there dozens of schools around here where you could sub?" he asked her, thinking, *why are you getting involved?*

Mona ignored the question and answered one he hadn't asked. "You had a relationship with Louisa, and now you have a relationship with me, so the missing link is a relationship between Louisa and me. I'm convinced that if I can just close that loop, it might heal past hurts in a way that lawyers and divorce papers and all that junk most certainly won't. It might bring understanding and unity."

"Oh, Mona." What was she even talking about? There was so much amiss that Nathan wasn't even sure what to address first. They weren't living on a commune. The goal wasn't unity; it was the opposite. How could Mona not understand that? A question flickered through his head: *Who is this person I left my wife for?*

Then he returned to the practical: Nathan knew that if he demanded or even asked Mona to stop subbing at Louisa's school, she'd only dig her heels in. So, he dropped it. "I'm tired. You're probably tired. Let's just have dinner and get the kids to bed."

Mona was the household night owl, but that night, Nathan was the one up padding around into the wee hours. He needed someone to talk to, but the only person he could think of—the one who knew when to dispense advice versus when to listen quietly or offer a comforting hug—was the last person in the world who'd want to hear from him now. It was a physical symptom, how much Nathan suddenly missed his wife.

CHAPTER 44

Mateo's Birthday

Mateo wasn't usually one to stress about getting older. He'd been on enough of those Forty Under Forty lists to feel like he'd accomplished a lot for his age. Plus, he and Mickey had always been the youngest parents at Mel's school and extracurricular events. For his whole adulthood, Mateo had felt that every year was better than the last; he'd put in a lot of work to build his life, and he'd also had a lot of luck along the way. He had no reason to believe the streak would break now. But there was something different about approaching forty. It seemed to tilt the ground beneath his feet, knocking him a smidge off balance.

Mateo had started waking up with headaches. He opened his eyes to the sight of Mickey's radiant smile, and felt worry. It wasn't just the pounding at his temples. With the opening up of their marriage, he sensed a chasm growing between his wife and him, despite the fact that they'd been having more sex than they'd had in years. When Mateo moved, he felt creaky in his bones, tight in his muscles, a stranger in his body.

Today he was forty.

He felt his wife's strong hands on his shoulders, working out the kinks. "I have a surprise for you tonight," she said.

How many years would it take Mickey to understand that she, not he, was the one who enjoyed surprises? But Mateo wouldn't snap at her: it had taken *him* years to realize that while that would make him feel better for a moment, the regret would linger much longer. "When?" he asked, hoping he might at least prepare himself.

"After your dinner."

"I hope you're talking about ice cream cake."

Mickey's mischievous smile, dimples on full display, indicated that no, she didn't mean dessert.

Mateo's only other friend who'd passed the fortieth birthday milestone had used the occasion to effectively light a match to his life. Mateo wasn't Nathan, not by a longshot. Nathan who'd earned a pittance for so many years as an adjunct professor, but never acted to make a change. Nathan who'd become a father and seemed peeved that his new responsibilities interfered with his chill time, who acted like he was the first person in history to be changing diapers in the middle of the night. Mateo loved his old friend, but

Nathan could be seriously immature.

Still, forty was a mindfuck. And now, since Nathan had asked to let his girlfriend tag along, their Giorgio's dinner would be a party of seven, not six. Was that a bad sign? Was it no big deal or a very big deal? Mateo wasn't sure.

But wait, no: Amy texted that she was sick. Had one of their sextet ever before been sick for a birthday dinner? Mateo didn't think so. Another possible omen. At least now the group would be back to six.

Until Louisa sent a barrage of texts: she wasn't coming, either. Or, she *was* coming but would be late. Actually, she was bringing a friend. Well, she wasn't sure, but she'd keep him posted. *What?*

Mateo's shoulders tensed again, and he half-wished he could bail on dinner, too. The beauty of the birthday tradition was its consistency, the reassuring reliability of food and friends amidst all of life's changes. Every single birthday, the six of them would sit together for the arc of an evening, from bread and olive oil to fat slabs of cake. No one was supposed to cancel last minute or request extra seats for plus ones. No one was supposed to announce that the night would end in a big surprise. It was supposed to be the six of them, six times a year, doing the same thing, over and over again, period.

Well, screw everyone else and their changes of plans. Mateo was forty goddamn years old. He'd be the grownup in the group; he'd show up and do his part.

———

Louisa didn't think twice when Poolehauzer's secretary handed her a thick envelope, her mouth set into a frown. The woman had a classic resting bitch face, plus Louisa usually left the school saddled with paperwork. It was a Friday, so she had the luxury of tossing the envelope on the mail pile in her foyer and forgetting about it for a while.

For the next two days at least, she wouldn't have to deal with the Students Against Testing protests, plus she had the house to herself for an hour before Mateo's dinner. She could take a bath, or a nap. She could pour herself a glass of wine, or two. She could watch TV or read a magazine. Of course, she spent so long luxuriating in all the possibilities that, before she knew it, forty minutes had passed. And her phone was flashing alerts. She read the texts in the order they'd come:

Nathan: "Can you remind me Laura's rate for sitting?" Odd, since she thought he'd taken the kids for the night so Mona could watch them during the dinner. Also, how was it that Louisa was no longer with Nathan, yet still had to play this role of reminding him of every kid-related detail?

Abe: "Need a lift tonight? Amy's sick, and I could use a copilot." She'd tell him no: she wasn't sure how it would feel sitting across the table from Nathan, and she wanted the option to bolt whenever she felt like it.

Mickey: "Mona's coming tonight. I'm so sorry! I just found out! Call me!" Louisa felt paralyzed; even her thoughts froze.

Nathan: "Also, heads up that Mona will be joining us."

Heads up?! Half an hour before they'd be meeting wasn't a heads-up; it was an ambush.

And that's when Louisa's eye caught on the folder she'd carted home—instead of the familiar River Mill insignia was a stamp that read "Massachusetts Probate and Family Court."

She tore it open and scanned the documents: summons, complaint, alimony, child support, rights and responsibilities. The shocks came fast and furious: Nathan had met with a lawyer and filed for divorce. He wanted Louisa to give up nearly a quarter of her income not only to support the kids but to support him, too. He'd filed for something called a "no-fault" divorce. Louisa didn't know what that meant, but she was pretty sure someone was at fault, and it wasn't her.

She could stay home. No one was forcing her to go, and everyone would understand. But the thought of reheating sad leftovers in the fridge then plunking down on the couch to surf Netflix and marinate in self-pity felt too depressing to Louisa.

She had another idea. Her fingers went flying on her phone, responding to none of her texts, but instead inviting DantheMan78 to the dinner. If Nathan could bring a date, so could she. Within moments, her one-night-stand replied, "cool count me in." Louisa stuffed the divorce papers in her purse, and stormed out into the night.

———

Again, Abe asked Amy to reconsider. It would do her good to spend time with friends, to eat a hearty meal, to be reminded of how wonderful their life was. Well, he didn't voice aloud this last part. Again, Amy declined, not even peeling her eyes from her laptop screen to answer. She said Mateo would forgive her absence, which she must've known wasn't the point at all.

So, Abe went solo. It was a mild May evening, the sun still idling on the horizon. For the first time that spring, Abe didn't need a jacket. This milestone usually put a literal skip in his step. It was a sign not just of warmer weather but also of the post-spring break slide to the end of the school year, to everyone congratulating everyone else on a job well done, then looking ahead to the promise of summer. Abe appreciated the cyclical nature of his job: the ebb-and-flow patterns of the year. He'd long since figured out how to ride out this or that storm that came with teaching high school. This year's ramped-up testing and backlash were particularly bad, but like everything at River Mill, it would eventually blow over.

Except Amy's words had shattered him. She didn't want the baby. Or, she didn't think she wanted it. Or, she didn't think she wanted it, but Abe thought she really did. Abe didn't know what to think.

The morning after the doctor's appointment, Abe hadn't been able to rouse himself for school. He'd hoped that Amy might stay home, too, so they could talk it through. But his wife had gotten up like normal, brushed her teeth and dressed and put on mascara (somehow this task in particular rankled Abe), and left for work, leaving Abe alone to try and contain his uncontainable feelings. He'd eventually taken a walk. The trees and grass were verdant, the air fragrant with new tulips; it felt like an assault to Abe's senses.

Abe had always thought of himself and Amy as a unit, particularly in their desire for a baby. The two of them hardly ever fought—it was a defining feature of their marriage—but in the rare case of a disagreement, they hashed it out and worked through it together. But here was a decision (*the most important decision!*) and not only had Amy experienced a complete change of heart, but apparently her opinion was the only one that mattered. It was mind-boggling; it made no sense. Abe respected that Amy was the pregnant one, but for the first time he reconsidered the notion of "her body, her choice." Why was it her choice alone? Didn't he count, too? He wanted a baby so badly. Only when an elderly neighbor walking a dog met his nod with a surprised stare did Abe realize he was crying. He was not fit for being in public.

Abe stayed out of work for three days. Meanwhile, Amy stayed late at the office each night, and when she finally returned home refused to engage in real conversation. She was processing, she said; she needed time. Abe noticed a bottle of prenatal vitamins had appeared in the medicine cabinet, though the seal was still intact. What did that mean? Abe knew he was losing it a little. For tonight, he'd pushed himself to shower and finally change out of sweatpants.

He told himself it would be good for him to get out of his head, and see his friends, and be out in the world.

In the Giorgio's parking lot, Abe was startled by a knock on the car window. It was Nathan, along with a young woman who peered in at Abe and waved. Abe felt like locking the door, restarting the car, and peeling off, but he stifled the urge and waved back.

Nathan was glad to spot Abe in the lot. Abe was one of Louisa's closest friends, which meant Nathan had barely seen him in the past six months, and he missed the guy. As nervous as Nathan felt about tonight, as hesitant as he'd been when Mona badgered him until he secured her an invite, the sight of Abe lifted his spirits. Maybe they could all just get along. Though Abe seemed to be taking forever to exit his car.

"So, you're the famous Abe Jones?" Mona said. "I'm Mona. I've been filling in for you this week at the school."

"Huh?" Abe looked like he was underwater, and Nathan was a little annoyed at Mona for this aggressive introduction.

"This is my girlfriend," Nathan explained. "She started subbing at River Mill this week."

"With Louisa?" Abe seemed to be surfacing.

"Not *with* her, but yeah, in the same building," said Mona. "For you, actually, as I said. Anyway, it's an honor to meet you. Your students really admire you."

"Thanks." Abe finally got out of the car, and Nathan noticed how harried he looked. It was not the kind of thing he usually noticed. He gave Abe a pat on the shoulder.

"Shall we go inside?" Mona chirped.

Mateo and Mickey were already seated, Mickey's arm wrapped around Mateo as if they were a single being. They even resembled each other: the short strawberry-blonde hair (Mateo's streaked with silver), the hazel eyes, the broad shoulders and rod-straight posture. It made Nathan wonder if people had ever thought that about Louisa and him: two tall figures slumping their way toward middle age. Would anyone ever think that about Mona and him, or would he continue to field the puzzled looks of people trying to discern if she was Nathan's niece or mentee?

"Nice to see you again, Mateo." Mona shook his hand, then reached out to Mickey. "I'm Mona. It's great to finally meet you. Your gym sounds amazing."

Mickey nodded cautiously and gave a tight grin that didn't even remotely resemble her usual smile. Nathan noticed that she didn't say, "Drop by anytime," "First visit is free," or any of the other welcoming sales lines she usually offered. He also wondered if Mona had rehearsed these greetings, repeating them like affirmations, surrounded by candles and a cloud of lavender fragrance. He banished the unkind thought from his brain.

"Happy birthday, man." Nathan clapped Mateo on the back, laughing weakly. "Welcome to the fifth-century club."

He sat down and Mona slid in next to him: in Abe's spot. Abe stood hesitating, until Mickey pulled out Amy's usual chair, next to her. She urged him over, saying, "I'm so sorry Amy's sick. We'll order her some spaghetti to go."

Only Louisa's chair remained empty. Nathan wondered where she was, but didn't dare ask. Mickey ordered wine, and they all sat waiting for it in silence, the non-presence of their sixth party member hovering over the group.

Mickey turned on her smile for Kimmy the waitress as she ordered the bruschetta and burrata and olives. Mona piped up with "And one order of stuffed mushrooms."

Sacrilege! Abe gaped. Nathan held his breath, fearing Mickey would scold her for the departure from tradition, but instead she smiled blithely. "Sure, why not switch things up for a change?" She proceeded to order garlic broccolini and antipasto skewers. "We'll need extra anyway, since Louisa's bringing a guest."

"A guest? Who?" Nathan demanded.

"We don't know him," Mickey said simply, then she turned to the waitress and winked. "Why don't you bring a couple extra bottles of cabernet. I think we'll need them."

———

Mickey was a bundle of energy. Mona intrigued her, with her big eyes and calm manner, with how little physical space she took up yet how unapologetically she'd wedged her way into this decade-long tradition and assumed her place at the table. Mickey had conflicting urges: to pull Mona aside to pepper her with dozens of questions and also to give her the cold shoulder. She tried to concentrate on the latter, out of solidarity with Louisa, who would likely show up any minute now. She didn't really think Louisa would bring a date; it had to have been a bluff to piss off Nathan.

Mickey anticipated that the main drama would go down after dinner. Although she knew Mateo was no fan of surprises, she'd decided to keep her idea a secret to give him less of a chance to chicken out. Anyway, he was the one who'd recently mentioned the night they first met, the threesome he'd never taken her up on, and how it might be fun to try one now. Mickey was in awe of her husband—her forty-year-old husband!—and all he'd opened himself up to in these past couple of months. That he'd followed her into this new marital territory was testament to his love for her and his willingness to discover new corners of himself. She knew it made him nervous. She knew it was outside of his comfort zone. And yet, here they found themselves, married for nearly half their lives, and always finding new ways to be together.

Mickey was so busy marveling at her husband that she nearly missed Louisa's approach. She barely recognized her friend. Louisa wore a slinky slip dress and red lipstick—she looked voluptuous, stunning—and her fingers were braided between those of a very cute guy. Wow, she'd actually done it: she'd brought a date.

"Hey Lou." But Louisa was distracted, on a mission. She dragged over a chair from a nearby table and sandwiched it between Mona and Abe, almost bulldozing over Abe in the process. "Skootch," she insisted, so Abe, Mickey, and Mateo all slid over one space. Louisa directed her date into the seat next to Mona and plunked herself down beside Abe. "There," she said.

Louisa was still bustling around, so she either didn't notice everyone gaping or was pointedly ignoring it. She finally settled, took in the table, and launched into her greetings: "Happy birthday, Mateo. Abe, I'm glad to see you're feeling better. Mickey, please pour me some wine. Daniel, meet Mona; Mona, Daniel. You two will have lots to talk about, being the two new ones of the group." Mona reached out a hand to Daniel, who shook it tentatively; he clearly had no idea what he'd walked into. Mickey braced herself for whatever Louisa would have to say to the one person she had yet to address. "And Nathan, now that we're in the same room together, do you think we should discuss this?"

She dropped the manila envelope in the middle of the table; a corner landed in a dish of olive oil.

"Oh!" Mona said, but it sounded like a hiccup. "Maybe you two should talk about that in private?"

Mickey went to snatch up the envelope, spotting the words "Massachusetts" and "Court" before Louisa swatted her away.

"In private!" Louisa yelped. Her eyes looked a little wild. "Why would we possibly conduct any part of this in private? Mona, my dear, let me bring you up to speed: Nathan announced that he wanted to end our marriage right here at this very table, oh, about four months ago. Then just this week, he got my boss' secretary to hand me this, in my place of work, which is about as public as you can get. Which actually, you would know, since you've decided to barge into my workplace, too. So, I don't think this is the moment to finally call for some discretion, you know what I mean?"

Nathan had yet to react, so Louisa waved a hand in front of his face. "Earth to my soon-to-be-ex-husband! Let's hash out this so-called 'no-fault' divorce, shall we?"

"Louisa," Mickey said, "would you please accompany me to the ladies' room?"

Louisa ignored her. Mickey caught the eye of this Daniel person, who looked like he'd stepped into a trap. She hoped her expression conveyed, *You can bail, it's fine, we got this.* But Louisa draped a possessive arm around the man's shoulders, pinning him in place.

Nathan mumbled something.

"Excuse me?" Louisa demanded.

"It had to be a neutral party serving the papers," he repeated. His face was drained of color; he looked near-catatonic.

"How about the fucking mailman, then, huh?"

He was still barely audible: "'No-fault' is just a technical term. I know I'm the one at fault. Louisa—"

"Damn right you're the one at fault. And you." She poked a finger into Mona's chest. "Is this part of the arrangement with the lawyer, too, for you to show up at River Mill and shake everything up?"

Mona started to speak, but Louisa silenced her: "Let me tell both of you something, okay? You want to take a quarter of my paycheck, Nathan? Fine. You know how I really rake in the big bucks working for the Department of Education. But guess what? The joke's on you, because if your little girlfriend gets her way and sabotages those state tests, then guess who won't have a job come fall? Your sugar mama, that's who! I'll have to leave the house either way. And now your children—remember them?—may end up with two unemployed parents, plus we'll both have massive lawyer bills after duking all this out. So, congratulations. Nice planning, you two."

Mickey had sort of lost the thread. She looked to Mateo to do something. He tapped his fork against a glass, but it barely made a clink.

Abe cleared his throat and announced, "Amy's pregnant!"

That did it. Everyone looked to Abe, who himself looked surprised that he'd spoken at all.

Mickey felt whiplash, but she tried to focus on this new bombshell. "A toast!" she exclaimed.

Everyone raised their glasses—even Louisa, even Nathan, even Mona and Daniel.

"Who's Amy?" she heard Daniel whisper to Mona.

Louisa retracted her grip from around her date's shoulders, and wrapped her arms around Abe instead. "I'm so happy for you, Jones. Cheers for Abe, he's gonna have a babe. Cheers for Abe—" She indicated for the others to join in, and they all complied, desperately relieved to have moved on to this new topic.

"Amazing news, man." Mateo clapped Abe on the back.

"Children are a miracle," Nathan said mechanically.

"So true," Mona added, gratuitously.

"No wonder Amy's home sick," Mickey said. "How has she been feeling in general? Should we call her on speaker?"

"No!" Abe barked. "Sorry. She's been having a hard time sleeping, so I don't want to disturb her."

"Congrats, buddy." It was Daniel, now getting up, finally managing to extract himself. "It was very nice to meet all of you, but uh, I have to go." No one put up a fight, because *come on*. Mickey wished he'd invite Mona to join him in taking her leave, too.

Louisa seemed to have forgotten she'd brought a date, and took a beat to catch up. "Wait, I'm coming with you."

The man looked reluctant, but what could he do? "Okay, I'll drive you home."

Louisa went around hugging half the table. "Love you, Micks. So happy for you, Jones. Happy birthday, Mateo." She took Daniel's hand. "Bye, everyone."

Mona was the one to pick up the manila envelope. "You forgot this."

Louisa snatched up the envelope, and they all watched her leave.

———

Abe couldn't believe what he'd done. What was wrong with him? His friends were all beaming at him, their happy gazes like lasers to his heart. He'd told the truth; he hadn't lied. And of course, he'd done it to save Louisa from further humiliation. And maybe a part of him had welcomed the playing out of the fantasy: the scenario that Amy's pregnancy was purely joyous news to be celebrated.

Once Louisa was gone, Abe couldn't bear to stay, either. "Excuse me," he said. He headed in the direction of the men's room, then continued on to the exit. He hoped his friends would forgive his abrupt departure.

Outside, he dialed Amy. No answer. He tried three more times, and three more times the ringing ceded to a recording of his wife's voice. He started to leave a message, to explain himself and apologize for revealing her news, but after lots of stuttering and backtracking, he said, "Never mind, I'll explain in person." He had to get back to his wife.

And then they were four. The main dishes hadn't even arrived when Mona and Nathan nodded at each other and Mona informed the table that they were taking off too, that after such a stressful evening they were going to swing by her yoga studio for some breath work—Mateo wasn't sure he'd heard that right—before they had to relieve the babysitter.

Mona wasn't as far away as she thought when Mateo heard her say, "What a shit show."

So, then it was just him and his wife at the long table, as Kimmy the waitress set down the plates heaping with pasta and cheese and butter and meat.

"Hungry?" Mickey asked.

Mateo laughed. "Not really."

His stomach brimmed with butterflies; he'd been clenching his fists for an hour. Maybe his wife's surprise had already happened: Surprise, your friends will bring dates to spite each other and yell about their divorce proceedings at dinner! Surprise, your other friend who spent years trying to conceive before deciding to adopt will announce that they're pregnant! Surprise, everyone will ditch your birthday party before the food even arrives!

"Oh, you've got to eat," Mickey said, dropping generous scoops of mushroom risotto and spaghetti carbonara onto both of their plates.

When Kimmy appeared with one final dish, Caprese salad, Mickey peered up at her. "Our friends have abandoned us. Please come sit and help us make a dent in all this."

Kimmy consulted her watch. "My shift's just about over, so sure, why not?"

Mateo got a funny feeling, the butterflies flitting faster. Hours later, Mickey would assure him that no, it hadn't all been choreographed ahead of time: everyone else leaving right in time for Kimmy to swoop in and dine *a trois*. She hadn't planned to loop in Kimmy until later. But there they found themselves, eating chicken parmigiana off each other's plates, feeding each other forkfuls of cacio e pepe, clinking and refilling wine glasses. What a relief to be rid of their friends with all their complicated baggage and entanglements; what a pleasure to sit and eat with his wife and this acquaintance who turned out to be very easy to talk to.

Mickey touched Mateo's hand, then she touched Kimmy's hand, then she brought his hand on top of Kimmy's, so he was touching both his wife's hand and the waitress' hand.

Mickey's voice was a tickle in his ear. "Is this okay?"

He liked to be asked. "Yes," he said, thinking it felt nice and warm, this stack of hands. He grew bold. "So what's the plan?"

"Follow me," said his wife.

The hotel was down the block. The suite smelled like sandalwood, the lights half-dimmed. There was Prosecco, and Maggie Rogers on the stereo, and a small mountain of pillows on the bed. The pictures on the wall were a notch classier than the usual hotel fare. Mateo focused on the details. Only from the corner of his eye did he register another one, that his wife's lips were pressed against the waitress'. Even when he faced them, he had to squint; it was like staring at the sun. A hand extended toward him, Mateo took it, and then there was no turning back.

He felt like he was watching the experience from above: Who was having things done to him by these two beautiful women? Surely not him.

Their clothes collected in little piles on the floor, and Mateo noted his blue button-down and Mickey's black satin bra mingling with unfamiliar pink lace. He backed up a step. Now that he was out of the fray, he could take it in. He could observe the women pressed together, their tits saying hello like new friends—the thought was so silly it made him laugh. Mickey winked at him, a small gesture that brought Mateo back into his body. He took another step back and tumbled onto the bed. The women followed. Mateo hung back and watched, enjoying the private show. He felt a little longing, a little jealousy, and a low thrum of nerves—a cocktail of sensations that fired him up in a way that he was pretty sure he liked. He knew he liked watching his wife enjoy herself.

After some time, he whispered to Mickey, "Can it just be us now?"

She took care of it. Kimmy gave long, lingering kisses to both of them, then Mickey led her out. Mateo let their goodbye chatter wash over him, the harmony of female voices, then his wife returned to bed. Mateo relaxed, now that it was the two of them. This is what he really wanted. He rolled over to her, the sheets still warm from the third body.

"Surprise," Mickey said, her finger pads stroking his belly.

"And I thought it was going to be cake."

"Oh, there's cake, too."

She slipped her panties back on, and tossed Mateo his boxers. She pulled a cakebox from the mini-fridge, revealing a perfect mound of cheesecake and two forks. They ate straight from the box, sprawled across the sheets. It was so delightful that Mateo had an urge to invite their daughter to join them: Mel loved cheesecake almost as much as she loved hotels. The thought of his little family unit made Mateo's eyes well up. He blinked away the tears, embarrassed.

Mickey kissed his chest and nestled against him, braiding her legs through his. For all these years they'd ended the day this way, and it always made Mateo feel that all was right with the world. "I love you," she murmured, already half-asleep.

"I love us together," he replied.

Amy saw nothing but blue sky and the occasional fluffy white cloud. She was a giant bird, soaring in sweeping arcs, so light, so free.

"Honey. Psst, Ames."

She was being nudged in her hip; she had a hip, and was no longer soaring and free; she was heavy and trapped under a tangle of blankets.

"Are you awake?"

Annoyed, Amy rolled over to see her husband and his sweet smile.

"Hi." The words were thick on her tongue. "How was dinner?"

"You don't want to know."

That perked her up. She turned on the bedside lamp. "Tell me."

Abe was a natural storyteller. Amy was rapt; she couldn't believe Nathan and Louisa's divorce papers became the table's centerpiece, and that she'd missed out on meeting Mona. For weeks, she'd been doing all she could to retreat from life, but now suddenly she missed her friends. She decided she'd call Louisa in the morning.

"Honey, I told them you're pregnant. It just slipped out." Then came the explanation, the apologies, the regret in Abe's eyes.

"I understand." She really did. She'd put her husband through hell, for which she felt terrible, and he was all mixed up inside. It made sense that he'd want to tell his friends the news; to him, it was a miracle. "I mean, I am pregnant."

"I'll fix it! I'll tell them whatever you want, that I was lying, or temporarily insane, or that you lost the baby."

Somehow this last idea made Amy's voice catch in her throat. "It's okay. I started taking prenatal vitamins." She didn't know why she said it, or why she'd finally broken the seal of the bottle she'd purchased over a year ago (the expiration date was still three months away). She supposed popping the pills made her feel like a good person, when so much lately made her feel rotten to the core.

"Okay," he said cautiously, clearly straining not to ask follow-up questions.

"I know this is torture for you," she said. "I don't know if it helps to tell you that it's torture for me, too."

"Oh Amy, that's the last thing I want."

"Well, I'm sorry. I'm confused. I feel lost, and stupid, and ashamed of the fact that I'm having doubts."

"I'm here for you."

"I know you are. And I know how lucky I am to have you. I'm just so tired."

Abe kissed her on the top of her head, and Amy let herself be wrapped up in her husband's arms.

She was somewhere between awake and asleep when she felt herself become the bird again, gliding through the air. Now she was descending, until the world came into view, and she made her landing on a familiar pair of shoulders: Abe's. But he didn't notice, because something was in his lap. A baby. He was singing and rocking it, and Amy felt hollowed out. Bird bones are hollow, right? It came to her suddenly: she was an albatross, weighing down on Abe, the literal embodiment of the metaphor. It felt ridiculous, and intolerable. But it also made a certain sense, and gave Amy an idea. She could have this baby and give it to Abe, then flap her wings and fly away to somewhere she truly belonged.

CHAPTER 45
Louisa

Louisa used to be a pro at that computer game Minesweeper, her fingers moving faster than her mind to clear the board without detonating any mines. It used to feel like a metaphor for how skillfully she navigated the world, relying on her smarts and intuition not only to skirt danger but to win, to set records, to rack up gold stars and accolades. It was amazing to think that she used to have time to play videogames.

Now, it felt as if Louisa was stumbling around ineptly, managing to explode every mine. This morning, in the middle of washing up after breakfast, Phoebe had removed her toothbrush from her mouth and asked her mother, "What's divorce?" Her baby, not even three years old, had heard the word and understood that it was significant to her life. Louisa would've preferred if she'd asked about death or where babies came from, the normal hard stuff. She'd responded in exactly the wrong way, getting all worked up, clutching at Phoebe's shoulders and demanding to know where she'd heard about divorce. *Brilliant,* teaching her child to be ashamed of asking a question! Phoebe burst into tears, and Louisa had to exit the bathroom to collect herself, leaving Finn to comfort his sister. Twenty minutes later, halfway to daycare, Louisa realized she'd left the kids' lunches on the kitchen counter. "Fuck!" she shouted, banging at the steering wheel.

"Bad word, Mama!" Finn scolded.

"Oh, give me a goddamn break," she snapped back. Then both her kids were crying.

"Dada and Mona don't talk so angry," Phoebe whined through hiccupping sobs.

"Well, good for them." Louisa felt the vein in her neck throbbing. *This is divorce,* she considered. *It's your mother forgetting your lunch and cursing and shouting at you and making you cry.*

School wasn't much better. Students Against Testing had expanded their efforts, and the hallways were papered with their messaging. Every flier felt like a personal affront to Louisa.

Then there was Poolehauzer's secretary, Mrs. Perkins, who told Louisa, "He's been ready for you," as if she were twenty, not two, minutes late for her meeting with the principal. Her expression was so smug that Louisa was tempted to clap back with some nasty vitriol.

But unlike earlier with her kids, she exercised will power and stayed mum. Idly, she considered how much was left unsaid over the course of a day, held in out of restraint or fear or social propriety, covered up with a tight-lipped smile. Relatedly, why *not* shoot the messenger, if the messenger happened to be a self-satisfied little prig named Mrs. Perkins? Again, Louisa marveled at Nathan's idiocy for choosing this woman to serve her the divorce papers.

The principal's office was so packed with mines that even the most careful maneuvering would leave Louisa with little hope of safety. Her supposed comrade, Chad Mack, stood erect, looking primed for battle; but Louisa knew they weren't really on the same side.

Poolehauzer pounded at his desk. "T minus one week, Ms. Bauer!" He was jumpy with excitement. "The exam packets are on their way: signed, sealed, and near-ready to be delivered." Louisa felt a spike of anxiety. "Oh, and I impulse-ordered buckets of these pencils, thinking it might motivate the students." Dr. P twirled a pencil between his fingers, demonstrating how the stripes of sparkly pink and blue looked to be climbing endlessly; it would be a perfect distraction for kids who were supposed to be concentrating on exam questions. "Also, my lovely wife was thoughtful enough to pick up cupcakes from a little bakery called The Test Kitchen." He winked. "Get it? Take one, take one."

Louisa reluctantly accepted a red velvet one. "Have you guys seen the student protests?" she asked, pointlessly, because how could they have missed them? "Unfortunately, I don't think colorful pencils will be enough to persuade the kids to cooperate for the tests." It was hard to be taken seriously with her fingertips coated in cream-cheese frosting.

Poolehauzer waved off her concern. "The students are just blowing off steam. It's like stress relief. If there's one thing about teenagers, it's that you've got to let them express their anger. Plus, it's on-trend to be anti-testing. But when it comes down to it, no kid will want a poor score on their record."

"Excellent point," said Chad.

Louisa tried to catch Chad's eye to see if he really shared their boss' nonchalance, but he stared straight ahead, as inscrutable as cardboard.

"Proceed as planned," Poolehauzer said. "You know the drill: When the exams arrive, sort them for distribution to the proctors, and remember, no tampering with the packets!" He wagged his finger at her in mock-jest, like she was a naughty child.

"I've got it," Louisa said.

"That's the spirit, Ms. Bauer."

She finished the cupcake on the way back to her office, her stomach already churning from the sugar, as meanwhile she fielded student glares and snarls; one kid defiantly passed her a Students Against Testing flyer. There was no doubt about it: Louisa was the face of the state tests, public enemy number one.

She hid herself away for the rest of the afternoon, staring at her desk: on one side, the upcoming testing schedule; on the other, the manila folder containing the divorce papers. Only after the last bell rang and enough time passed for most everyone to filter out of the halls did Louisa step out.

Just her luck, another landmine: Mona. She must've gotten on the permanent sub list, filling in for whoever was out.

To avoid her, Louisa ducked around a corner and found herself face to face with a Students Against Testing sign penned by a wannabe rapper: "We're requesting no infesting us with B.S. testing! We're suggesting investing in our future! We're S.A.T. and we're protesting!"

Louisa began riffing on a protest rhyme of her own, muttering it under her breath: "We had our tiffs, we had a rift. Now I'm defendant and you're plaintiff. Our marriage has experienced irretrievable breakdown. Now you're coming for a shakedown."

"Clever kids, huh?" Mona had found her.

Louisa tried to modulate her breathing, but couldn't keep the tremor from her voice: "Listen, apparently I can't help that we share a place of employment. But I can choose not to interact with you."

"I know, but listen." When Mona touched her arm, Louisa flinched. "They're planning a walk-out for day one of testing. So far, a third of the school has signed on. I just thought you'd want to know."

Every muscle in Louisa's face tensed. Again, she considered the concept of shooting the messenger.

"Louisa? Are you okay?"

"Are you seriously still standing here?"

Mona recoiled, then skittered away. The hall was now empty. Louisa stared at the sign, the *requesting, infesting, testing, suggesting* scrawled in rudimentary magic marker. She felt disgusted. *How hard was it to just sit for the stupid tests and let the state know how much you know?*

At first it was just a corner. But the sound of the tear was so satisfying that Louisa craved more. She ripped the poster in half, directly through the "B.S." She peered around her—coast still clear.

So, she tore the thing to shreds, tossed the pieces in the air, and stomped on them when they landed. She had visions of continuing down the hall, clawing at more posters, punching through banners, destroying every last piece of Students Against Testing propaganda.

"Bauer?"

She spun around to find her friend ducking out of his classroom. "Jones? What are you—why are you still here? I didn't think ..." Faltering, her throat went dry.

"I stayed late to grade. What are you doing?"

His voice was gentle. Louisa crumpled to the floor and dropped her face into her palms. The tears felt automatic.

"Hey, it's okay." Abe sat down beside her.

She was doing that blubbering thing where she could barely get a word out. "It's just, Nathan, and the kids, and the students. Why can't they just suck it up and take the tests, you know?" Abe failed to suppress a smile. "What?"

"We just did a whole unit on the history of peaceful protest. I'm sorry they're making your life hard, but I've got to say, I'm proud of the students."

"Oh, screw you, Jones." Louisa gestured to the construction paper confetti surrounding them. "Can we keep this momentary lapse in judgment between us?"

"I don't know," said Abe. "I might just report you to the S.A.T. ringleaders. Annabelle is infamous for showing no mercy."

"Gee, thanks. Anyway, what are you still doing here? Why aren't you home nursing your wife through morning sickness?"

Abe let out a puff. "I'm avoiding her."

"What? Why?"

"She doesn't want the baby."

"What do you mean?" Louisa spoke carefully, flashing back to Amy spending the night at her house; her questions, her fear, all of it.

"That's what she says, at least."

"Abe, I'm so sorry." Now Louisa was the one offering comfort, rubbing her friend's shoulder.

"I really don't know what's going to happen."

Louisa had so many questions, but there would be time to ask them later. For now, she said simply, "Me neither."

The two of them sat there, butts on the cold linoleum, contemplating their uncertain futures.

CHAPTER 46

Melody

It felt like a magic trick, how Melody could look in the dressing room mirror in just her bra and panties and feel okay, maybe even better than okay. How her mom could pass her a handful of dresses from the next stall over and say, "I bet one of these will look fantastic on you," and Melody could actually believe her.

Since they'd started dating, Bryce had been telling Melody she was cute, pretty, beautiful, even sexy. Of course, her parents and friends had been paying her the same compliments her whole life (except the last one). But, filtered through the mouth of her first boyfriend, it was like Melody was hearing the words for the first time and only now understanding their deepest, truest meaning. She performed a little spin in the dressing room, feeling cute and beautiful and pretty—even sexy. Emboldened, she winked at herself in the mirror, then rolled her eyes at herself.

"Try the purple first!" Mickey called out

Another bit of magic, that the mere fact of her mother suggesting something didn't make Melody want to do the opposite. When had this shift happened? Melody pulled on the purple gown, the racerback straps emphasizing her strong shoulders and the slinky satin falling just so. It wasn't just Bryce's words that had transformed Melody's feelings about her body. Her body itself had changed. Before she'd been built like a box, but this past year she'd shot up three inches without gaining a pound. Swim season had left her limbs lean and strong, her stomach flat, and her waist cinched. Her acne had cleared up and her posture had improved. Even her boobs had finally grown a bit.

"Let me see!" her mom called out. When Melody ventured out, she got the delighted gasp she was hoping for. Mickey clapped. "I just knew you would look stunning in that one."

It wasn't just mother's intuition. Melody stood face to face with her mother and it was like looking in the mirror: same height and hair, matching features, identical figures. Even a few months ago, this would've driven Melody crazy, but now she felt proud. Mickey was a knock-out, and it followed that she herself wasn't so bad either.

That was the other thing that had changed: namely, Melody's feelings about *everything*. For most of high school, so much had felt impossible, but recently something had loosened inside of her. It was like she'd emerged from a raging storm into the sun. Part of it was Bryce. Another part was her college acceptance letter. Knowing she would soon be moving across the country to start a new, independent life made Melody more tolerant of her current circumstances, more appreciative of all the people populating her life. So much of growing up had mystified and mortified her, all the changes that felt totally out of her control, the constant quest to figure out who she was, with no satisfying answers. It could be so dispiriting. But lately Melody had stopped overthinking every little thing. She'd settled into herself, relaxed a little.

"The silver next?"

As Melody wiggled her way into the silver dress, she half-listened to her mother's monologue on the other side of the dressing room door. "I cannot believe my daughter is going to the senior prom. On my birthday, no less. I may just treat myself to a fancy dress, too, declare my birthday dinner a formal event. Why not usher in the last year of my thirties in style, you know?"

Mickey seemed to have changed recently, too. She'd always been a force to be reckoned with, the biggest personality in the room, plus Melody's hero (though she never would've admitted that aloud). But Melody detected a new lightness in her mother lately, and it made her more fun to be around.

"Let's see, let's see!"

Melody tuned out her mother's pleas, wanting a private moment to marvel at her own image. *This* was the dress: strapless and floor-length, studded with sequins that winked in the light, hugging her in all the right places. It was like nothing Melody had worn before. It made her feel like the best version of herself.

She imagined Bryce seeing her for the first time in all this shimmery glory, affixing a corsage to her wrist, and telling her she'd never looked so beautiful. Her school didn't do the prom-queen thing, and Melody had gotten the full anti-princess indoctrination as a girl, but at the moment she felt like royalty. She wanted a matching tiara; she'd pay for it with her own babysitting money if she had to. It would be the perfect outfit to wear on the night of her first time. She pictured Bryce's fingers removing her crown, unzipping her, and taking her virginity. Melody hadn't yet shared this plan with her boyfriend, also a virgin, although she knew he'd be on board. She'd been holding it in, her own special secret.

A knock on the dressing room door. "Are you stuck in there? Come on, show your mother!"

Melody emerged with a big smile on her face.

"Oh, that's the one, no question."

"Definitely," Melody agreed.

"My baby's all grown up!" Her mother's hug turned into lifting her off the ground and spinning her around. "When you walk in there in that dress, everyone's going to try to make out with you."

"Mom, gross." Okay, so Mickey still did have the ability to mortify her.

"Oh, and I grabbed us these, just for fun." Mickey held up two hangers with matching gowns that were long and red with deep plunging necklines and cut-outs at the waist. "You try that one and I'll try this one."

"Um."

"Come on, humor me."

The gown was super-trashy but also sort of spectacular. Slipping it on made Melody feel like a different person.

"Ready when you are!" Mickey sang out.

"One, two, three." They emerged together from their dressing rooms and both devolved into giggles. Seeing her mother in the gown was even more ridiculous than seeing it on herself.

"You, Melody Quinn Moran, look hot," Mickey said.

"I can't believe I'm saying this, but you do, too, Mom."

"Not so bad for an old broad, huh? Just add a bunch of makeup and jewels and we could be mobster girlfriends."

Lizzo started up through the store's speakers, and Mickey began bopping around. She called out to the saleswoman. "Hey, would you turn it up?"

It never would've occurred to Melody to make such a request, but her mom hadn't even thought twice. Mickey reached for Melody's hands, and the two of them danced through the dressing rooms. Striking poses in front of the three-way mirror, they spotted the saleswoman behind them. Again, Mickey didn't hesitate: She drew the woman into their little dance party, and by the next chorus all three of them were busting out their silliest moves and cracking each other up.

"Ahem."

Melody noticed her dad before Mickey did. She stopped short and folded her arms across her chest, suddenly embarrassed, even as her mom kept moving. The saleswoman slipped away.

"What's going on, guys?" He sounded wary.

Mickey performed a final spin, stopping to plant a kiss on Mateo's mouth. "Hey, babe. Mel found herself a prom dress. Isn't it gorgeous?" She winked at her daughter.

The look on her father's face could only be described as aghast, and Melody's mouth went dry. "You're joking." Before either of them could explain that yes, she was joking, he said, "You're not twenty-five, Melody. And you," he addressed Mickey with a scowl, "you're not twenty-five, either."

"Wait, we're not?" Mickey said. "Could've fooled me."

It drove Melody nuts when her mom did this: stoked her dad's anger with sarcasm. She thought both her parents were being dumb.

Mateo dug his heels in. "It's so typical for you to encourage our daughter to wear a prom dress that makes her look like a ... like a floozy."

Mickey tried to catch Melody's eye with her smirk, but as ridiculous as her dad's word choice was, Melody refused to get involved with whatever was going on here; she sensed it had little to do with her.

Mickey turned to Mateo. "Mel can wear whatever she wants to wear to her prom."

"Uh, not if what she wants to wear is *that.*"

The way he pointed at her made Melody want to put on a sweater. She'd had enough. "What the hell is wrong with you people? Dad, you sound so sexist, and also from like a century ago. Mom, why are you acting like I actually want this ridiculous dress? We were just messing around. Both of you are insane!"

She stomped back to her dressing room and slammed the door, quickly changing into her jeans and sweatshirt, leaving the red monstrosity in a heap on the floor. She slumped onto the bench, trapped by her parents' whisper-arguing on the other side of the door. She overheard one of Mickey's favorite lines, "It's the principle of the matter." Meanwhile, her dad was accusing her mom of something. He mentioned the saleswoman. He got louder, saying he felt like taking a shower, and he didn't even know what was going on anymore, and that Mickey always had to take things a step too far. Mickey scoffed and called him a prude.

This was the kind of shit Melody was not going to miss when she went away. What would happen to her parents, she wondered, without her there to mediate when her mom turned into a drama queen and her dad got a stick up his ass, without her reminders for everyone to simmer down and act like a goddamn family? Well, that wasn't Melody's problem; she was leaving.

CHAPTER 47

Amy

One week. That was the timeline Amy gave her husband, for when she would finally be ready to hash things out, to really talk. Amy was good with a deadline. She liked knowing what was expected of her and when, so she could plan things out and pace herself accordingly. But now, the days were ticking by.

Of course, a bigger, realer deadline loomed over Amy, which she was reminded of when she slunk out of the office on her lunch break to visit the bizarrely named Bright Skies Clinic and the receptionist asked her how many weeks along she was.

"Eleven," she said. "I'm not ready to ... I don't ... I'm here for a consult, I just want to talk."

"Sure." The woman seemed unphased by Amy's unintelligible sputtering. "A doctor can meet with you in about twenty minutes."

"Thanks."

The waiting room was like any other: full of people flipping through magazines and staring at their phones and zoning out. It was mostly women, ranging from teenagers to ladies who seemed well above child-bearing age, and there were a couple of men, too. They were a mix of races, although no other Asians. No one chatted, and it was hard to tell who was with whom. Amy settled into a chair, then she got antsy and paced from the magazine rack to the water cooler and back. How come everyone else seemed so calm? It was freaking Amy out, how little everyone else was freaking out. She felt a buzz in her pocket; without looking, she knew it was Abe texting her a heart. He always texted her a heart during his sixth period break at school.

"Ms. Sullivan-Jones?" A woman in scrubs appeared in the doorway; she looked Indian. "The doctor is ready for you."

Less than ten minutes had passed. Doctor's offices were always running late, not early, so what was going on here? Amy felt jittery and the first rumbles of panic were gaining traction in her belly.

"I'm sorry," she blurted out.

She fled the clinic. Out on the sidewalk, she bent over, hands on knees, gasping for air.

Then it was the next day, Amy's next lunch break, one day closer to her self-imposed deadline to speak to Abe. Her meandering walk led her through the double doors of a store as absurdly named as the clinic: Buy Buy Baby. It should've been the name of an adoption agency. But this place didn't actually sell little bundles of joy; it sold all the gear you never knew you needed for your bundle. Amy felt like a visitor in a foreign land. It was totally overwhelming, navigating the aisles of strollers and seats and swings that vibrated and sang songs and had seventy-two different settings. She took a sharp turn to the clothing, where at least most items were recognizable (although what on earth was a magic sleep suit?). She kept moving. What finally stopped Amy was the "mother" section, the shelves of nursing bras and pump parts and nipple creams and other mysterious paraphernalia that apparently would be needed were she to accept this new identity of "mother." Amy had no clue how any of it worked, or how any of it might relate to her.

An employee surprised her. "Welcome to Buy Buy Baby! How far along are you?"

It was presumptuous, but Amy answered anyway, "Um, eleven weeks."

"Fantastic! Would you like to set up a registry? A consultant can meet with you in about twenty minutes."

Amy's jaw dropped. It was nearly the same thing she'd been told at the clinic. She couldn't get out a response.

"Or maybe you're just browsing? That's fine—it's a lot to take in." Amy couldn't help it, her eyes filled with tears. The saleswoman smiled and touched her elbow. "May I make a suggestion?"

She must've taken Amy's lack of response as assent, because she led her back to the clothing section. The endless combinations and permutations of organic pastel cotton were mind-boggling, as if infants had dozens of events to attend, all with different dress codes.

"Go ahead and pick out an outfit. Just one, something you really love. It'll give you a picture in your mind to focus on, and help you get excited about everything to come."

"Thanks," Amy managed.

The woman left her alone, and Amy decided to follow her advice. She zeroed in on a onesie so tiny it was hard to believe humans came in such small sizes. It was white with pale green stripes and scalloped edges, and there were matching pants and booties. Amy observed herself pick up a pom-pom cap to complete the look. How odd to discover that her taste in baby clothes included pom-poms. She arranged all the pieces, cap to booties, like she was laying out tomorrow's outfit. She tried to envision the baby who would fill the clothes: fidgeting limbs, round belly, chubby cheeks. She felt Abe's sixth-period text buzz again in her pocket. She snapped a photo of the outfit, but decided not to send it.

The line for the register was epic: women with toddlers hanging off them like extra limbs, babies call-and-response screaming, and one lone man wearing noise-canceling headphones and whistling. Amy waited for five minutes, then someone bumped into her and asked, "Excuse me, are you in line?" It was the woman's belly that had bumped her; she looked about forty-five weeks pregnant. Amy honestly wouldn't have been shocked if her water had broken right there on line. It made her panic.

"Uh, no, sorry."

She abandoned the baby clothes and stumbled out of the store. In the parking lot, she stood panting, trying to catch her breath.

CHAPTER 48

Abe

One day before the end of Abe's marital embargo, when his wife had agreed she would finally sit down to talk about the elephant in the room—er, the baby in the womb—state testing began. The whole school seemed on edge, which made Abe feel less alone with his own anxiety. And although he wouldn't have admitted it to his earnestly outraged colleagues, he was looking forward to the break from teaching. He needed a rest.

Abe accepted a cookie from a student before he noticed the "S.A.T." icing. In the lead-up to the exams, the anti-testing group had stepped up its game, creating a logo and talking points and apparent plans for a school-wide walkout. Abe was privately impressed with their efforts, even as he remained publicly neutral. He felt conflicting tugs of loyalty to the students and his fellow teachers and to Louisa. More to the point, this wasn't a battle he had the energy to fight.

Abe overheard the students psyching each other up: "You guys pumped?" "You ready?" "We've worked so hard—today it all pays off!" They exchanged fist bumps and pats on the back, like they were heading into a championship sports game.

Abe watched as Mr. Mack invaded the kids' huddle, soliciting high-fives. "Don't leave me hanging," he said. One boy lifted a limp hand. "All right, all right," added the dean. "Everyone's gonna do great in there." The muffled snickers trailed him down the hall.

Teachers weren't allowed to proctor their own subjects; Abe was assigned to eleventh grade Math, where two of the S.A.T. ringleaders, Leo Feit and Annabelle Smith, sat front and center, backs rigid, eyeing Abe's every move. It put him on edge. As he tore open the teacher packet, he imagined it igniting. Dictating the instructions, he focused on sounding as steady as possible. "Please read all exam directions carefully. When you see an arrow at the end of a page, turn to the next page."

Leo cut him off with a cry of "No!"

Annabelle added, "When we see an arrow at the end of a page, we will not turn to the next page!"

Cheers, giggles, a few groans.

Abe did his best to ignore them. "When you see an X, you have finished the section. Check your work and wait until the session is over."

This time when Leo shouted "No!" the rest of the class knew to chime in, "We will not check our work and wait until the session is over!"

This chanting went on, until Abe had no choice but to start the test session. It wasn't as bad as he'd feared. Leo and Annabelle crossed their arms over their chests and glared into the void, while a few other students dozed or created pointillism-style art out of their Scantron sheets. But the majority hunched over their test booklets and bubbled in answers, jaws strained with concentration.

After the break, Abe was mildly surprised that every student returned to their seat. This time when he read out the instructions, there were no interruptions. The session set off smoothly, with most kids taking the test in earnest. Still, Abe held his breath.

Apparently, the morning had just been a warm-up. Ten minutes into the afternoon session, the classroom intercom crackled to life. A voice that clearly did not belong to a faculty member called everyone to attention, "Testing, testing, one, two, three. Testing, testing, ZERO!" The last word was screeched, eliciting a collective wince in the room. Leo and Annabelle exchanged smiles. "Jay Robinson here, officially announcing the Students Against Testing walk-out."

Every single student in Abe's classroom stood up, abandoned their tests, and walked out.

CHAPTER 49
Louisa

Louisa was loitering pathetically outside the teachers' lounge, hoping to catch wind of idle chatter. Did the faculty, too, think the morning session hadn't been so bad? Louisa's peeks into classrooms had revealed the majority of students in test-taking mode, with just a smattering opting out. For the first time in a week, she'd relaxed. She'd let herself believe that it would all work out: the students would ace the tests, the school would retain its full funding, and her job would be safe.

So, she was caught off guard by the stampede.

The swarm of students overwhelmed her. "Walk out, rock out! Walk out, rock out!" The shouts grew louder and rowdier. For fear of getting plowed over, Louisa cowered by the bulletin boards. A boy she'd suspended at least twice made hostile eye contact, grabbed his crotch, and may or may not have whispered "Walk out, cock out" as he passed by.

The kids flooded through the double doors, exiting the building twice as fast as they did during fire drills. Louisa's panic took a moment to catch up to her. By then, she realized several teachers' heads were poked out of their doors—proctors had strict instructions not to leave assigned rooms during test sessions—and they were looking to her for guidance.

"Everything's under control," she pronounced, as if she were playing Opposites with her twins. She pulled out her walkie-talkie and radioed Poolehauzer and Chad Mack. Predictably, no response.

She invented instructions on the fly. "All teachers not on proctor duty, report immediately to the courtyard to monitor the walk-out. Any significant development, any hint of trouble, page me stat."

Why wasn't Louisa going out there herself? She was needed in the building, she told herself; surely some kids were still in classrooms dutifully sitting for exams. In truth, Louisa wasn't sure she could handle the scene outside. She feared it would be the final step to meltdown. She didn't trust herself that she wouldn't muscle into the crowd and pummel those little shits, Jay and Leo and Annabelle, to a pulp.

So, she paced the halls, feeling like an unhinged Victorian heroine roaming the misty moors, on the precipice of flinging herself into the icy sea.

A bell sounded through the intercom, mockingly marking the end of the test session. The few rule followers skulked into the halls then out to the courtyard to join their bolder peers. Next came the proctors with their stacks of tests and Scantrons, bundled in their assigned manila envelopes. Louisa wanted to hear their take on all this, but they maintained poker faces as they dropped the exams off on her desk.

The ice cream sundae social had been Louisa's idea, back before Students Against Testing swept the school. A treat to reward the kids for all their hard work leading up to the exams, and for making it through day one. The cafeteria workers would've been setting up all morning, lining up the dozen flavors and toppings Louisa had pleaded with the PTA to fund. Chad Mack was supposed to supervise. She could picture him holding court over an empty cafeteria, obliviously lapping up a mint chip cone. Would any of the students show?

Louisa tried to be inconspicuous, peering through her office window down to the courtyard. The student body barely fit into the space. Masses of kids stood shoulder to shoulder, clapping and chanting. The security guards were off to the side in a clump, one of them performing back stretches. Was there more to the plan? And how long would it last? And, wait a minute, where were the ringleaders?

Louisa's walkie-talkie went spastic: "Vice Principal Bauer, come to the courtyard, come to the courtyard right now."

Just then, she watched Jay, Leo, and Annabelle storm through the double doors into the courtyard, carrying giant cylinders of—what? Oh. It seemed to happen in slow motion, the three of them reaching the ice cream scoopers into the massive tubs and lobbing scoops into the crowd. There were squeals and shouts. More tubs and scoopers were passed around, and more and more kids got in on the action. They pelted each other, pressed ice cream into cheeks and hair, licked it off bodies. Faces looked joyful, deranged, belligerent.

Louisa's own face was frozen, as she catalogued the appearance of the flavors she'd ordered: vanilla, chocolate, strawberry, coffee, mint chip, mocha, M&M. The commands of the security guards were ignored.

Finally, Poolehauzer materialized. The crowd parted slightly, which created just the opportunity for Jay to grab a fistful of cookies and cream and fling it right in the principal's face—a perfect shot. *Holy shit.* The security guards pounced. Louisa's walkie-talkie rumbled again, and she watched through the window as her furious boss paged her, dessert dribbling down his cheeks. "Ms. Bauer, report to the courtyard immediately!" She drew her window shade and collapsed into her chair.

Stay calm, stay calm. The mantra howled in Louisa's brain over her racing heart. She dropped her forehead to the stack of manila envelopes on her desk. Every muscle was flexed, on high alert. Seconds passed before she could lift her head. She stared at the envelopes stuffed with exam answer sheets: the catalyst of a thousand students, the spark to the veritable riot going down outside.

Her instructions were clear. She was not to tamper with the tests. She was not to handle the Scantrons. She was to place them in their assigned plastic baggies, seal them shut with the official Department of Education stickers, package them in the state-issued box, tape it up, and mail it out. Simple.

Well, she would just peek. She selected a random envelope. The first Scantron was bubbled in only through question five. The next one was totally blank. A third one's bubbles spelled out a vertical "FUCKD."

Fucked—exactly how Louisa felt. Nathan's leaving was like pulling at a loose thread, and in the past six months the whole fabric of her life had come undone.

But she couldn't just give up. Somehow, she had to stitch it back together. She knew she wasn't thinking clearly, but she had to at least try to save the school and the students—and herself.

Her cell phone buzzed and buzzed. Through her walkie-talkie she heard her boss' voice; he sounded livid. "Vice Principal Bauer, where—are—you? Get yourself outside *now!*"

Everyone was outside; everyone but Louisa. She picked up a number-two pencil, cracked open a test booklet, and began reading. The passage was about the history of aviation, mind-numbingly dull. But Louisa had always been good at concentrating, to a fault. She diligently noted the attributes that qualified the Wright Flyer as the first airplane: it was powered, dirigible, et cetera. She was so focused that she didn't register the knock, or the creak of her office door opening, or the person standing in front of her desk—until she spoke.

"Oh! Sorry!"

Mona. Fucking Mona.

Louisa dropped her pencil—what was she even doing? What had she been thinking? What was her plan? This so wasn't her. "May I help you with something?" she asked, as calmly as she could, her heart in her throat.

Mona was already backing away. "Sorry. I was just checking on you, since I didn't see you outside. I was worried. I didn't mean to interrupt. I'm so sorry."

Louisa's walkie-talkie roared to life, her boss' bark filling her office: "Ms. Bauer, if you don't report to courtyard this very minute, you will be in more trouble than you can imagine!"

She powered off the device and set it down. She retrieved her bag. She stood up and took Mona by the shoulders. "You never saw me today, okay?"

The girl nodded obediently.

She walked out of her office, out of the school, and out to the parking lot, where she got in her car and drove off, never once looking back.

CHAPTER 50

Mickey's Birthday

Mickey was in her element. Flitting around the yard, greeting the kids in their fancy duds, passing out tater tots and pigs in blankets (coating their stomachs before the big night out). All the parents had pitched in for a professional photographer. Victor was a tall Frenchman with a scruffy beard and piercing amber eyes. He moseyed around capturing candids of the kids: girls fixing each other's hair, Mel's best friends James and Gus adjusting each other's bowties and stealing kisses like the adorable couple they were, a group of guys idling at the edges. When he passed Mickey, she cracked jokes, making him laugh. She directed him to snap a shot of Mel pinning Bryce's boutonniere to his lapel and Bryce securing Mel's corsage. Observing her daughter discovering romantic love was a joy for Mickey. The air was fizzy with romance.

Victor leaned in to Mickey's ear. "And who's your prom date?"

"Ha ha. No prom for me, but it is my birthday."

"I sensed it was your special day." As he hummed "Happy Birthday," he turned his camera on Mickey, and she posed dramatically. She could feel people's eyes on her, and she knew she looked good, all dressed up in her new jade halter jumpsuit with gold hoops and matching wedges. She was the only mom there who might've possibly been mistaken for a high school senior. Not that it was a competition, plus none of the others had gotten pregnant at age twenty and none owned a gym. But Mickey couldn't help that it made her feel good.

Mateo passed by with a plate of appetizers, and Mickey grabbed the back of his shirt, then called Mel over to their huddle. "Family photo time. Everyone say 'cheesy prom'!" After Victor got the shot, Mickey squeezed her husband's bicep. It hadn't been his choice to host half the senior class in their backyard for photos. But it was his only daughter's prom night and his wife's birthday, and he was being a good sport—handing out drinks, shaking hands, even helping one of the girls mend a broken sandal strap. Mickey spotted him chatting by the drinks stand with Kiki Smithson, mother to Mel's friend Ezra. Kiki was attractive in an old-stock New England way: fresh-faced, with good teeth, clad head to toe in L.L. Bean. Mickey meandered over to eavesdrop.

"I was terrified to leave home for college," Mateo was saying. Not exactly the flirtatious chatter she was expecting. "Thinking about Melody leaving feels the same."

"Don't I know it," Kiki replied. "Ezra can barely get himself dressed. I figure I'll be driving to Rhode Island every weekend to do his laundry."

Mateo laughed along with Kiki, but Mickey knew that's not what he'd meant. Mel was strong and capable; she could do her own laundry, plus ace a course-load of A.P.s while killing it on the swim team. Mateo wasn't scared for her; he was scared for himself: How could they possibly fill the Mel-shaped hole in their home? How would it be after he was left behind?

Mickey swooped in, smiling at Kiki and slinging an arm around her husband. "Hey, how's my number-one?" she said. It was part-reminder, *I'm your wife—remember me? And I'm not going anywhere.*

"Good, good. I should probably check on the next batch of tots. Excuse me, ladies," Mateo slipped out from under her arm, leaving Mickey to field Kiki's bland commentary about this significant milestone in their children's lives.

When the line of limos pulled up to the curb, Mickey contributed to the cheers. She hadn't attended her own prom; unlike Mateo, she'd been laser-focused on getting out of her hometown and on with her life. So, it was fun to finally join in on this sweet, kitschy tradition, even vicariously. She'd snagged her daughter's purse from her room earlier and popped in a few goodies: chocolate kisses and a Sephora lip gloss, plus a couple of condoms. She pulled Mel close for one last hug. "Have the best night. I love you."

"Love you, too. Where's Dad?"

It was a good question. Mateo often went missing during major moments with their daughter, when it all got to feel like too much. Mel's friends were starting to pile into the limos, and James and Gus were calling out to her and Bryce to join them, but Melody told them to wait a minute. She ran inside, and found her father; he'd been watching from the foyer. Mickey observed as father and daughter hugged; there were tears in Mateo's eyes. It was sweet.

But the longer they held on, Mickey—who never felt jealous when pretty women flirted with Mateo or (rarely) vice versa—began feeling envious. Unlike his romantic passion for her, Mateo's paternal passion had never waned over time; if anything, he'd seemed to grow more and more attached to Mel. Why wasn't it that way with Mickey, too?

The embrace finally ended, and Mel and Bryce went off with their friends. Mickey waved the limos goodbye, then joined her husband. She reached out to squeeze him in the same way their daughter had, trying to capture some of the intensity she'd observed. Mateo hugged her back, but just for a moment before pulling away to pat her on the back.

———⟶

"You're shitting me!" "No way!" "Holy shit!" Amy felt like an exclamation machine, punctuating every line of Abe's story with shock and awe as they drove to Giorgio's. His job often sounded like it took place in another universe, but this was new: a school protest turned walkout turned food fight.

"The principal's face getting pummeled with ice cream is an image I won't soon forget," Abe said. "And the sound of the cheers as they dragged away the perp."

"What about Louisa?" Amy asked. "I hope she wasn't targeted, too."

"I honestly couldn't even find her. The courtyard was utter chaos, and she wasn't picking up her phone. I'm sure she was neck-deep in suspensions and clean-up and who knows what other muck."

Amy shook her head. "The most dramatic moment of my work-day was when I typed the wrong bracket and had to redo twenty minutes' worth of work."

Wasn't this nice, wasn't this easy? Amy rested her hand on Abe's, and at the next red light, he leaned over to kiss her for the duration of the stop. For twenty-four more hours, baby talk was off the table, and what a relief to focus on Abe's school drama instead. Even the birthday dinner felt like a nice distraction. If nothing else, Amy was looking forward to the food; her stomach was rumbling.

When they arrived at Giorgio's, only Mickey and Mateo were at the table. Both stood to greet them.

"Wow, Mickey," Amy said, taking in the length of her friend; she looked like a movie star. "Growing older suits you. You look stunning."

"Well, you're glowing. Bring it in, mama! Finally, I can congratulate you in person!" Amy acquiesced to the hug, saying nothing.

Amy started to feel off-kilter as the first plates of food arrived. Her stomach kept rumbling, then seized up at random. She tried to detect a pattern in the jolts of pains, to no avail. Mateo and Mickey were talking about their daughter's send-off to prom, and how in the blink of an eye it would be Abe and Amy's turn with their kid. Abe, bless him, steered the conversation away from their future and back to Melody: was she still dating that River Mill boy, where was the prom, and would there be an after-party? No one seemed to notice when the cramps hit Amy so hard that she had to double over to cradle her belly. She made like she was reaching down to dig through her bag—conveniently, she found Tylenol. She ordered a seltzer.

"What do you mean, is there an after-party?" Mateo asked. "The prom isn't enough?"

Mickey rolled her eyes playfully at her husband. "There's a sleep-over at Gus' house. Mel claims it'll just be the gays and the gals, but I tucked a couple condoms into her purse just in case." She winked.

Mickey seemed to love being provocative to get a rise out of Mateo, but Amy didn't stick around for his reaction. Because something bad was happening to her insides. And in her underwear. She bolted up, muscle memory carrying her to the ladies' room.

When she tugged down her pants, there was no mistaking it. This wasn't the rusty brown of her period—no, a bright red stain marred the white cotton of her underwear. Amy's stomach tightened again, sending drops of the same red into the toilet bowl.

Amy felt detached as she watched the red dilute the water and swirl into the pinkish streaks. She felt like her younger self doing a science experiment with a dropper and food coloring to learn about solubility. She kept observing and observing, resisting forming a hypothesis. Maybe she could just sit there seeing the drop, drop, drop of blood from her body into the toilet, until eventually all would return to normal. Another seizing up was followed by a gushing wet-ness. Amy gathered a big wad of toilet paper and reached down to wipe. Between her legs was an oozing, thick and viscous. It soaked right through the toilet paper and pooled in her palm. She held her hand up to her face, slick with red. In the fastest flash, she thought, *My baby*. Then nothing, an absence, a buzzing between her ears.

"Does anyone have a pad?" she called out, though she had no idea if anyone else was with her in the bathroom. Miraculously, a hand reached under her stall, and it was one of those horrible thick pads that made Amy think of school nurses' offices, exactly what she needed. She felt a warmth toward the sisterhood of fellow menstru-ators who'd come through for her in her moment of need.

The tears starting up, and terrified that a single one would unleash a flood, Amy commanded herself to snap out of it and focus. She had to clean herself up. It took half a roll of toilet paper plus most of her mini-tube of hand sanitizer for her hands and inner thighs. The job done, Amy pulled up her pants. Her belly was still an angry wreck, but at least she was steady on her feet. In a way, she felt steadier than she had in months. She glanced back at the bathroom stall and took a mental snapshot, guessing she might want to call it up later in her mind: The space was understated, simple, cool. They were descriptors Amy once would've used to characterize herself, although not lately. But maybe, she thought as she left the bathroom and reentered the restaurant, she was now headed back to herself.

———

Nathan could fill notebooks with all the things Louisa did that had driven him absolutely mad, things he'd felt he couldn't tolerate for one more day and was desperate to be free of: Her irritating ability to come up with the perfect thing to say or do to soothe every baby fit and toddler tantrum, when nothing Nathan did had ever worked; her way of turning stoic and steely in stressful situations; how she refused to wear socks to bed, preferring to press her ice-cold feet against his calves at random intervals throughout the night; her habit of picking up any glass set down for a single second and whisking it away to the sink, sighing as if she were surrounded by helpless slobs; the truly terrible voices she did for Daniel Tiger and Peppa Pig and all the other characters that populated the kids' storybooks; her simplistic, self-satisfied interpretation of Nathan's research that she refused to let go of, insisting that Markov chains represented a kind of aspirational life philosophy of dismissing the past as irrelevant and looking only to the future. Except all of these things now seemed endearing to Nathan, quirks rather than character flaws. When he was honest with himself, he missed them. He missed her.

The feeling rushed over Nathan when he spotted Louisa walking toward the table, looking like a shell of his capable and headstrong wife. Something had happened to her, something bad, and Nathan yearned to embrace her and reassure her that everything would be okay. But he knew he'd given up the right to play that role in her life. Plus, there was a good chance he was the cause of her distress. He'd woken up the morning after Mateo's birthday and felt utterly disgusted with himself. For months he'd been acting like an asshole, taking out all of his disappointments and frustrations on Louisa, imagining the obvious answer was to call it quits on their marriage and find something better, and feeling superior for having found this solution. The last straw was serving his wife the divorce papers at her school, demanding so much when she'd done nothing wrong. And look at Louisa now: she looked wrecked. How Nathan wished in that moment that he could believe in her ideas about Markov chains; how he longed to erase the past four months and say, "Oops, sorry, never mind, can we go back to the way things were?"

Nathan had overheard Mona talking to a friend, debating the merits of Silver Lake versus Los Feliz. He'd confronted her to ask whether she was planning to move to Los Angeles, and she'd shrugged. "I'm thinking about it. All this divorce and alimony talk has been messing with my energy; I'm feeling it in my back. So, it's probably time for me to move on. You could come if you want." She said the last bit so half-heartedly that Nathan laughed, and she did, too. It was kind of a nice moment, actually. Nathan realized that although he felt sad about the possibility of Mona leaving, it was only a little sad.

But it wasn't just about Mona. Nathan missed his life. The past few months had been a lot of things: exhilarating and freeing and sexy, but also messy and sad. At first, he'd felt like he was finally becoming the man he was meant to be. But lately he realized how delusional he'd been, how he'd transformed into a coward who believed life was supposed to be all fun and games. Nathan was tired of himself. He knew he'd lost his way.

The big question was, could he find his way back? Would Louisa take him back, and could things be different between them? That afternoon, Mona had texted him "School=total anarchy!!!" and Nathan's first thought was, "Is Louisa okay?" He'd pinged back a dozen questions, but Mona had turned silent. The intrigue of Mona was wearing off, too. Once upon a time, Louisa would've never not responded to a text from him; Nathan had taken that for granted, too, and now he craved that reliability. As he watched Louisa sit down beside Mickey at the table, it was clear that she was not okay.

"Louisa," he said.

A flicker of panic crossed her face. "Is Mona here?"

"What? No. I shouldn't have brought her last time. I'm sorry—"

"Where is she?"

"I don't know. Her graduation's tomorrow. She's probably out with friends." Nathan felt impatient with the direction of this interaction. "Forget about Mona. How are you?"

But they were interrupted by the waiter, a new guy. Where was Kimmy? As far as this server knew, this was the group's first time at Giorgio's. Nathan felt impatient during the stumbling recitation of the specials; afterward, it was too late: Louisa was avoiding Nathan's gaze, focused on Mickey. When Abe asked her, "Do you want to talk about today?" Nathan saw her shake her head, then drain her glass of wine in one swig.

Nathan wasn't hungry or thirsty; he mostly forgot about the

spread in front of him. Instead, he spent the meal inwardly berating himself for being such a screw-up, and trying to think of ways to un-fuck everything he'd fucked up. Could he offer to drive Louisa home and then simply follow her inside, go upstairs, hug his children, and slip into bed beside his wife? Could he make an appointment with his department chair and grovel and apologize his way back to a job? Could he happen upon a time machine, jump inside, and rewind back to his old life?

"No," Louisa said. But she wasn't talking to Nathan. She wasn't talking to him at all.

———

Deep breaths. Louisa told herself she could do this.

"Happy Birthday!" she said to Mickey. Mickey thanked her.

"How are you?" she asked Mateo, doing the double-cheek kiss. He said he was fine.

"Hi," she said to Abe and Amy, hugging them both. They said hi back.

"Hi," she said to Nathan, waving from a distance. She asked if Mona was coming. She was not. Where was she? Out with friends. All right.

Okay, this wasn't so hard. Being sociable. Going through the motions. Louisa had had months of practice pretending that her life hadn't imploded, so she simply kept up the charade. It was a helpful distraction, actually, behaving as if all was well.

She sipped her wine. She smiled at the young waiter, said "please" and "thank you," ate her dinner. She participated in a conversation about prom dresses; hers had been purple with spaghetti straps, very nineties. She'd had an okay time at her prom—she'd gone with a friend, nothing dramatic or traumatic, a barely memorable night.

What exactly had Mona seen, or thought she'd seen, in her office earlier? And what had Louisa been thinking walking out in the middle of the school day, in the midst of an emergency? She'd eventually had the presence of mind to text Poolehauzer that she was sick with what she believed was food poisoning, since no one could argue with that; he hadn't even responded.

Huh? Questions were being asked of Louisa. She wasn't keeping up. The cracks were starting to show. She gave up, and gave in; she buried her head in Mickey's chest—the one soft part of her friend—and let her eyes close. Mickey didn't ask what was wrong. She just petted Louisa's head in a mesmerizing rhythm.

She sat up with a jolt, and thought, *I have to talk to Mona.* But to say what exactly? To berate her for continually butting into Louisa's business: first her marriage and now her place of her work, her private office even? Or, to beg her to take pity? She'd already left Louisa's marriage in shambles, so might she at least keep her mouth shut to let Louisa keep her job? Oh, there was nothing to say to Mona. Louisa's career was over, ruined, kaput.

She had to leave the dinner. She stood up.

She let herself be hugged by Mickey and Mateo and Abe. She was waiting for an embrace from Amy, too, but her friend took a full minute to stand. For the first time that night, Louisa got a good look at Amy. She was pale and splotchy and quaking. Louisa squeezed her close and whispered into her hair, "You look like something terrible has happened."

Amy responded with, "Yeah. You do, too."

They both stood there blinking at each other, in a weird, surprised communion. Then Louisa kissed Amy on the forehead and said, "I love you, but I have to go. I'll check in on you first thing tomorrow."

Nathan had been trying all night to stare Louisa down with his stupid puppy-dog eyes. There was no avoiding him now; he blocked her way to the exit. He took her by the shoulders and she tensed all over. "Louisa, are you all right?"

She choked out a bitter laugh. "No, Nathan, I'm not." She slithered out of his grip and was gone.

It was difficult to account for the next stretch of hours. Louisa didn't go to bed, but she wasn't exactly awake either. Pacing the halls like a sleep-walker, she might've been trying to work through her conundrum and formulate a plan. But her thoughts were caught in a loop of "What is wrong with me?" and "What now?" and "I'm screwed." Eventually, against all odds, the sun came up and her children called out to her.

———

For the third time, Abe asked Amy if she was all right. She'd been in the bathroom for ages, and now she sat slumped over in her chair, looking pale as a sheet.

"I'm fine," she insisted, but when he reached for her hand, she rebuffed him, reaching for the plate of spaghetti instead. Ever since she'd told him she was pregnant, Abe couldn't help but ask her constantly how she was feeling. The hormones made her sick and moody and hyper-sensitive, so he never knew what he was going to get, and he was still trying to figure out how to navigate that.

He'd give her some space. He pulled out his phone and saw an email from the adoption agency. "This almost never happens so fast," it began. "Luck is on your side!"

Abe reread the opener, confirmed the sender, and scanned the rest of the message: "baby girl," "three months old," "travel arrangements to China." He placed his phone screen-down on the table. His heart was pounding. He didn't know what to do with his hands. He reached for a breadstick.

It couldn't be true. The whole day had been surreal. The student walk-out and the ice cream fight, then he and Amy in the car giggling and kissing like teenagers, followed by her about-face at the table, and now this.

He took another breadstick, and caught himself drumming the pair of them on the table. He checked his phone again; the email was still there, and the information the same: a baby was waiting for Abe and Amy to adopt, should they choose to follow through. Abe had imagined this moment so many times. The elation of having finally reached a destination they'd worked so hard to get to, the way he and Amy would come together in sweet relief and excitement. But now, Abe just felt confused. His wife was clearly unwell, plus irritated with him. And he didn't even know what she wanted for their future.

How implausible that after years of them yearning for one baby, the universe was granting them two. Abe remembered Louisa's shock at finding out she was pregnant with twins, her excitement and terror: those twinned emotions. Abe felt similarly now, only the duality reflected two possibilities: that Amy would come around again to the idea of motherhood, or that she wouldn't. Maybe, Abe let himself hope, knowing that this infant existed on the other side of the world—a real, fully-formed person who needed a family, just like Amy had once been—would re-warm her to parenthood, in a way that the bundle of cells in her uterus had not. When they talked tomorrow—finally!—Abe would find the best way to bring this up.

Abe tucked his phone away and noticed that Amy was drinking wine. This was new. Her doctor had said it was perfectly safe to enjoy a single drink a few times a week, but Amy had been feeling too nauseated to imbibe. Abe had to admit it: Despite the doctor's okay, he found it a little upsetting to see his pregnant wife consuming alcohol. Not to mention that the glass she'd poured looked to be a lot more than the medically approved four ounces. It was just one time, he told himself, trying to relax; he wasn't going to be the pregnancy police. Plus, he knew his opinion wouldn't be welcome. But after polishing off the glass, Amy reached for the bottle again and poured herself another generous glug-glug-glug: seven or eight ounces, at least. Abe saw Mickey take note, then decide not to say anything. Abe grew worried. Deep breathing wasn't working. He had to intervene. "Hey," he whispered to his wife. "Want to maybe slow down there?"

Her eyebrows shot up in accusation and her voice was cutting. "Oh, give me a goddamn break for once in my life."

Abe's mouth went dry; never once had Amy spoken like that to him. He didn't mean to drag her from the table, but he had no desire to hash this out in front of an audience. In a corner of the restaurant, he said, "Is this your way of telling me you're going to end the pregnancy, Amy? Because it's a pretty immature tactic, not to mention cruel."

Amy didn't even have the decency to respond. Abe felt his face heating up as he grew angrier. He'd catered to his wife's ridiculous request to take the baby conversation off the table for a week, and to her waffling, and to the fact that after all the time and effort and money they'd spent trying to become parents, the moment it became a real possibility she suddenly wasn't sure. He wanted to shake her, but settled for wagging his finger. "You could have the decency to be direct with me, and not humiliate me in front of our friends. You're always so cool and cavalier, but guess what? I'm not. My future is on the line here; my heart is about to explode, and I've been doing everything in my power to cater to your every whim—"

Amy got right up in his face and spat out the words, "I had a miscarriage."

Abe stumbled back. "What?"

"You heard me. It happened just now, in the bathroom."

"Oh." Abe couldn't process this news. Even as concern for his wife flooded his nervous system, the anger didn't dissipate. The implications hit him, too, that the baby was gone; their biological child was not to be. He didn't know what to say. Eventually he managed, "How do you feel?"

"Awful. Crampy and leaky and gross."

"Emotionally, I meant." It just came out; correcting her like she'd gotten the answer wrong, like she was one of his students and just needed a bit more coaxing.

But Amy was too preoccupied to rebuke him. "Numb, I guess. At least now I don't have to make a decision." She looked at her feet. Abe felt desperate to know what her decision would have been. He tried to analyze her expression, whether it was more sad or relieved; he couldn't tell. The email from the adoption agency suddenly felt like it was burning a hole in his pocket.

"I assume you haven't checked your email?"

She looked at him like he was crazy. Right, she'd been having a miscarriage; she wasn't scanning her inbox.

"The adoption agency has a baby for us. I mean, if we want her. She's three months old, and—"

"What the fuck, Abe?" Amy never swore at him, and now she'd done it twice in ten minutes. "Can you not let me sit with this massive thing that just happened to me for like ten minutes before you lay another massive thing on me?"

"I'm sorry. I guess I was trying to …" But he didn't know what he was trying to do. Cheer her up, maybe? But why would that cheer her up? He was thinking of himself, of how this other possibility cheered *him* up. "I'm sorry."

"The other thing I feel is starving. For the first time in months, I want to eat until I'm so stuffed I can't stand upright. So, I'm going to go back to our table, okay? And tomorrow, as planned, we can talk about all of this." She made a dismissive gesture at "this," which Abe felt encompassed everything he cared about, their life and their future.

Abe followed Amy back to the table, because what else was he going to do? She was his wife, and he would do his best to be there for her however she needed him, even if that meant shutting the hell up for the rest of the night or, as she indicated with a snap, passing her the bread basket and the bottle of wine.

⟋

Mateo had ceded the night to his girls—to seeing his daughter off to her prom and to trying to give his wife the birthday of her dreams. He'd succeeded at the first task, but the second was not going so hot. All of their friends seemed to be in moods. Plus, Mickey was clearly disappointed that Kimmy had the night off (Mateo was relieved—as much as he'd enjoyed their wild night, he was now embarrassed to recall it, and would've felt mortified to have Kimmy serving their table).

As everyone said their goodbyes, all Mateo wanted to do was go home and veg out on the couch with his family. But Melody wouldn't be coming home that night, apparently, and Mickey would want to salvage her birthday after the disappointing dinner. So, Mateo willed himself to rally, to push himself out of his comfort zone and try something different and spontaneous, something that would please his wife. He texted her gym partner, Keisha. She would know a fun place to go and—he asked sheepishly, not knowing how to phrase it—did she know how to procure any substances to enhance the evening? She wrote back immediately with an address and a "yes."

Mateo hadn't even known clubs like this existed near River Mill. It had been a decade-plus since he'd stepped foot in such a place: the low lighting and pumping music, the sweat-slick bodies bumping on the dance floor, the circular enclaves tucked away on the perimeter. It was both cheesy and cool, the kind of place the receptionists at his office might frequent after changing into skimpier outfits and bolder makeup at the end of the day. Again, he decided to submit to the night as Keisha led him and Mickey to a lounge area in the back and pressed little pink capsules into their hands. Mickey reached for a second one, and Keisha leaned in and said, "Your husband arranged this."

"Is that so?" Mickey raised her eyebrows. As she swallowed her capsules, her lips brushed past Keisha's, nearly touching, before landing on Mateo's.

Oh, Mateo thought, swallowing his own capsule.

That's as far as he got in processing what was happening, because Keisha grasped both his and Mickey's hands and led them into the flashing lights and strong beats of the dance floor. Mateo liked dancing, he remembered, though he couldn't recall the last time he'd really done it, besides the obligatory bopping around at weddings or the swaying with Mickey in their living room when she felt moved by a song. This was different. This was arms swinging and hips dipping and shoulders shaking, this was his body telling a story across space among all the other bodies telling their own stories; this was skin pulsing and blood pumping and soul singing. Why didn't Mateo spend all of his spare time dancing?

Keisha was at his side, shouting, "This DJ is a genius."

"You're a genius for taking us here."

Mickey was on his other side. "You're a genius for inviting Keisha."

The music shifted to something slower, a simple beat and then a sultry female voice came in singing about the color pink. The dance floor transformed into a rosy glow, and it felt like the hue was saturating him. It felt like vibration, and connection, and desire, and this exact moment. Mateo was gliding and floating between his companions, these two goddesses who treated their bodies like temples, who were worthy of worship. Mateo couldn't believe he'd lucked into this scenario. He placed his hands on each of their waists and they ceded to his touch. Hands went to his waist. They were moving together as a trio. Keisha whispered something in Mickey's ear and Mickey's eyes shone. Then Keisha leaned in and kissed his wife—on her cheek, down to her jawbone and neck, then up to her lips. Mickey was kissing her back, hands spread across Keisha's ass. Mateo could barely contain himself. He wanted in. He pressed a hand over Mickey's, and asked "May I?" to Keisha. She turned toward him with a welcoming look. The three of them grinded their bodies against one another, exploring along with the music. Mateo felt he could dance forever, or maybe they'd move to one of those dark banquettes in the back; they could be discreet. Mateo was aware of every tingle on his tongue, every breeze against his skin, every sensation in his—

"Oh my god, Dad?"

Mateo froze. He snapped his eyes shut. Bowling balls banged around his brain. His breath raced. He hiccupped. He had to be imagining it. The familiar voice was just a trick, part of the drug doing a crazy number on him.

"Hello, Dad? And Mom?! And Jesus Christ, is that Keisha?" That was definitely Melody's voice—or a version of it, shrieking like she was in physical pain.

Mateo opened his eyes. There she was: his beautiful daughter in her glimmering silver gown. Her boyfriend, who looked about ten years old in his tux, wrapped a protective arm around her waist. "What are you guys even doing here? This is not happening! Someone please tell me this is not happening!"

"Oh honey." Mickey, high as a kite, Mateo now realized, reached out to their daughter. She wore a blissful smile, like wasn't this all a funny coincidence? "We're out dancing, just like you."

Melody ducked away from her mother's touch. What had she seen? From the look of disgust on her face, a lot. Keisha, wisely, had excused herself.

"Melody." The synapses in Mateo's brain weren't firing fast enough and he didn't know how to express what he needed to express. Worry and shame gathered and settled like sludge in his core.

"Ew, Dad. You're all sweaty and gross. I basically expect Mom to be this embarrassing, but you? Is this what you guys do? You've got this secret perverted life where you go to clubs where everyone's half your age and you make out with your friends? Is your entire life goal to mortify me? Oh god, I'm going to be sick."

And she was—all down Mateo's shirt. It felt fair. After fun and games, there was always a comedown, a reckoning. After the antics of the past few months, he deserved to be punished. The odor snapped him back to sober. He took his daughter's limp hand, and she didn't flinch. "Oh honey. Come on, I'll drive you home."

The boy—Bryce—intervened, in a comic attempt at authority. "With all due respect, Mr. Moran, I don't think you're in any shape to drive anyone home. I'll take care of Melody. Come on, let's get you a seltzer." The young couple escaped into the crowd, and Mel didn't even glance back.

The speakers were now blasting a song that everyone knew the words to, and they all looked like they were bouncing on pogo sticks, Mickey included. She took Mateo's shoulders and only then seemed to notice his shirt. "You can probably just ditch it," she said, unhelpfully, continuing to jump.

"Mickey, our daughter just saw us making out with Keisha."

"I know. She's upset. I get it. It's a big shock. But she'll cool down. We'll talk to her. She's cool. She's Mel. She's cool. It'll be *juuust fiiine.*"

Keisha had reappeared. "Do you want me to go after her?" she asked.

"Thanks, but no," Mateo said. "This isn't your mess to clean up."

Mickey pulled Keisha back into her orbit, and soon the two of them were dancing again, rolling their necks and dipping their shoulders to opposite sides, choreographing on the spot. Mateo was stunned by his wife's nonchalance. "Come on, babe," she told him. "Forget about it for now. We were having so much fun."

It was true, they had been having fun. But that was over. "Let's go home, Mickey."

"And miss the rest of my birthday celebration? No thank you very much."

Mateo saw there would be no convincing her. "I'm going home," he said to no one.

Navigating the crush of people to the exit, wincing at the deafening bass, Mateo couldn't believe he'd found this scene enticing just a few minutes ago. Now he yearned to be in the comfort and quiet of his home, hugging his daughter and wife close. But the fantasy was ruined when he caught a whiff of himself. He had literally made his daughter ill. He felt like he might be sick himself.

CHAPTER 51
Mona

Mona was amazed how little her yoga practice translated to cardiovascular activity. Racing up and down the corridors had left her panting like a dog. But she didn't stop. There were just a couple of hours before her graduation, and she had to find Louisa.

The vibe at the school was subdued, like everyone was hungover from the excitement of yesterday's walk-out and ensuing ice cream fight. Jay, Leo, and Annabelle were all suspended. Without their trusty S.A.T. leaders, the rest of the student body seemed neutered. Or maybe they'd gotten the rebellion out of their systems, and now were prepared to sit obediently for today's tests. Mona didn't know and, honestly, she didn't care. All she cared about was locating Louisa. "Excuse me, have you seen Vice Principal Bauer?" she asked student after student. Most didn't even manage a "Huh?" in response.

During her third lap around the building, Mona stopped again at Louisa's office and again banged on the door. She wanted to tell Louisa that her secret was safe with her. She had no intention of outing her, about the tests or her sudden absence. While it was obvious that education didn't mean bubbling in Scantron sheets for standardized tests—Mona assumed that Louisa knew that, too—desperate times called for desperate measures. And figuring out the right thing to do was rarely clear-cut. She didn't judge.

Mona wanted to say all that to Louisa, and to apologize, too. She wanted to tell Louisa that she knew she'd messed up; that for Mona, too, the maybe-wrong thing had looked right. Or that maybe the wrong and the right could co-exist. Mona wanted to confide how it had always annoyed her that she'd been named after a character from a play whose main traits were "nice" and "meek," and how she'd always resisted those expectations. But maybe she'd gone too far. And now she was trying to repair some of the damage she'd caused: she would soon be far away, off to California. She thought Louisa would be relieved to hear that. She hoped Louisa might even forgive her. Mona had come to really like Louisa, probably more than she liked Nathan. Louisa was such a badass, and underappreciated. Mona looked up to her. She had so much to say to her—if she could only find her. She banged even harder on the office door.

"May I help you?" It was the dean with the stick up his ass: Mr. Mack.

"I'm trying to find Ms. Bauer. Have you seen her?"

"I have not." Mr. Mack consulted his watch. "But it's five minutes into first period, so you're right to expect her on the premises." His laugh was ugly. "However, when it comes to Ms. Bauer, where she *should* be does not always translate to where she *is*."

What was he blabbing about? "Did she maybe call in sick?"

The dean expressed a little puff of air. "I wouldn't be surprised if she did, considering her test prep initiative was such a flop. Perhaps she doesn't have the guts to face the fallout." As he kept talking, Mona wondered, why was this dude throwing his colleague under the bus so cavalierly, confiding in a random sub like they were BFFs?

"Would you please shut it?"

Mr. Mack's jaw dropped, exposing a too-white set of teeth. How could he work in a high school and be so easily rattled?

Mona went on, "Louisa is going through a hell of a divorce and her ex is trying to sue her for child support *and* alimony, despite the fact that *he's* the one who cheated on *her*, plus he went and lost his job. She's got two little kids, and this stupid stressful job where she doesn't get any of the credit she deserves. On top of all that, she has to work with guys like you who wear pants that are way too tight."

The man actually looked down at his pants, as if this was the most upsetting thing Mona had said. It took him a moment, but eventually he seemed to remember he was in a position of authority over her. He straightened his spine and narrowed his eyes. "You are done here. Your temp position is terminated. I suggest you leave immediately, or I can call security to escort you out."

"Fine."

"Fine."

"Fine," Mona said again, mostly to see if Mr. Mack would keep it going.

"Fine."

Mona suppressed a smile. "But if you see Louisa, will you please tell her I'm looking for her?"

Mr. Mack just laughed. Mona saw herself out, feeling defeated. She hoped Louisa was all right.

CHAPTER 52
Louisa

It was a brand-new day. The sun had come up in a show-offy mood, and now every sidewalk speck and steel building edge glinted in its glow. The sky was cloudless and—Louisa felt a little silly even thinking it, but yes, it really was—cerulean. The air felt crisp against her skin, the day's humidity still hours away from settling in. After everything, the nice weather felt like a gift.

And so, after depositing the twins at early daycare drop-off, Louisa planned to treat herself to a latte at the schmancy café a few blocks west. It was so pleasant out, she decided to walk.

She'd never made it to bed the night before, and now she felt light with sleeplessness, like she simply might drift up from the sidewalk and float away with the breeze. She was amazed to discover her heart at ease. It felt like acquainting herself with a long-lost friend.

At two or three a.m., she'd opened her laptop, typed "Dear Dr. Poolehauzer," and let her fingers tap out a letter of resignation. It wasn't just the right thing to do, it would also prevent her from having to live in fear of Mona reporting what she'd seen, then enduring the drawn-out humiliation of an investigation. Louisa was grateful to Mona, in a way, for putting a stop to something Louisa almost certainly wouldn't have gone through with, but a small part of her did wonder. Printing out the letter, she thought she'd feel devastated; instead, she felt relieved. Never again would she have to sit through a meeting with the inimitable duo of Dr. P and Chad Mack. Or plan weeks of bullshit test prep then demand an entire faculty get in line. Or escape to Stairwell F when she felt panic nipping at her heels. All of it would soon be over.

Clearly, there were practicalities to consider: how she would manage to keep food on her family's table and a roof over their heads and health insurance in their names, especially now that Nathan's income consisted of an occasional check for three or four hundred dollars. But Louisa would figure something out—she always had. Screw it: She could swallow her pride and ask her parents for a loan, or she and the kids could move into their basement, and Louisa would become a Starbucks barista for the benefits. It would be awful, but probably no more awful than her current situation. It was a freeing thought.

After she'd folded and sealed her resignation letter, Louisa moved on to the next set of paperwork: the divorce papers. She'd signed every line that asked for her signature and initialed every box that asked for her initials, the tears only coming as she penned in her last "LB." Both sets of papers were now tucked into her purse, ready to be disseminated. Louisa didn't know all the coming steps that would officially detach her from her job and from her marriage, but at least she was on the right path.

She stepped off the curb to cross the street. She didn't have the light, but she glanced in both directions, the way she'd drilled her kids to do; though maybe she wasn't paying close enough attention. Maybe for a split-second she let her eyes flutter closed and tilted her chin to the sky to feel the sun on her face. The last thing she remembered was a powerful force hurling into her hip, the clunk of her skull against the concrete, and a cry from the depths of her being, "Nathan!"

CHAPTER 53
Amy

As Amy lay in bed, head pounding and belly cramping, Abe brought her everything she asked for (Tylenol, coffee, water, toast), and other essentials she didn't think to request (a heating pad, scrambled eggs, a blueberry muffin), plus a slew of other items meant to mitigate her misery (her iPad opened to Netflix, and her Kindle loaded up with *Little Women*, which she'd been meaning to reread for years). It was all so thoughtful that Amy wanted to cry. She did cry. She felt rotten in about a dozen different ways, including the fact that it was obvious that Abe was walking on eggshells, careful not to upset or crowd her.

But even that was sweet; her husband was doing his best. Amy was over her irritation at him, and she was too tired to be angry.

"We don't have to talk," he said. "I mean, if you need more time, I understand. I mean, not to say that I understand what you're going through, just—"

She reached for his hand and tugged him closer. "It's all right. Let's talk."

Abe faced her, focused and open; he was being so completely Abe that Amy had to close her eyes to get out the words she needed to say. "I can't adopt that baby."

She opened her eyes to see her beloved husband, her wonderful Abe. He was nodding like it was a tic, working so hard not to cry, to be here with her and understanding of her needs. Amy could see that he couldn't formulate a response.

"I am so sorry, Abe. For not communicating earlier that this is how I feel, for not even really understanding it, and for dragging you through all of this, for years. It's unforgivable, and I'm so ashamed."

He was shaking his head, but Amy knew what a piece of shit she'd been. She wished she could shake off a layer of herself like a snake shedding its skin, and just walk away from the person she'd become. "I would do almost anything to make you happy." She owed him more of an explanation. "That was the thing. Since the first time I met you, I knew how much you wanted to be a father. I love you so much that I yearned to give that to you. And because you wanted it so badly, for a while it made me believe that I could, too, like the power of your wanting could spill over into me and that would be enough. But it turns out it isn't. I would give so much to change that, to give you the thing you want most in the world." She looked down. "I am so, so sorry."

Abe was still shaking his head. "You don't mean this, Ames. You're scared. You're overwhelmed. You need time. You—"

"No, Abe." She said it as gently as she could. "This isn't about time. And for the first time in a long time I'm not feeling scared of what I want. My whole life, I've hated being different, the only Asian face in a room, the only kid who didn't know her real parents. My mom and dad always talked about parenthood like it was the holy grail, how they'd fought so hard for it, and how meeting me was the greatest moment of their lives. You're like that, too, aching so much for a child. And all our friends are parents; it's like, having kids is just what people do. So, I forced down the little voice in my head that told me that once again, I was the odd one out, for wanting something else. I went through the motions, hoping everything would work itself out. Well, it won't. It can't. And I'm truly sorry I didn't tell you all this before, but for all of those reasons, I couldn't. So, I'm telling you now."

Abe was looking her right in her eyes. "May I ask, why don't you want a child?"

Amy swallowed hard. "I don't think I have it in me to care for another human like that. Taking care of myself is hard enough. My work is my joy and I don't want what I see with the mothers at my office, having to balance everything, and make compromises, and feel guilty about not having enough to spread around. I think of my own mother, too; for all her talk of how much she yearned to be a mom, she gave up a big career to raise me, and I always got the sense that she'd regretted it, as much as she would've denied that. Plus, I mean, look at Louisa."

Abe protested, "But you're not Louisa or your own mother or the other women in your office. It could be different for us. What if I left teaching for a while and stayed at home? I would do all the caretaking, and you could be just as focused on work as you are now."

Amy had never considered this possibility. But no, that didn't sound realistic. Plus, she'd made her decision; she was past the point of entertaining Abe's ideas for compromise. "The truth is, I'm not sure if I have the perfect explanation, but I just know in my heart that I don't want a child, the same way you know in your heart that you do."

Abe took her hands, and Amy saw his eyes wet with sorrow. "This is a lot to take in, Ames. I hear you, I do. And I know I have a great life. I have you, and my friends, and my students, and all of that will just have to be enough." Tears started streaming down his face. "We can't always get what we want, right? If a baby isn't in the cards for us, then, okay, we'll find another way forward." His voice cracked.

"Abe." Amy knew this part would be the hardest. "I can't stay with you and bear the guilt and shame of denying you your biggest desire."

"What do you mean?" Abe squeaked. His hands began trembling in hers.

"I mean, you should adopt that baby and be her father, and I will step out of the picture."

"Step out of the picture, as in, leave me?" His tone was shifting. He sounded angry, which caught Amy off guard. She thought she could count on her husband to remain the same old Abe: understanding, conciliatory, kind.

Amy's nod was small, and Abe scoffed. "Surely you know a single man can't adopt a baby from China. Amy, you must know that."

"Oh, I, um—" she stumbled. Had she known that? She didn't think so, but maybe she had; maybe she'd conveniently forgotten the detail that would foil her very neat plan of Abe getting his baby and her receding into his rearview mirror. Her heart started racing. "Abe, I know you'll figure out a way to become a father. You'll adopt from somewhere else. Or, you'll have no problem finding a partner who wants to be a mom. You're such a great catch!"

"A great catch, Amy?"

Amy realized what a lame thing it was to say. Abe was shaking his head incredulously. He looked like he couldn't decide whether to blow up at her or collapse into a pile of misery.

"Abe," she said. "I would never forgive myself if I was the reason you didn't get to be a father. I love you too much to do that to you."

"This cannot be happening." Abe stood up. "I love you, too, but I can't talk to you right now." He sounded profoundly sad.

"Abe," she said. He waited, but when it became clear that Amy had no follow-up, he left the room.

Amy lay there, feeling maybe the worst she'd ever felt. Her gut clenched, her ovaries cramped, her joints ached. The knowledge that she was the lowest form of human life shivered over her in devastating waves. And yet, in the briefest breaks from her wallowing, she heard a little voice in her head saying, *You did it. You listened to your heart and you'll be okay.* A tiny sliver of Amy believed it.

CHAPTER 54

Mickey

Mickey's bedroom was gray. She'd never before noticed how monochromatic it was, but the walls, the curtains, the furniture, the sheets and comforter: everything was gray. The morning air appeared gray, too, and when Mickey blinked her eyes shut, she saw gray behind her eyelids. Even the pulsing din behind her forehead was tinged gray, if it was possible for a sound to have a hue.

When she recalled the previous night, her brain hurt. She couldn't reconcile the warm joy of dancing with the cold comeuppance that followed. She couldn't understand how she'd been feeling so free on the dance floor, then in an instant, because of an unfortunate coincidence, she was expected to transform into mother mode: selfless, responsible, nurturing, plus deeply ashamed to have been caught by her daughter expressing a different side of herself. And when she didn't comply, how outraged her family was at her.

Mickey loved Mel more than any other person on earth. But there was something messed up about the fact that her daughter's appearance (in the world, at the club) was supposed to force Mickey into that very narrow version of herself—at least, according to Mel and Mateo. Mel was seventeen years old; surely that was old enough for her to understand that her mother was a sexual being. Yet, Mel and Mateo had both stormed out of the club in a huff, abandoning her, and on her birthday. Mickey felt abandoned now, too: Mateo had left for work before she even woke, and Mel was still at her slumber party.

Her phone rang from inside her clutch, flung onto the floor beside the bed from the night before. The screen read "Western State Medical Center."

"Hello?" she hiccupped.

"Is this Mickey Moran? I'm Hope Johnson, a nurse practitioner at Western State Hospital. I'm calling about Louisa Bauer. We found your card in her wallet, and—"

"What happened to Louisa?"

Mickey was in her car in under five minutes, blinking back tears and trying to stay focused on the road. *There was a car accident,* the nurse had said. *Pelvic fracture, internal bleeding, concussion.* Mickey begged to know if her friend would be okay. She was in surgery now, and there would be a road to recovery, but yes, most likely she would be okay. All right. Okay. All right. Mickey sucked in deep breaths, thinking about what needed to be done. Had they called Nathan? The nurse hadn't said. When Mickey dialed him, he screened her call, the prick. So, she left the basics of what she knew (not much) on his voicemail and told him to get his ass to Western State. She dictated texts to Mateo and Mel: "Louisa was hit by a car. She'll be OK, but she's having surgery at Western State. Heading over now. I love you. ♥♥♥♥." If any moment called for an excessive number of heart emoticons, it was now.

Louisa was still in surgery when Mickey arrived. There was no way she could sit among the other worried waiters, held hostage by the chipper lifestyle show playing on the mounted TV. Pacing the halls turned to calf raises and lunges, and soon Mickey had created a workout, deep-squatting by the nurses' station and triceps-dipping at the entryway. The more she exerted herself, the less she had to picture her best friend being cut open on the operating table, and the bone-crunching incident that had brought her there.

Mickey had completed three circuits by the time Nathan appeared, looking pale and red-eyed. As Mickey hugged him, his body felt clenched and cold. She knew he was the type to transmute his fear into anger: she'd seen it before. He marched right up to the intake desk and demanded to speak to Louisa's doctors, barking out questions that no one had the answers to. Mickey admired how calm the staff remained; she never would've had the patience to work in a hospital.

When Nathan stepped away from the front desk, she was surprised to see him slump into a seat, drop his head into his lap, and burst into tears. Mickey placed a cautious hand on his arm; he was clearly in a volatile state. "I fucked it all up," he said between sobs. "I'm such a fuckup."

"Shh, it's okay." Mickey resented that she'd been put in this position. She didn't want to hear the regretful ravings of the man who'd devastated her friend and now had the audacity to be upset that she was even more hurt. But he was the father of Louisa's kids, so Mickey made herself comfort him.

"I came as fast as I could." It was Amy—Nathan must've spread the word. Thank god for a distraction from his wallowing. "Abe is on his way. How is she? Any updates?"

"She's still in surgery," Mickey reported. "Come be with us." Amy looked terrible. She'd seemed sick last night, too. "The vending machine has ginger ale, if you need it."

Amy opened her mouth, then shut it, then opened it again, like she couldn't decide whether or not to share something. "I miscarried," she finally said. "But it's, whatever. I'm okay about it, I think. Oh, and I'm leaving Abe."

Mickey laughed; she didn't know why. "Melody caught Mateo and me hooking up with my friend from the gym. I think they both hate me now."

Now it was Nathan and Amy's turn to laugh. Then both women turned to Nathan, like he was up next. "I'm still in love with Louisa," he admitted. "I've been such a moron. As soon as she's conscious, I'm going to beg her to take me back."

The three of them sat in a row, squeezing each other's hands and staring straight ahead, all of their confessions hanging in the air. It was sort of humbling to realize that, here in the emergency room, their personal dramas were dwarfed by broken bones and ruptured organs and worse, traumas that required teams of doctors and cutting-edge technology to fix. They sat together in quiet communion, meditating on their own problems, and each other's, and on their absent friend. Their lives were so full of pitfalls and perils, it was a miracle any of them made it through any day. And how absurd, that for all the work they put into maintaining their relationships and advancing their careers and honoring their own needs and wants, it could all be decimated in an instant, by the crushing force of a ton of steel. They were all one potential moment away from destruction. And yet, they endured; what else could they do?

The hours moved like oil in a lava lamp, expanding and contracting in oozy blobs. Eventually, Abe joined their vigil, wordlessly taking a seat beside Amy. Mateo and Mel arrived next. The six of them sat in a line, drinking crappy coffee, fidgeting, no one saying much. Mickey tried to reach out to her husband and her daughter, but neither would meet her eye; Mel stayed hunched over her phone, perking up only when Nathan offered to split a bag of chips. Mickey overheard Mel asking him if he needed help with Phoebe and Finn; she said she could do daycare pick-up and spend the night so he could stay at the hospital. Nathan sounded grateful for the offer, and Mickey's heart swelled; what a kind, gracious girl she'd raised. But then Mel intercepted her smile with a cutting look. If she didn't feel so hurt, Mickey might've been impressed by her daughter's ability to shift on a dime from sweet to vicious. Her husband still wouldn't make eye contact, either, but as their daughter left to pick up the twins, Nathan's car keys in hand, Mateo pressed a palm against Mickey's back. It was a concession: Even if he was still mad, he was there.

Finally, a man in scrubs approached the group. "Louisa Bauer is out of surgery, recovering in the ICU." Mickey exhaled in a way that made her feel like she hadn't breathed in hours. "Who's family here?"

"I'm her husband," Nathan declared, rising from his seat. Mickey had to stop herself from rebutting this claim as he was led away through a set of double doors, leaving behind the rest of Louisa's loved ones: her true, if not actual, family.

CHAPTER 55
Louisa

Louisa was in a white room, that much she could tell. She felt heavy and cold. Her head seemed to be stuffed with cotton. Where was she? Where were Phoebe and Finn? Were they okay? She couldn't hold onto the questions long enough to try to formulate answers.

It seemed wiser to stay still, to not even attempt to lift her eyelids. Except suddenly, someone else was in the room, holding her hand. "I know you can't hear me right now," she heard. "You're resting, doing exactly what you need to be doing, so please don't mind me." Who was it—Nathan? Yes, Nathan. Louisa relaxed a notch, wavering in and out of sleep, catching snippets of his words.

"I know we fought a lot. But remember how afterward, there was always that moment when it could go either way? Like, we might invite each other back in, and let ourselves be vulnerable. Or, we might put up shields, and end up on opposite sides of the house pretending everything was fine but really feeling totally hollowed out. It used to be, we did more of the coming back together, you know? Before things shifted the other way. I know you noticed it, too. It was eating me up inside. And that's when—"

Louisa slid back into sleep, lacking the energy to join Nathan on this journey down marital memory lane. She came to again during his apologies. "I'm so sorry I took our life for granted. I know I'm a pathetic cliché. Seeing you like this is—it's unbearable. But, if you'll let me, I'd like to be there for you to help you heal. I'd like to work to earn your forgiveness. I'm really going to try, you'll see. With you, the kids, everything. I'll always regret losing sight of my love for you these past few months. I love you, Louisa. I've always loved you. I always will love you."

Louisa couldn't handle any more verb conjugation, or the rest of it, either. With great effort, she peeled open her eyes. "Can you please tell me what happened to me?"

Nathan laughed—that big, hearty laugh that melted something inside Louisa. "You're awake!"

He gave her a run-down of what he knew, about the driver blinded by the sun's morning glare and the ensuing collision into her side. Louisa tried to jog her memory. She remembered the strong sun and the bright feeling filling her up—and she remembered calling out for her husband. Otherwise, her mind was a blank.

Nathan's look was too intense for Louisa's liking, like he was going to propose they renew their vows right then and there at her hospital bedside. But she forgave him the impulse, knowing how dramatic events could dredge up all kinds of emotions. Louisa, for one, was most concerned with easing the sharp pain in her hip.

"Could you bring me another pillow?"

Nathan hustled. He brought her two. It felt good to be propped up, and Nathan seemed to get that Louisa wasn't interested in further conversation.

"Well, I won't hog visiting hours," he said. "The others will want to see you."

"The others?"

"Everyone's here. We've all been huddling together rooting for you. I'll tell the nurse they're family so they can come in."

Louisa could picture her group of friends, the five of them. How nice, she thought, to have an "everyone" you could rely on at times like this.

"Send Mickey in," she said, then closed her eyes, preempting any further expressions of sentiment from her ex.

———

Louisa woke again to an odd sensation on her lips. It was Mickey with a tube of lipstick.

"Oh good, you're up. I thought some MAC Peachy Keen would do wonders for your post-surgery lewk."

Louisa discovered laughing made everything ache. "Please distract me from my pain."

"Certainly. Boy do I have a tale for you."

"Oh good."

Mickey always came through with a story, and this one, about her late-night club adventures, was as engaging and titillating as Louisa hoped for.

"I can't decide if you're the most or least evolved person I know," she said.

Mickey's eyes twinkled. "Both, probably."

"But you have to talk to Mel."

She shrugged. "She'll come around."

"No Mickey, you have to apologize. Can you imagine how traumatizing it would be to see your parents in that position?"

Mickey made a face. "You can't compare my parents to Mateo and me. We're still young and hot, or at least young-ish and hottish.

Happy birthday to me."

"But you're Mel's parents. You're supposed to be her stable home base, not two-thirds of a ménage à trois she happens upon in a club. I don't say that with judgment. You know how brilliantly Nathan and I have been doing at providing a stable home base for our kids lately."

Mickey fluttered her lips. "It's not just Mel who hates me at the moment. Mateo seems half-ready to flee to California, too."

"Maybe it's time to rethink your priorities." Saying this jostled something in Louisa's brain. "Hey, do you know where my purse is?"

Mickey shrugged. "No, but I can ask."

As Mickey left to find a nurse, Louisa pictured the paperwork. Had her divorce papers and resignation letter been scattered to the wind or obliterated under tire treads? She wondered whether it was a sign from the universe. But then Mickey was back with Louisa's purse—it was fine, just a little scuffed up. A peek inside revealed the papers intact, barely even crumpled. If Louisa wanted, she could've called Nathan back in and handed him the divorce papers right then. But she tucked the papers away and asked for Abe instead.

———

"How the hell are you, Dauer?" Abe asked, balancing himself on the edge of the bed.

"I'm a mess, clearly," said Louisa, "but I'm sick to death of talking about it. Tell me about you, instead."

"You sure?" She nodded, so he went on. "All righty. Well, what a coincidence! I'm a mess, too. I'll just come right out and say it. Amy lost the baby, she put the kibosh on the adoption, and now she says she's leaving me."

"Oh no." The shock of Abe's words pierced through Louisa's brain fog. He must've been devastated about the baby, and the adoption. But Louisa didn't understand the last part; he and Amy were always the most solid, the deepest in love. "What do you mean, she's leaving you?"

"She said she couldn't handle the guilt of knowing she'd let me down, the shame of devastating my dream. And after finally admitting to herself that she doesn't want to be a mother, she needs to be on her own. Or so she claims. It's the classic 'it's not you, it's me.' She wants me to find someone else to reproduce with." He laughed weakly, looking miserable.

"Oh, Jones. Amy's been through so much. It's a huge deal to miscarry, even if it also comes as a relief. Maybe she just needs time."

"Maybe." But he didn't sound hopeful.

Somehow, Louisa's hospital room had become a makeshift confessional. What would a priest tell Abe? "This too shall pass." Louisa's version was a snippet of a Robert Frost poem floating through her head: "Nothing gold can stay." It seemed a little harsh given the circumstances. There was a reason people expressed themselves in platitudes: It was so hard to know what to say, and how much could words help anyway?

Louisa reached for Abe's hand, ignoring all the tubing tributarying down her palm. Abe sighed and said, "Life sure can be disappointing."

"That's the understatement of the hour." They both laughed.

"Speaking of disappointment," he said, "I'm sorry for going on about me when you're here in this state."

Louisa waved him off. "It's nice to not think about my own disaster for a few minutes."

"You should know Chad Mack nearly shat himself with smugness over your unexplained absence this morning. I admit I enjoyed breaking the news to him about the accident (sorry), and watching him do a one-eighty into concerned, compassionate mode. He spent about thirty seconds pretending to consider dropping by for a visit. I assured him that it would mean a lot to you." Louisa conjured the strength to smack Abe's hand. "I imagine Dr. P's wife will be sending over the world's most garish flower arrangement. Along with a memo from her dear husband with instructions about what's expected of you when it comes to planning graduation from your hospital bed."

Was the dizzy disorientation Louisa felt from the surgery or from hearing Abe talk about River Mill High like it was a world she was still a part of? Suddenly she needed to not be alone with her news, and what had let up to it. She fished the resignation letter from her purse.

Abe read it, then looked up in shock. As he searched for what to say, Louisa filled the silence. "First I had a momentary lapse in judgment where I considered tampering with the test Scantrons, which Mona walked in on. Then I walked out and left the school, mid-student demonstration. I just couldn't deal anymore."

Louisa didn't detect any judgment in his features, but Abe was a surprisingly good poker player. She continued, "So, now you know how I felt ten minutes ago when you dropped your bombshell on me. Anyway, if Mona decides to report me, at least I'll already be gone."

"I don't think she will," said Abe. "She was running around trying to find you all morning. She seemed really concerned."

"Huh." Could it be true? Might Mona actually have her back? Abe handed back the letter. "Do you really want to do this? It's not a crime to contemplate fudging the tests to meet an impossible standard so you can keep your job."

"Don't forget abandoning my post during a crisis as my boss called repeatedly for my help."

"Meh." He shrugged.

Abe was the most ethical person Louisa knew, so it meant a lot to hear him downplay her misconduct, even if he was just trying to make her feel better in the wake of a seriously terrible twenty-four hours. Louisa also realized that a part of her had probably been hoping to get caught, as an out from such a toxic workplace.

She considered the letter. "I was sort of looking forward to turning this in."

"Well, whatever you decide to do, I'm glad you didn't resign yet. No job means no health insurance. And this whole situation is going to cost a pretty penny."

Louisa sighed, anticipating the inevitable Aetna nightmare. There were so many disappointing parts about adulthood—healthcare being one of them things that had been decidedly absent from her childhood fantasies of growing up. She reached out to Abe. "Give me a hug, Jones. Amy's an idiot to leave you. I mean, she's a brilliant woman who obviously gets to choose whether or not she wants a child. But also, she's an idiot, and I'm so sorry. I'm here for you, always."

Abe held on to the hug for a moment longer. "Thanks, Bauer. You should rest. After Chad Mack pops in for a visit, that is."

"Screw you. Scram."

Once again, Louisa was reminded how much laughing hurt. It was a cruel joke, how everything was the opposite of what it was supposed to be: laughter led to pain; optimism preceded a car crash. Good marriages failed; bad marriages, well ... Louisa was worn out from all the rumination.

CHAPTER 56

Melody

Growing up apparently happened slowly and then all at once. As Melody made a slow revolution around her bedroom, she felt she was seeing all her stuff with newly mature eyes. Her fish-patterned bedspread, the desk she'd painted gold on a snow day, the photo collage of her and James and Gus that decorated her closet door, her phone dangling with charms; all of it belonged to the child version of herself: none of it suited her anymore. If she could've, she would've set a match to all of it. But her stupid parents were insisting she go through everything item by item, separating it into piles to take, leave, toss, and donate. She groaned in annoyance.

She cranked up her music so high that her eardrums pulsed. She was daring her parents to come tell her to turn it down. Every time they'd tried to talk to her since The Incident, Melody had met them with looks of death, and they'd backed down. Her stubborn strength filled her with pride.

She picked up a photo from her dresser. In it, her mother was tilting her head just so, blocking half of Melody's face. Melody couldn't believe she'd once liked the picture enough to print, frame, and display. She'd felt proud of having such a pretty, cool mom, compared to all the other moms with their lame, outdated jeans and identical blonde highlights. But the other moms wouldn't do what Mickey was doing in this picture: obscuring her own daughter just to display her so-called good side to the camera. The other moms weren't constantly competing for the spotlight in photos, in the pool, in their love lives (Melody shuddered). They were content just to be moms, and to let their daughters shine. Whereas Mickey was always fighting against her mom-ness, reminding Melody of all the things she was in addition to being her mother. This was supposedly to set an example, to present Melody with the endless possibilities of what a woman could be. But Melody knew better. It had nothing to do with her, which was exactly the point; it was really about Mickey proving something to herself. Micky had become a mother when she was just a few years older than Melody was now. Ironically, it had both forced her to grow up fast and left her forever stunted. At least, that was Melody's take. The upshot was, it could really suck to be her daughter. Melody chucked the picture into the "toss" pile.

She turned to her closet. The sight of her prom dress, a crumpled heap on the floor, made Melody's eyes pool with tears, despite her personal pledge to remain stoic. Prom was yet another thing her mom had ruined for her. Her dad, too, but Melody knew in her gut the fault was Mickey's. It had been Gus' idea to stop by the club on the way to the after-party, to test out the fake IDs James' older cousin had made them. It was exciting to hand the laminated plastic to the bouncer, to track his bored glance, then be granted entrance to a forbidden adult space. Bryce had taken Melody's hand and she swore she felt sparks. *This is the guy I'm going to lose my virginity to,* she'd thought. *Tonight.* He led her to the dance floor, where—*bam!*—it all went sour. Because of course, after seeing her parents being so totally disgusting, and with Keisha, who Melody basically considered a part of the family, the last thing she wanted to do was have sex. She didn't want Bryce to touch her shoulder, never mind any other part of her body. She didn't even want to *have* a body. But being physically incapable of either crawling out of her skin or dying of mortification, Melody demanded Bryce drive her to the party (there was no way she was going home), where she marched to the nearest couch and tried to pass out. She'd been avoiding Bryce's texts and calls ever since. Now Melody fingered the gown's silver sequins; she'd decide later which pile to put it in.

All of her summer clothes she transferred to a suitcase. She wasn't sure if it got cold enough in L.A. for sweaters, but she guessed probably not before Thanksgiving, which was far enough away that she could imagine visiting home then. It had only taken a couple of days for Melody to change her summer plans; as an incoming student, she just had to fill out a few forms to enroll in summer classes and secure a single in a dorm. It was probably a lame dorm if it still had open rooms at this late date, but Melody could hardly afford to be picky. And speaking of hardly being able to afford stuff, the one-way flight had wiped out her savings. Still, Melody knew it was worth it. She'd printed out her plane ticket yesterday morning, and kept it in her pocket like a talisman ever since. Only three more nights of sleeping in her childhood bedroom, under the same roof as her despicable parents. Seventy-two hours until freedom.

It had become her routine all week to visit Louisa each afternoon in the hospital. The two of them had come to an agreement: Louisa was allowed to spend three minutes lecturing Melody about reconciling with her parents before she left for college, and encouraging her to fill them in on her plans for early departure, then she had to shut up. Then Melody would prod Louisa with questions about her own college days, plus all the terrible things students had done during her years at River Mill. Heading out for today's visit, Melody removed her plane ticket from her pocket and dropped it on the kitchen counter.

CHAPTER 57
Amy

Amy lay on the elephant-print rug and stared up at the colorful pinwheels whirring in the fan's breeze. She understood why parents hung mobiles over their babies' cribs; what she didn't understand was why adults didn't hang them above their own beds, too. Who couldn't use a little extra soothing to sleep?

Amy was supposed to be packing; she was returning to work tomorrow, and it would be easier to do this without Abe here. But she'd spent the past few nights staring at the ceiling, and she was now discovering that severe sleep deprivation was incompatible with figuring out what parts of her life to salvage versus what to ditch. Nearly every item in this house felt both safe and suffocating.

She was drawn to the nursery—or would-be nursery—the one room in the house that didn't feel like the embodiment of her and Abe. It was mostly empty, save for a bookshelf, the elephant rug, and the pinwheel mobile, which they'd bought about a hundred years ago. It had been their third or fourth date, on a day trip to the Newport mansions, where they'd spent hour upon hour fantasizing about a decadent alternate life. Neither of them was ready to let go of the imagining as they poked around a gift shop. The spinning pinwheels drew their gazes; then they locked eyes, both certain the other wanted it, too. Buying the mobile felt romantic, their first joint purchase. Only later did it occur to Amy that Abe might've assumed she'd been dreaming of a future child while watching it spin, just as he'd likely been; Amy had just thought it was pretty.

Until today, it hadn't occurred to her to come visit the mobile. Now she lay sprawled out like a starfish across the precise spot they'd pictured a crib, experiencing the tail end of this ordeal, wearing one of the giant sanitary pads Abe had bought her mere hours after she'd told him she was leaving. "To be more comfortable," he'd said, making space in the bathroom cabinet for the box, at which point Amy had wondered if a heart could actually physically break.

The mobile's movements were mesmerizing.

It felt strange to grieve something that never was, wrong to memorialize a future she'd decided she didn't want. But there Amy was, in the half-formed room that never came into its own, mourning the absence of the crib, the maternal feelings, the infant smells, the intertwining of mother and child. A part of Amy longed to cocoon herself in all that loss, to make it feel realer, to justify the echoing emptiness it had left inside of her. She could really lean into it and start mourning the loss of her marriage, too—feel the rug beneath her turn to quicksand—but there was a limit to how deeply Amy could let herself sink into sadness in one afternoon. All she knew was that she couldn't be here anymore, in this house, with this man, in this version of her life. She forced her gaze away from the mobile. Standing up left her lightheaded.

Since she'd admitted to herself that she didn't want a child, Amy felt okay admitting that she was in need of some mothering herself. She'd called Adele and asked to return to the nest. It was comforting to picture how it would go: She'd wear sweatpants, work from her childhood desk, take frequent snack breaks, maybe tag along with her mom to the animal shelter to cuddle some puppies; she'd let herself regress a little.

But before she could relax into that scene, Amy had to do the work of deciding what to pack for now, what to set aside to take later (Abe had cleared out space in the garage), and what to say goodbye to for good. Abe had given her free rein. If Amy liked, she could've taken every piece of furniture and every last kitchen utensil, and Abe would just be happy to imagine her using all their things—or so he claimed. Amy guessed that if Abe allowed himself a sliver of space to acknowledge his anger, it would open up the floodgates. Anyway, Amy couldn't pick apart their home; she couldn't do that to him, or to herself.

She gave herself ten minutes, grabbing pants and shirts at random and stuffing them into a duffel. On a whim, she added one of Abe's gym t-shirts from the hamper, figuring she'd allow herself an occasional whiff of the man she'd been loving for a decade. She decided to grant herself one more indulgence: She dragged a chair into the non-nursery, and stood on tippy-toes to unhook the mobile from the ceiling. She laid out the wires and pinwheels gingerly on top of her things and zipped up her bag.

CHAPTER 58
Mona

Mona was singing along to The Byrds' "Turn! Turn! Turn!" She had a soft spot for songs that perfectly encapsulated an experience. This transition felt joyful. It felt right. Her body moved easily, free of pain. Each item she picked up, she took a moment to hold and appreciate before placing it in a box. It was just stuff, Mona knew. She was careful not to form such strong attachments that she started believing her clothes or gadgets defined her. But she couldn't deny that each thing she packed away was infused with meaning: the feather dream catcher she'd made on a yoga retreat, the perfectly peach Lydia Davis book from her short story course, the thin gold hoops Nathan had given her on the night they moved in together. A life was a collection of experiences, and Mona liked to surround herself with concrete reminders of them.

She sang along about the changing seasons, the building up and breaking down, the dancing and mourning.

In this season of her life, Mona had been a student and a teacher, a friend and an enemy, a girlfriend and even sort of a mother. Now the seasons were changing, and it was time to move on. Time to turn away from this cold, stark landscape and head west, to the great unknown. Well, it wasn't totally unknown: Mona had connected with a yoga studio in Silver Lake and was set to start a teaching trial the same week a bedroom was opening up in her friend's apartment. The rest she'd figure out. She'd waitress, she'd whatever.

She sang about love and hate, war and peace, embracing and not embracing.

She would miss Nathan. His clever connections, how he'd cared for her so tenderly, and how he'd opened himself up to meditation and yoga, embracing beginner's mind like a pro. His crazy kids. Even his wife. While Mona had once cast Louisa as an insensitive nag, she now considered her someone she might've been friends with in a different life. As for Mona's role, well, some might still consider her the villain or the victim, the naïf or the seductress, the schemer or the dupe. But Mona hoped that most of all she'd been a catalyst. It was good to shake things up, to get swerved off your path. Literally or metaphorically, a car crash that didn't kill you forced you out of cruise control ... or something like that.

At the chorus, Mona herself turned and turned and turned as she sang.

Since the crash, she'd taken on a new rule as a crucial cog in the machine. While Nathan basically lived at the hospital with Louisa, Mona had picked up the slack with the kids, carpooling and bathing and cooking for them. Nathan and Louisa's friends were all busy with their own lives, but now that Mona had graduated, her days were open; she was free to help. She was waiting until the time felt right to visit Louisa. Mona wanted to reassure her that not only would she not rat her out, she respected what she'd done at the school. Good for Louisa for looking out for herself.

Mona's temporary River Mill ID lay on a pile of junk mail, and she tucked it into her wallet. She hadn't taught much of anything during her stint as a substitute teacher, but she'd sure learned a lot.

When Nathan finally appeared, the whole bedroom was boxed up and overflowing out of industrial trash bags. They were both moving out—Nathan tomorrow, to return to the house for Louisa's recuperation, and Mona next week. They stood facing each other, weighing their options. Nathan looked hesitant, but Mona had never been one to refrain from embracing.

She kept her eyes open. It was romantic and bittersweet to know that it would be their last time making love. Mona flashed back to that first statistics lecture, when she'd seen something in this man that made her entire being feel seen. So what if their time together had only lasted a couple of seasons?

CHAPTER 59

Mateo

Surrounded by the chaos of the airport, Melody was a picture of serenity. She answered every one of Mateo's questions with polite patience, even when he asked for a third time if she had her ticket and her ID; he couldn't help himself, and maybe he was trying to rile her up a bit, to get at that moody teenage version of his daughter that had suddenly been replaced by this near-adult venturing off into the world. There was so much he'd hoped to do with Mel over the summer: take her to baseball games and concerts, go on tandem bike rides, teach her how to use a drill and cook a few decent meals.

Having a child could feel like the slowest, most torturous form of loss. At the beginning, you knew every detail, from the exact configuration of their face when they were hungry or happy or in pain to the timing of each bowel movement. You knew their whole world: it was orchestrated by you. But then one day, they could crawl away, then toddle, then run off to discover and explore things beyond you. Their world became their own.

Mateo thought of Melody around age two, when she'd become obsessed with penguins, despite the fact that they had no toys or books about penguins and had never mentioned the birds in her presence. So where had Mel learned about them? Mickey had shrugged off the idea that they, as parents, had ever been the gatekeepers to their daughter's world. She claimed that Mel had always been her own person, and that one of her favorite things was looking at their daughter and marveling at what wonderful private imaginings were going on in that little head of hers.

That was a fundamental difference between Mateo and his wife: She celebrated the mysteries of their daughter, while he wanted more of her. "What's on your mind, Mel?" he asked now. It caught her off guard, his first question of the day that wasn't strictly logistics.

"I'm excited," Mel replied with her characteristic confidence. But Mateo sensed the hum of nerves under her words.

"I'm excited for you, too, sweetheart."

He'd tried a dozen ways in the past week to apologize to Melody, to talk to her about what she'd seen, to explain how one day she'd come to understand the complexities and contradictions of marriage, and to reassure her that he was still her good old dependable dad. But she'd brushed him off every time. Now she leaned into his shoulder, which Mateo took as a step toward reconciliation.

They both spotted Mickey speed-walking across the terminal, clutching a pair of oversized Jamba Juices. Melody stiffened. Mateo whispered in her ear, "Please be nice." He didn't like to team up with his daughter against his wife, but he thought Mel might be receptive at the moment.

Mickey burst in with her usual turbo energy. "Sorry that took ages. Juice Spot is closed, so I settled for the Double J. Mel, I thought you'd dig this apple ginger cayenne concoction."

Mother and daughter faced off—same height, same profile, same rail-straight posture. "I can't bring juice through security," Mel said, pronouncing "juice" as if it were "cancer."

Mickey stayed chipper. "Well, the security line's pretty long, so you can drink some of it, anyway."

She extended the cup, and Mateo willed his daughter to take it. *This is how your mother is showing her love,* he pleaded silently. *Same as when she spent half the night shouting at you about your surprise summer plans.* Eventually Melody accepted the cup, although she held it far from her body, as if it might be contaminated.

Mickey turned to Mateo—her wink made him wince—and held up the second cup. "I figured we could share."

"I bet you did," Mel said, not quite under her breath.

To Mickey's credit, she pretended not to hear. "Should we get in line?" she said.

"The line's for travelers only." Mel was suddenly a stickler for the rules.

"Okay!" Mickey answered, voice still bright.

Mateo took his wife's hand. It felt sad how her determination to keep things cordial was suppressing any real sentiment. She was bad at goodbyes, anyway. When Mel had whined about her parents planning to see her off from inside the terminal, Mickey would've caved: patting Mel on the back and sending her on her merry way from the parking garage. But Mateo had insisted they escort her inside.

Luckily, Mateo's telepathic choreography was working. Mickey reached out to hug her daughter, and Mel let herself be hugged, before briefly hugging back. Mateo saw Mickey mouth "I love you," and Mel respond, "Me too."

Then it was his turn to hold this grown-up child—this childish grown-up—in his arms. Words abandoned him.

"They're making me take stats," Mel said into his shoulder. "I'm going to suck at it, so you better help me."

"You bet." Finally, Mateo let go.

Mickey would've denied that she was tracking Mel's every move through the snaking security line along with Mateo, but the nails she was digging into his flesh told another story. Mel probably believed she was out of her parents' sight when she chugged the rest of her Jamba Juice before chucking it into the trash beside the frowning TSA officer.

"That's my girl," Mickey said.

Mateo had the same thought, but about his wife. He'd been mulling something over all week, and it was finally time to say it.

CHAPTER 60
Mickey

As Mickey watched her daughter disappear through the terminal, she thought about the moment she'd spotted Mel's plane ticket on the kitchen counter—and the relief she'd felt. Oh good, she'd thought, now she wouldn't have this angry, moody creature moping around all summer ready to attack her with a cutting remark the moment she let her guard down. Mickey never would've admitted that to Mateo, who was devastated to lose his daughter, and months earlier than planned. And it didn't stop Mickey from flipping out at Mel, because how dare she go behind their backs to make these arrangements, then communicate them so passive-aggressively.

Respect was the only parenting philosophy Mickey had ever subscribed to. Right from the start, she'd treated her daughter like a real person with her own individual needs and wants, her own perspective and opinions. No baby talk or arbitrary rules just to show who was boss. It had worked for years and years; Mickey and Mel had been best pals more than mother and daughter, because their relationship was based on mutual trust, not a power-authority dynamic. Mickey was proud that they didn't succumb to the same squabbles she'd witnessed between other mother-daughter duos.

Well, until recently. Maybe it was because Mel was ready to leave. It was what Louisa described always happened to the seniors at school: the closer graduation got, the more terrible they turned. Louisa claimed it was developmentally appropriate. Mentally, they'd already moved out of their childhood homes and on with their lives, but physically, they were still stuck. (It made no sense to Mickey that college acceptance letters arrived well before high school ended.) This discrepancy bred rage and frustration, which the kids targeted at their teachers and parents; i.e., their jailors. Previously, Mel had appreciated Mickey for who she was as a person, but now Mel had become very strict about what she felt was and wasn't allowed for her mother. Mickey couldn't share Melody's same taste in pressed juice, for example, or wear midriff-revealing shirts. She certainly couldn't have a sex drive. She was supposed to be different, other—*mother, period.*

So yes, Mickey admitted she was glad for this version of her daughter to leave. Living away from home changed a person, and Mickey thought it would do Mel good to learn all that she still had to learn, to discover that she was much more naive, much less prepared than she thought she was. She'd been coddled in a way that Mickey never had been as a kid. Mel had never even held a job, for god's sake. (As much as Mickey disliked how puritanical her daughter had become, she hated even more hearing herself take on the role of know-it-all mother anticipating her daughter's stumbles.)

Mickey tapped Mateo on the butt, and tried to ignore how he flinched. Since her birthday, he'd barely touched her or let himself be touched. "Let's skedaddle," she said.

They headed one way to the parking garage just as Mel headed the other way to her gate. It would be healthy for them all to get some space; important for her and her husband to begin building the foundation of their new normal. For starters, Mickey thought, she'd take Mateo out for breakfast.

But her Jeep was proving elusive. Mickey didn't even realize it until they'd made a giant circle in the lot, and Mateo headed to the stairwell, saying, "Maybe it's upstairs."

But it wasn't on that level, or the next one up either. Mateo always handled the logistics, while Mickey mostly daydreamed. But he must've been too wrapped up in his daughter's departure to register their parking spot. Mickey was thinking about how sweet that was, when Mateo railed around to face her.

"Honestly, I can't do this anymore."

Mickey laughed at the outburst. "Okay, so should we cut our losses and Uber it over to a car dealership?"

"I'm not talking about the car, Mickey." Her husband looked dreadful, but Mickey assumed it was on account of their suddenly empty nest. "I mean this." He gestured back and forth between them, and Mickey froze. "The way we've been conducting this relationship, you know, the openness. It's not working for me."

Mickey relaxed the slightest notch: he wasn't talking divorce; he wasn't pulling a Nathan (or an Amy). Still, she felt defensive. "It seemed to be working for you just fine the other night, until our daughter showed up. And now there's no chance of a surprise pop-in, since Mel's gone."

Mateo looked like she'd punched him in the gut. "I was trying to be open to you, and your wants. Sure, I had fun, but the cost has been too high." Mickey opened her mouth to speak, but Mateo continued. "And I've got to say, your continued flippancy about that night is sort of disturbing. Everyone makes mistakes, but it's a problem if you can't admit it when you do. We screwed up, Mick. Mel wasn't over-reacting." He took in a sharp breath. "This whole situation has been a mistake for me. I'm not going to stop you from being with other people if that's what you need, but you don't get to do it and still be married to me. So, it's your decision." He waved a dismissive hand, like he was over everything, then walked off.

Mickey felt stunned, and confused. Because, despite the other night, hadn't their sex life improved? Hadn't they been having fun? Wasn't life more exciting now? Mickey truly believed that more was more; yet, here was Mateo insisting the opposite.

But that wasn't even what was making her feel so dejected, her legs like two tons of concrete, incapable of going after her husband. She was in disbelief that he could just walk away from her, and from their marriage. He was looping the lot, and right before he came back into view, Mickey heard his voice echoing through the garage, "You know what, fuck that." Despite herself, she felt her hopes lift. "I'm not letting you go so easily. Screw everyone else. We belong together and that's that. It's us. It's always been us. You and me, baby."

Mateo swept her off of her feet, concrete limbs and all, and kissed her in the most familiar, beautiful way.

"You mean it?" she asked.

"Mickey Moran, I love you more than I know how to begin to say. I've loved you since the moment I laid eyes on you, and I've been loving you more and more each day since. This love"—he pressed a finger to her chest and then to his own—"it's my oxygen. It's what makes everything else possible. I need it. I need you. You're my Mickey. I'm your Mateo."

He released her back onto the ground, then spread his arms wide and shouted as loud as Mickey had ever heard him shout, "I love my wife!" The words echoed through the garage, causing a teenage boy heading their way to do an about-face.

This is what Mickey had needed all along: her husband. She needed him to fight for her, for them. She needed him to shout out his love and take up space with it, not just have it humming along in the background of their lives. Sure, Mickey wanted other people, too. But something that most people learned very early and that Mickey was just figuring out is that you can't always get what you want. And maybe people who understood that also knew that not getting everything made the things you did get that much sweeter. And that those things were worth fighting for.

Mickey took Mateo's hand. "You and me, baby. For life."

They strolled hand in hand through the garage, Mickey scanning left, Mateo scanning right. They were partners, a team. Mickey found her mind wandering to her daughter. Had she apologized to Mel?

Not exactly. Her flight was scheduled to take off in five minutes. Mickey sent her a text: "I'm sorry for everything that happened this week. I'm sorry I brushed off your feelings. I love you. Go get 'em out west." Then she tucked her phone away. It didn't matter if Mel responded; she was just a kid, and she was hurting. Mickey was the mother, the one meant to comfort and soothe.

The Jeep wasn't even backed into some dark corner. It was parked in plain sight, in the middle of a row they'd passed at least twice. Mateo clapped his hands together like Mickey had seen him do watching one of his beloved Red Sox turn a double play. Like he did watching Mel win the fifty-free, like he did when Mickey crossed another triathlon finish line. This was her guy.

She wanted to ravage him in the rediscovered vehicle. But she had a hunch that what Mateo would really want was to share a plate of eggs and toast, after which they'd return to their big, empty home, where Mickey would lead her husband up to their bedroom, just the two of them.

CHAPTER 61

Abe

Abe was on high alert monitoring Finn's raging around the playground, driving himself crazy trying to figure out when to step in and when to let the kids work it out among themselves. Finn stealing a boy's ball: Abe demanded the boy apologize; Finn cutting a girl in line: he gave the boy a stern look; Finn stomping up the slide despite the line of kids waiting at the top: Abe gave up. All the admonishments to "wait your turn" and "say you're sorry" seemed to be for the benefit of the fellow adults, anyway; the kids didn't care. And why should Abe engage in performative parenting when he wasn't even a parent? He cut himself some slack. He left Finn to his reign of terror and stole occasional glances at Phoebe loitering by the tire swing, pushing imaginary riders this way and that. When Abe caught himself counting down the hours until he could unload the twins and return home unencumbered, he realized the silver lining to Finn acting the playground Godzilla: sometimes he felt grateful to be childless.

Abe had volunteered to pick up Louisa from the hospital and settle her back in at home. But apparently Nathan was taking care of it, plus moving back in to help out with her recovery; Abe had been on the verge of questioning this arrangement when her warning look shut him up. So, he offered to take Phoebe and Finn for the afternoon instead. Beyond altruism, Abe was trying to keep himself occupied—particularly today, which marked Amy's official departure. They'd said a vague goodbye. It was all Abe could handle. He wouldn't even let himself touch his wife, worried that the feel of her skin would cause his throat to close up, his heart to stop pumping, his body to crumple into a pile of flesh and bones. They'd see each other again soon, whenever Amy decided to come back for the rest of her things. Anyway, Abe knew he couldn't really begin to say goodbye to his wife until she was gone.

When Abe heard a high-pitched wail, he guessed Finn was to blame. It took him about five seconds to spot Finn triumphant at the helm of a mock ship and to deduce that the crying boy next to him had been forcibly demoted from captain to castaway. Social mores dictated that Abe assume responsibility for the perpetrator and try to diffuse the conflict, just as he knew that within moments another adult would arrive to comfort the victim. He climbed the three shallow steps to the ship's bow, and sure enough, as he was chastising Finn, a woman whose flaxen curls matched the wailing boy's appeared at his side, followed by a man who shared the boy's profile. As the woman brushed the hair out of her son's eyes, the man crouched down and whispered in his ear. Abe overheard, "Sharing is caring. Everyone gets a turn."

The boy moved his lips along with his father's, then said, "Sharing is caring. We all need to learn."

Then all three of them chanted together: "Let's be kind and let's be fair. Here, there, and everywhere." Both parents kissed the boy, then each other.

Finn narrowed his eyes at the trio, his curiosity now trumping his rancor. Abe narrowed his eyes, too, fighting the urge to do something to mar this picture of family unity. "Come on, Finn," he said, forcing himself to walk away.

Finn skipped off to the swings, Phoebe was over at the slide, and Abe slumped onto a bench. Until this moment, it had been working: looking after the kids to keep his mind off Amy. But now, Abe felt himself spiraling. Everywhere he looked were happy couples, happy families, happy people. It was unbearable. He squeezed his eyes shut and began humming "Fire and Rain." He'd recently been one of the happy people, too; but without Amy, Abe didn't know who he was.

Soon Finn was at his side, tugging at his shirt, saying he was bored and hungry. "Okay, where's your sister?" Abe asked. The boy shrugged.

After scanning the playground twice, Abe started to freak out. Phoebe was nowhere. "Phoebe!" he cried, louder than he knew he was capable of. "Phoebe!"

All those happy people picked up on his panic. The playground grew frantic with shouts of the girl's name; nothing united a group of parents like the search for a lost child. Abe scooped up Finn, who kicked and squirmed, every inch of his body resisting Abe's grip as they dashed around the play structures, looking, looking, looking. Abe worried his fear was blinding him, so that he wouldn't even see Phoebe if she appeared in front of him. He was spiraling again. Like, no wonder the universe was preventing him from fatherhood, if he couldn't even keep a couple of kids safe for a couple of hours; and obviously his wife was abandoning him; and clearly his friends would be next, when he'd have to break it to them that their daughter disappeared under his watch. He was such a pathetic shit.

How long did the panic last? It felt outside of time.

The woman with the flaxen curls was the one to spot the unlatched gate, to bolt out and reappear moments later with Phoebe on her hip. Phoebe wore the same dreamy expression as when she was pushing the tire swing. She was fine, unaware she'd caused such a stir. She'd had a promenade, she said, pronouncing it to rhyme with "lemonade." All the adults laughed, desperate to release the tension of the search. Abe knew it tickled Louisa to teach the kids old-timey vocabulary, and Phoebe had a knack for whipping out the words when people were in need of amusement. He'd never felt so relieved.

With all the commotion, Abe had momentarily forgotten about the writhing creature in his grip. He set Finn down, at which point the boy unleashed his fury, delivering a one-two punch to Phoebe's stomach and Abe's thigh. The boy could hit: Abe clutched his leg, as Phoebe's body folded in half. She gasped for air.

Again, the fair-haired woman swooped in. She placed a hand on Phoebe's back and instructed her to take slow breaths. Abe couldn't help thinking of Amy, who'd soothed Abe similarly on so many occasions. Finn stood blinking at the scene. He must've decided the reaction he'd caused didn't live up to his hopes, because he took off running. Abe flew after him, his thigh stinging where he'd been punched. He tackled Finn to the ground under the wobbly bridge. The boy kept thrashing and screaming as Abe hugged him close.

"I know," Abe sighed. "I know. I know."

Abe could feel the vibrations from Finn's little body, the rage at his whole life being turned upside-down, the turmoil of never knowing which home he'd be shuttled to, or by whom, and to top it all off, the shock of finding his mother broken and frail in a funny-smelling hospital room. Abe knew the kids had only gotten to see Louisa in snippets, during which she stayed in bed and they were instructed to be gentle with their hugs. Abe could picture Louisa squeezing her son's hand and saying, "I'm here, I'm here," when she wasn't really. Finn needed his mom, and she was unavailable to him. Abe knew the boy was terrified he wouldn't get her back.

These feelings were much too big to be contained by a toddler. Abe wished he could absorb some of the hurt. But the best he could do was be there and hold him. It was probably the best anyone could do for anyone else.

"I know, I know," he said, because he did know what it was like, sort of. Eventually, the boy's wails gave way to whimpers, until he went limp, burying his head in Abe's neck. Patting Finn's head, Abe felt comforted, too.

They needed a change of scenery. Abe would take the kids back to his house for a snack. He took each of their hands and together they walked the couple of blocks south.

In front of his house, Abe stopped short. There she was, loading a suitcase into her car, wearing that simple green dress he loved, her hair in a low ponytail. She looked beautiful—she always did. As much as Abe wanted to maintain his dignity and to honor his wife's wish to leave, he also wanted to get on his hands and knees and plead for her to stay—for today and for the rest of their lives.

Amy finally noticed him on the sidewalk. She waved. They locked eyes, and Abe's gaze asked what he was going to do without her. Her smile communicated her faith in him. It was confusing, his deep trust in his wife's judgment competing with the blasted-out feeling at his core.

Abe's friends sometimes talked about their marriages like the light had gone out, like they were lucky to find a glowing ember now and then, reminding them of the love that had once burned bright. But it had never felt that way for Abe. Even through the last couple of years, Abe's love for Amy had been a raging fire. It never went away, the sense that touching her would send up sparks. A decade in, he still felt the pulse of love, that insatiable desire to know all of his wife, inside and out. Abe knew how lucky he'd been. And it was beyond his powers of imagination to conceive of his life without the glinting thread of Amy—and his love for her—sewn through every inch of its fabric.

"I don't ..." Abe's voice faltered. Tears fell from his eyes.

"You don't have to." Amy looked at her feet.

Abe knew sincere expressions of emotion made Amy uncomfortable, so he wiped his cheeks dry. "I've loved you for a very long time, Amy Sullivan-Jones. I don't imagine I'll stop anytime soon. Please don't go."

"Abe, I have to."

"Will you reconsider?"

She was still looking down, shaking her head. "I don't know."

She might have said more, but she was interrupted by the shouts of Finn and Phoebe. "Ice cream! Ice cream! Ice cream!"

Amy responded in a flash, finally looking at Abe: "I think they want broccoli. Is that what you heard?"

Every ounce of Abe wanted to collapse in a puddle onto the sidewalk, but he summoned the wherewithal to remain vertical and stay in this silly exchange. "Yep, I heard that, too. Should we all go eat some broccoli?"

"Noooo!" the kids wailed, thrilled with their outrage. "Ice cream! Ice cream!"

"Oh, I could've sworn you said broccoli," Amy said. "I'm glad we cleared that up."

She turned to Abe, eyes suddenly sparkling with unspilled tears. "You'll be okay, I promise."

She squeezed his hand, then walked to her car, got in, and was gone. Abe was left to mull over the fact that she couldn't possibly promise a thing like that. Still, Amy's confidence had always bolstered his own, so for the moment he chose to believe her. The person he loved most in the world had said he'd be okay. Maybe he would, maybe he wouldn't. In the meantime, there would be ice cream.

CHAPTER 62
Louisa

The symbolism was hard to miss. Step by tiny step, bearing as much weight as she could tolerate on her left leg, the one with the fractured femur, Louisa was learning how to walk again. And it was fucking grueling.

She could be forgiven for having thought that recovering from getting hit by a car might involve a generous dose of R&R. But no, after a couple of days, she was transferred to a rehab hospital, where Louisa was put to work. The physical therapists noted the weaknesses in her left quads and glutes, and her poor range of motion in the knee and hip, giving her exercises that were laughable in their simplicity yet nearly impossible to execute. The one that made Louisa laugh out loud, despite the pain and frustration, was what they called "gait training." Because of course, it was the perfect coda to this mess that Louisa would have to re-learn to walk.

Louisa had observed her children learning to do this very thing, and it had not been like this. They'd figured out how to stand, then cruise around with help from the furniture, then finally in one fateful moment—and it really had been the same moment for both of them, in that crazy twin synergy that Louisa had believed in ever since—they'd taken a leap of faith, let go, and *walked*. It was perfectly natural, their bodies built for it, their miniature muscles and joints working in concert to propel them forward.

That's how it always was, right? The stuff that came naturally to kids was so often so difficult for adults: playing, expressing your needs, giving and receiving love, and apparently also learning to walk. Louisa felt pathetic as she struggled with another shuffle-step, then another, making infinitesimal progress across the room.

But Louisa was also a little in awe. Something she'd always done without thought or consideration turned out to be quite complex. The fact that her hips and pelvis were shifting to her injured leg made her trunk lurch to the right to compensate, which in turn caused her left glute to give way and her pelvis to drop to the right. Part of the therapy was observing her gait in a mirror, and it looked like she kept missing a step. The world's least sexy sashay.

Meanwhile, the person guiding her movements looked like sex itself, even in an oversized tee and yoga pants. "Tighten your abs, lift your knee, more weight through your leg, squeeze your butt, don't let your hip drop, keep your pelvis level, breathe, breathe." Mona's small hands were pressed against her hips. Louisa groaned and took what was more of a suggestion of a step than the thing itself. Mona cheered. "That's it!"

Did it surprise Louisa that Mona had shown up for her in this way? A little. The first time she'd appeared in Louisa's hospital room, Mona had located her P.T. worksheets and studied the sketches of androgynous figures performing leg lifts and heel slides. Then she stated her qualifications: training in rehabilitation yoga, a couple of courses in kinesiology and anatomy, plus a decade of managing her own scoliosis. After other visitors' pleas of "How can I help?" followed by the expectation that Louisa come up with a task for them, it was a relief to hear Mona's offer to help in this very specific way.

Was Louisa embarrassed to have Mona of all people assist her at her most vulnerable? Again, a little. But the girl had a real knack for it, the hands-on adjustments and verbal cues as well as the encouragement. She seemed to really understand how hard this was. After she came around a couple times on her own, Louisa asked outright if she could return the next day. She'd been showing up every day since. Louisa would miss her after her departure to L.A.

Now Louisa was back home. After ten mini steps, which got her from the couch halfway to the TV, Mona helped her onto her back for stretching. As she lifted the leg with the fractured femur, she instructed Louisa to think of funny things her kids had said, to distract from the pain.

But Louisa focused on Mona instead, manipulating her leg this way and that, working on her range of motion. "I get why Nathan fell for you," Louisa said eventually. She could feel Mona holding her breath. "I don't have these qualities of yours: patience, calm, attention to the minutest detail. All that inspirational quote crap, which turns out to mean something." Mona held Louisa's leg still. "See, like right now, how you're just being here and taking it all in."

"Where else would I be?"

This made Louisa laugh. Back at the apartment. Out with her friends. Off to California already. There were dozens of other places Mona could be instead of helping her soon-to-be-ex-lover's possibly-soon-to-be-ex-wife rehabilitate her shattered leg.

"Look," Louisa said, "I'm not going to say this is all for the best, or that everything happened for a reason. For starters, I currently can't walk. Not that I can pin *that* on you. Second, Nathan's career is done."

"Louisa, I'm really sorry for the hurt I caused."

"Thank you." Louisa's voice wavered. It was surprising how important it felt to hear Mona's apology. "My point is, we've all survived, right?"

"We have."

The more time Louisa spent with Mona, the less ill will she felt toward her. Watching her with Nathan proved gratifying, too. On the drive home from the hospital, as he'd engaged in his hyperactive radio scanning, Mona had caught Louisa's eye in the rearview mirror and they'd shared an eyeroll. The things Nathan had accused Louisa of being so uptight about were clearly starting to grate on his girlfriend, too. Louisa realized that even if Mona weren't moving away, this fling would've proven to be exactly that.

During that first visit to the hospital, Mona had also confessed that she had no intention of telling anyone what she'd seen on the day of the test walkout. She felt it wasn't her place, and she was sure Louisa had her reasons for doing what she'd done. The only thing she didn't regret about butting her way into River Mill High was that she'd gotten to see Louisa at work, and how she was a true leader. No wonder Nathan had married her, she'd said with a blush. Louisa didn't admit it to Mona, but she felt grateful the girl had walked into her office that day, jolting her back to her senses. Mona's sentiments now made Louisa imagine mentoring her; that is, if either of them had stuck around at the school.

Because that morning, Louisa had called Poolehauzer to resign. She could tell he was scanning his email as they spoke: she'd watched him do it on phone calls with countless others. His split attention made it easier to talk. "I'm sorry I abandoned my post that day," she said. "I was not in a good place, and—"

"You certainly weren't, because you were here at River Mill! Get it?" Poolehauzer honked out a laugh. "Well, I didn't think you had it in you." It was funny how he said it, like he half-admired her gumption.

His sigh was loud in her ear. "What a shit-show, am I right, Ms. Bauer?"

"You are right, sir."

"Well, your resignation makes my life a lot easier, given that—surprise, surprise—our funding has been slashed. Either you or Mack were destined to get the boot. That man should bow down and kiss your feet for your lapse in judgment. An entertaining image! Anyway, if you're looking for an in-home nurse, we hired a fantastic one when Vanessa fractured her toe last year. My poor wife, she was a wreck about missing a month of cardio barre."

"Thanks, I'll let you know," Louisa said, laughing to herself; a part of her would miss Poolehauzer's ridiculousness.

"I'll have someone box up your things and send them over," he said. Louisa would've told him not to bother—Abe was already on it— but she knew he wouldn't follow through anyway. "Well, Ms. Bauer, without you around, this den of hormones and depravity will only deteriorate further."

Louisa knew that was the closest she'd get to a thank-you from her boss. "Thanks, Dr. P. I wish you well."

"Go Lions, roar!" It always made Louisa smile, Poolehauzer's uncanny ability to make the school mascot's call sound weak and cowardly.

"Roar," she replied in the same tone.

One stressful call down, Louisa had turned to the next: Aetna. The first wave of hospital bills had trickled in, with dollar amounts so astronomical they drew noises resembling laughter from Louisa, though she felt the opposite of amused. But after the healthcare representative typed in her information and Louisa was preparing to make her little speech—her only defense being "Surely this can't be right!"—the rep thanked her for her prompt payments and asked how he could help her today.

"Prompt payments?"

Her account balance was zero. It took several exchanges for Louisa to understand that this wasn't an error; some good Samaritan had paid off her bills. The rep couldn't divulge payment info, but Louisa knew. Mateo had visited the hospital and told her about an office manager position at his company that was hers if she wanted it, whenever she was ready; it was beneath her qualifications, of course, but it would tide her over until whatever came next. When he mentioned the salary, Louisa thought she'd misheard; it was double what she'd been earning at River Mill. He'd give her an advance on her first paycheck if she needed it; he said it as casually as if he were offering her a cup of coffee.

Maybe money didn't make you happy, but it sure could vaporize heavy clouds of anxiety hanging over you. Louisa knew an act of charity when she saw one, and it made her a little uneasy. But she also knew that Mateo and Mickey loved her, and what would make such a difference to her was of little consequence to her friends. She'd find a way to pay them back, monetarily or otherwise.

When a beep sounded outside—Mona's ride to the airport—Mona rested her hands on Louisa's shoulders, an intimate gesture. "You've made so much progress."

"And so have you," Louisa said, and they both laughed.

Mercifully, Mona and Nathan must've already said goodbye, upstairs, which was still off-limits to Louisa due to her leg. They'd spared her having to witness their final intimacy, a kiss or an embrace, tender words, maybe tears. Louisa was curious how it felt to Nathan: like a devastating breakup or a great relief? More likely, something in between.

"All right," said Mona, "Catch you later."

"Sure." But Louisa couldn't imagine she would; sometimes people left your life for good.

⸻

Then it was back to basics: Louisa and Nathan. From her perch on the living room couch, she could hear him padding around upstairs; the old house announced every step with creaks and wheezes. When they'd first moved in all those years ago, Louisa had sat in this very spot and listened to similar sounds from the ceiling, not quite believing that all this space was theirs. It had felt like they were playing at adulthood.

Now it felt like they were playing at something else, although Louisa wasn't quite sure what. Nathan had been there nonstop, caring for the kids, making the meals, cleaning the house, attending to Louisa's every need. He'd stay on as she continued to heal (she wouldn't be calling Vanessa Poolehauzer's nurse). He had managed to break the lease on his apartment with only a small penalty, and neither of them had brought up the divorce papers since the accident. It was all working out, in a sense. And when Louisa was back on her feet, well, who knew what would happen then?

Louisa rang the schlocky "Get whale soon!" bell that Mickey had bought at the hospital gift shop—featuring a beluga with an ice pack on its head and a thermometer in its mouth. Nathan was by her side in seconds.

"Naptime for me."

She was prepared to limp her way to the makeshift bedroom he'd set up for her in the sunroom, but Nathan scooped her up in his arms. Louisa relaxed into his familiar feel and scent, too tired to fight the comfort. She figured she'd sleep for an hour or two, mustering up the energy to greet her kids when Abe brought them home. But when she opened her eyes, she realized many hours had passed: All was dark, the house silent. Louisa reoriented herself in the sunroom, and pictured Nathan asleep upstairs; the last time he'd slept in that bed was the night he announced he wanted a divorce.

Louisa breathed through her pain and stiffness, performing the visualization exercises that Mona had taught her. When it wasn't enough, she rang the bell.

Nathan arrived in an instant, sat her up, and dispensed a pill.

"Thank you," she said, locking eyes with her husband. "I can't tell you how much it means to have you here."

"It's nothing," Nathan said, although his smile indicated that he knew it wasn't.

As Louisa drifted back to sleep, she could sense Nathan at her side, keeping vigil. He stayed. In the morning, she was awakened by the quick thuds of little feet above her head. She turned over to see her husband curled into a blanket on the floor. Within moments, the thuds reached the sunroom. The pair of children in pajamas leapt onto their father and nestled their delicious cheeks into Louisa's chest. She took a mental snapshot: This was her family.

CHAPTER 63

Louisa's Birthday

It happened during the fallow summer-through-autumn stretch of no birthdays in the group. Nathan noticed it on the drive to his new job, as a data analyst at an ed tech company. Mickey and Mateo saw it while out on a run, training for the half-marathon that Mickey had cajoled her husband into registering for. Amy heard about it from colleagues brainstorming their next happy hour spot. Abe came upon it on a stroll with the new Spanish teacher he'd started spending time with. They all felt pangs of nostalgia and regret, maybe a touch of relief. Louisa didn't find out until a couple of weeks before her December birthday, when she called to make a reservation that she wasn't even sure she'd keep. The line rang and rang until a recording regretted to inform her that Giorgio's had shut down and thanked her for over a decade of joy in serving their customers with the finest Italian fare; the owners had retired to Florida. Louisa held the phone up to her ear for a full minute after the message ended.

Well, it had to be a sign. The tradition had run its course. It had been (mostly) good while it lasted. Louisa began brainstorming a different kind of birthday: a day off work, maybe lunch out with her kids, or drinks with Mickey, or even just a bundled-up walk on her own by the river. She still felt grateful to be walking again, with near-full mobility.

It was Mickey who called a week before the big day. "What's the plan, Lou?" She brushed off Louisa's suggestion of cocktails, and encouraged her to include the whole group. The six of them hadn't gathered in months, and everyone was depending on her to bring them back together, she said. Louisa's birthday was the highlight of the holiday season!

Louisa was skeptical of these claims, but she lacked the conviction to fend off her friend. Fine, she told Mickey, but it had to be different; it had to be new. Mickey agreed.

The morning of her thirty-seventh birthday, Louisa woke up feeling every day her age, older even. Her left leg still sometimes announced itself with cracks; she was constantly stretching and readjusting, and it seemed like she'd be doing her PT exercises forever. A year ago, the few silver strands framing her face had lent her an air of mystery, whereas now her waves were full-on salt and pepper. Mickey was gifting her a trip to the hair salon for her birthday, and

Louisa was still deciding whether she'd just get the gray washed out, or go for a bold blonde or even one of those trendy pastel-streaked styles.

Louisa stood in the kitchen doorframe and observed her children standing on chairs at the counter with Nathan, the three of them hunched over a plate and giggling.

Her daughter spotted her first. "She's up!"

Phoebe presented it proudly: a pancake with banana-slice eyes, a bulbous strawberry nose, and a lopsided blueberry smile. Finn brandished a card heavy with crayon.

Louisa gathered up her kids and inhaled their morning scents, the most intoxicating perfume. "This is exactly what I wanted for my birthday," she told them.

Nathan stood back shyly, a dish towel over his shoulder, his large hand clutching a small box. There had been so many years of Nathan's birthday gifts. He'd never picked up on Louisa's hints about the cute earrings she'd spotted in a store window or the fact that all her yoga clothes had grown threadbare. His presents were often projects, like a marble chess set—he'd teach her!—or an antique radio she could take apart and reconstruct according to her preferences. Or they were gadgets intended to improve some aspect of her life that Louisa didn't feel needed improving, like a computerized device for a window box planter guaranteeing optimal growth. It was Psych 101: Nathan's gifts to her were things he wanted himself. Depending on Louisa's mood on said birthday, this either irritated her or endeared him to her.

Inside the box was a watch that looked to be made of steel. It weighed about three pounds. "The battery's supposed to last a decade, there's an LED light, and you can store three time zones and four separate alarms." Nathan was getting worked up. "It's water- and mud-resistant. It's what the NAVY Seals use."

"Perfect for when I find myself in the midst of a muddy war," Louisa said. She could now rib him in a way she never used to be able to do; he actually laughed.

"Well, you never know what life will bring."

"Very true." She strapped it on. It looked ridiculous next to the dainty silver loop of a watch she'd worn for years. It was the last watch on the planet she would've chosen for herself.

During their marriage, it had always felt hard to know how much to give in versus how much to resist. Louisa had sat through several chess lessons, and even suggested the two of them play on occasion. A semi-success. She'd tried tinkering with that radio. But she'd never even unboxed the window planter device.

When should you stand firm, clutching at your dignity, and when should you swallow your pride and let things go? How much internal negotiation was too much? And what was the end goal? How much did any of it matter anyway? Louisa would drive herself mad turning these questions over in her head, often at two or three a.m., pro-and-conning it ad nauseam as if she might eventually reason out the right answer. As if there were a right answer. Since the accident, though, she'd stopped obsessing over this stuff.

Louisa knew she'd often done the same thing with Nathan's presents, buying him sweaters and scarves that were her own taste more than his. It was a sign of love, right, like a twist on the golden rule? Then again, wasn't the golden rule a little selfish, assuming others wanted to be treated the same as you wanted to be treated? Louisa had read about research that found the closer you were to someone, the less you listened to them. You thought you knew the person you loved, so you grew deaf to them. Well, Louisa and Nathan were listening to each other now.

"Thank you," she said, and kissed Nathan's cheek.

With her new military-grade watch strapped on, Louisa reviewed her recent battles: She'd come very close to manipulating the state exams, then she'd walked out of the school in the middle of a crisis. No one who knew seemed to care, except Louisa herself. She considered herself a person of integrity, and she'd let herself down. She swore to do better.

Louisa felt less clear about her marriage. For the past six months, she'd needed Nathan for everything, and he'd been there for her in every possible way. He was like a new person, nurturing and attentive, focused single-mindedly on their family, a partner she could truly count on. Louisa, too, felt transformed. It was as if she'd put on corrective lens and could see clearly all that was truly important. There was so much that simply didn't matter, that she'd wasted so much time and energy on; realizing it relaxed Louisa. And now, her leg was basically healed, and Nathan was *still* there. They'd swapped rooms after she'd re-mastered the stairs—Louisa back up to her bedroom and Nathan settling into the sunroom. It was an economical arrangement. And easier, since they were still trading off nights with the kids, albeit under the same roof. They were also careful not to ask questions about each other's whereabouts on off nights. Louisa had had a few sleepovers with other men, though nothing to write home about.

More and more, they all ended up hanging out together: Nathan stir-frying at the stove and Louisa chopping a salad while the kids wreaked havoc at their feet, then all four of them around the table. Nathan asked questions about their days and listened to their answers; again and again, he told them how grateful he was to be there with them. In the old days, they'd rarely eaten dinner together as a family. Now, after the kids were in bed, she and Nathan might do their own things, or they might end up on the couch together. Just last week, they'd shared a blanket and watched a movie, a rom-com that Nathan never would've tolerated in the past, then Louisa had let him trail her up to bed. She'd thought maybe it was a mistake of muscle memory—until he reached for her, hesitating for a moment to gauge her response. Louisa reached back. They ended up entangled, bodies once so familiar newly acquainted, both of them panting with pleasure and surprise.

Louisa's life, once so black and white, had shifted into this blurry gray space, and she was okay with the ambiguity. When Mickey or Abe asked what was going on with Nathan (or when she asked herself the same question), it felt fine to throw up her hands and say she didn't know. There was no plan and no expectations. They were taking it day by day. For the first time in a long time, Louisa felt light, optimistic even.

"Everyone ready?" she asked.

Louisa typed the address of the new Mexican spot into her phone, and they piled into the car. From the passenger seat, Nathan placed his hand over Louisa's on the steering wheel. "Happy birthday, Lou."

Louisa was idling by the hostess stand, taking in all the details that were different from Giorgio's, when she was caught by surprise by two sets of arms, a bear-hug sandwich.

"A very merry un-birthday to you," Mickey sang out, followed by Melody's, "Who me?" then Mickey's, "No, her!" She kissed Louisa's cheek.

This is what she got for requesting that they keep her birthday low-key: no fancy food, no fine wine, no seating chart, no cake. Home after her first semester of college, Melody looked even more her mother's twin, and Mickey glowed with the joy of reuniting with her daughter. The two were friends again, making a scene, magnets for attention. Mateo stood on the sidelines with a young man, both wearing matching expressions of embarrassment mixed with amused pride. That must be Arjun, Mel's new boyfriend from college; very cute.

Abe arrived with a woman Louisa had heard about. She'd been

imagining Elena as kind of a hologram, not quite real. But laying eyes upon her now—a tall brunette with sharp angles and dark brown eyes—it hit Louisa that there was nothing ambiguous about it: Abe was dating her.

"Everyone, meet Elena. Elena, meet everyone."

Louisa extended a hand but the woman grazed her cheek against Louisa's cheek instead; Elena had moved here from Texas to teach Spanish at River Mill. With a bittersweet pang, Louisa understood that Elena had replaced her as Abe's work confidante. She wondered if the pair took breaks up Stairwell F to the roof. That was one of the things Louisa missed about the school: those views of the water, the heart-to-hearts with her old friend. Her desk at Mateo's company looked out onto an office park, and though she was friendly with everyone, she'd yet to make a close friend at her new job. Working with educators had been different; everyone was there because teaching was a calling, not simply an occupation. Louisa knew she'd find her way back to that world eventually.

"How many are we?" Nathan took a headcount. "Nine adults, two kids?"

"Eight adults," Abe corrected

Louisa squeezed Abe's hand. For months, she'd reached out to Amy every couple of weeks; she wanted her friend to know that she was thinking of her, even as she respected her distance. Amy would usually take a day or two to respond. Once she'd mentioned that she missed the crew, so Louisa invited her to the lunch. Amy replied that she could probably make it for dessert, if it was all right with Abe. Louisa asked Abe, and his face lit up at the possibility. It gave Louisa hope. As content as he seemed with Elena, it was clear he still longed for his wife.

Louisa allowed herself a moment of mourning for the original birthday six, for the group that had felt like home, that had been her first happy family, and that she'd assumed would remain together forever.

Then she was pulled back to the present by Phoebe and Finn, each child underfoot and clutching a leg to pin Louisa in place: their favorite new game, hindering her, oh so charmingly. Behind her were Melody and her new boyfriend, Arjun, incapable of keeping their hands off each other, deep in young love. Around her stood her friends of a decade-plus: Mickey making Mateo laugh, and Abe whispering in the ear of his new girlfriend. And there at her side was Nathan, who was—how else to put it?—her person, despite it all. And here was Louisa, still standing, celebrating another birthday.

The group had morphed, the venue had changed, and they'd all survived another year. Louisa took in the lot of them milling about and waiting to be seated, nothing more ordinary. But as always, under the hum of the everyday—of marriage and kids and career and friendship and a birthday meal out—were enough pings of the extraordinary to make one marvel at it all.

A waitress held out her hands in welcome. "Party of ten, right this way."

The End

ACKNOWLEDGMENTS

Thank you to the following people:

You, the reader. It's because of you that I've had the privilege to continue publishing stories and connecting with fellow book lovers like you. I am so grateful you picked up this book, and I hope you found something in these pages that resonated.

My brilliant agent, Joelle Delbourgo, who has remained a steadfast advocate and trusted advisor through the years.

Nancy Cleary, for falling in love with this story and bringing me in to the Wyatt-MacKenzie family.

My teachers Max Apple, Tom DePeter, and John Browne, who taught me so much about writing, the power of storytelling, and being human.

My teacher colleagues Becca Gordon, Steve Martin, and Rebecca Fabricant, whose friendship and humor carried me through a few intense years of classroom teaching, a period which served as inspiration for sections of this book.

My early readers and dear friends: Juli Breines, Jessi Breland, Paula Derrow, and Cristina Silva. I am so grateful for your wisdom, generosity, and invaluable feedback.

More early readers: Ariel Djanikian and Alicia Oltuski. For me, a silver lining of covid was reconnecting with my college writing group—all of us Max Apple devotees who signed up for his Tuesday afternoon seminar every semester. Nearly two decades later, I found myself in a (Zoom) room workshopping fiction again with Ariel and Alicia, two of the finest writers and humans I know. Your insights improved this novel immeasurably.

Steve Ji, for a math fact-check, and for keeping up a continuous Slack conversation that's carried me through remote work. Shaun Logan, for a physical therapy fact-check. Svana Calabro, for a family law fact-check. Any errors are my own.

Zick Rubin, for pro bono legal expertise, book after book.

Amber Bryant, my writing buddy: Despite an end to our sessions at The Greene Grape Annex (RIP) and The Center for Fiction, I still imagine you beside me while I write, and feel inspired by your tapping of keys and companionship.

The bookstagram community, a special group of book lovers who do so much to promote and support authors such as myself.

A special thanks to the indomitable Ashley Spivey: I'm so grateful to have you in my corner.

My parents, Nancy and Al Palmer, for your unconditional love and support, which recently included taking in my family during the pandemic, and allowing me to turn your bedroom into my work space.

My daughter, Emilia Keber, who alternately tells me that writing books is cool and that it looks very boring, and who groans when I go to work then greets me with boundless enthusiasm when I'm finished.

My husband, Damian Keber, who never groans when I go to work and who values my need to make up stories and believes in the process perhaps even more than I do. There's no one else I'd rather have at my side.